BREAKING STORIES

*Democracy demands
a free press*

JOHN ARMSTRONG

AUTHOR'S NOTE

In my view, dedications are the riskiest part of any novel. Who does the author mention and who is left out? For those who make the cut, what do you say, and how do you say it? It's a classic "lose, lose" situation. So, at the risk of also losing the reader before page one, I'm going to play it safe. But I'm going to play it straight too. *Breaking Stories* is dedicated to my wife, Valerie Hance Armstrong. She is my Anam Cara, my soul mate. Val, I will be forever grateful for all our years together, and your help in writing *Breaking Stories* is the least of it.

Everyone has a story. If truth be told, several stories. Some we would be happy to share. Others we'd prefer to remain private. Taken together, they give a trajectory to a person's life, sometimes bending upward, then pausing before reversing itself. This dynamic continues to play out until, inevitably, the story breaks for good or ill, ending in something like redemption or perdition. Sometimes, the break is so newsworthy that a relentless reporter, like Jake Morris, gets hold of the story and it becomes "breaking news."

To those who turn the page and enter the world of *Breaking Stories*, I hope you find yourself in one or more of its characters, and I hope it causes you to better appreciate your own story—or stories. Just try to stay out of the news.

BREAKING STORIES

ONE

"MORRIS! GET YOUR IVY LEAGUE ASS IN HERE!"

You often heard Hunter Dane's voice before clapping eyes on him as if he were giving you fair warning. Today was no exception. Dane's bellowing spilled out across the newsroom floor as Jake Morris made his way toward the office door of the managing editor of *The Times Union*. It never boded well to be summoned to the command post, and Jake suspected why he had been called in.

For several months, he had been investigating some dubious activities of the local state senator, Ben Anderson. Jake covered politics for the paper. Most of the time that meant sitting through interminable public meetings, filing public records requests, or tagging after candidates at 4H Fairs. But this mission was different. Jake had been working on a deep dive into the dark world of campaign fundraising as practiced by one of the masters of statewide politics. Anderson was immersed in a campaign for a fourth term in the senate, but that wasn't the real contest. Everyone, at least everyone on the inside, knew that he was working to position himself for next year's gubernatorial run.

It had all started with a tip Jake got during the campaign from a young woman working on Anderson's staff. She had taken a sabbatical from college to volunteer on the campaign, and Jake had met her at a fundraiser. After standing together for hours on the periphery listening to several testimonials, they finally heard from the man himself. Later, they shared a few drinks and then, eventually, the remains of the evening.

At some point, Carol, or so he remembered her, began talking about the Senator's friend, Max Grabel. Grabel owned several nursing homes around the state. He and Anderson had apparently become quite close, to the point that they had just returned from a vacation together at Grabel's villa in the Turks and Caicos.

None of that seemed to register with Jake until a few days later when he was reviewing a list of upcoming senate committee meetings. The senate Health and Institutions Committee had scheduled hearings on nursing home safety. That inquiry was triggered by a recent fire at one of the homes that cost several lives. The hearings would be led by the Committee Chair, the Honorable Benjamin Anderson. Jake had learned there are few coincidences in politics. That's how this whole thing got started.

Before plunging in, Jake had made the tactical decision not to seek Dane's official sanction of the venture. Jake had been on the political beat for three years now. He had learned how to do it without breaking a sweat, but this project would be different. He knew that the paper had limited resources to fund a special investigation. Nor did Hunter Dane seem to have the appetite for one.

It was not that Dane lacked the guts for it. Despite a bit of a paunch, he certainly hadn't gone soft after nearly fifty years in the newspaper business. Recently, he had displayed his grit by throwing the paper's publisher out of his office when she attempted to cut editorial staff. It was rumored though that Dane was burned some years ago when he ran a series about an alleged pedophile priest. The reporter had misidentified the target of the inquiry, and an innocent priest had taken his own life. That incident had apparently left its mark. With that in mind, Jake decided to freelance this story while still making all his usual deadlines. He surmised now that he had somehow blown his cover, and he would have to face the wrath of Hunter Dane.

Dane had just finished blistering the hide of his copy editor who shambled past Jake on his way out the door. Dane was known around the paper as the "Great White". Now he was looking over his glasses at Jake. His bared teeth were jammed down on an ever-present unlit cigar.

"Who the hell do you think you are?" Dane's cigar swept the air, pre-empting any response.

He was just getting started. Dane was reputed to be one of the great creative cussers of all time. Usually, if you did not pass his saliva test, he would compare the object of his vitriol to a specific human body part or to a particular member of the animal world. Even a cultivated lady, such as the paper's publisher, noted that Dane's language on occasion was "somewhat pungent." But Dane dispensed with the preliminaries that day.

"What in the name of God were you thinking?"

Apparently, Jake had left his computer on the previous night. Dane was usually the last to leave the office. He happened to see something very interesting on Jake's screen on his way out the door. Now Dane pulled up

Jake's story on his computer. His tirade over, he silently read through the story again.

Jake had a moment to recover. He suspected that the managing editor was a bit intrigued by what he read. Whatever interested Dane could very well captivate the US Attorney if the information ever got into his hands.

Initially, what Jake learned seemed like just another sleazy politician sucking up to a wealthy donor. But after weeks of interviewing Anderson's current and former staffers, all for background only, obtaining emails from various sources, and reviewing years of financial disclosure statements and other public records, Jake had stumbled upon the filings of a non-profit organization known as Senior Moments Counselors which had Anderson's wife listed as its executive director. Its stated purpose was to provide counseling to family members of dementia patients. After more digging though, Jake discovered that the organization had received funding in the hundreds of thousands from another non-profit formed by Grabel Health Systems. He was not able to discover much activity involving Senior Moments other than a consulting agreement with a local gerontologist. This arrangement just might have had something to do with the recent decision of the senate Health and Institutions Committee to abandon its inquiry into nursing home safety and the adequacy of staffing at state nursing homes.

When Dane finished reading, he sat back in his chair, stroking his chin. Then he turned his chair away and stared out the window for several moments. Suddenly, he swung back around and looked solemnly at his young reporter.

What happened next nearly took Jake to his knees. He asked how soon the story would go to press. Dane studied him carefully and then quietly said, "Last time I checked, I make the calls on what stories we publish in this paper."

Now it was Jake's turn to let loose. "Are you kidding me?"

If he expected a response, he didn't get one. Dane just sat silently behind his desk, his eyes revealing a hint of sadness. Jake was shaking as he stood up. "I'm out of here."

Walking unsteadily out the door, Jake went to his desk, picked a used paper bag from the trash, and filled it with a few personal things. He then passed through the doors of *The Times Union* newsroom, likely for the last time.

TWO

Now began a time in Jake Morris's life that he would one day refer to as "The Odyssey." Like his ancient counterpart, Jake would be driven off course, engage in some swinish behavior, and be tempted by his own Circe. He would face some circumstances as daunting and ultimately life-changing as any that faced that Greek warrior. But for now, Jake was left to lick his wounds, and he did so in the grand tradition of the many frustrated journalists before him. He went on a bender that would have made Papa Hemingway proud.

After shaking the dust from *The Times Union*, he walked downtown to his favorite pub, Liam's Hideaway. Liam's was the real deal with its owner straight from County Cork. The Guinness was always fresh because it turned over so quickly. Jake had his first taste of it during a college semester abroad at Trinity College Dublin and he enjoyed its creamy tartness. The fish and chips were also delicious, and the patrons included many recent arrivals from the auld sod so "the craic was grand", as they say on the Emerald Isle. Jake was counting on all of that to stifle the anger and hurt he felt.

It was only mid-afternoon, so he had his choice of seats at the bar. He picked a spot at the end, nearest the musician's corner. Jake planned to be there for a while, so he knew he was well-positioned for when the players arrived. He ordered a pint, but then thought better of it and asked for two fingers of Tullamore Dew for accompaniment. Before long, he'd be redis-covering the words to some good old rebel songs.

The beer and whiskey came and went like the tide, and, when closing time came, Jake felt like he was trapped in a force 12 gale. He slid off the stool, hitched up his pants, and made his way to the exit with his buddy, Liam, as a guide. Fortunately, Liam had called a cab. He poured Jake into the back-seat, gave the cabbie directions, and Jake his final blessing.

Jake awoke the next day with a pounding head and a full bladder. He stumbled into the bathroom in only his boxers, and swaying over the bowl, managed to splash the seat only a bit. He turned and looked at the appa-rition staring back at him in the mirror. It vaguely resembled himself. Tall and thin, the face pale and lightly freckled, with hazel eyes and a full head of light brown hair. The dark circles under the eyes were a bit concerning but, hopefully, he would not get used to seeing them. With that, Jake began his first day among the unemployed.

After slipping on jeans and a sweatshirt, Jake turned on the coffee machine and began to forage through the kitchen, not a difficult task since he was never a cook and didn't keep much food on hand. He did find a half-eaten Danish in the refrigerator. That would do for breakfast. He then opened the front door of his apartment and retrieved the day's edition of *The Times Union*. He dropped it on the table, and the main article below the fold happened to be his last story, a report on state budget cuts to mass transit. That story was boring even for him, so he turned the paper over as he nibbled on the Danish and sipped his coffee. There, top front, was a photo of that smug bastard, Ben Anderson. He was standing with his wife and two kids next to a group holding signs reading "Seniors for Anderson." How ironic. Anderson looked trim in a custom suit with no tie. His angular face had a wide smile, framed by a thick head of silver hair. Anderson's wife appeared every bit the marathoner that she is, gazing proudly at her spouse. Their two kids were doing their best to look like they were enjoying it all. He thought for a moment that maybe Anderson had been clued in that Jake's investigative work would never see the light of day.

Suddenly, Jake looked up and saw the small thumb drive next to his keys on the counter. He had used it to copy the story on the way out yesterday. He couldn't help muttering to himself as he glanced at Anderson's photo, "Well, don't be so sure of yourself, buddy."

Jake put the paper down and looked out the window. He could see over the tops of smaller buildings extending eastward toward the river. The sun was still low, and it cast a brilliant sheen upon the water. He could make out two racing shells coursing ahead. Each had eight-man crews working together as if they were a single rower. "Beautiful," he thought, "but what the hell am I going to do now?"

Already he could feel the anger slipping away, but the hurt remained. Jake began to run through his possibilities. He didn't think that *The Times Union* would assert any proprietary rights to his story so it was possible that he could shop it to another publication or even publish it himself on the net. Anderson would obviously fight back hard. Could Jake withstand the pressure without the muscle of a major publisher behind him?

There must be something more behind Dane's behavior. What could it be? That question gnawed at Jake as he weighed his next move. Seeking a distraction, he picked up his cell phone to check on any overnight texts. No juice. He had put it on silent last night and, given his condition, he neglected to recharge it when he got home. He plugged it in now, and the screen exploded with messages from his former co-workers wondering what had happened yesterday.

Several people were in the newsroom when he left. They watched his abrupt departure in amazement. Obviously, there was a blow up between the Great White and Jake, and everybody wanted the scoop. He knew that he could not disclose the real reason for his departure, so he just spread the word that he and the Boss had agreed that Jake should pursue other opportunities. No one would buy it, but they would just have to accept it. Even if he couldn't. He did agree though to meet up with a few of his buddies from the paper that night for wings and watching football at Toppers, a popular spot catering to young guys on the prowl.

Jake knew he had to get out of his apartment for a while. He went down to the street, got into his much-neglected VW Jetta, and drove out into the suburbs. Almost instinctively, he headed for his old neighborhood. Not much had changed since he left for college almost twelve years ago. The neighborhood was all tree-lined streets, neatly laid out with modest homes on small lots. He stopped in front of one, a Cape Cod with white siding and Kelly-green shutters. The basketball pole and backboard were still there but the net was missing. There was a bike with training wheels turned over in the driveway. Otherwise, the old homestead looked pretty much the same. He had not been back there since his mother died.

While Jake was still in kindergarten, he learned that he'd been adopted. He soon got past the news. Nobody in school made a big deal about it, especially because his adoptive parents were so popular with the other kids. They were into middle age by that time, but they still had a lot of energy, and their house became headquarters for Jake and his friends. His parents didn't have a lot of money, but Jake never lacked for the essentials, and he certainly knew he was loved. His mom and dad were there at every game and every school assembly. He remembered now how proud they were, sitting in the front row as Jake gained the highest academic award at grade school graduation. He received a scholarship to the local Christian Brothers Prep and continued to excel academically and otherwise. He was a four-letter track star, winning the state championship in the eight hundred meters in his senior year. From there, he went on to Dartmouth and his visits home became less frequent.

After graduation, Jake returned to the area, first taking a job at his old prep school, and then moving on to his stint at *The Times Union*. He got his own place and tried to get back home as often as he could to check on the folks. He wished now he had tried harder. His mom was diagnosed with pancreatic cancer five years ago and died within a matter of months. His dad already had advanced Parkinson's disease. With Mom gone, he was placed in a nursing facility and didn't last more than a year after that.

In his mom's last days, Jake had stepped in to straighten out his parents' finances. He was shocked to find out that, over many years, he had been the beneficiary of a trust. His family's lifestyle certainly did not reflect it, but that explained why his parents had been able to pay for much of Jake's educational expenses and for special events like his semester abroad.

He had discovered correspondence to his parents from an attorney, Henry Battalini, Esq. Jake called him and met him over coffee one day, hoping to unravel this mystery. He judged that the gentleman was in his late fifties, conservatively dressed, and with an air of quiet refinement. Jake was unable to find out much about him, except that Mr. Battalini was a sole practitioner. He learned even less about the circumstances of the trust. He was simply told that the identity of the benefactor could not be revealed. Mr. Battalini was the trustee of what he described as a sprinkling trust, an arrangement whereby the trustee has almost unlimited discretion to determine the amount and timing of financial distributions. Until their deaths, any funds given to Jake had been through his parents. Jake was told that any future distributions would be made to him directly. Mr. Battalini already knew his address, his employer and pretty much everything else, it seemed.

Jake sat quietly behind the wheel for a few minutes more, then started the engine and headed back into the city.

That night, he got together with his friends at Toppers. The event had much the same ingredients as the night before. Jake was a bit more in control though, and he resisted any efforts to wheedle out of him the details of his dust-up with Dane. There was one interesting development. Toppers had a bartender who caught Jake's eye the moment he walked into the place. She was a tall redhead with an open smile and a friendly manner that quickly made her customers feel at ease while also clearly conveying that she was all business. Jake got the message. He decided he would test her resolve another time. Meanwhile, he hoped he had made as favorable an impression upon her as she had on him.

His pals wanted to know Jake's next move. That was an easy one. He told them he didn't have one yet. Any shift to another paper would require him to leave the area. Jake didn't rule that out, but it was not his preferred choice. He could try to do some freelance work, maybe writing magazine features, but he was just not ready to pull the trigger.

THREE

JAKE'S NEW LIFE SOON TOOK SHAPE. IT WAS NOT A THING OF BEAUTY. Each day seemed to melt away, and yet he awoke one morning surprised to realize that his period of unemployment was now entering its sixth week. Most days, he rolled out by ten after another night of carousing. After some coffee and toast, he would take a long run along the river, shower, and then jump on the computer.

He soon learned that the reports of a recession in the print media were accurate. Jake had thought he might be the exception. After all, he had won multiple Stapleton Awards for political reporting while at *The Times Union*. Somehow, that didn't seem to count. So, after he got past his reluctance to relocate, he extended his search. But to little avail. He did get an offer to work as a technical writer for an industrial publisher, but Jake had no interest in what would have been a dead-end job writing about things like solenoid ball valves rather than the endless variety of characters he found in the world of politics.

In the first few days after leaving the paper, Jake wondered how he'd pay his bills. His credit cards were nearly tapped out, and he soon learned he was temporarily disqualified from receiving unemployment benefits since his separation from the paper was deemed voluntary. But fortunately, Mr. Battalini came through for him. Two weeks after his last paycheck, he received a check from his trustee which, oddly enough, closely matched his bi-weekly take-home pay. Even stranger, after a few weeks of that, he began receiving two checks, one payable to his landlord toward his monthly apartment rent and one payable to him. It was as if his trustee were aware of Jake's growing bar bills. Something had to break, and he hoped it would be soon.

Jake's mind often wandered back to his time at the paper, and particularly his experiences with Hunter Dane. When Jake came to *The Times Union*, he was pretty green. Jake chuckled as he thought of the choice of that word. His only real journalistic experience was working as a reporter for the Big Green's school paper, *The Dartmouth News*. It touted itself as the country's oldest college newspaper, founded in 1799. He had the chance to write some interesting pieces, including one about a student protest of a controversial commencement speaker. That one got him featured on the national news. However, those experiences did not really prepare him for the pressures he faced at *The Times Union*, ferreting out information from his sources, writing the columns, ensuring their accuracy, and making tight deadlines. He had to admit that in his inimitable fashion, Hunter Dane had taught him all that.

When Jake arrived at the paper, he had just gone through a bad patch. In the prior year, he had lost a wife and a job. He should have seen signs of the divorce, but his departure from teaching was unexpected.

Having majored in English, Jake left Dartmouth, unsure of his next step. Near the end of his senior year, his future father-in-law offered to arrange Jake's entry into the financial services world, but Jake had no appetite for it. The law was another consideration, but he just wasn't sufficiently inspired to spend another three years in school at this point. So, for the moment, teaching seemed the default choice.

Jake got word shortly after graduation that his old prep school, Christian Brothers Prep, had an unexpected opening in the English Department. A long-time teacher had been diagnosed with leukemia and was unable to return. The headmaster, Brother James, reached out to Jake, who had been one of his favorite students. So it didn't take long for him to join the faculty there. The fact that Jake was both an alumnus and an Ivy League grad made it an easy sell to the school's Board of Trustees.

It was much harder for Jake to pitch it to his new wife. He had already disappointed her by turning down her father's offer to join his private banking firm. Now, he was asking her to leave her family in Greenwich, Connecticut so that he could come back home to take a low-paying job teaching mostly underachieving adolescents. How many chances would she have to find a job there in her field of interest, Impressionist Art? Slim to none. Pippa Montgomery was not pleased.

Jake and Pippa had been members of Dartmouth's track team. Jake was initially attracted by her long legs, tawny blonde hair, and fine features. Pippa found him both cute and funny. During their last year at Dartmouth, they were inseparable, becoming engaged in January and marrying in June. When Jake took the teaching job, Pippa privately hoped that his tenure would be brief and that they would then move onto something more substantial. After the move, she spent her days working on the computer in their small apartment, drafting copy for an art exhibit catalogue. Her only relief came through her long afternoon jogs along the river. When Jake returned from school each night, he spent much of his time preparing lesson plans and grading papers. Slowly, communication broke down, and they each began to question privately their marriage commitment. They both had a stubborn streak though, wide enough that neither of them could fully stretch out and grasp the truth. At least, until the day that Jake announced that he was leaving his teaching job.

Jake had started off well at the Prep. Most of his students took to him. He was only a few years older than they were, and his track accomplishments at the school were still talked about. The students also responded well to his somewhat unorthodox teaching techniques. In addition to his classes, he coached track and cross-country and moderated the school paper. He had no other life except school although it seemed that only Pippa was aware of it.

The end came suddenly. He had assigned a major essay to one of his less-advanced senior sections just before the Christmas break. Performance on the essay would have a major impact upon the students' semester grade at a time when transcripts were to be sent to supplement their college applications. When the papers came back, a single essay stood out from all the rest. One of the more pampered members of the class handed in a paper that was striking because of its clumsy effort to appear scholarly. After reading the essay twice, Jake began to Google certain passages. Not surprisingly, he discovered that they had been lifted from several academic treatises. Many of the plagiarized excerpts made no sense based upon their context. "How stupid," he thought. Under his established standards for the class, Jake decided he had no choice but to assign the offending student a grade of zero.

When the papers were returned, it was not long before all hell broke loose. The student's father was an alumnus of the school and a major donor. He was furious and dead set on seeing that this "discrepancy," as he called it, was resolved quickly so that his son's revised grade would go out to his targeted colleges on time.

Jake refused to budge. He reminded the headmaster that the school was touted as a place for Christian gentlemen. Christian gentlemen don't cheat. At least, they aren't rewarded for doing so. It turned out to be a losing battle. After multiple efforts to change his mind, the headmaster determined that Jake had lost his objectivity. Perhaps, he had not explained the rules against plagiarism clearly enough. Another teacher was brought in to deal with the problem. She decided that the best way to bring it to an end would be to allow the student to write another essay over the holidays. It would be graded during the break, and the new grade would be incorporated into the student's transcript. The student and his parents were satisfied. Jake was not. He emailed Brother James and told him he would not be returning after the Christmas break.

That evening over dinner Jake broke the news to Pippa, and she exploded. "You what? We are less than six months into this marriage, and you decide to quit your job without giving me the courtesy of talking about it beforehand? Is that how little you think of me"?

Jake stared back for a moment, and then with a slight shake of his head, he turned away. Pippa stood up, turned, and walked toward their bedroom. Then, she wheeled and fired one more shot. "Jake, did you ever consider that the punishment here might be greater than the crime? We both know the outsized importance placed today on being accepted by an elite college. Parents hammer that home to their child every chance they get. If you held to your self-imposed standard, this young man might have gotten locked out of consideration by the school of his dreams. And his parents might not let him forget it. Couldn't you have imposed some other penalty, equally onerous, but not with such drastic consequences?"

Again, Jake had no response.

"Well, that's what I would have counselled you. But it's now too late."

Pippa handed Jake a blanket and pillow and then shut the bedroom door. After a brief discussion the next day, she called her parents and then booked a flight back to Greenwich. She'd pick up her life back there. Jake would now have to figure out what was left of his.

FOUR

IT WASN'T LONG AFTER JAKE'S PRECIPITOUS DEPARTURE FROM teaching that his mom approached him about an opportunity in journalism. His parents knew a guy in management at *The Times Union*. Apparently, they were looking for a cub reporter to cover the local scholastic sports scene. Jake seemed to fit the bill with his college journalism and sports experiences. He had nothing else lined up, so he took the interview. As he sat outside the office of the managing editor, he worried that his Dartmouth pedigree might work against him. He didn't want anything to create the impression that this job would be treated by him as just a placeholder until a better one came along. Even though he hoped that's what would happen.

As soon as Jake entered the office, he could see that the occupant was a throwback to another era. The place had an air of barely controlled chaos. The desk suffered from long-term abuse, the wood scuffed, and the finish faded from the random banging of chairs, spilled coffee, and the rub of sweaty hands. The top was mostly covered with recent editions of the paper and a few other publications, as well as drafts of future articles and yellowed memos. All of it arranged randomly so that nothing could be quickly located, except by the occupant. There was a credenza on the side wall opposite a single window, its thin veneer of dust interrupted only by a few pieces of memorabilia. A brownish autographed baseball, a few tarnished trophies, and a dog-eared program from an early Super Bowl. There were only a few hangings on the walls, and there was no evidence anywhere of a life beyond the newspaper. The only concession to modernity was a computer station set on a small table next to the desk. It was not turned on.

Hunter Dane got up from behind the desk, walked quickly around and offered Jake his hand. Dane was about six feet and heavily limbed. He was somewhere in his late sixties, with white hair, closely cropped. A nasty look-ing, unlit cigar stuck out of the side of his mouth. Jake would always recall that Dane's most prominent feature was his penetrating blue eyes, now in-tently fixed upon him.. Dane offered a concessionary smile as he gestured for Jake to take a seat. He chose not to retreat behind his desk but pulled up a chair facing Jake directly.

As Jake would come to learn, Dane handled the interview like everything else in his life. He grabbed the reins and never gave them up.

"Mr. Morris, what makes you think you want to get back into the newspaper business?"

Jake thought for an instant, then said, "I don't know yet."

Dane's eyes blinked. "I guess that's a good start."

Dane obviously had absorbed everything in Jake's bio, but as the conversation continued, it seemed like he had done some additional research.

"Why did you decide to take on the entire establishment at Christian Brothers Prep? Seems like you may have a problem with authority, Mr. Morris."

Jake tried to explain what drove him out the door. He wasn't sure of Dane's reaction. His story elicited just a bit of a grunt from the old man.

After a wide-ranging conversation covering Jake's personal history, his academic credentials including his time with *The Dartmouth News*, and his views on the responsibilities of a journalist, Hunter Dane concluded their meeting by letting Jake know what to expect.

"You are being hired to cover scholastic sports. That means you will be traveling all over the city and suburbs watching games until you want to find a sensory deprivation chamber somewhere. I know you are a sports nut, but you will have to learn more about every sport than most of the coaches you will get to know. On Friday and Saturday nights, you will be on the phone until midnight, grabbing box scores, and getting quotes from coaches and players. And you better not get it wrong. I don't want to be fielding calls from pissed-off parents because their son grabbed more rebounds than you reported. Remember. You are not this current generation's version of Bob Woodward. At least not yet. In theory, journalism is simple. You gather the facts, make sure they're accurate and then you write the story in a way that makes people want to read it. I know in practice it's not that easy, but you can't lose sight of the essentials. If you successfully cut your teeth on the sports beat, maybe you'll get a chance to write about more momentous subjects. But we're getting ahead of ourselves. You'll start Monday morning."

Two minutes after he responded, "Yes, sir," Jake was out the door.

He was taking over for a veteran of the local sports scene. They worked together for two weeks before his predecessor's retirement. Jake basically shadowed him for the first week. He was introduced to a bunch of coaches and athletic directors but didn't get most of their names. He also quickly learned a bit about the politics of high school sports, watching a parent joust with a coach trying to improve his son's chances for a college scholarship. By the end of the second week, Jake was pretty much doing the job on his own.

It took a while, but he came to like the work. He most enjoyed meeting the kids and watching them grow as young men and women. Sometimes he had the opportunity to write a feature story on one of them, and it felt good to do something to boost their confidence, much like what he had tried to do as a teacher.

Every so often, Hunter Dane would have cause to offer Jake a refresher on the basics of journalism. Like the time that he reported on a championship basketball game and got the scores reversed in the story. That conversation left a bruise that never fully healed. Dane read his paper from front page to back every day, and nothing in it escaped him. He was always the first to know when a certain reporter was back on the sauce, or if one of his employees was scouting out another job. In every instance, he swept in quickly and dealt with it.

Although Jake felt the lash of the Great White more than once, he also witnessed his other side. When Jake's mom and dad died, Dane attended each of their funerals, sitting through the full service each time. After he had been at the sports desk about three years, the guy covering state and local politics up and left without notice. Dane had to find a replacement quickly. He chose Jake. Working the politics desk was a much higher stakes game. Dane kept a close eye on Jake, quick to offer advice when asked and criticism when needed.

Once, Dane discovered a piece in which Jake had described the atmosphere at a public meeting as "soporific." Dane hit the ceiling. "Maybe you think you are already working for *The New York Times*. Or maybe *The Times* isn't good enough for you. Perhaps *The Paris Review* is in your future. But until you get there, Morris, while you are here don't you ever again use a word that can't be understood by the average tenth grader. I don't want my readers having to stop to Google every other word you write."

On the other hand, when Jake received his first Stapleton Award for a series on bid rigging in the mayor's office, Dane was at the awards ceremony. Afterward, he did something Jake did not expect. As everyone was filing out, Dane suggested that they adjourn to the bar for a nightcap. The boss ordered two glasses of single malt, neat. He turned to Jake, raised his glass, and said, "It's good to know that neither of us is wasting his time. Well done."

Thinking back now, Jake continued to be mystified as to why Dane hesitated to run his story. It took some time, but Jake came to believe that there was no way that Hunter Dane was on the take or that he was intimidated by anyone. There must be a good reason and an equally good one for why he was keeping it to himself. For now, Jake decided to sit on it as he sorted things out. In any event, he had likely burned his bridges and he now wished he hadn't.

FIVE

S Jake spent his days in his monk's cell contemplating his future, he considered a recent offer to write a feature story for a men's magazine. They wanted him to live the experience of men in a dangerous occupation, telling their stories firsthand. He would be fully immersed in this new experience for several weeks, if not months, and Jake was beginning to think that he needed that right now. Yet, every time he tried to focus on the assignment he found himself distracted by thoughts of the redheaded bartender at Toppers he encountered some weeks ago.

Jake's breakup with Pippa had left a bitter taste, and for a long while he had no interest in chasing after anyone else. Sure, there were occasional dates and a few overnighters, but the hectic pace of his job seemed to fill that void in his personal life. Until now.

Jake had been back to Toppers more than once since his first encounter with Tess Reilly. He had asked one of the other bartenders her name. He knew she would find out, but he didn't care. He was certainly drawn to her good looks, the peaches and cream complexion and high cheekbones, all framed by her sculpted red hair. However, there was more to her than that. He watched her interacting with other customers, trying to listen but not be discovered. She had the professional bartender's gift for gab, but he also recognized a certain detachment. It was something in her eyes when she wasn't engaging with customers. Just a hint of sadness. "This woman has been through a lot," he thought to himself.

Jake had the good sense not to move in quickly. Tess obviously dealt with aggressive men every day on the job. He did not want to be considered just another occupational hazard. On each visit, Jake would find a seat near Tess's station, stay only briefly, but try to chat her up. She was cordial, but he didn't pick up any indication that her interest was more than professional.

All that changed one night. Jake came in late, and he sat down next to a guy who obviously was past his limit. He was loud and getting sloppy. He called for another round, and Tess came over to suggest politely that he call it a night. The drunk didn't take it well. Grabbing Jake's drink, he threw it in Tess's face. Jake reacted quickly, pinning the guy against the bar until the manager arrived and took over.

Jake looked across the bar at Tess. She was shaking and trying to hold back tears, as another bartender tried to comfort her. Jake stammered a bit as he told her how terrible he felt while she tried to pull herself together. She thanked him and said, "It's just my luck to keep running up against guys like him."

Immediately, he saw his opportunity. "I would like the chance to change your luck."

Tess seemed to look right through him.

He followed up with, "How would you like to meet me for breakfast tomorrow morning?"

Tess thought for a moment. "How about the Perfect Pancake at 10?"

He responded, "You're on. See you then."

Jake paid his tab and quickly left.

He got to the restaurant early the next morning. It was a Saturday, so he wanted to be sure to have a table when Tess arrived. He picked one near the front windows and was into his second cup of coffee when he saw a blue van pull into the parking lot. Tess walked around the van as a young boy stepped out of the passenger side. She opened the sliding door behind it and a ramp dropped down. Stepping inside, she made some adjustment and then slowly backed out while guiding a wheelchair. Another smaller boy was in the chair. His head swayed from side to side as Tess pushed him toward the front door while the older one trailed behind. When they arrived at the table, Jake stood and pushed a chair away so that Tess could guide the wheelchair into place. Then they all sat down.

Tess immediately took charge.

"Jake, let me introduce you to my sons." Gesturing to the older one, she said, "This is Thomas. He's eight." Then she placed a hand on the wheelchair and said, "And this is Michael, but we call him Mikey. He's six."

All the while, Tess was watching Jake closely, searching for his reaction to these surprise guests. He didn't hesitate.

"Good to meet you, boys. Do you like pancakes?"

As they waited to be served, Jake did his best to adjust to the distraction of two young boys out for breakfast. Thomas was talking about his basketball team while Mikey attempted to join the conversation. But he could only utter sounds that were unintelligible to Jake. Meanwhile, the boy's head rolled back and forth and his lower body spasmed from time to time. With all that going on, Tess was still able to manage a conversation, commenting generally about last night's unpleasantness, and asking Jake about his work. When breakfast arrived, conversation ceased. Tess concentrated on feeding Mikey and reminding Thomas of his table manners.

After the plates were cleared and the bill paid, Tess apologized but said that she and the boys would need to get back home. Her mom was waiting to take charge of Mikey while she took Thomas to his game. Outside, when the boys were settled in the van, Tess thanked Jake for breakfast. She hoped that he was not put off by the unexpected guests, but she had no choice but to bring them along. Without thinking, he replied, "Well, this is probably the most unusual first date I've ever had."

She looked at him curiously. "First date?"

Jake was visibly embarrassed. "I guess I'm getting ahead of myself."

Tess smiled and said, "Maybe not. I'll give you my number in case you'd like to try for number two."

While driving back to his apartment, Jake tried to process what had just happened. Tess had somehow felt comfortable enough to show her cards, or at least to turn one over. She had tested him. He wondered how many guys would have politely walked away from that scene, afraid of what they might be getting themselves into. Well, Jake was not walking away, at least for the moment. From what he had observed, he was more interested than ever in Tess Reilly.

SIX

Ben Anderson's days began early and ended late. As usual, he awoke at 5:00 a.m. His wife, Brooke, did not budge as he eased his way out of bed, completed his morning ritual, slipped on a robe, and went downstairs. It was nearly daybreak when he walked outside for the newspaper. As he sat down to fruit and cereal, he quickly scanned the headlines. Ben was immediately drawn to a story at the bottom of the front page. "Hickey Appoints New Lieutenant Governor," it read.

Governor Jim Hickey had a little over a year left in his final term. The state constitution prevented him from another run. His former lieutenant governor had died suddenly, and Hickey was bound to select a successor, if only for his short time left in office.

As Anderson pushed toward election to his fourth term in the senate, through threats and promises, he had extracted from Hickey a commitment that he would not put any obstacles in Ben's way in his own drive for the governorship next year. That promise included putting no one in as lieutenant governor who could use it to challenge him. Then, Anderson came up with a better idea. Why not put his most serious rival in the job, but hogtie him so that he would have no chance to make a run for the top spot? Lieutenant governors only do what governors allow them to do. Hickey would control all his movements in office, making sure that he was given trivial projects that kept him out of the news. The guy would be stuck doing chores like chairing a commission studying whether to extend the deer hunting season.

After Anderson considered the field of potential candidates, he suggested that Hickey appoint Assemblyman Nick Fazio. Fazio was a hard-charging legislator who ached to be the state's chief executive. He had a background as a tenacious prosecutor before entering the legislature. He was handsome and had an equally photogenic family. Anderson judged him to be his only viable competitor, and now Fazio had taken the bait.

As he sipped his coffee, Ben smiled and muttered to himself, "Nicky boy, you finally screwed the pooch this time."

Fazio thought he would now be just one step away from the governor's seat, poised to capture it next November, but he was well on his way to political oblivion.

The Senate was not in session, so Anderson planned to spend the day in his district office, receiving constituent visits and preparing his remarks for the Cardinal's annual charity banquet that evening. He put on a blazer, open collar shirt, and casual slacks. By seven, he was in the backseat of his car with his chief of staff next to him and his administrative assistant driving.

Meg Holland was Anderson's alter ego. They had been together ten years now. She was as tough as they come in the business. She knew everything about every politician on the scene, including things their spouses would be shocked to discover. If Anderson thought it, Holland had already acted on it. She would soon be taking on the dual roles of chief of staff and campaign director. His administrative assistant, Stan Mosca, was still green, just a few years out of undergrad at Fordham, but smart and aggressive. They worked well together.

Ben Anderson had always touted his openness to receiving visits from the public every third Wednesday of the month. It tried his patience, but the publicity it generated was worth it. Stan always sat in, taking notes, and then seeing that either he or one of their other staffers followed through, providing a response to the aggrieved party. The requests were generally mundane, requiring his staff to plunge into the bureaucratic quagmire of state government and get the wheels turning. Sometimes nothing could be done, but it was paramount to demonstrate that an effort had been made.

Anderson left the afternoon open to get ready for his evening event. Each year, Cardinal William Boyle held a lavish dinner at the Dunham Arms, ostensibly for the purpose of raising money for Archdiocesan charities. It accomplished that and a lot more. The event drew about a thousand dignitaries: businesspeople, labor leaders, academics, clergy, and every statewide politician whose campaign coffers could cover the ticket price. It was strictly black tie and had been a stag affair until recently when the Cardinal realized the need to add females to the mix. He was concerned about the hits that the Church had been taking lately. No sense in fueling more claims of misogyny among its ranks.

The Cardinal's dinner was just about the hottest ticket among the state's power brokers. It was an ecumenical affair. The only common bond among the attendees was their ravenous pursuit of power and money. Past dinners had been the catalyst to launch certain political campaigns and to ruin others.

Both business mergers and dissolutions were accomplished over the course of the evening. Alliances were formed and enemies made.

Ben Anderson looked forward to it every year, but especially so this time. The Cardinal had made a point of informing him that he would be seated on the dais next to him. The Governor would be on the Cardinal's right and Ben on his left. Apart from wanting to advance Ben's plans for higher office, the Cardinal was also expressing his appreciation for Anderson's work on behalf of the Archdiocese in the senate. Ben had been successful in bottling up in committee a bill which would have opened a one-year window for claimants to sue for alleged sexual molestation even though the normal statute of limitations had run out. He was particularly proud of that piece of work. It played out so slowly that the media lost track of it, distracted by the constant churn of daily news. Ben was happy to see that his efforts were now bearing fruit.

The parade of petitioners had passed through Anderson's offices by early afternoon. Mosca was tasked to run down their requests. Hopefully, he would resolve their problems, but in each case, he would prepare a written response which Anderson would sign personally.

Ben retreated to his office for his usual lunch of cottage cheese and sparkling water. He sat there and thought about what he would say that night. He would only have a few moments at the end of the program, just before the Governor spoke and the Cardinal made his final closing comments. That would be more than Fazio would get. He would have a non-speaking role in the audience.

Anderson couldn't help but smile. "Doesn't he know how useful it is to bundle a $100,000 in contributions to the Cardinal's fund?" he thought. He sat for a few minutes, made some notes, grabbed his jacket, and headed back home.

When he arrived, he met Brooke in the driveway coming back from her daily run. They both would be attending that night's event; however, Brooke would be at one of the tables on the floor with Max Grabel and his wife. They both had become friendlier with the Grabels over the last few years, leading to Brooke's involvement with Senior Moments.

It had taken some time for Brooke to adjust to her husband's life as a politician. When they married twenty-four years ago, Ben was a young lawyer, struggling to make partner in the largest and most influential firm in the city. Ben saw politics as a means to advance himself in the firm. So, when an opportunity to run for the assembly came up, he jumped at it. Initially, their goal was for him to make money, but Ben soon became more attracted to the allure of politics. When the senate seat opened, Ben saw his chance. That was twelve years ago, and Ben's focus had not changed. He loved working the levers of power, but Brooke had come to tire of it. She always wanted to be the spouse of a successful attorney. Although Ben was still a partner in the firm, he hadn't really practiced law in years. He was paid $150,000 a year to be listed on the letterhead and perform various public relations roles. That plus his senatorial salary did not exactly meet Brooke's expectations. It had been a source of contention between them for years now. That had led to their decision to accept Max Grabel's offer.

From the beginning of his political career, Ben Anderson had played up to and occasionally beyond the lines, ethically and legally. He quickly learned to finesse the rules prohibiting "pay to play" in accepting political donations. Ben always avoided any contacts with donors where he specifically agreed to perform a service in return for payment. But that was until he met Max Grabel. Grabel did not amass his considerable fortune through subtlety. He knew what Anderson could do for him in the senate, and he recognized how much more he could accomplish as governor. Grabel contributed heavily to Anderson's campaigns, both personally and then by bundling payments through third parties. His hold on Anderson was further tightened through their guy weekends for golf at his villa where Grabel also supplied the female accompaniment. But his idea to draw Brooke into his web was masterful.

Grabel knew that Brooke was hungry for money, so he suggested to Ben that they set up two dummy non-profits. Grabel's would appear to fund various worthy charities, including what eventually became Senior Moments. Brooke's involvement as executive director seemed to be for the purpose of advancing her husband's concern for senior services; however, apart from some meager support for some academics studying the impact of dementia on families, Senior Moments' true purpose was to launder over $100,000 each year to Anderson personally, disguised as executive compensation to his wife. The crowning touch for Grabel was that his bribe would not just be well hidden. It would also be tax deductible.

SEVEN

WHEN BEN AND BROOKE ENTERED THE BALLROOM, BEN COULD SEE that more than a few conversations were interrupted, with heads craning to watch them, checking for indications of where they stood currently in the political pecking order. Ben shook hands, squeezed arms, and tapped shoulders while Brooke air-kissed her way through the crowds as he escorted her to a table with the Grabels. He then made his way to the podium.

The Cardinal led the assemblage in offering grace before dinner, and Ben quickly and casually crossed himself before and afterward, as if he were a true son of the Church rather than a nominal Presbyterian. He made sure to be seen sharing some casual conversation with both the Governor and the Cardinal and ordered a single pinot noir to go along with the prime rib. Ben then settled back and endured the parade of speakers ahead of him on the agenda.

When Ben's time arrived, the plates were being cleared, and he could see that the audience was getting restless. Only he, the Governor, and the Cardinal remained to speak before the masses could adjourn to the outside bar. Ben would try to be both brief and memorable.

He stood and stepped to the microphone, pulled a wad of paper from his jacket, then looked at the crowd. He could almost hear their collective sigh. Then he smiled, put the paper away and said, "just kidding." The laughter in response set the tone for what followed.

First, Ben thanked the Cardinal for his work in promoting so many worthy charities and the Governor for his leadership on behalf of the people of this state. He then took a moment to congratulate his good friend, Nick Fazio, for his ascendancy to the office of lieutenant governor.

"Nick, I know you will be a great success in the job, but I recommend that you wear your track shoes every day if you are going to try to keep up with our Governor."

He looked down at Fazio, who was beaming as he turned around to accept the scattered applause. For a moment, Ben locked eyes with the

Governor who did not seem especially pleased at his taking the opportunity to spike the football.

Ben next noted the fine turn-out for the event. He did say that he had heard a complaint from an unnamed monsignor earlier in the evening that there were too many politicians attending this year. He said that he had asked the monsignor a question: "Monsignor, how can you tell the difference between a professional politician and an amateur? He didn't know so I told him that all the 'professionals' are wearing Roman collars."

That brought the house down, with the loudest guffaw coming from the Cardinal.

Ben concluded by saying that both politicians and the clergy have one thing in common. "We both deal in the art of the possible, and this event, the Cardinal's Annual Charity Dinner, makes a better life possible for many families and individuals in our community."

He sat down to a standing ovation.

EIGHT

JAKE HELD OFF A DAY BEFORE CALLING TESS. HE TOLD HER HOW much he enjoyed his breakfast with her and the boys. She thanked him and said that Thomas and Mikey had fun also. Jake asked if he could exercise that option for date number two. Tess paused for a moment.

"What do you have in mind?"

He suggested dinner the next Saturday night at Emilio's, a fancy Italian restaurant. Tess agreed. She would have her mother available to watch the kids. Jake wrote down her address and said he would pick her up at six. "Game on," he thought. He had not felt so excited about anything in a long time.

That Saturday night, Jake stood at the door of a modest, but well-kept, townhouse in a nearby suburb. An older woman opened the door, smiled at him, and said, "You must be Jake. I'm Mary, Tess's mom. Come on in."

Jake walked into the living room and found the boys watching a ballgame. Thomas said "hi" and Mikey just smiled at him. Tess came in from the kitchen. She greeted Jake warmly and then reminded her mom to keep an eye on the crock-pot and have the boys in bed by 9:30. With that, they were out the door and on their way to dinner.

As they sat down at their table, all of Jake's attention was upon Tess. She wore a simple green dress which complemented her tall, slim frame. He thought she seemed more relaxed than their breakfast encounter. As they each looked over the menus, Jake asked her if she had any favorite entrees.

Tess laughed and replied: "Never ask an Irishwoman what her favorite Italian dish is. She'll just say spaghetti. Besides, I don't get out much, so why don't you order for the two of us?"

Jake smiled. "Selecting food and drink is one of my few talents."

When the waiter returned, Jake ordered eggplant rollatini as an appetizer and veal Osso Buco for them both. He also asked for a bottle of a decent chianti classico.

"We're off to a good start," he thought to himself.

The conversation over dinner was light, ranging from Tess comically describing her more eccentric customers, to Jake talking about some interesting exploits covering politicians. They finished their espressos and Jake suggested that they adjourn to the bar for a sambuca. As they sat sipping their drinks, Jake asked Tess how she came to be a bartender.

Tess stared back at him for a moment before saying, "I guess what you are really getting at is what's the story with Tess Reilly. Well, you paid for my dinner, Mr. Morris, so I guess you're entitled to hear it, just as long as I hear yours also."

As Tess talked about her life, the light in her eyes seemed to fade, a reflection of what he had seen at Toppers that night. Her dad died suddenly when Tess was 19, while she was studying to be a teacher at the local community college. She was the youngest of four. A few months after her dad's death, one of her brothers, a local cop, introduced her to a friend of his on the force. Paul was handsome and he made Tess laugh, helping her to get through a very tough spell in her life. They became close quickly, and a few months later, Tess discovered she was pregnant. Although she was not a particularly devout Catholic at the time, her mom was, so when she found out the news, she encouraged Tess to bring the child into the world.

"I am so grateful now that I took her advice. Thomas is pure joy, and he is so kind to his younger brother. The advice that I should have rejected, however, was her urging me to accept Paul's offer of marriage."

Tess related how her relationship with Paul started to unravel even before Thomas was born. Paul worked undercover and his hours were erratic. She sometimes would not see him for days, and she certainly couldn't count on him for family events or other social gatherings. He would often come home under the influence of one thing or another. It got worse though.

With Paul absent most of the time, Tess had to drop out of school when Thomas arrived. Although Mary helped when she could, Tess was essentially raising the baby alone. When she discovered she was pregnant again, Paul cut loose on her. He was furious and came close to striking her more than once. He told her that the baby was all her fault and that she should have an abortion. When she refused, he moved out. Paul blamed Michael's diagnosis of cerebral palsy on her, and he only paid support when she threatened to take him to court.

One day Tess saw Paul's picture on TV. He and his partner had been arrested for stealing drugs from some major dealers, using it themselves and bartering some of it for sex with prostitutes. Paul was convicted and sentenced to ten years in prison. As awful as it was to hear the news, Tess was almost relieved. She later learned that Paul had died in jail under suspicious circumstances, an apparent victim of one of the people he had helped put away. At least he was out of her life altogether.

Tess paused for a moment and took a sip of her drink.

Jake couldn't stop himself. "How did you ever recover from that?"

She thought for a moment. "I'm not sure I have. When Paul was dismissed from the department, all our income stopped. We lost his pension and our health insurance coverage too. It wasn't long before we also lost the little house that we owned. Skyrocketing credit card debt forced me to file for bankruptcy. We moved in with my mom which is where we are now. We qualify for Medicaid but it doesn't cover all the health care we need, especially with Mikey's cerebral palsy. I tended bar before, and I was able to get the job at Toppers. I work Tuesday through Saturday nights from seven to two. You've seen what I put up with, but the tips and Mary's Social Security are enough to barely hold things together. She also covers for me when I'm at work, making sure that the kids get bathed and are in bed on time. I'm able to take Thomas to school and pick him up, take Mikey to his therapy, make dinner for them, and generally keep the place up. Recently, I've gone back to college, taking two courses this semester. It's a grind but I put myself in this situation. We're getting by, but with Mom getting up there and Mikey becoming a bigger challenge over time, I try not to think too far ahead. Well, can you top that story, Mr. Morris?"

"I'm not sure I can."

Jake talked about his adoptive parents, the stable childhood they provided, and the recent revelation of a secret benefactor who helped with the finances. He described his experiences at Dartmouth and his short marriage to Pippa. He then told her about his brief teaching experience and his work at *The Times Union*. Without going into specifics, he talked about his recent departure from the paper after discovering a scandal involving a local politician and then Hunter Dane's apparent decision to shut down the story. Finally, he shared with her something about the offer he was considering to write a piece about men in a dangerous occupation.

When he finished, Tess smiled and said, "Well, I guess we both have had our share of missteps."

In the car on their way back to Tess's house, Tess turned to Jake. "You probably figured out that I brought the boys to breakfast because I didn't want you to have any illusions about me. Now you know the full story. I can't afford any more mistakes. I must protect my boys, and I can't have another jerk in my life. Don't take that personally, Jake. You seem like a good guy. I like you. I like you a lot. If all that doesn't turn you off, I am ready to take the next step, but only if you let me control the pace. How does that sound?"

Jake stopped the car in front of her house. He was clearly rattled by her candor. He turned to Tess and said, "Sounds good to me."

"Alright then. No need to see me to the door. But next time let's not go to such an expensive place."

She then leaned toward him, placed her hand under his chin, and planted a kiss directly on his lips. She was out the door and up the walk before he could say or do another thing.

NINE

Hunter Dane leaned over his desk as if he were about to launch himself toward Jake's successor, Liz Schiller. His face was beet red, almost the color of the many strikeouts and interlineations he had made on the draft of her story of the Cardinal's dinner the night before. Dane was in attendance, and Schiller's account bore little resemblance to what he had observed. He dropped it in front of her and directed that she clean it up as best she could without missing deadline. Reflexively stubbing out his unlit cigar, he dismissed her with a slight wave of his hand. As she walked back into the newsroom, the other reporters immediately recognized what had happened. They all had the same experience at one time or another. Liz and her bloodied draft both looked like they had been ambushed, and in a way, they had.

Dane tried to regain his composure. Maybe this new reporter will work out. Maybe not. She's certainly no Jake Morris. Jake would have gone beyond a simple recounting of the proceedings. He would have picked up the subtle and not-so-subtle subplots involving Anderson, Fazio, the Governor, and the Cardinal. Jake would have deftly sewed them into the fabric of the story. And he wouldn't have resorted to highfalutin words and obscure metaphors to do it.

"At least I cured him of that," Dane muttered.

Dane was nearing the end of his career and he knew it. The newspaper business bore little resemblance to what it was when he started. Print circulation and advertising revenue continued to trend downward, and although the paper now had a digital edition, it just wasn't the same as holding all the news together in your hands. People scanned their smart phones and read the headlines that interested them, but usually not the whole story. Sure, there still were *The Times* and *The Post* and a few regional outliers like *The Times Union,* but each day more folks were dropping their subscriptions and getting a distorted version of events from their chosen cable network.

"Pretty soon print media will be extinct," he thought.

He smiled as he looked across his office at the one object hanging on the far wall. He thought of the many first-time visitors to his office who, while walking out, could not suppress a quizzical look when they saw the diploma and discovered that he was a graduate of Columbia University's famed School of Journalism. Dane was quietly proud of that accomplishment, but he certainly did not fashion himself an Ivy Leaguer. With his rumpled suit, loosened tie and shirt unbuttoned at the top, he knew he looked more like an old door-to-door salesman than a media colossus. And that's just the way he wanted it.

As far as the rest of his world knew, Hunter Dane had no life beyond the walls of *The Times Union*. But, in fact, he did.

After college, he had offers from a few national publications, but he wanted to return home. Both of his parents were not well at the time, and his brothers and sister were scattered across the country. Besides, he liked the area. It was big enough to have some good sports teams. It had a bit of culture and some notable restaurants. And it had rolling hills overlooking a broad river. He also was tired of the frenetic pace of bigger cities based upon his experience at Columbia.

Dane was lucky to get a position with *The Times Union*, even though he had to start at the bottom. For the first year, he was basically a gofer for the city editor. Occasionally though, he did have a chance to write a local interest story for the Sunday magazine. His best article was an interview with one of the last surviving veterans of World War I. The man was ancient and hard of hearing, but Hunter got him to open up and the story revealed a lot about both the man and a forgotten war.

As with Jake Morris, Hunter had his first break reporting on local school sports. He eventually moved through the chairs, and twenty years ago he became managing editor.

Over that time, he had gone nose to nose at one time or another with his publisher and with just about anyone in the area who felt that they could control the news or, in other words, control Hunter Dane. Dane's record was not perfect, but he certainly had a favorable won-lost record.

A few of the veterans at the paper recalled that Dane once had a wife and a daughter. They claimed he was divorced many years ago, and it was rumored that his daughter had some involvement with drugs and may have died of an overdose. In any event, they all agreed that whoever was responsible for writing Hunter Dane's obituary had their work cut out for them.

TEN

LIZ SCHILLER SPENT THE NEXT FIFTEEN MINUTES IN THE LADIES' room. It took that long for her to pull herself together after her session with the Great White. She had come to *The Times Union* after having worked two years at *The Chicago Tribune*, a job she took immediately after graduating from Northwestern. She was certainly not a rookie before her recent assignment to the politics desk, although she wondered whether Hunter Dane would agree with that.

She knew what she was up against when she took the job. Everyone told her that Dane was a tough boss and that she was replacing Jake Morris, an award-winning journalist. Although everyone was ridden hard by Dane, some in the newsroom had detected a special connection between Dane and Morris. Liz wondered now if that might be affecting her relationship with the boss. Maybe, he was still hurting over the loss of her predecessor.

Liz tried to put all those thoughts aside as she re-worked the story of the Cardinal's dinner. She added certain details that brought color to the interactions among the principals of the piece. She had to admit it. Dane was right. There was a story behind the story that she had to report. In fact, there were several stories including the "scratch my back, I'll scratch yours" relationship between the Cardinal and the pols, the rivalry between Anderson and Fazio, and the Governor's delicate dance between the two of them.

As usual with Dane, it had been a tough lesson but a necessary one. When she completed her edit, she forwarded the draft to him. She waited expectantly, and within ten minutes, she received the verdict. "OK, go to press," was his succinct reply.

Liz let go with a sigh of relief and she was soon out the door. She needed a drink and someone to enjoy it with.

Liz found both waiting for her at McGuinn's, a hole-in-the-wall bar known to generations of reporters. She had texted ahead, and Cody Walton was waiting for her at the bar with an ice- cold Moscow Mule. She smoothed her hand across his shoulder and slid onto the stool next to him. Cody was a staff photographer at the paper. They had partnered on several assignments and had learned to work together well.

One night, after they came back late from covering a political debate upstate, they stopped for a drink, which led to a few more drinks and then to a night of lovemaking at Cody's apartment. They had come together with an intensity that was also tender. Although they hadn't been conscious it was happening at the time, their collaboration at work had led to something more, as they observed the civility they both showed to the subjects of their stories. The newspaper business often reveals people at their worst. It's easy for those on the inside to become cold and cynical. But they both shared a compassion for their subjects.

That was three months ago, and they were still together professionally and otherwise. Word had gotten round about them, and even in their world they had turned some heads: a tall, good-looking Jamaican and a dark-haired Jewish girl with beautiful eyes.

Cody and Liz discovered that they had certain common interests apart from their attraction to each other. Each had a taste for sushi, and they were both serious skiers. In fact, they had planned a long weekend in the mountains over the upcoming holiday until they were assigned to cover a Martin Luther King Jr. commemoration that Monday at Mount Zion AME Church. They commiserated with one another as they sipped their drinks and discussed when they might reschedule their trip.

ELEVEN

A S EXPECTED, BEN ANDERSON BLEW OUT HIS COMPETITION IN THE senate race in November, winning with just under 70 percent of the vote. Near the end of the year, he skillfully opened his run for governor. He had to craft his public announcement carefully, since he had only recently pledged to serve his constituents for another full term. So, over the late winter and early spring, he would orchestrate very public appeals from certain influential party leaders imploring him to change his plans in the best interest of the state. Initially, he would maintain that he could not turn his back on the people of his district, but gradually he would soften his response when he had successfully stoked what appeared to be a spontaneous groundswell of public support for his gubernatorial candidacy.

It was now early January, and his strategy was beginning to unfold. He had introduced legislation to reduce both corporate and individual income taxes under the banner of unleashing the power of the private sector to create jobs and prosperity. He claimed that the additional private revenue would increase tax collections without the need to cut public services. Although the opposition howled, his party's base ate it up.

There was one notable exception among that base. Nick Fazio. Publicly, Fazio mouthed his full-throated support for Anderson's tax reform bill. Privately, he seethed as he watched Anderson's game plan take shape. He pleaded with the Governor to allow him his own platform to make a run. He asked to be put in charge of a statewide program to combat opioid addiction, an issue which had finally come out of the shadows, and surveys showed it as a major concern for likely voters. Instead, the Governor chose to undertake that effort himself along with a popular sports figure who had lost a son to drug addiction.

With Fazio stuck in the gates, Anderson's stealth campaign cruised along. His next step would be to participate in a highly publicized brotherhood celebration on Martin Luther King Jr.'s birthday. There he would have an opportunity to portray himself as a leader intent upon healing the racial and social divisions in society in the company of the most respected clergy in the state. He couldn't wait to see what that would do to his poll numbers.

However, there was one small bump in the road leading to the governor's mansion. Although Anderson's daughter, Britney, maintained an unblemished record in her senior year of prep school, her brother, Blake, was swept up in a scandal at the state university. He had been part of a hazing incident at his fraternity. Two pledges had been injured in the melee. Although their injuries were not serious, the school administration had come down hard on the fraternity brothers involved. Blake was suspended for a year, so he was now home trying to find excuses for his behavior.

Ben and his son had always butted heads but, after Blake's return home, things got even worse between them. Ben wanted Blake to volunteer with an overseas youth mission until his return to the university next fall. Blake threw it back at his father, claiming that Ben just wanted to get him out of the way with this mission idea as a cover to avoid any political splashback. After that exchange, any communication between them was through Brooke.

TWELVE

After their dinner date, Tess and Jake's relationship moved into high gear. They caught an off-Broadway play the next weekend, and Jake was invited to family dinner at the Reillys the following Sunday. He came prepared with a bottle of chardonnay, flowers for Tess's mom, and pie and ice cream for the boys.

Jake was a bit on edge when he arrived. Although he liked kids and had always found it easy to connect with them, he felt the pressure of wanting to be accepted by Tess's boys. The obvious communication challenge with Mikey increased his anxiety. He also knew that Tess and her mom were close, and Jake would be the first man entering the household since Paul left.

Five minutes after his arrival, Jake realized that he had no reason to worry. When he walked in, Mary greeted him with a hug. She thanked him for the flowers and took his packages into the kitchen. Mikey was sitting on the living room floor next to his big brother who was playing a computer game. He smiled up at Jake, and Thomas invited Jake to play along with him. He was focused on the screen when Tess came downstairs.

"Don't stop the game for me. I've got things to do in the kitchen."

He was quickly eliminated by his video competitor, so he walked back into the kitchen and sidled up to Tess, hugging her from behind as she stood before the stove and kissing her on the cheek.

"Can I give you a hand?"

She smiled as she half-turned to him and said, "That's certainly something I haven't heard from a man in a long while. How about opening the wine? The corkscrew is in the top drawer."

As he popped the cork, Jake felt more relaxed than he had in a very long time.

Tess's fried chicken was exceptional, and after the boys had finished their apple pie à la mode, she put on some music intended to relax Mikey. She took him through a brief vocabulary session as Jake sat on the couch and helped Thomas with math homework. Mary did the dishes and then retired to her room. After the boys had been put to bed, Tess and Jake sat downstairs together while Tess shared with him a family photo album.

When they finished, Tess got up and returned with a bottle and two glasses.

"This is the last of my dad's supply of Irish whiskey. I hope you enjoy it."

Jake perused the label as he broke the seal and popped the cork. "Midleton's. Are you kidding? This stuff is as smooth as it is expensive."

She poured two fingers full in each glass and sat back down. After a few sips, Jake's arm dropped down and encircled Tess's shoulders. They turned toward each other and shared a long, deep kiss. Before Jake could go further, Tess placed a finger on his lips and said, "Sorry, Jake. It's not the place and time. But don't give up hope."

THIRTEEN

A BEAT-UP GRAY PICKUP PULLED DOWN AN ALLEY BEHIND THE church on a Thursday morning in early January. It was cold and gray and no one else was in sight. Two men stepped out of the truck, each in their mid-thirties, wearing work clothes and indistinguishable one from the other except that one was a few inches taller. Both were nondescript, except that they were white men in an otherwise African American neighborhood. The only thing noteworthy about the truck, if anyone was around to show an interest in it, were two small decals on the rusted back bumper. One was a replica of the Confederate flag and the other of a sniper rifle.

The taller one reached into the truck bed and hauled out a tool chest. Both men then walked down steps leading to a basement doorway. One tried the handle and the door opened. They looked at each other and smiled as they entered. After five minutes, both men were back in the alley and into their truck.

As they slowly drove away, the smaller one, who was driving, chuckled, and said to his partner, "This will be even easier than we thought."

FOURTEEN

IT WAS NOW THREE MONTHS SINCE JAKE'S DEPARTURE FROM THE paper. He felt increased pressure to do something, brought on by too many idle days. The checks from Mr. Battalini kept coming, but he wondered if he would ever work his way back into journalism. If not, what else would there be? His time was typically spent in front of his computer job hunting. Otherwise, he had plenty of time to second-guess himself about his abrupt decision to quit *The Times Union*. He even considered contacting Hunter Dane and offering to apologize. The trouble, however, was that Jake still felt he was right about the need to publish his story. Besides, it would do no good anyway. The paper had found his replacement. Jake had met her recently when he was having some drinks with a few of his former co-workers. They had talked a bit, and Jake had to admit that he liked her and was impressed with her credentials.

As for the story, it was more relevant than ever as Jake kept track of Ben Anderson's accelerating drive toward next year's election. Jake had first thought he needed a publisher with the firepower to back him up, thinking Anderson would come after him with guns blazing. He had extended his search to include several East Coast papers. So far, he hadn't gotten any further than a few interviews.

But, over the last several weeks, Jake had come to admit to himself that there was another reason why he had not acted on his story. He could have easily found an online publisher that would have taken it. But he also grudgingly acknowledged that his concern about retaliation from Anderson was overblown. Jake had come to surmise why Dane seemed reluctant to run the story. It was his way of telling Jake, "There be dragons here." Jake didn't know how but he needed to find out what Dane was shielding him from. And he knew he would never get it out of Dane himself.

Without any other job prospect now, Jake turned his focus back to the offer he had received from a men's adventure magazine called *Stalwart*. He had put together a proposal to work for a time with a logging crew. Logging is still the most dangerous occupation in the country despite recent industry improvements, and he would be imbedded with loggers for several months sharing their daily experiences. Hopefully, his story would reveal what it takes to survive the perils of that kind of life.

The only thing holding him back from committing to the assignment was his desire to be with Tess. His budding relationship with her was the one positive thing he could hold onto right now, and he was not sure how a lengthy separation might affect it.

FIFTEEN

JAKE WAS NOT THE ONLY ONE WEIGHING THE NEXT STEP. TESS Reilly had now spent enough time with Jake to recognize that there might be a future with him, and that thought left her both thrilled and terrified. After little sleep, she awoke early on a dreary and cold Monday, got into her running gear, and headed out for a long run. She often found that the solitude of early morning and the quiet rhythm of her body helped her to focus her thoughts. She needed that now.

Over the last several weeks, she and Jake had seen a lot of each other. They'd been to a show, another dinner, and then Jake had taken her out along with her mom and the boys for pizza. He had shared Christmas dinner with them, and they both spent New Year's Eve drinking champagne and watching the ball drop on TV. Her mom and the boys took to him quickly and that was a big relief because, although she did her best to hide it, Tess had fallen hard for Jake. So why was she still scared to death? She had to sort that out.

Tess had spent her life among dominant males. Although she had been the princess to her dad and brothers, their efforts to shelter her had been smothering and her disastrous marriage to Paul nearly finished her off. Since then, she had made her way in the world alone. At times, the loneliness was overwhelming but that was the price she paid to avoid the risk that another man might hurt her and her boys. Jake did not seem like that kind of guy, but she needed to be sure. When she was around him, she felt secure and at the same time sexually excited. But she knew that was just not enough.

Tess finished her five miles and then slowed to a walk about a block from home. By then, she had come to a decision. Recognizing what she had gone through, Jake had been understanding of her reluctance to trust him. She had held back the pace until now, but she knew that could not continue much longer. Either she would have to take a chance or shut the whole thing down. And she couldn't do that now. From what she had seen, Jake Morris was the best chance she'd have for a lasting relationship with a man. Jake had been talking about the two of them spending a weekend at a country inn. She would suggest that they get away over the upcoming Presidents' Day weekend. Meanwhile, they would continue the dance.

SIXTEEN

The Reverend Micah Washington was probably the most respected clergyman in the state, at least among those capable of ceding that title to a Black man. He was recognized both because of what he had done and what he represented.

Young Micah had been present during the turbulent birth of the civil rights movement of the Sixties. As his father had done before him, he went south to study at Morehouse College in Atlanta. There, he sat in the pews at Ebenezer Baptist Church, transported by the uplifting message of the Reverend Martin Luther King, Jr. He travelled to D.C., standing on the Ellipse on April 28, 1963, along with a throng of 250,000 others, to hear King's iconic speech. It offered a dream for an America free of the scourge of racial bias. Those experiences motivated him to enter the seminary, intent upon leading a life committed to achieving that lofty goal.

In his early years in the ministry, he had marched and participated in sit-ins promoting voting rights and access to public accommodations. He had known nearly all the leaders of the movement, but he quickly separated himself from the likes of Malcolm X and Eldridge Cleaver who both rejected King's non-violent tactics.

Forty-five years ago, Micah had assumed co-pastoral duties with his own father at Mount Zion AME Church. There, he had started a mentorship program for young men returning from incarceration. He directed youth programs fostering both athletics and scholarship, job training for high school dropouts, and he presided over an annual fellowship service on the anniversary of Reverend King's birthday.

All these activities established Micah Washington as a man who never faltered in pursuit of an America blind to prejudice of any kind. That's why he was admired by so many throughout the state and beyond.

Old Micah awoke on this day dedicated to the birth of Reverend King, and as with every morning, he began it in prayer. He prayed for many things and many people, but he especially prayed that the celebration of racial, ethnic and religious harmony that he would host that day would brush the hearts of those in attendance and that it would move them to do something to bridge the growing chasm in his community.

As he sat down to breakfast with his wife, Esther, Micah looked out at his back yard covered with a thin crust of snow. The ominous, gunmetal grey sky and the lightly falling snow added to his concerns.

Esther looked up from the newspaper and saw the look on her husband's face. She had seen it often during their fifty-two-year marriage. His furrowed brow, tightened jaw, and the distracted look in his eyes.

"Micah, stop worrying. You do this every year. The weather is supposed to clear up. You'll have your usual overflow attendance."

"I'm more worried about what I have to say and whether it will make any difference. This event is supposed to bring us all closer together, but every year it seems we are further apart."

Suddenly, Micah's expression changed. In a panicked voice, he asked, "Esther, I need to review my notes. Have you seen my reading glasses?"

Esther smiled. How many times had they gone through this ritual? Feigning exasperation, she pointed her forefinger at her forehead, and Micah reached up to his to retrieve his glasses.

"Micah, as long as you can find your glasses on the pulpit today, you'll be fine."

SEVENTEEN

THEY FILED INTO THE CHURCH BY TWOS AND THREES, ALL MEMBERS of Mount Zion's celebrated Bible choir, arriving an hour early to run through a final practice for this morning's observance. Led by their conductor-organist, Bessie Hamer, a formidable lady in her late sixties, the choir was made up of twenty-five men, women, and children, ranging in age from ten to seventy-six. The oldest was Micah's wife, Esther, and the youngest his granddaughter, Cissie. After thirty minutes, they were ready. They nodded and murmured approvingly to one another as they spread their robes and sat back in the stall to the left of the altar. The crowd of visitors had begun to arrive.

Among them was Ben Anderson. Reverend Washington had personally invited him during a recent visit to the Senator's office to solicit his support for a bill to expand gun owner background checks. Anderson was seated in a roped-off area for dignitaries in the front two pews. Surrounding him were several Protestant and Catholic religious leaders as well as rabbis, imams, and Hindu and Buddhist priests. Interspersed among them were also members of the business community, social activists, and other political figures.

Behind these notables were perhaps another three hundred guests, filling the remaining pews, spilling into the aisles, and out into the vestibule. Two traffic control officers, having performed their duties, were among the last to press into the back of the church.

The media had the event well covered. Among them were a film crew from the local NBC affiliate. Liz Schiller and Cody Walton set themselves up next to the fifth pew on the far left. Cody had his camera well-positioned for a wide angle shot of the altar which would include the choir and Reverend Washington. He could then swing around and capture much of the congregation.

Reverend Washington, dressed simply in a black suit, with a silver cross hanging from a chain around his neck, stepped into the chancel and faced the congregation. The choir stood, followed by the entire assemblage. The organ played the introduction to, "Lift Ev'ry Voice and Sing," and the celebration began. It was a joyful sound, and the visitors were soon swaying along with the church members. The choir then led them into, "We Shall Overcome."

Afterwards, there was a moment of silence, broken only by the shuffling of the choir members as they sat back down. A young girl stepped out from among them and walked to the center of the sanctuary. The organ started again, and little Cissie began to sing with a high but certain voice, "This Little Light of Mine."

When she finished, the crowd erupted with clapping and a chorus of "amens". She bowed slightly and returned to her seat. The assembly was on its feet now, cheering, as her grandfather made his way to the pulpit. Only those close by could see the glimmer in his eyes.

Pastor Washington began.

"It is fitting that a young child has reminded us today that each of us is called to bring our own light into this world and to sustain it against the forces that might snuff it out. That was the message delivered by our brother Jesus, and it was the same message that our brother Martin attempted to convey. It is a message shared by all the religions represented here today. We all must do what we can to promote peace and reject the message of those who would sow violence among us. As found in John 1:5, 'The light shines in the darkness and the darkness has not overcome it.' On this day celebrating the birthday of Martin Luther King Jr., we must affirm his dream that all of us, regardless of race or religious affiliation, live together as brothers and sisters in peace, sharing with one another the light that glows within us.'"

His message concluded, Reverend Washington stepped down from the pulpit. The choir stood and began to sing "The Battle Hymn of the Republic." Everyone else rose and joined in. Except for two shadowy figures who appeared, barely visible, standing just beyond an entry on the front right side of the church. They had as panoramic a view of the proceedings as the media, but for a far different purpose.

Before the hymn ended, the first shots rang out. For a single moment, it competed with the sound of the organ and accompanying voices until the sound of their music ended abruptly. Replacing it were discordant screams and wails echoing off the walls, mixing with staccato bursts of semi-automatic weapons.

The taller man trained his AR-15 on the altar. Micah Washington was the first to fall. He stood only thirty feet from his assassin. The first round blew off the top half of his head, and the second hit just below his stomach.

He collapsed and was dead before he hit the floor. The shooter then swung his long gun toward the choir stall. Seven choir members were struck before the others had time to dive down below a wooden partition. It offered them only slight protection. He then trained his weapon on the assembly in the pews and aisles.

His partner had already taken down a handful of worshippers with his 9 mm Luger. Many had dropped to the floor or attempted to hide within the pews, but both shooters continued to fire, fanning their weapons from one side of the church to the other. Each firearm had a high- capacity magazine, the AR 15 holding thirty rounds and the Luger 15 rounds. When one man swapped out a magazine, the other continued to fire, keeping their victims pinned down.

It only lasted a few minutes, although those who survived the ordeal would later recall that it seemed interminable. The walls and floors were splashed with blood, and bits of bone and clumps of hair were everywhere, along with wood splinters from the blasted pews and plaster chipped from the walls. The air was heavy with the acrid smell of gun smoke.

The carnage was cut short by the courageous act of one of the traffic officers. When the shooting began, he immediately dropped to the floor. He then crawled down the center aisle, making his way over and around bodies until he reached the front of the church. With his service revolver in hand, he turned the corner of the first pew to face the side aisle and the attackers just a few feet away. Before they could react, he put two rounds into the taller one who staggered and fell. The other officer had hunkered down in the back of the church, calling in on his radio and helping those around him to escape out the front door. Sirens erupted in the distance. With that, the remaining assailant backed quickly out the side door and was gone.

Within seconds of the attack, Cody Walton had pulled Liz Schiller to the floor, covering her with his body. He lay still while feeling intense pain from his left hip, as if he had been struck by a hammer. He noticed a pool of blood spreading on the floor around them which he assumed came from his wound. But when the firing stopped and he rolled away from Liz, he saw the source of the flow. Liz had been struck in the upper chest and she was losing blood fast. She would not regain consciousness and would bleed out before help arrived.

When the paramedics had done what they could and the survivors had been transported to area hospitals, a grisly tally was taken. Eleven had died, twenty-eight wounded, with six of the latter in critical condition. Two of them would die within the next twenty-four hours. One of those would be young Cissie Washington; the other, the wounded assailant.

Of those who miraculously survived, many were in shock. One was Ben Anderson. A priest seated next to him had been one of the first fatalities. Ben's suit was covered in the man's life blood. The Senator was taken to a nearby hospital for evaluation. By that time, all the local media outlets were on the scene, and reporters from the national networks were on their way.

When Ben was discharged, Brooke was there to take him home. As they walked toward their car, a news crew suddenly confronted them, and Ben had a microphone thrust in his face. The camera captured his blood-drenched suit and the shock in his eyes. Ben simply said that everyone should pray for the victims and their families. As he slumped down in the passenger seat on the ride home, his head began to clear. He began to consider how his involvement in this nightmare might impact his upcoming campaign.

EIGHTEEN

Word came quickly to Hunter Dane. One of his reporters burst into his office with news of the shootings. He immediately tried to reach Liz Schiller's cell phone but his call went straight to voicemail. He then called Cody Walton. By then, Cody had received emergency treatment for his leg wound. He was now lying in a hospital bed waiting to see a doctor. When he heard Hunter's voice, he quickly broke down. His only intelligible words were, "Liz is dead." After Hunter was assured that Cody's condition was stable, he hung up and gathered all available staff in his office. He told them what had happened and then laid out for them their coverage assignments. Before they were dismissed, he had someone run down the address of Liz's parents.

Hunter now sat alone in his office, trying to process it all. As he did, he was overcome by a near-paralyzing sadness. He had faced plenty of crises, but it had been a long time since anything had struck him this hard. He offered a silent prayer for Liz and all the other victims and their families. Then he stood up, grabbed his overcoat, and walked out the door. He dreaded what was coming next, but he had to tell the Schillers about their daughter. If they hadn't received the news yet it would be better if they received it from someone who knew her. He owed Liz that.

As Hunter drove across town to the Schillers' home, he tried to prepare himself for what he would face. He knew that the couple were academics. Barry Schiller was a professor at a local college, and his wife, Rachel, taught high school. They would be off for the MLK holiday, but would they be at home? If they had heard of the incident on the TV or radio, would they connect it to Liz? He had no way of knowing. He only hoped that he would reach them first.

As he picked his way through traffic, his thoughts turned to his own daughter. Fiona had been about the same age as Liz when she died, although the circumstances were far different. Hunter and his wife had agonized over their daughter's struggle with addictions—first marijuana, then cocaine and, finally, heroin. Over the last two years of Fiona's life, she had tried three times to get clean. For a while, it worked. She stayed on methadone for three months, but some of her user friends sucked her back into their world. Early one morning, they got a call from a local ER. Fiona had overdosed and they couldn't bring her back. So, Hunter Dane knew all about losing a daughter. As with the Schillers, she was his only child. He hoped that he might be able to draw upon that loss to somehow ease their pain.

When Hunter pulled up to the house, he was relieved to see that there were two cars in the driveway. He rang the doorbell and heard approaching footsteps. The door swung open, and Rachel Schiller greeted him with a quizzical half smile.

"Can I help you?"

Hunter chose to bring things to a head as quickly as possible.

"Mrs. Schiller, I am Hunter Dane, your daughter's managing editor. May I speak with you and your husband?"

Her smile vanished, replaced by a look that revealed the building dread his words had triggered. She turned and, standing at the foot of the stairs, called out, "Barry, please come down here right away."

The Schillers sat on a couch across from Hunter, and even before he began, Barry reached across for his wife's hand.

"Mr. and Mrs. Schiller, I am so sorry to have to tell you that Liz is dead."

Barry Schiller blinked hard. Rachel screamed and turned toward her husband, burying her head in the crook of his neck. Hunter waited a moment and then shared with them only the minimal details they needed to know at that point. They asked if he could call their rabbi for them, and Hunter waited until he arrived. He then excused himself and left the Schillers to their grieving.

NINETEEN

MOUNT ZION AME CHURCH WAS NOW A CRIME SCENE. A TEAM made up of the FBI and state and local investigators secured both the interior of the Church and surrounding grounds. Spent shells, empty magazines and the AR 15 were inventoried as well as a padded rifle case found in the basement heater room. Outside, there were deep ruts in the snow and mud, evidence of what appeared to be truck tires. Investigators walked up and down the alley, knocking on doors to discover if anyone had observed the truck, the men, or anything else out of the ordinary.

It didn't take long to identify the shooters. The one who was wounded never regained consciousness, but the other was found speeding west on the interstate, his truck having been seen by a motorist who heard on the radio a general description of the vehicle. He surrendered without a fight. It turned out that both men were former military, unmarried, and frequent visitors to several White supremacist websites.

For the next three nights, the Mount Zion Massacre, as it came to be called, was the lead story on every national news broadcast. Viewers learned about the victims and their killers. The story of the murder of Reverend Washington and his granddaughter in plain view of his wife assumed almost biblical overtones. Cody Walton was interviewed about his last moments with Liz Schiller, his colleague and lover. His grief was felt by viewers across the nation. The public also learned of the killers' numerous hate-filled rants published by certain radical right-wing media outlets.

Forensic pathologists from across the state were called in to complete autopsies of the thirteen bodies as quickly as possible, while funeral arrangements were made by the families. All the bodies were released by the coroner within two days. The dead shooter was quickly buried in a private service. Arrangements for the others were more complicated. In addition to Reverend Washington and his granddaughter Cissie, there were five more members of the Mount Zion community among the dead. The church building was deemed unsuitable for a memorial service. It would bear the marks of the massacre that occurred there for some time. In addition, it was too small for the expected number of mourners. The church elders met with Esther Washington and the other next of kin, and they all agreed that there should be one communal funeral service. After discussion with other local pastors and with city officials, it was decided that the service for all deceased church members would be held in the city convention center the following Saturday.

Among the other victims was an imam, a Catholic priest, and two representatives of local social service agencies. Arrangements were made for each of them. That left Liz Schiller. In accordance with her Jewish tradition, her service would be held at a local funeral home within twenty-four hours of the body's release. The community braced itself for the painful days ahead.

TWENTY

THE FUNERAL HOME WAS FILLED BEYOND CAPACITY. A NUMBER OF dignitaries were present, but most of the attendees were just people Liz Schiller had known at some time in her life. When everyone else was in place, Barry and Rachel, Barry's mother, sister, and brother-in-law entered the room, taking seats reserved in the front. In the Hebrew tradition, each of them wore the traditional black ribbon bearing a slight tear to signify the life that had been ripped from them.

Their rabbi, David Bacharach, took the lectern. He stood heavily before them as if weighed down by a grief that he had assumed on behalf of all those present. His eyes swept the entire congregation, and then they settled upon Liz's parents. Barry and Rachel sat still as stones. Their eyes were fixed upon the casket resting before them.

The rabbi began to recite selected passages from the Book of Psalms. He spoke softly, as if the words might serve as a balm to heal their collective wound. He then requested a moment of silent prayer. Finally, there came his greatest challenge, the hesped, his eulogy for Liz Schiller.

He spoke of knowing Liz since she had first been brought by her parents to pre-school. He noted her inquiring mind and her concern for others even as a young girl, and he asserted that this sensitivity had matured into a strong sense of social justice which animated her life, especially as a journalist.

"Why would such a person be suddenly and violently torn from us, especially from parents who love her as dearly as Barry and Rachel? I suppose we will not know the answer in this world, but I suspect it has something to do with what we do now to honor her memory. Liz lived her life loving, trusting, and caring for others. We know little about her assailants except that it seems they were consumed by anger, fear, and hatred. In reaction to their horrific acts, we are tempted to respond in kind. But we must not. We will grieve the loss of Liz and the other victims of this tragedy. But to honor them, we must continue to live our lives as a testimony to those lives we have lost. Remember Liz. Accept the sadness we must feel now but know that her spirit endures, and it implores us to overcome despair with trust, fear with hope and hatred with love."

For several moments after the eulogy, there was silence. Then Rabbi Bacharach directed the congregation to stand and conclude the service by reciting the Kaddish, the Hebrew prayer which glorifies God even amid such devastating loss. When it concluded, Rachel heard a soft but deep sob coming from the pew directly behind her. She turned around and reached out to grab the hand of Cody Walton.

Four pallbearers escorted the simple wooden casket out the front door to a waiting hearse, followed by a cortege of family and friends who were directed to their vehicles for the trip to the cemetery. The remaining mourners then made their way to an outside plaza where they waited respectfully for the entourage to leave.

It seemed like they lingered to absorb together the rabbi's message. Small groups formed based upon their shared connection with Liz. Political figures were gathered in a corner where they attracted the attention of the media in attendance. Ben Anderson could be seen in the distance, no doubt recounting to the press his role in this sad event. Jake and Tess were there and, as they walked outside, Jake spotted a contingent from *The Times Union* with Hunter Dane at its center.

"Well, Tess, I guess the time has come for you to make the acquaintance of the Great White."

As they approached the group, Hunter looked up at Jake and their eyes locked upon one another. There was a palpable feeling of tension among the others present until Hunter broke the mood with a warm smile.

"Jake, how are you doing?"

"Tolerably well, especially since I met this lady. Let me introduce you to Tess Reilly."

Hunter held both of Tess's hands in his as he said to her, "It is a true pleasure to meet you. Jake's fortunes have certainly improved."

As they got into their car, Tess shared her take on Hunter.

"I like the man. He obviously still has strong feelings for you. Maybe, you should find a way to re-open the door unless your ego will not permit you."

Jake just gave her a sidelong glance. Little else was said on the trip home.

TWENTY-ONE

BEN ANDERSON WAS ANNOYED. NO, HE WAS FURIOUS. MORE THAN that, he was also a bit anxious. Max Grabel was becoming a real pain in his ass. In fact, he was slowly taking control of Anderson's life. After the Schiller funeral, Ben scrolled through a ream of text messages. He saw one from Grabel asking him to call and one from his chief of staff, Meg Holland, simply reading, "He's at it again!" He called Meg and she quickly told him that Max had taken advantage of his temporary inaccessibility to commandeer one of his staffers, assigning him to find out why a new wing to one of his nursing homes had not received a final state inspection.

By the time Anderson stalked back into his office, his tie and jacket were off, and he threw them both in the general direction of his couch, with Meg trailing behind him and closing the door.

"The gall of the guy!"

Ben slumped into his desk chair as Meg walked behind him and began to massage his shoulders. As Meg did her best to ease the tension, Ben was momentarily distracted. He reached behind to run his hand up the inside of her thigh.

"Stand down, Senator. Remember the rules. Not during business hours. Besides, we need to focus on the problem. You are well ahead in the polls. Your opponent doesn't have a clue. Now, as if we needed yet another star in our constellation, you find yourself cast as one of the tragic figures in the Mount Zion Massacre story. We are about to glide into the governor's mansion, but your only liability is Max Grabel. We made a calculated decision to accept his patronage even as we knew what a reckless son-of-a-bitch he is. So how do we create some separation without alienating him?"

Anderson leaned forward, both hands now back on the desk.

"I don't know, but we'd better figure something out quickly because we both know that if Grabel goes down, he takes us with him."

TWENTY-TWO

THERE WAS MORE GRIEVING AHEAD, AND FOR THE REMAINDER OF that week, much of the city was immersed in its shared anguish. Each memorial service was scheduled so as not to interfere with another. The next was a traditional Muslim funeral for the slain imam. Then, a Protestant service for the local, non-profit agency representatives killed in the shoot-out. The funeral Mass for the murdered priest was a more elaborate affair. The church was packed to the rafters. Twenty co-celebrants stood elbow to elbow at the altar, with the Cardinal and two bishops on either side. The ritual might have been different, but the pall of suffering that hung over the mourners was the same as that visited upon the other faith communities. There remained only the service for the deceased Mount Zion Church members.

Elaborate preparations had been underway ever since the decision was made to hold a common burial service for the seven Mount Zion church members at the city's convention center. A small army of city, state, and federal officials were engaged in planning the logistics, including extensive security measures to thwart any possible copycat shooters. Initially, there was speculation that the President might attend the service; however, the decision was made not to cancel a scheduled state visit to Poland that weekend. Before leaving for Warsaw, the President issued a statement of condolence to the families of the victims, decrying the barbaric act of two demented minds and calling for increased efforts to identify and to treat mental illness.

Although the Governor, both United States Senators, and a raft of other politicians planned to attend, none of them were asked to speak at the service. Instead, apart from the prayers to be led by certain chosen clergy, there would be a single speaker who would offer a eulogy for those lost, Martin Washington, Reverend Washington's eldest son.

Saturday morning arrived clear and frigid. Promptly at 10:00 a.m., the doors to the convention center opened and a mass of citizens from every part of the city spilled inside for what would be a four-hour visitation before the service itself. They moved slowly up the center aisle toward the stage, before which were arranged seven plain wooden coffins, each closed, except for one. Six were aligned together, but the small open one was centered below the rest. It contained the remains of little Cissie Washington. Unlike the others, her wound could be hidden by the white choir gown she wore. A simple silver cross hung from a chain around her slim neck. Most memorably, the sides of her mouth were slightly upturned, offering a suggestion of comfort and peace.

A seemingly endless line of mourners passed before the coffins; some somber and silent, others unable to control their grief, wailing and moaning as they made their way. The air was laden with the scent of the numerous floral arrangements covering the stage and the floor below. The press of people filing by soon caused the cavernous hall to become uncomfortably warm. The families of the deceased stood by as long as they could to greet the many well-wishers; however, eventually, they were forced to sit down and fan themselves. Finally, the lines thinned, but many remained in the auditorium, taking their places for the service to follow. Nearly all 7,000 seats were filled by that time.

Representatives of several church choirs across the city had prepared all week for their role in the service. They were seated together on the left half of the stage, some fifty voices prepared now to honor the dead. Six chairs were randomly placed among them, each with a single rose placed on the seat. Five red ones and one white rose on a smaller chair, each signifying a deceased member of the Mount Zion choir.

On the right side of the stage, several area clergymen were gathered. In the center was a larger armchair and draped across it was a stole with brightly colored panels, each panel bearing an embroidered Byzantine Cross. It was Reverend Washington's pastoral cloth.

David Bacharach, the Schillers' rabbi, rose to deliver a reading from the Old Testament Book of Wisdom. His words reflected the awful circumstance.

"But the souls of the just are in the hand of God, and the torment of death shall not touch them. In the sight of the unwise they seemed to die, and their departure was taken for misery, and their going away from us, for utter destruction, but they are in peace."

The words seemed to act as a balm to the sorrowful audience, but when he reached the passage "The just shall shine and shall run to and fro like sparks among the reeds," Esther Washington could not hold back an anguished cry as she thought about her granddaughter and how she had made her little light shine.

When the prayers and readings were concluded, the choir rose and led the assembly in singing the old Negro spiritual, "Walk Around Heaven All Day", followed by "Amazing Grace." It was now time to hear from the eulogist.

Martin Washington waited for several moments after the music ended, then stood and slowly approached the lectern. He was a tall man, clean-shaven, with a receding hairline of closely cropped gray hair. He began to speak and his deep, rolling voice reminded many of his father.

"Friends, I have been given a difficult task today. I have been asked to convey for all of you our sorrow for the loss of seven innocent souls. My burden is even heavier because two of those souls are my father and my beautiful niece. Nevertheless, I will do my best to speak on your behalf."

Martin began by describing what it was like to grow up as the pastor's son at Mount Zion AME. He spoke of each of the victims, some of whom he referred to as "Aunt;" others he identified as playmates from his childhood. He talked of his father's influence upon him, and how he had impressed upon him from the very beginning the importance of justice and the majesty of the law.

His voice caught for a moment though when he spoke about the joy his father felt to hear little Cissie sing in the choir.

"These were all good folks walking through life humbly with their God. They were cut down suddenly even as they were joined together singing His praise. Now, we are left behind to carry on their mission. Are we up to that? Can we bear the pain of their loss and avoid the temptation to turn that sense of loss into bitterness and hatred? We can and we must."

"In the aftermath of the First World War, the poet W.B. Yeats described the prospect of chaos taking hold in the world. He wrote, 'Things fall apart; the centre cannot hold; mere anarchy is loosed, and everywhere the ceremony of innocence is drowned; the best lack all conviction, while the worst are full of passionate intensity.'"

"Yeats could well have written those words about our country today and with the event of this last Monday in mind. Ladies and gentlemen, we occupy the center in our bitterly divided society, and we must hold. Every day and every moment of every day, we must be mindful of our common humanity, regardless of whatever superficialities distinguish us one from the other. And we must act on that knowledge. We must stay connected with one another. That was the core purpose of the celebration at Mount Zion that was so abruptly and violently suspended."

"So, in closing, I ask you now to affirm your belief in that common humanity by standing…every one of you. Stand up and turn to your neighbor on the left and right and all around you. Exchange a handshake or even a hug if so inclined."

Seven thousand stood as one and greeted one another over the next several minutes. But Martin Washington was not finished.

"Now, I want you all to remain standing and direct your attention to the words on the message boards above us, as this magnificent choir leads us in concluding this service by singing, "The Battle Hymn of the Republic.""

There was a mix of both tears and smiles among the crowd as they streamed out of the convention center and into the late afternoon.

TWENTY-THREE

Hunter Dane left the convention center and decided to walk the mile back to *The Times Union*. He usually did not work late on Saturdays, but he needed to check on the stories in progress for the Sunday edition. Half the staff was assigned to cover every aspect of the Mount Zion Massacre and its aftermath. Obviously, the lead would be the convention center service, but there would be a recap of the murders and a profile of each of the victims. Another would describe the current state of the gun violence debate, and various politicians would offer their latest bromides to deal with the issue. As he trudged along, Hunter realized that this edition might well be the most momentous one for the paper in his long tenure.

The temperature had dropped even more, and there was a feel of snow in the air as the lights of the city came on. As Hunter made his way to his office, he recognized something that he had experienced only a few times in his long career. He felt a collective energy in the newsroom, as reporters huddled together in discussion while others hunched over their keyboards, all of them straining to get their stories right while meeting deadline. In a few minutes, he had their work before him on his computer screen, and after only a few minor edits, it was ready for production.

He was hunched over his desk, glasses off and rubbing his eyes, when he heard a knock. His door opened partway, and Margaret Opdyke poked her head inside.

"Hunter, do you have a minute?"

"Sure, Peggy, anytime for you."

Peggy Opdyke was the editorial page editor. She had that job for almost as long as Hunter had been managing editor. They had been through a lot together, both professionally and otherwise. Peggy had been the only one at the paper that Hunter had ever let into his private world. She had discreetly helped him through the death of his daughter and his later divorce. He had been there for her when her first husband died. She was one of only a few at the office who called him Hunter, and, except for the publisher, he was the only one who called her Peggy. They were both aging icons of journalism, offering one another some comfort in the waning days of their careers.

"Peg, as usual, you got it just right in describing how this city has responded to the events of this week. I've never seen so many people reach out to others who would have been invisible to them before this happened. But the question raised by Martin Washington remains. How long will this last? How long can the center hold when so much else is pulling us apart?"

"I don't know, Hunter, but we need to do what we can. Editorially, I hope that this paper will have a renewed focus on reporting good news as well as the steady flow of depressing stuff."

Hunter grunted his assent and added, "More than that, I think that sometimes our zeal to uncover the truth can cause a lot of unintended harm. Innocent lives can be ruined in the effort to turn over every rock. Was it Justice Brandeis who said that sunlight is the best disinfectant for democracy? If so, he didn't account for the collateral damage that disinfectant can cause. I don't know. Maybe, I've lost it. Maybe, it's time."

"No, it's not, Hunter, so stop talking like that. You and I both have a few more lessons to teach this current generation before we are cashiered out. By the way, what plans do you have to replace Liz? Have you heard anything about Jake Morris? Any chance he might return?"

Hunter hesitated for a moment.

"I don't know what I'm going to do yet about the politics assignment. I did see Jake after the Schiller funeral. He has a new girlfriend who seems nice. We were civil to one another, but I don't think that Jake will ask for his old job back, and I'm not about to offer it to him. What's done is done."

"That's a shame. But for now, I recommend that you get the hell out of here. Hunter, you've had one of the toughest weeks of your life, and I don't like the look of you. You're pale and you look exhausted. Go on home."

TWENTY-FOUR

THE REGION WAS HIT WITH A MAJOR SNOWSTORM THE NEXT weekend. Jake showed up at the Reilly household on Sunday afternoon with a sled and two large inner tubes. Tess, Jake, and the boys piled into the van, and they slowly picked their way through the barely plowed streets to the local arboretum. It featured a long, steep hill. Over two hours, they made several runs on the course, bumping and careening down the slope, with either Tess or Jake holding onto Mikey all the way. Jake had taken to calling him "Mighty Mike," carrying him on his shoulders for each trip back up to the summit. Happy and exhausted, they got back to the house as dusk was settling in. Mary had prepared her famous chili and homemade bread. They were all exhausted, so Jake left early after helping prepare the boys for bed.

The next morning, a light snow was falling. Because of the storm, all classes and Mikey's therapy were cancelled, so the boys were still sleeping, and Tess had a rare open day. She was seated at the kitchen table with her coffee and newspaper in hand as Mary came through the door. It would take more than a winter storm to keep Mary Reilly from daily Mass. She stamped her feet on the doormat, and took off her down jacket and knit cap, concluding the ritual with an exaggerated shiver.

"It's colder than a witch's nose out there! Would you believe that Father Skelly overslept again today? Pat Flynn had to bang on his window to get him up. One of these mornings, he'll wake up in eternity, and then I guess they're going to have to ordain me to say morning Mass. So, what's going on between you and Jake?"

And that's how the session started.

Mary Reilly had never been one to hover over her children, so Tess was not offended by the question. In fact, she was anxious to hear her mother's views on her new romantic interest.

"Right now, I don't really know where this is going. It has been a whirl-wind four months. I enjoy being with Jake. He's funny and kind. He's smart and intuitive. He has made a big hit with the boys, and I judge with you also.

But he's also impetuous and a bit hot-headed. I guess that may be partly responsible for his short marriage and his sudden departure from *The Times Union.*"

Mary couldn't resist interrupting. "Well, you have a few smudges on your record also, young lady."

With an exaggerated grimace, Tess regained the floor.

"Given that history, I have a hard time trusting men even when they seem as good as Jake looks to be. I need time to sort things out, but I know that if I wait too long, Jake will likely drift away. That's why I agreed to the upcoming overnighter, and I appreciate you covering for me with the boys."

Mary took a moment as she wrapped her hands around her coffee mug.

"Your dad and I were married for thirty-six years before he was taken from me. They were good years, some better than others. We all have our shortcomings. Michael had his, and I have mine. But we came to accept them, both in ourselves and in each other. I know all that you've been through. You married a bad man. That doesn't mean that you can't find a good one. But don't expect him to be perfect. If that's what you want, you will wake up one day a bitter old woman."

Tess reached across the table and took her mother's hand.

"You have always been the rock in this family, and you still are."

Mary shrugged. "Well, I feel like the rock of ages these days. Guess I'll go up and check on the boys. You start breakfast. We can use the leftover bread for French toast."

TWENTY-FIVE

EN ANDERSON WAS GASSED. THIS WAS HIS SIXTH SKI RUN OF THE afternoon, all the time chasing Max Grabel down the mountain. It got more embarrassing each time. Grabel had twelve years on him, but Anderson was over-matched both physically and technically. Each year, Grabel invited Ben and Brooke to his slope-side chalet at Jackson Hole. And every time, Anderson prepared as best he could. He heavied-up on his training sessions, working his core, quads and hamstrings, and sneaking away, if he could manage it, for a long weekend in Vermont. But none of it was ever enough. Brooke and Grabel's wife, Beverly, would take a few runs on the bunny slope and spend the rest of the day shopping. Max and Ben would stay on more challenging terrain, most of the time on the famous Alta Chutes, each of them steep and studded with trees and rock outcroppings. Most nights brought fresh powder to the mountain which added to the challenge, requiring Ben to remember to sit back a bit on his skis and carve his turns.

This would be Ben's last run. He watched Grabel work smoothly down the slope, his legs pumping like synchronized pistons, picking his way through the trees, plumes of powder arching outward and marking his course until he was no longer within sight. Fortunately, he did not observe Ben's skis chatter to a rickety stop above him, perilously close to a steep side drop. Ben looked up and saw a guy pointing at him from one of the quad cable cars above, and he could see that he and his friends were enjoying Ben's predicament. He gingerly backed away from the precipice. Ben plodded along through the rest of the run, his burning thighs turning to jelly. By the time Ben made it back to the chalet, Max was already in the hot tub offering him a cold beer.

Before he left for Wyoming, Ben held a late-night planning session with Meg Holland. They discussed how he might approach Grabel to get him to back off from his heavy-handed reliance upon Ben's political influence. It would be awkward for him to broach the subject while availing himself of Grabel's hospitality, but they agreed Ben had no choice. Grabel's shenanigans were putting them both at risk. Besides, there was never a chance to catch Max off guard. He moved like a veteran boxer, working his opponent around the ring, hitting, and moving and slipping a punch when you thought he was cornered. It might as well be on his turf as anywhere else.

Ben wisely waited until the final night to make his pitch. Grabel hosted a farewell dinner at the finest restaurant in Teton Village. The Grabels were regulars there, so they were quickly escorted to a table with the best view of the mountain as the sun dipped below its crest. Grabel ordered for the men the finest Japanese whisky available and an excellent French chablis for the ladies. In doing so, he reminded the maître d' that the staff should be at their best tonight because they would be serving the next governor of his state. Ben winced and nervously looked around at the adjacent tables, guarding against the off chance that he might be recognized by a constituent.

Max invited Ben to select a quality red wine with dinner. However, when the sommelier arrived, Ben's choice of a 2012 Margaux was overruled. Grabel advised that 2015 was a superior vintage. "Not an auspicious beginning to the evening," Ben thought to himself. After a delicious meal of elk and bison chops, they adjourned for the evening to the Grabel lodge.

Brooke and Beverly retired early so the men were left to smoke their Montecristos and sip their cognacs in Grabel's study. As they sank into leather armchairs before the fire, Ben looked up at the snarling visage of a grizzly's head mounted above the mantle. He hoped that what he was about to say would not produce a similar response from Grabel.

He began cautiously. "Max, as always, Brooke and I had a fantastic time with Beverly and you this week. You both are gracious hosts, and we look forward each year to spending time with you in this beautiful home. More than that, over the past several years, you have become a good friend and a loyal supporter. So, it's difficult for me now to raise a concern with you."

Ben looked across at Grabel. He had set down his glass. His eyes narrowed. They were now fixed intently on Ben.

"What concern?"

"Before I start, is it safe to talk here?"

Grabel shot back. "Boy, you really are paranoid. Do you think it's come to that? Besides, I do a lot of business when I'm out here, and I have set up a sophisticated anti-bugging system. So, tell me what's got your panties twisted, Benny."

Ben always hated Grabel using a nickname that he thought he had shaken after third grade. He brushed it off now. With Grabel's limited attention span, he knew he had better make it short and persuasive.

"We are both under a microscope now. Me, because it's obvious that I'm running for governor and without a serious challenger in the primary. You, because you have become the leader in the senior care industry at a time when its practices have come under increased scrutiny. Our professional and private lives have become intertwined, and we know that certain of our dealings together are subject, shall we say, to being misconstrued."

Grabel couldn't help himself. "Misconstrued? What you really mean is that we stand a chance of getting called before a grand jury someday. Isn't that what you mean, Benny? Do you think I don't know that?"

"I know you do, Max. It's just that we need to avoid the perception of improper influence. I have seen more than one politician brought down because he wasn't careful. There are people watching us. If the optics are suspicious, they'll talk about it. When you show up at my office without notice and direct my staff to intervene for you with a state agency, don't you think that people take notice? Legislative staffers run in packs. One of mine might share that story with a friend working for one of my enemies or, worse, with a reporter. If I don't step on my johnson, I stand a good chance of being the next governor. If so, we can continue to be useful to one another. But, if either of us stumbles, it's likely that we'll both go down."

Grabel finished his drink and stubbed out his cigar. "Message received, Senator. But you had better not neglect me as you move into this campaign. I will line up the donors, and I am also going to arrange for an increase in this year's grant to Senior Moments. But speaking of perceptions, can you get your wife off her ass to do a bit more to make it look like a legitimate operation? For $100K a year, she needs to do more than arrange for a few lectures on advances in dementia treatment. And one more thing. You had better find a way to shitcan that bill raising the state minimum wage. Do you know what that would do to my bottom line? Enough said. We'll see you off in the morning."

TWENTY-SIX

JAKE HAD JUST FINISHED MAKING A CALL TO TESS, CHECKING IN on the boys and her, when he got the text. The guys were waiting for him down in the street. One of Jake's boyhood friends was getting married, and he had asked Jake to be a groomsmen. With that came the obligation to join in the traditional bachelor's party. Tonight was the night, and Jake, somewhat reluctantly, piled into a rented limo for a night on the town. The groom and his two other attendants were already exchanging shots of bourbon as they made their way through heavy traffic to their first stop of the evening. His host handed Jake a glass and shared a generous pour.

The first stop on their pilgrimage was Aunt Millie's. Millie Trapani and her bar had become legendary in the life of the city. Millie was now somewhere north of eighty years and hardly stood above bar level, but she was always in full control of her domain. Each morning at 6:00 a.m., except in the event of a blizzard or hurricane, she could be found outside her front door scrubbing the steps. She finished her day at midnight, presiding over closing time, collecting the receipts, and supervising clean up. In between, she made the best roast pork sandwich anyone ever tasted, juicy thick slices with garlic and peppers, drenched in gravy and nestled in a hard Italian roll. Sinatra was reputed to have a plane flown in from Palm Springs just to pick up an order. Presidential candidates paid homage to Millie every four years so that they could be photographed chomping down on one of her gastronomic wonders. At least one aspirant stumbled when he approached the task too delicately, asking for a knife and fork. He wound up losing the state vote.

Jake and his buddies settled into a booth and placed their orders, heavy on the gravy, along with a round of beers. As they waited, they speculated about the groom's capacity to fulfill his marital duties, and then their focus shifted to Jake and his new romantic interest. Jake refused to engage them except to say that he had never met a woman like Tess, which was met with hoots and predictions of another bachelor party on the horizon. After sandwiches and several beers, they loaded back into the limo for the next event.

Snookers was a fancy pool hall. They took two tables, ordered the first of several rounds of shots and beers, and the competition began. After a few hours, it devolved into a contest as to which of them could still manage to make even a single shot. Before things got totally out of hand, the limo arrived for the last leg of the evening's entertainment.

They drove through a commercial neighborhood past a string of auto dealerships until they got to their stop. It was a cavernous, one-story structure, its walls washed with blue lighting. Looming over the entrance was an immense electronic sign. On it was a heart-shaped figure of a woman's buttocks with a shot glass poised on top of each cheek. The flashing sign below identified the enterprise as "Bottoms Up. A Sophisticated Gentlemen's Club."

As a former English major, the double entendre was not lost on Jake. They tumbled out of the limo and entered the premises.

After a cash exchange with the doorman, they were led to an alcove off the dance floor. They collapsed into a worn and weary-looking couch and ordered yet another round of drinks. The drinks came quickly, and the tab mounted at a dizzying pace. By the time the first of the dancers approached her assigned pole, each member of the team had slid down into the couch and was nearly supine. Their senses deadened, it was now all a whirl of legs and breasts. When the dancers finished their routines, the groom and his guests struggled to place bar-soaked bills in the location suggested by the dancers.

Finally, the groom announced that he had arranged a special dance. He had written each of their names on a slip of paper. One of them would serve as a partner for one of the dancers. A tall dark-haired woman approached. Curiously, she was wearing pasties in the shape of exclamation points, barely covering the nipples of her billowy breasts. She picked a slip out of a glass and called out the name, "Jake." Jake blinked stupidly and slunk down further into the couch.

The dancer began with slow undulations, moving back and forth in front of Jake as fierce looking security staff stood close by, as if Jake or any of the others was capable of mayhem. The dancer moved closer and closer until she turned around and settled onto Jake's lap. The movement started again, slowly gaining in intensity and grinding hard against Jake's nearly recumbent frame. Jake's face had a fixed expression which could not be confused with ecstasy. He was visibly in pain. Nevertheless, as the song ended, Jake gamely placed an index finger over one of the exclamation points and presented a glazed smile to the cell phones pointed at him.

As they drove away, Jake turned to his friends and slurred, "I was always a stickler for punctuation."

TWENTY-SEVEN

Cardinal William Boyle had presided over the Archdiocese for five years now. It had been a homecoming of sorts for him to return to the city where he was born and raised to serve as shepherd to its some one million Roman Catholics. That number represented all those self-designated members. The exact number of active Catholics today was certainly much less.

The Cardinal closely watched periodic reports from his two hundred parishes. They documented a disturbing trend. Mass attendance and financial contributions were dropping steadily. The Archdiocese could no longer afford to maintain all these parishes and their elementary schools as well as its ten regional high schools. In response, three years ago, the Cardinal had commissioned a study that recommended closing fourteen churches and assimilating their congregations into adjoining parishes. Twelve elementary and three high schools would be shuttered also. When the study results were leaked, panic set in among those affected. The Cardinal faced open revolt in two parishes, including a "pray-in" at one that lasted for several days. Many parents transferred their children to public schools. The consolidation was now completed but the net result was an even more dramatic drop in church attendance and revenues. This Church was certainly different than the one Boyle grew up in. Its members were no longer willing just to "pray, pay, and obey."

He understood that much of the blame for this crisis lay with the shadow the priest pedophile scandal cast upon the Archdiocese, as it had upon the Catholic Church in America and across the world. The Archdiocese had recently been the subject of a state grand jury report which identified ninety-three former priests who over the past fifty years had either been convicted or credibly accused of child molestation. Many of them had remained in ministry long after evidence had been presented to the Cardinal's predecessors. It was commonly known now that priests had been shuffled from one parish to another as they came under suspicion. Boyle had been brought in to attempt to put out the fire when the last archbishop came under public scrutiny for his dereliction. Ironically, the attorney general leading the inquiry, Mary Beth Karpinski, had been a student of Boyle's. He wondered now whether he might find himself in the crosshairs of a similar investigation into one of the dioceses where he previously served.

The Cardinal was aware that the Church's trouble went well beyond the current child sex abuse crisis. Its roots lay in the historic structure of the institution. Too many modern Catholics, at least those from the United States and other developed countries, were no longer willing to accept the authority of the pope and the hierarchy. Maybe it all started when Pius VI issued the encyclical *Humanae Vitae* way back in 1968 condemning contraception. That, of course, led to the ongoing conflict over abortion and the Church's active involvement in the push to overturn Roe v. Wade. But even beyond these positions impacting the intimate lives of lay Catholics, it seemed to him that more and more Catholics just no longer wanted to accept the Church's dominion over them in anything at all. Wherever this was going, Bill Boyle knew one thing. He was a true son of the Church, and he would die one. Whatever it would take to hold together this Archdiocese, he would do. If that troubled his conscience, then that's why the Church offers absolution to sinners.

The Cardinal was still ruminating as his car entered the drive leading to his residence. It was nearly 7:00 p.m. His long, official day had concluded with his presiding over the confirmation of twenty eighth graders at Saint Aloysius Church. His private secretary, Reverend Austin Cabot, also served as his driver. The young priest retrieved his boss's vestment bag, and they both entered through the kitchen. Theresa, the Cardinal's cook, waved as they passed through. They were struck by the aroma of braciole simmering in gravy on the stove. The Cardinal fell in love with Italian food when he was a seminarian in Rome. It was there that he cultivated the paunch that he and his fellow students came to call the "Roman Stigmata." Since then, he had always insisted upon having an Italian cook wherever he was posted. Irish housekeepers, but Italian cooks. He smiled approvingly at Theresa, announcing, "Perfetto," as he showed his appreciation by twisting his thumb and index finger against the side of his mouth. His suit coat was off now, and he loosened his tab collar, unbuttoned his shirt, and headed upstairs to wash up and change. They had guests for dinner.

He was back down in a matter of minutes, now in civvies: plaid shirt, green V-neck, and khaki pants. Father Cabot had already made a batch of martinis. He poured one for his boss, straight up with a twist. They sat and joked about Saint Aloysius's pastor who had momentarily forgotten the Cardinal's presence during the confirmation ceremony.

Soon the guests began to arrive. First, Edward Fegley, general counsel for the Archdiocese. Fegley had served several vicars over his long career, proving himself a crafty practitioner, though not well known as a student of the law. His intimate knowledge of the city and everyone important for advancing the Church's causes overcame any of his legal deficiencies.

The Cardinal's secretary greeted Fegley with his usual scotch on the rocks. Under instructions from the Cardinal, Father Cabot discreetly served a cheaper blend reserved for him, not one of the well-aged single malts saved for the Cardinal and his more valued visitors. Fegley was onto it, but it was only one of the many slights he had to endure to maintain a longstanding client that brought in over a million in fees for his firm every year.

Tom Matthews arrived next. He was owner of the largest insurance brokerage firm in the area, handling all the Archdiocese's coverages. He also served as chairman of the Cardinal's charitable fund, "Open Hearts". Tom was a member of the Knights of Malta, a Catholic lay order tracing its origins to the time of the Crusades. The Knights engage in humanitarian efforts worldwide. The Order includes certain men and women chosen by the Vatican for their charitable activities and other valued service to the Church. The Cardinal had orchestrated Matthews' selection as a Knight. Matthews had become his trusted, confidential advisor. As usual, Matthews declined an offer of alcohol, limiting himself to sparkling water.

The last to arrive were the Cardinal's special guests, Senator Ben Anderson and his chief of staff, Meg Holland. Their apologies for their lateness were waved off by the Cardinal.

"Ben, I know that you and Meg have a packed schedule. We're honored that you've made time to join us this evening. What can Father Cabot offer you by way of a libation?"

Within minutes, Cabot returned with two scotches, served neat. Fegley did not fail to note the rich amber color of their drinks. Obviously, they warranted the good stuff.

After a few minutes of light banter, they adjourned to dinner. The Cardinal began with a prayer, all the attendees blessing themselves afterward, including Ben, the only non-Catholic at the table. The fare was simple but delicious. Antipasto salad followed by steaming bowls of pasta fagioli soup.

The Cardinal had directed Cabot to decant two bottles of his finest wine before dinner. The secretary now poured everyone the first of the Brunello di Montalcano, a dark, earthy red, reputed to be the finest of all Italian wines. The Cardinal lifted his glass and offered a toast.

"May all of us find success in this coming year, especially our honored guest, the Senator."

As the guests enjoyed their food, the Cardinal told them about his introduction to this vintage wine.

"It was an Italian cardinal, an influential member of the Roman Curia, who introduced me to it. As a young priest, I served in the Vatican as the cardinal's secretary. He was a fierce defender of doctrinal orthodoxy in the Church. He was right on that account, and he was certainly right about this wine."

Theresa then appeared with the main course, serving everyone slices of the braciole accompanied by a side dish of linguini with garlic and olive oil. She was never one to hold her tongue. "I made this special for the Cardinal before he told me that he had invited some medigans tonight."

After she returned to the kitchen, Ben asked, "OK, I bite. What's a medigan?"

The Cardinal smiled. "It's an expression for a non-Italian. I was first called one by a paisan in the seminary. Only later did I find out it stems from the phrase 'merde de canne.'"

"Now, what does that mean?" Meg inquired.

The Cardinal chuckled. "Literally, it means dog shit."

When the laughs subsided, Meg Holland asked him if she could get the recipe for the braciole from Theresa.

"It's not her recipe. It's mine. You can find any number of recipes on the internet, but none like mine. I have a secret ingredient. To get the recipe, you will need to offer a bigger contribution to my charities than it takes to become a Knight of Malta."

As the espresso and cannoli were served, the conversation shifted to more serious matters.

"How is the race shaping up, Senator?" the Cardinal inquired. "Or maybe I should ask the real source. How's it going, Meg?"

Meg offered her best attempt at a blush and deferred to Ben. "Well, Your Eminence, I see a clear path through the primary, but it will get trickier from there to the general. At this point, the opposition's current favorite is Congressman Harper. He has a consistently liberal voting record so he can rely upon the unions, anti-gun activists, and pro-choice proponents. I have done my best to avoid agitating those elements. But, at the same time, I have quietly squelched legislation to expand gun restrictions and supported a bill to make abortion clinics affiliate with local hospitals. I should do well in the rural areas. Harper will do his best to get out the African American and Hispanic vote . Our city and the surrounding suburbs will be pivotal. I sure could use your help there."

The Cardinal sat for a moment, taking it all in. "Ben, you know how careful I must be to avoid losing our tax-exempt status. Besides, if I come on too strong, I will hear it from my boss. I can do this for you though. This October, I will issue a pastoral letter to be read in all the parishes. In it, I will remind the faithful of the urgent need to uphold human life from the moment of conception and of their duty to hold our public officials accountable for where they stand on that issue. I wouldn't attempt to tell you how to run your campaign, but a well-timed speech by you defending the unborn might be serendipitous."

The Cardinal could see that he had Ben's rapt attention, so he went in for the kill.

"You could do something for me also. I am sure you are aware of the Attorney General's recently released grand jury report. My sources tell me that the next step will be to issue subpoenas to the Archdiocese demanding documents related to my predecessors' conduct in dealing with accused priests. Mary Beth Karpinski is a practicing Catholic. As her spiritual leader, I have certain authority over her in ecclesiastical matters, but I must be careful not to appear to abuse that power in an effort to influence her prosecutorial actions. Frankly, I wish I could. I'd even consider denying her the sacraments if she doesn't give in."

He raised his hands and laughed a bit too loudly.

"Just kidding, of course. But, Ben, you are in a different position. You control funding for the AG's office as a legislator, and you will be at the head of the ticket when Mary Beth runs for re-election next November. Whatever you do to slow down, if not stop this inquisition, would be most appreciated. In addition, it would help if you provide me with whatever advance notice you can of any new developments in this inquiry."

Now it was Ben Anderson's turn to pause and consider a response.

"Cardinal Boyle, I will do everything that can be done legally and ethically to assist you."

The Cardinal sat back in his chair. "I suppose that's all I can ask. By the way, how is our good friend, Max Grabel, these days? Give him my regards when you see him next."

As Ben and Meg drove back to the office, Meg brushed Ben's hand away from her thigh.

"You know that the Cardinal was offering you a *quid pro quo* back there, don't you? No help in the pews next fall unless you tamp down the AG's investigation."

Ben turned toward her. She saw the fear in his eyes.

"And there was one more message from His Eminence. His reference to Grabel was a clear threat. He knows about your relationship with him. How much, we don't know yet. But he wanted to make you nervous, and he sure succeeded."

TWENTY-EIGHT

O N THE MORNING AFTER THE BACCHANAL, JAKE MORRIS CONFINED himself to bed except for a few urgent trips to the john. He slept fitfully, and when he finally roused himself sometime after noon, he moved tentatively around his apartment. He had a violent headache. Although he was exhausted, he also felt wired, a hypertension produced by the slowly receding blood alcohol level in his system. He discovered an old pizza box in the refrigerator. The two slices it contained were limp and the dull translucence of the cheese would have caused him to dump it all in the trash if he were sober. Instead, he opted not to use the microwave but simply gnaw away at the cold leftovers. He passed over a six-pack of beer and chose a bottle of spring water to wash it down. Even in his impaired state, he was beginning to reflect upon last night's performance. "Maybe Tess is right," he thought. He could have a bit of a drinking problem.

Slowly, the reflexes were returning. He reached for his phone and scanned his text messages. There were several waiting to be opened, most of them with an attachment. As he scrolled through them, he recognized the names of the crew from last evening as well as a string of other friends. Each message followed the same theme, attempting a clever commentary on his exploits at Bottoms Up. Each also included a photo of Jake pinned down on the couch by his dancing partner as he pointed toward her punctuated breasts.

Scrolling through, Jake froze when he saw the text from Tess. It also included the same incriminating attachment along with a brief message. "I see that you have now branched out into photojournalism. I suggest you cancel the reservation for our visit to the B&B unless you want to take your new dancing partner along. In any event, good luck in your new career."

The phone dropped from his hands, and Jake looked out toward a crew race on the distant river. Panic quickly set in. It caused him to confront a feeling which had been building inside him over the last several weeks. He had come to believe in a future with Tess and her boys. That assumption had guided all his actions, not just when he was with her, but in how he conducted himself each day and in how he assessed his future. There was one exception and that was his performance last night. He did not view it as an act of infidelity, but he had certainly let them both down. Why did he do it? Why in the past had he gotten himself into similar situations? Alcohol was only a partial explanation. He didn't have an answer yet, but he suspected that he might have plenty of time to search for one. For now, though, he had to do whatever he could to salvage their relationship.

TWENTY-NINE

RECENTLY, TESS HAD GONE BACK TO SUNDAY MASS. EVEN THOUGH she got home from work in the wee hours, she was up by 7:00 making breakfast for the boys and then getting them washed and dressed. As always, Mary was a big help. The four of them then piled into the van for the short trip to Saint Matthew's, her childhood parish. Mary attended Mass every day so she could not disguise her joy over Tess's recent change of heart.

This morning, as she struggled with Mikey to get him ready, Tess silently questioned her motivation to return to church. She had attended Catholic schools through high school, never questioning her religious instruction back then, except that early on she had become uncomfortable with the practice of confessing her sins. The thought of revealing her impure thoughts to a strange man partially hidden behind a small, curtained door sent anxious tremors through her. It was even worse when she confessed to a priest whom she knew. Over time, Tess gave up on confession, and gradually, she also distanced herself from other church doctrine. By the time of her marriage to Paul, Tess had become what was then known as a "Cafeteria Catholic," picking and choosing what she would believe, but keeping her differences to herself. Later, with the revelations of priests abusing children and the efforts of the hierarchy to cover up these crimes, Tess gave up on the Church altogether. She came to link that scandal and the Church's inflexible positions on doctrine all as a means of maintaining earthly power over its members.

So why was she going back now? She hadn't changed her mind about any of the things that had driven her away. She knew a part of it was because she felt that her boys needed some religious experience to reinforce the prayers and simple theology she tried to give them. Also, she herself missed the liturgy and the comfort and strength gained from participating in an ancient ritual that dared to proclaim the transformation of bread and wine into a divine personhood. She had resented what she viewed as the Church's control over her access to that sacrament. If necessary, she would block out any message from the celebrant that would intrude upon her private worship.

During Mass that morning, Tess included in her litany of prayers a plea for Jake and herself. She would have liked to pray that they would marry, but that was too presumptuous. Instead, she asked only that they both be honest with one another and accept whatever might come.

All of that changed, however, when she checked her text messages on the way out of church. A girlfriend who dated one of the other groomsmen forwarded her the photo of Jake with his dance partner. The shock she felt reminded her of the day that she saw her late husband in handcuffs on the nightly news. She shoved her phone in her pocket and somehow regained enough control to drive home safely.

Although it was lost on the boys, Mary sensed something was wrong. When they got in the house, she immediately took charge, sending Thomas upstairs to work on a school project and settling Mikey in the living room to watch one of his Disney movies. She then walked into the kitchen. Tess was seated at the table with her hands wrapped around a cup of tea, her eyes welled with tears. Mary poured herself a cup and sat down across from her daughter.

"Is it something we can talk about?"

Tess reached for her phone, brought up the photo, and passed it across the table.

Mary studied it a moment. "Not exactly Jake's finest moment, I'd say."

Tess grimaced. "That's an understatement."

Mary sipped her tea and took a moment to let Tess settle down.

"What are you going to do now?"

Tess took her phone back and pulled up the text that she had just sent Jake. She showed it to her mother.

"Well, I hope you give the guy the benefit of a trial now that you just hanged him."

Tess huffed a bit and responded. "He knows my history and I know his. I made it clear that he was on trial from our first date. He's had all the due process he'll get from me."

Her phone rang and Tess immediately sent the call to voice mail. She expected a visit from Jake shortly and she was preparing herself for it. She took a sheaf of paper and began to write. When she finished, she placed the note in an envelope, handed it to Mary and said, "When Jake shows up, please give him this and tell him I do not want to see him."

As predicted, Jake was at the door within the hour. By then, Tess had retreated to her upstairs bedroom, and Mary was left to finish the job. She opened the door to find Jake standing immobile on the step. He had the look of someone who had just gotten a terminal diagnosis.

"Mary, can I come in for a moment to see Tess?"

She hesitated, not wanting to deliver the news.

"I'm sorry, Jake. Tess told me to give you this."

She placed the note in his hand, and for a moment, she could see in his eyes the thought of pleading his case to her in her daughter's absence.

He shrugged and said, "Please tell Tess how sorry I am. I never intended to hurt her, and now I know I've lost her trust. Maybe I'll never have a chance to get it back. But tell her that I will always remember her and the boys, all of you, really. I have decided to take a reporting assignment in Montana which will take me out of the area for some time. When I get back, I'll try again. Who knows?"

Mary couldn't hold back. She hugged Jake, kissed him on the cheek, and closed the door. Half-hidden behind a window shade, Tess watched as Jake walked down the sidewalk, slipping the note into his pocket before getting into his car and driving off.

THIRTY

IT WAS LATE FEBRUARY. A MONTH HAD PASSED SINCE THE MOUNT Zion Massacre. Interest faded among many in the city, but for others, life would be different from now on. For them, shock and sorrow slowly receded but loneliness filled in the gaps as survivors were left to puzzle out an uncertain future.

Esther Washington bore perhaps the heaviest burden. Since entering their seventies, both she and Micah had spoken often about their deaths, planning final arrangements, and speculating with a tinge of dark humor on who might be the first to go. Micah contended that he should go first since his inability to get through a day without her guidance would leave him wandering aimlessly, left as a charge upon the rest of the family. Well, Micah's wish had come true, but in a way that neither of them had fathomed. Without an opportunity for a last goodbye, Esther's sleepless nights were haunted by the memory of Micah's assassination.

Even more difficult to accept was the loss of her little granddaughter. Cissie had brought great joy to their lives. She lived a few blocks away, and she had made a practice of stopping by daily to visit her grandparents. She was a kind, talented, and intelligent child. Even at her young age, she spoke about becoming a professional singer. Now, that would never be. Esther remained to console her daughter and her family just as they sought to comfort her.

Tragedy took a similar shape among the families of the other victims. It fell hard upon Rachel and Barry Schiller. Although their friends and fellow congregants did what they could, without other children or any family in the area, they were left to lean upon one another. There was one exception though. Before her death, Liz had spoken about a new man who had entered her life. They had sensed something different about how she spoke of him. Unfortunately, their first meeting with Cody Walton was at their daughter's funeral when Rachel and Cody reached out to one another in their shared grief.

Cody called a few days later and came to visit them. He shared with them his story of traveling as a young boy from Jamaica to New York City to live with an elderly aunt who raised him there. He studied photography at City College until taking a job with *The Times Union*. Cody's aunt died a few years ago. She was his only family member in the States. Rachel and Barry could see how much Cody was suffering. They shared Liz in life, and they now would share her loss together. They invited Cody over for Sunday dinner a few weeks after the funeral. It would become a ritual over time.

Meanwhile, the world was learning about the tormented life of Jonas Martin, the surviving shooter. Investigators from several law enforcement agencies took pains to uncover every rock which may have offered him shelter during his short life, attempting to glean his motive for killing and wounding so many innocent people. Jonas had lived in a ramshackle house with his mother. He worked part-time stocking shelves at a local supermarket and had few friends apart from Macy Blankenship, his dead co-conspirator.

Ample evidence was harvested from his computer to support the prosecutor's decision to treat the murders as a hate crime. Jonas had been a frequent visitor to several White supremacist websites. Macy and he had been part of the neo-Nazi demonstration in Charlottesville a few years ago. In the days before their fateful visit to Mount Zion AME Church, there were several emails and texts exchanged between the two of them in which they plotted to take down "as many niggers, Jews and other mongrels" as they could. Jonas's lawyers had him plead not guilty as they quietly negotiated with the prosecutor, hoping to escape a death sentence through a guilty plea in exchange for life without parole.

Those negotiations appeared to be going nowhere until, one day, the prosecutor received a visit from Esther Washington and Rachel Schiller.

They urged him to accept the defendant's offer. Although that view was not shared by all the victims' survivors, their entreaties were enough to convince the prosecutor to agree to recommend the deal to the court. All the families of the deceased would have an opportunity to make a statement to the judge at the time of sentencing. They would have to be content with that.

After sitting shiva, Rachel had reached out to Esther, and they had met for lunch. Even apart from their common loss, they were soon drawn to one another. Their discussion ranged from the people they had lost to how their lives would now change. Eventually, they were left to ponder what might cause someone to inflict such harm upon another human being. Rachel believed that both these young men had been so consumed with hatred that they viewed their victims as no better than animals they might hunt in the wild.

Esther shook her head.

"But even animals treat each other better than that."

They had read in the paper the interview of Jonas's mother. She had been asked that same question. She replied that she had no idea what had gotten into him. She broke down as she said how terrible she felt for the victims and their families.

As Esther and Rachel talked, they both came to the same conclusion. They would pay a visit to Mrs. Martin. After clearing it with the prosecutor, they traveled twenty or so miles into the country until they reached a tiny hamlet. There was a small convenience store and gas station surrounded by about a dozen run-down homes. They quickly found the Martin residence, a two-story structure with a sagging roof, paint flaking off the clapboard siding, and derelict Christmas lights surrounding the door and windows. The hulks of two abandoned cars stood guard by a large TV dish in the side yard. An American flag served as a curtain covering the front window.

They nervously approached the front door, knocked, and waited. After a second try, they could see through the smudged window a figure approaching. A woman's face filled the glass, appraising them for a moment before opening the door.

"What do you want?"

Esther and Rachel identified themselves, and after studying them for a moment, the woman opened the door wide and quietly said, "Well, you must have some reason to make the long trip out here, so come on in."

Hazel Martin was a woman who bore the marks of every battle she had fought in her fifty-some years, and she had apparently lost most of them. Despite the winter weather, she wore a sleeveless jersey over a pair of sweatpants, padding across the room in flip-flops. A tangle of long brownish hair framed a broad head anchoring a fleshy torso. Heavy bags hung below her lifeless, gray eyes. She pointed the ladies toward a couch from which she swept three startled cats. Hazel crumbled into a faded recliner, raised it upright and turned to face her visitors. Without so much as offering a glass of water, she waited to hear what they had to say.

With a silent nod from Esther, Rachel began. "Mrs. Martin, both Mrs. Washington and I want to thank you for the sympathy you expressed in your newspaper interview. We wanted to tell you that directly and to say that we recognize that you also are a victim of this tragedy. You have lost a son."

Hazel cut her off.

"I didn't lose a son. He was already lost. At least his father gave up whuppin' on me and found somebody else to torture. His son hung around so that he could suck off the tit as long as he could. I am sorry for what happened to all you good people, but I'm glad to have that loser outta my life. To be honest, I hope that they're goin' to put him down."

Esther couldn't help herself.

"Dear Lord! Please don't say that. We are supposed to forgive one another, as we hope to be forgiven. Rachel and I are not quite there yet, but we're trying. And you should too."

Hazel looked away for a moment and then turned back facing the two of them.

"I don't see that happenin' anytime soon."

Esther and Rachel were left with no other words to offer except to thank Mrs. Martin for her time. They were soon out the door.

Rachel and Esther had learned to share quiet times in the weeks since tragedy had brought them together. Others tried to offer comfort, but their show of sympathy often fell flat, leaving each of them exhausted by the effort to respond in a way that was expected. They sat in silence now as Rachel steered the car onto the interstate.

Finally, Rachel broke the silence.

"Isn't life strange? That woman wishes her son dead, and I would give up my life right now to bring my daughter back."

Esther reached across and squeezed Rachel's hand.

"I know. Every morning I wake up and for a moment everything seems normal. Then I realize that it's not and never will be again. I ask God why it happened, but I haven't gotten an answer yet. I fall back on a passage from our New Testament. 'For now, we see through a glass, darkly, but then face to face. Now I know in part, but then shall I know, even as also I am known.'"

Rachel smiled and nodded. "That may not be from a book that I read, but I agree with the message. How about joining Barry and me for dinner before I drive you home?"

THIRTY-ONE

J AKE'S MIND RACED AS HE DROVE HOME FROM TESS'S HOUSE. HE hadn't read the note yet, but he pretty much knew what it would say. His first impulse was to stop at a bar, but this time he resisted the urge. That was how he got himself into this mess in the first place. That and a couple of other character flaws that Tess had made him aware of. "She's right," he thought. "I am impulsive. I tend not to think things through. Just jump in and expect to work out the details as I go. And when things blow up, I look elsewhere for excuses. Well, nobody else made me drink myself into oblivion on Saturday night."

Whether it was over with Tess or not, Jake knew he had to make some changes in his life.

When he returned to his apartment, he brewed himself a cup of coffee, sat down at his kitchen table and opened the note. As he predicted, there were no surprises, except for its tone. Tess explained, once more, the importance of stability for her and her boys after her chaotic marriage. She needed a reliable partner, and absent that, she was prepared to soldier on alone. She had hoped that Jake might be the exception from all the other men who had wandered through her life, but his performance at the bachelor party proved otherwise. It was a symptom of some unresolved issues that he needed to confront. Tess could not afford to take a chance that she and her boys might be stuck with a guy wallowing in self-imposed misery. She thanked him for his kindness to her and her family and she wished him the best.

Jake understood, although he wished that she had offered some hope of reconciliation. He dropped the note into an empty fruit bowl where it would lie indefinitely. He sipped his coffee and sat back, reflecting upon what Tess had said. He then opened his laptop and emailed a note to the editor of *Stalwart* magazine. He was heading out for Montana, and he would be gone for a long while.

Jake made the proposal to *Stalwart* shortly after his departure from the newspaper. The magazine had made a name for itself through articles about men facing unusual challenges, whether in the business world, sports, the military, academia, religion, arts and entertainment or just about anywhere else. The writing was of a high quality and the publication had gained a small but loyal audience. Jake pitched them on a story about loggers, a calling with the highest mortality rate of all occupations in the country. He suggested that he be imbedded with a logging crew for several months. He would learn their skills, endure their hardships and, hopefully, reveal the toll the work took on them, both physically and otherwise.

For several weeks, Jake heard nothing in response, so he focused on a few special assignments as he scouted out more traditional reporting jobs. Then, two weeks ago, he received a lengthy email from the *Stalwart* editor. He had contacted a small logging operator in northwestern Montana who expressed interest in Jake's proposal. The owner explained that his company had a contract with the US Forest Service to thin out areas of a national park, removing dead or otherwise unproductive growth to reduce the risk of wildfires threatening tourist areas and nearby communities. The loggers would also harvest a limited number of selected trees that would fetch a higher price. Most of the timber would be suitable for sale to a nearby saw-mill. Some would be processed for mulch. Because of the need to save most of the healthier trees while culling out the derelicts, and because much of the work would be on steep slopes, the loggers would not be able to utilize much of the newest tree-cutting machinery, placing a premium on their use of chain saws and other hand equipment.

Jake was impressed with the detail of the company owner's response. He did not yet know a lot about logging, but he had seen the new equipment on the internet. Operators were shielded in protected cabs. They employed sophisticated technology. He learned that these improvements had significantly reduced the number of workplace accidents. But none of that would be available to Jake and this crew. He also read that the most dangerous place to be at a logging site was on the ground. That's where he and his future co-workers would be operating most of the time.

Over the next two weeks, Jake stayed busy planning for his new experience and putting everything else on hold. His arrangement with the magazine required him to work full-time for six months as a member of the logging crew while living within the local community. He would not be paid by the logging company but would receive a modest advance from *Stalwart*. Final payment would come when he delivered an extensive article, due within sixty days of the end of his logging experience. The advance would be enough to cover his living expenses out West, while he would rely upon his remaining savings and some help from the trust to pay his apartment rent and other expenses back home. He needed to discuss these arrangements with the trustee, so Jake called the offices of Anthony Battalini, Esq. to schedule an appointment.

Since their first encounter, Jake had spoken a few times over the phone with Battalini to keep him informed of his finances and job prospects. They had also met once at a local restaurant so that Jake could sign some trust documents. This was his first visit to the trustee's office. It was in a mid-size, downtown office building that housed various professional and business firms. Battalini occupied a small suite on the fourth floor where he conducted a law practice limited to handling trusts and estates.

When Jake entered the office, he quickly saw that the décor matched the personality of the trustee. The dark leather seating and oriental rug in the reception area were complemented by a few pieces of art on the walls depicting rustic scenes of the Italian countryside. A well-tended terrarium graced the glass coffee table. Dignified but not pretentious. Comforting but not comfortable. He could imagine a decedent's family waiting there for the will to be read to find out which of them had been favored and which had not.

Jake was greeted by Battalini's administrative assistant who offered him a cup of coffee. Within a few minutes, he was escorted in to meet with the trustee who rose from his desk and shook his hand, motioning for Jake to take a client's chair. Battalini sat back, looking across the desk with a slight smile that conveyed a certain professional amiability.

"So, what brings you here today, Jake?"

Over the next half hour, Jake laid out his plans, including his financial requirements during his six-month relocation to Montana. The trustee assured him that the trust would cover his rent, utilities, and other fixed expenses while he was away. He also volunteered that his paralegal would check in on Jake's apartment periodically. He then took down the address where Jake could be reached, confirming his email address and cell phone number.

Then, he softly inquired, "You can tell me it's none of my business, but I'll ask anyway. Why are you doing this?"

Although Jake was aware that the trustee had an obligation to husband the trust's assets, the question still surprised him.

"I have always wondered what it would be like to work at something physically demanding, knowing that if you don't do your job right it might cost lives. Also, I must admit that there have been things going on in my life I'm not happy about, and I think I need a change of routine to, maybe, shake things up. I figure that spending time in Schuyler, Montana, might just do that. Does that make any sense?"

A gentle expression returned to Anthony Battalini's face.

"If you think that putting yourself through this crucible you've set up for yourself will help, then maybe it will. Good luck to you, Jake, and keep in touch with me. And let me know if there is anything you want me to check on while you're gone."

The two shook hands and Jake was quickly out the door. Riding down the elevator, his thoughts were fixed upon the trustee's last comment. "What did Battalini mean about checking on things? Did the trustee know about Tess? If he does, how would he have come by that information?"

THIRTY-TWO

Hunter Dane was wrapping up his day. He had just met with the newest member of *The Times Union's* editorial staff. After Liz Schiller's death, Hunter pulled the resumes of those others who had applied to replace Jake. He remembered a young man who impressed him nearly as much as Liz, but who had the disadvantage of being a white male at a time when the paper was striving to bring more diversity to its staff. Hunter contacted him and he quickly accepted his offer.

Steven Chadwick was a product of the state school system. He had progressed from a local community college to the state university where he was editor-in-chief of the paper. He then worked briefly at *The Cleveland Plain Dealer.*

After only a few weeks on the political beat, Hunter handed him Jake's work on the Anderson investigation. He directed Chadwick to broaden the inquiry to include the relationship between Max Grabel, and Anderson and his wife, as well as their contacts with the Archdiocese and Cardinal William Boyle. Although nothing yet linked them together, he was instructed to compare notes with the reporter assigned to cover the pending state grand jury investigation of the Archdiocese's handling of the pedophile priest scandal.

As Hunter shepherded Chadwick out the door, he thought to himself, "I just may have given that young man an opportunity to win a Pulitzer Prize."

An hour later, Hunter was engaged in a different sort of shepherding, as he guided his old friend, Father Ron Harbourt, through a crowded restaurant to the back table where their friends from the seminary were seated. They met every third Thursday of the month. Ron was recovering from a stroke, so Hunter had volunteered to chauffeur him tonight.

The group called themselves the "Sole Survivors". They had started off together on the way to ordination but a few, like Hunter, dropped out along the line. Some others left for various reasons after years in the priesthood. Jeff Baldwin became an Episcopal priest. Of the original fifteen, death, disability, and other causes had reduced their number to ten. Father Nick Marino was the titular head of the club. He called them to order, and before their drinks arrived, he called on Hunter to provide the blessing.

"Heavenly Father, we ask your blessing upon this gathering of your sons. We pray that you will strengthen us as we continue our earthly journey. Temper justice with mercy. Bring peace where there is conflict. Comfort where there is sorrow. Hope where there is fear. Finally, please let there be pot roast on the list of specials tonight. Amen."

Hunter Dane's prayers were at least partially answered. The pot roast was delicious, the drinks flowed, and the conversation was spirited. As usual, those still in active ministry spoke of the difficulty of holding on to their vocation. In one fashion or another, they found ways to live with the depression that came with a celibate life. Some of their brothers tried to deal with loneliness through dependence on alcohol or drugs or through illicit relationships which provided some passing comfort. Worst of all, some others had chosen to impose their will upon the most innocent, achieving brief sexual gratification along with the momentary illusion that they were in control of their miserable lives. As for the Sole Survivors, they depended upon prayer, each other, and an occasional cocktail.

They had read the news reports of those predators among them, and they all shared some degree of guilt for these crimes. For years, word had spread among them of priests who were quietly shuttled from one parish or diocese to another as their bishops did whatever was necessary to silence the victims and diffuse the anger of their loved ones. But that was no longer possible. The word was out, and even those priests who had kept their vows and served their flocks faithfully were now looked upon with suspicion.

One member of the group described a recent encounter at an ice cream store. He had stopped after Mass for a cone while still wearing his clerical garb. A little boy was sitting at a table crying, as the ice cream dripped down his chin. The priest walked over to comfort the boy and wipe away the mess. The boy's mother had been standing in line a few feet away. When she turned around to see her son being helped, she immediately jumped out of line, swept up the boy and walked out without a word.

They agreed that every priest would pay now for the sins of the guilty, but none of them could predict what impact this scandal might have on the Church in the long run. As bad as things were though, they knew that it was about to get even worse. The ongoing state grand jury had its sights on the hierarchy, and they knew that their former classmate, Cardinal Bill Boyle, was in the direct line of fire. All of them turned to Hunter, since they surmised correctly that *The Times Union* was on his trail.

"So, what can you tell us, Hunter?" Father Nick asked.

"Nothing. I will not even acknowledge that there is an ongoing investigation. My lips are sealed as tight as yours when you leave the confessional, Nick. I can only tell you that the era of the silence of the lambs is over."

THIRTY-THREE

IT HAD STARTED AS A BUSINESS MEETING, BUT NOW BROOKE Anderson found herself on her hands and knees searching for a lost earring underneath the office couch of Max Grabel.

She went to Max's office ostensibly to discuss a speaker's series she was arranging for families dealing with aging parents who had recently been diagnosed with dementia. She also wanted to make her case to Max for an increase in funding for Senior Moments. Brooke was hoping to be able to raise her own compensation considerably. Not that she really deserved it. She typically spent about five to ten hours a week on the job. Not bad for $100K a year. Nevertheless, Brooke walked confidently into Max's office wearing a beige dress suitable for a business meeting except for a large gold zipper which traveled down the back from the neck to below her waist, complemented by snakeskin half-boots. Max escorted her in and directed his assistant to hold all calls for the next hour.

They sat next to one another at Max's conference table as Brooke presented resumes of prospective speakers. Max showed little interest. After about fifteen minutes he stood up and walked over to a sideboard to refill their coffee cups. When he returned, he put down the cups, stepped back behind Brooke's chair and placed both his hands on her shoulders. He then began a slow massage. After a few minutes, Max leaned down and kissed Brooke behind her ear.

"Stand up."

It sounded more like a command than a request, but Brooke did as she was told. Max pulled her chair away, pulled down her back zipper and the dress dropped away. Brooke stepped out of it and removed her boots. Max then picked her up and carried her to the couch.

Their intimate encounter lasted a longer time than Brooke had ever experienced. Although nearly twenty years her senior, Max's appetite for sex was almost more than Brooke could handle, but when it was over, Max was quickly back to business.

As they were dressing, he joked, "I guess this serves as your interview for increased funding this year. Well, you will be appropriately rewarded for your services. However, in addition, I want your Senior Moments to refer its dementia clients to my new memory care centers."

On the way out the door, Max asked Brooke about her husband's campaign.

"I wouldn't know. He comes home late, if at all, and he's back out early the next morning."

Max struck a sympathetic pose. "Sorry about that. Give him my regards when you have the chance, and thanks for our own 'senior moment.'"

THIRTY-FOUR

O N THE MORNING OF HIS DEPARTURE, JAKE AWOKE BEFORE 5:00. HE dressed quickly, grabbed two duffel bags which he had packed the day before along with his laptop and then took an Uber to the airport. It was a gray, drizzly March morning and the weather matched Jake's mood. By 9:00, he was on a flight to Missoula, Montana.

As the plane dropped low for its approach to the runway, Jake got his first look at Montana in late winter. Except for the runway and terminal apron, everything else was shrouded in white. The pilot announced that another foot of snow was on its way. Jake was glad that he brought along his ski parka, gloves, and knit cap. Along with his insulated boots and long underwear, he figured that he had what would be his standard gear until the spring thaw came. From what he had read, that could come as late as May.

Jake arranged for a long-term car rental and within the hour he was headed north in an extended cab pickup. There was a light snow falling. Although the road had been plowed, it still was covered with a layer of packed snow, so Jake stopped at a truck stop and installed chains. He also grabbed a thermos of coffee.

As he walked back to his truck, Jake was stunned by the topography. On the left were the Mission Mountains with the Swan Range to the right, both a part of the massive Rockies. The snow served to flatten out the mono-chromatic landscape, but it was still an immense spectacle.

He had a long ride to Schuyler under the best of conditions, and that wasn't the case today. Along the way, he passed the great expanse of Flathead Lake and skirted the Flathead Indian Reservation. Jake drove straight through, only stopping briefly for a sandwich he ate behind the wheel. Sunset still came early, and Jake did not want to be traveling through unknown terrain in darkness and, perhaps, in a driving snowstorm.

By the time Jake pulled into Schuyler, his headlight beams formed cones of thick swirling snow. After hours of concentration trying to follow narrow ribbons of tire tracks, he was relieved to see the lights of town. He turned onto Main Street where a sign read "Welcome to Schuyler—the Friendliest

Town in Big Sky Country—Population 1,437." Jake hoped that would prove to be true. Up ahead, he saw the lights of a small motel. It looked passable, so he pulled into the parking lot and booked a room for the night. Nothing fancy, for sure, but the room was warm and clean. Even better, it was next to a bar. Without taking off his coat, Jake trudged next door, hoping for a beer and maybe even a decent meal. He got both at Cupid's Place.

Over the coming months, Jake would become a regular customer of the bar and would get to know its owner who was actually named Cupid—Cupid Kincaid. She was a formidable woman somewhere in her forties with a face that still retained its youthful beauty. Jake settled at the bar, and Cupid came over to take his order. She wasted no time on preliminaries, returning quickly with a large draft after putting in his order for a grilled steak.

The place fit Jake's expectations of a small-town watering hole in the West. Mounted trophies of bison, bear, and elk glowered down upon him. On the far wall, a stone fireplace blazed away. In front, some beat-up tables and chairs circled a small dance floor. Near the entrance was a long bar with law enforcement patches, dusty ball caps, and other memorabilia gracing the wall behind it.

Jake looked around and judged that the storm had kept most of the regulars home. There were two couples having dinner at one of the tables and five or six patrons at the bar. Jake was seated near the door. At the other end of the bar, he took note of three men, apparently in their late twenties, who seemed to be sizing him up. As he worked on his first draft, Jake watched as the trio put down multiple shots and beers. The one in the middle acted like the ringleader. He had stringy dark hair, a scruffy beard and a loud, high-pitched voice. At one point, he gestured toward Jake and said something which produced guffaws from his drinking partners.

Jake's steak arrived, and he ordered another beer. When Cupid returned with it, he tried to chat her up. He must have piqued her interest because she stuck around, washing out glasses and initially confining herself to a discussion of the storm. He knew what she really wanted to know. What was this stranger doing in her little town in the middle of a blizzard? He decided to end the suspense, so he asked Cupid if she happened to know Emil Brunson.

"Of course. Everybody in Schuyler knows Emil. His family logging company has been a part of this town for at least four generations. What business do you have with Emil?"

Jake laughed. "You sure are fast getting to the point. I have an appointment with him tomorrow morning about joining his crew this season."

Cupid stopped drying glasses and looked at him as if for the first time. Jake could see that she was sizing him up, trying to judge if he was serious about what he had just said.

"Well, if you are good enough to work for Emil Brunson, you're a better man than I judged when you first came in here."

THIRTY-FIVE

WHEN JAKE DROVE INTO THE YARD OF BRUNSON LOGGING COMPANY the next morning, the sun was breaking through the clouds and the temperature had risen to just above freezing. A few men could be seen working in the open bays of the garage, and smoke was rising from the chimney stack of a small building which Jake correctly judged to be the office.

Upon entry, he was met by a woman in her late forties with long, ash blonde hair. A handsome woman with an athlete's body. She introduced herself as Ingrid Brunson, and she pointed to her husband. Emil Brunson got up from his desk and made his way toward Jake, all six feet four and two hundred fifty pounds of him. He greeted Jake with a bone-crushing hand-shake, offered him a straight-backed chair, and then brought him a cup of coffee poured from a pot thinly crusted with an accretion of grounds built up over time. Jake took a sip and tried to suppress the effect of the dark, molten brew as he worked to restore circulation in his right hand.

Brunson threw another log into the fire box of a corner wood stove and then sat down at a desk that he obviously did not spend a lot of time behind. Despite the season, he wore only a T-shirt over heavy duck pants held up by wide red suspenders that stretched across his broad frame He had short gray hair and a well-groomed beard. One massive bicep was adorned with a tattoo showing a globe and anchor with the inscription "Semper Fi" below .

Jake quickly determined that Emil Brunson was a force of nature for reasons well beyond his imposing physical presence. Emil sat back and held Jake with a steady gaze that made clear he was considering whether he had made the right decision to allow him to join his crew.

"Let me be clear from the beginning. I agreed to this arrangement because I believe in this way of life. I want the word to get out that logging is a worthy pursuit for young people, both men and women, who appreciate working hard outdoors and then seeing what they've accomplished. I want them to know that logging operations provide a valuable product for our economy, and, if done responsibly, preserve our natural resources. I am the fourth generation of Brunsons in this business, and I have two sons and a daughter. I want them to decide for themselves what they wish to do with their lives, and that includes being a logger if that's what interests them. My hope is that after your experience here you will tell that story. Of course, that's up to you. But let me tell you what isn't up to you. While you work for me, you will take orders from me without question, and you will do nothing that puts my men in danger. I was a company commander with the 1st Marines in Fallujah in 2004, and I lost a lot of good men there. Unfortunately, I have seen loggers die too. I never want to see that again. So, if you do something stupid on the work site, I will not hesitate to send your butt back East. Is that understood?"

Jake blinked and responded, "Yes, sir."

THIRTY-SIX

Steve Chadwick had never met Jake Morris, but after reviewing the notes of his investigation, he quickly concluded that Morris had been onto something. Some in the newsroom thought that Morris was a bit of a prima donna, but nobody could tell him why he up and quit when Steve could see he was apparently on the brink of breaking the biggest story of his career. In any event, he was now charged with picking up where his predecessor left off. Dane was providing him with back-up to cover the run of more mundane political stories so that he could focus on the Anderson investigation. He would work along with Ellen Conway who was reporting on the grand jury inquiry into Cardinal Boyle and the Archdiocese.

First, he ran down all of Morris's sources just to be sure that his information was accurate. It all checked out. Senior Moments' tax returns showed annual revenues of around $150,000 over the last two years with at least $100,000 coming from Grabel's non-profit. There was $130,000 or so of administrative expenses, including $100,000 in compensation to Brooke Anderson, the Executive Director. The rest mainly went to a local gerontologist, a Dr. Norman Barkoff, for consultations and speaking fees.

Steve soon concluded that, once the story got out, it would be enough to prompt a senate ethics investigation into the relationship between Senator Anderson, his wife, and Max Grabel. That would likely derail Anderson's bid for the governorship and possibly launch a federal criminal investigation. But he knew there had to be more. It was now late March, and given the upcoming primary season, Steve understood that he had at best a few months to put it all together. The voters were entitled to know what they had found before they went to the polls. The Great White was paying close attention, demanding daily updates. Steve found that curious. Obviously, this was a huge story, but he also got the sense that Dane had a personal stake in its outcome.

Having done his homework, Steve was now ensconced in a booth at his favorite diner, pondering Dane's hidden motivation, as he nibbled on a tuna fish sandwich. Suddenly, his thoughts were interrupted by a swooshing sound as Ellen Conway landed on the seat cushion next to him.

"Why do they pick a nice Catholic girl like me for a dirty job like this? Is it just because I'm gay?"

Without looking up from his cell phone, Steve replied, "Could it just simply be because you're good at what you do?"

Ellen lightly cuffed him on the head and hailed a passing waitress, ordering a pastrami on rye. She was back from a trip to the state capitol attempting to ferret out some news of the grand jury convened to investigate the priest pedophile scandal, and she was looking for some comfort food. She reached across him and grabbed a french fry.

"You're not going to eat all those, are you?"

Steve met Ellen in his first week at *The Times Union*. They clicked immediately. From the start, he could see there was no hidden agenda with her. She looked straight at you through round, horn-rimmed glasses framed by short brown hair, cropped in a pageboy style. The effect was owl-like, and her friends in the newsroom would typically greet her arrival with a chorus of "whoos." Ellen just took it in stride.

Although Steve and Ellen appreciated the chance to work together, neither of them could see much overlap at the moment between Ellen's probe of corruption among the local clergy and Steve's scrutiny of the dealings between the Andersons and Max Grabel. After lunch, they were to meet with the Great White to brief him on their work so far, and they hoped then to gain some insight as to why Dane had ordered them to collaborate with one another.

THIRTY-SEVEN

Hunter Dane was sipping a cup of soup as Steve and Ellen entered his office, his unlit cigar nearby in a clean ashtray. He put his lunch aside and trained his sights on his young journalists.

"Tell me something I don't know."

It didn't go well. Ellen explained that her usual sources had nothing to report on the grand jury's work. Although she was aware that subpoenas were served on the Archdiocese and the other dioceses in the state, seeking documents related to internal investigations and assignment transfers over decades, so far Attorney General Karpinski had prevented any leaks of the investigation.

Ellen had no idea what, if anything, was turned up and who might be a target of the inquiry. However, several present and former priests had already been prosecuted for child molestation. So, the expectation was that the AG was now moving up the food chain, looking for evidence that their superiors were aware of their misconduct, shielding them from the law, shuffling them around from parish to parish and, if necessary, from diocese to diocese to keep things under wraps. Hunter grunted and suggested that she seek out former priests to see if they would speak to her, even if off the record, about what they may have heard. He could have offered up some names, given his network of old seminary friends, but he would never do that.

Steve had not fared much better. He found out about the Andersons and Grabel enjoying a ski vacation at Grabel's chalet in Wyoming, but that added little to what was already known about their cozy relationship.

Again, Hunter was not impressed.

"You need to establish a corrupt bargain between Anderson and Grabel. Something of value that Grabel received for his campaign contributions, his phony grant to Brooke Anderson's non-profit, and his other gratuities. Otherwise, it can be spun simply as one friend helping another."

"But what about any connections between the Cardinal and the other two?" Ellen asked.

Hunter leaned back in his chair and studied them for a moment as if he were about to conduct a seminar in forensic psychology.

"To appreciate that, you've got to understand the nature of power. Power can be used for good or ill. All three of these men are powerful, and although there may be times when they exert power for the benefit of others, they have become intoxicated by it and, for each of them, amassing power has become an end in and of itself. Wealth to them is simply one currency by which they can measure their accumulation of power."

Hunter stopped for a moment to let his words sink in. Then, he began again.

"Powerful men, and, in our culture, it is most often men, are drawn to one another. They see that they stand apart from the rest of us, and they look to one another either as rivals or, if possible, as collaborators exchanging one form of power for another. These three are drawn to one another by that common obsession. That was clearly shown by their public interaction at the Cardinal's annual charity dinner. With some more digging, we just might find out that their relationship is deeper and darker. We might or might not, but it's worth a try. So, both of you need to share what you discover and see where the connections take you. Now, get back out there and let me know what you find out."

THIRTY-EIGHT

FTER THREE WEEKS, JAKE MORRIS WAS ADJUSTING TO HIS NEW surroundings in Montana. Emil and Ingrid Brunson seemed to be reserved by nature, and Jake judged them to be especially so toward him initially. They had agreed to share their lives with a total stranger who would be recording that experience for a national publication. Even so, it was difficult for them. Nevertheless, as he learned about their logging business, they gradually opened up.

After Emil's safety warning that first day, Ingrid took Jake down to the bunk house to show him where he would be staying. It was a spartan one-story structure across from the pole barn where all the vehicles and equipment were stored. It had a dormitory with six bunks, each of them next to a small dresser. Adjoining it at one end was a shower/toilet room and a small kitchen at the other. Jake had not known about these accommodations, but he quickly learned that each member of the Brunson crew was strongly encouraged to stay there during the week. Emil Brunson still operated on military time, and this arrangement assured that each of his workers would report promptly for duty on workdays which Jake learned began at 6:00 a.m. Each occupant was responsible to make his bed, share the cost of any food purchased, and keep the premises clean at all times. No drugs or alcohol were permitted, and tobacco smoking or dipping was only allowed outdoors.

Winter was slowly loosening its grip on western Montana. Logging operations would begin in early May. Over the winter, three of Brunson's workers took jobs elsewhere, grooming the slopes at a nearby ski resort. He kept two men on to work with him plowing the local roads under contract with nearby towns and maintaining his vehicles and equipment. Jake would be helping them over the next several weeks as he tried to learn as much as possible about logging before he went out with the crew. That interval also gave him time to become acquainted with his new boss and the men with whom he would be working and living with in the coming months. He would also get to know the good folks of Schuyler, Montana.

Jake quickly discovered that Brunson ran a motley crew. They ranged in age from their early twenties to late forties. Miguel Ramos, who went by Mig, was a Mexican of questionable legal status with a wife who was a Flathead Indian. They lived with their son on a nearby reservation. During the logging season, Mig would travel back and forth each weekend, along with Nelson Begay, who was himself a Flathead and had family on the reservation. Israel Jackson, Iz for short, was African American, apparently single and the oldest of the bunch. There were two local men who also abided by Emil's request to stay at the bunk house. Martin Ramser had dropped out of high school, first doing menial jobs, before taking on a more important role on the crew. The latest member, apart from Jake, was Jimmy Maxwell. Brunson had apparently known the Maxwell family all his life. Jimmy's dad was a close friend who had played football with Brunson back in the day. Jimmy was recently released from a halfway house after a drug overdose. Despite strong reservations, Emil had agreed to take him on.

There was one more member of the crew for the upcoming logging season, Emil's middle child, Matt. Eighteen years old and about to graduate from high school, Matt worked summers for his dad since he was fifteen. He had been recruited to play football for the University of Montana Grizzlies, and he would be leaving for Missoula in August. He expected to major in forestry and land management, with hopes of someday taking over the family business. His older brother had taken a different path, also inspired by his father. Brett was in his third year at the US Naval Academy where he was a starting offensive lineman for the Middies. Their younger sister, Sarah, was in her second year of high school. Her dad described her as an A student who was also a promising basketball player. Emil was obviously proud of his children, and from the family photo on his desk, it was apparent that his children, blonde, tall, and athletic in appearance, shared their mother's good looks.

Jake's days now began at 5:00 a.m., every day but Sunday. In the first week, he shadowed Emil as he got ready for the logging season while also responding to calls for snow plowing. On several days, Jake traveled with Emil out to the logging site which was in a national forest about ten miles west of town. The crew would be working on a steep range that stretched for two miles above a winding river gorge. It was accessed by a narrow dirt road off the nearest highway.

Emil's contract with the US Forest Service had come with strict permit conditions to assure that the forest was carefully thinned while also sustaining sufficient growth to prevent erosion and threats to wildlife. As the crew moved upslope, at regular intervals they would cut a clear path across the terrain to create additional fire breaks. Emil, Jake, and a Forest Service representative spent hours walking the slope and marking the timber designated for harvesting. Jake was overcome by the enormity of the countryside as he hiked among ponderosa and lodgepole pine, Douglas fir, aspen, red cedar, and other species. Some were a hundred feet high and as much as three feet in diameter. The experience left him humbled and also conscious of the dangers facing any intruder into this paradise.

Except for an occasional foray into town, typically highlighted by a visit to Cupid's Place, Jake's evenings were spent huddled over his laptop, taking notes of his days, or communicating with a few friends back home. He tried to avoid replaying in his mind the breakup with Tess. But he thought about her every night, wondering how she and the boys were. He learned from a mutual friend that Tess had pulled back into her former life, avoiding social encounters and spending her free time with the boys and her mom. More than once, Jake stopped himself from attempting to contact her. If ever there would be a reconciliation, he knew that now was not the time to attempt it. Strangely, he found peace in that knowledge. It occurred to him that this forced separation might be doing him some good.

THIRTY-NINE

EN ANDERSON SLID INTO HIS CHAIR ON THE DAIS TO THE FAR right of the chairman of the senate Judiciary Committee as the body was gaveled to order. There was a single matter on the agenda—a public hearing on Senate Bill 753 which would amend the state firearms law to prohibit the sale of assault-type weapons and limit the capacity of ammunition magazines.

The hearing room was packed, the audience roughly evenly divided between the bill's proponents and Second Amendment devotees in opposition. Among the former were representatives of organizations advocating for more limitations on gun use, as well as some of the survivors and family members of the victims of the Mount Zion Massacre. In the first row, directly in front of Anderson were Esther Washington and Rachel Schiller. They caught his eye, and Anderson solemnly lowered his head in recognition.

The bill's opponents were noticeably unruly. In addition to representatives of various gun rights groups, there were members of self-described militias, many of whom were decked out in camo gear and holding placards with incendiary messages. One of the signs read, "Go ahead and make my day. Just try to take my guns away." Camera crews had been set up at the front of the room and other media representatives were huddled together in the back.

Although everyone had been screened for weapons beforehand, security personnel constantly scanned the room for any sign of danger. The air was charged, as if a storm were about to break out. On one side of the room, faces looking up at the legislators bore expressions of somber resolve reflecting, in many cases, the loss of a loved one. On the other side were found those who could only barely restrain their fury over the fear of losing something they considered their birthright.

As with every issue he confronted, Ben Anderson viewed the debate over guns through the prism of his political future. Over his years in the senate, he had gained a reputation as someone who was both tough on criminals and supportive of lawful gun use. Although he came from an urban district, he had spent many days and nights out in the hinterlands, attending events ranging from pig roasts to turkey shoots. He had learned to fire a gun and very publicly joined his fellow hunters each year on the first day of duck season—although his hunting garb always made him look more like a model for Abercrombie and Fitch. He expected that all that effort would pay off at the polls next fall, but his involvement in the recent church shooting complicated things.

Anderson had gone that day to Mount Zion AME Church to punch his ticket as a politician whose appeal extended to both minorities and moderate suburban voters, but he had wound up nearly becoming a victim of gun violence himself. His experience had forced upon him a perspective not shared by many of his peers. It presented both a challenge and an opportunity. Gun control supporters assumed he was one of them. Across the aisle, however, some Second Amendment people now viewed him with suspicion, wondering what he was doing in that church in the first place.

Somehow, he needed to draw votes from both camps. As he looked out at the audience now, he knew that each side wanted to hear from him, and each knew what they wanted him to say. Anderson wondered whether he could thread the needle again today, somehow leaving both sides thinking he was with them, just one more time.

First, he had to sit through hours of testimony. The bill's backers presented the current tally of deaths from mass shootings across the country. They emphasized those incidents involving shooters using assault rifles and expanded capacity magazines. In each instance, they calculated the amount of time and the number of rounds expended to produce the number of lives lost. They speculated about the lost opportunity to stop the perpetrator if he had not had such firepower.

Survivors of the Mount Zion Massacre offered emotional accounts of the carnage they witnessed that day and the trauma which continued to haunt them. Their message was that assault weapons and high-capacity magazines serve no lawful purpose. Outlawing their sale would not prevent all shootings but it would certainly save some lives.

The opponents wisely chose to express their sympathy for the survivors, but they then argued that the proposed restrictions would be only the start of a campaign to take firearms away from law-abiding citizens, leaving them defenseless against criminals who would always find a way to obtain guns. Their expansive reading of the Second Amendment called for no limits on the rights of citizens to bear arms since the Founding Fathers recognized this right as fundamental to a free society. Those words were met with cheers from the men and women in camo whose signs implicitly threatened violent overthrow of their own government if it came after their guns.

Finally, Ben Anderson's moment arrived, but it came in a manner he had not anticipated. Near the end of the public comment period, Rachel Schiller and Esther Washington approached the microphone. They identified themselves, and then Esther directed a question to Senator Anderson.

"Senator, has your experience living through the carnage at my church altered your thinking about the need for gun regulation?"

All heads turned in Anderson's direction. And he was ready for them.

He began slowly and in a tone of voice as if he were having an intimate conversation. Although he periodically panned the room, he was focused primarily upon Esther and Rachel. He talked of the deafening sound of gunfire, the horror as he watched bodies blown apart, and the shock as blood and flesh were splattered on him when the man next to him in the pew went down. He stopped several times for a moment to allow the words to sink in. A few people in the room began to sob quietly. Anderson knew then that he had them. The bill's supporters would believe that he was on their side, whatever quibbles he might have with the wisdom of the legislation. He had earned that right because of what he had lived through with them. Then, he pivoted rhetorically.

"The question now is what we can do practically to prevent a recurrence of that nightmare. It seems to me that there are common sense steps we can take. We can improve our network of mental health providers to reach those who are drawn to violence before they have time to act. We can strengthen our law enforcement agencies, giving them the capacity to monitor those individuals and groups who use social media to foment hatred toward our fellow citizens. We can provide grants to improve security in churches and other public buildings, making them harder targets against attack. For those steps to be effective, however, we need widespread support, including from the vast majority of lawful gun owners. We cannot accomplish these things if those law-abiding citizens believe that a random act of violence, no matter how barbaric, can become an excuse to deprive individuals of their Second Amendment rights. Sadly, I do not believe that legislation which would alienate those citizens should be adopted based only upon the hypothesis that it might afford a better chance of stopping an attack. There are more effective measures to reduce gun violence."

When Anderson concluded his remarks, the room was silent for a moment. Then, murmurs were heard from each side of the room. Both camps were trying to decipher what he had just said. The bill's supporters were drawn to the speaker because of their shared emotions, but they were obviously struggling to accept the rationale offered to oppose it.

The other side was also initially perplexed. At first, it sounded as though the Senator was about to abandon them, but then it began to seep in. He had found an artful way of justifying his support for them while also touching the hearts of their opponents. Despite the barely suppressed anger in their ranks at the start of the hearing, Anderson had presented them as people of good will, ready to work with their opponents to support real efforts to stop violent criminals. The Senator had stuck by them, and in their view, he had won the debate.

Ben Anderson might have pulled it off, but for his insatiable appetite for publicity. As the room cleared, he was approached by a TV news reporter who asked him to elaborate upon his comments. He should have tempered his remarks about gun rights, and he certainly should have seen that Esther Washington and Rachel Schiller were hovering nearby. Before the interview was over, they both set upon him. Esther pointed her finger in his face, furious over what she described as his shameless trafficking in their grief. Rachel then weighed in.

"Senator, this is just a callous effort to advance your political career by toying with the emotions of people who have suffered enough already."

All of it was captured on camera and would be run again and again on both the local and national news. Anderson had just snatched defeat from the jaws of victory.

FORTY

IT WAS AFTER 2:00 A.M. ON A SATURDAY IN LATE MARCH. TESS REILLY had just finished her shift at Toppers. She was being escorted to her car by the bar manager, a precaution taken since a night a few weeks back when she was accosted by a drunken patron in the parking lot who tried to force his way into her car.

Tess thanked her boss as she slid behind the wheel, locked the doors, and warmed up the car. It was a cold night and the lights outside cast an opaline glow through the frosted windshield. Tess reached under her seat for the scraper, then remembered that Thomas had accidentally stepped on it, and she had neglected to replace it—just another broken or missing part of the machinery of her life. It would take a few moments for the heater to do its work, so Tess turned on her favorite jazz station and was left for a few moments to reflect upon her current state.

It was now a month since the breakup with Jake. The first few weeks were the worst, especially dealing with the boys' questions. They had both become attached to Jake. Thomas would ask when Jake would be back, and Mikey would launch into a chorus repeating "Jaaaaake" until Tess could find something to distract him. Mary was no better, although her admonitions were non-verbal. She would simply look mournfully across the dinner table at Tess, wanting to help but only making matters worse.

It's not that Tess didn't have moments when she questioned her decision. In a short time, Jake had won her heart. Apart from her physical attraction to him, Tess enjoyed their conversations. She loved his sense of humor, and, importantly, he obviously cared for the boys and Mary.

Not that there weren't caution signs from the beginning. Like herself, Jake was strong-willed and impetuous. Unlike her, he had a reckless side. Although she had been widowed now for three years, her former husband still cast a long shadow. Jake bore no resemblance to Paul; however, not only was Jake's alcohol-fueled performance at the bachelor party a very public humiliation, it also raised the possibility of an addiction that might consume their relationship.

She had learned enough from her own failed marriage, as well as from her observations at work, to know that she could not take a chance with another guy. Her boys had been through a lot, and she would not have them live through the kind of abuse she had experienced. Nevertheless, Tess realized that she had not given Jake an opportunity to explain himself before she showed him the door. Now, she wished she had but it was too late. She didn't know where she was headed, but she was beginning to think she would have to face it alone. The windshield was finally clear. Tess put the car in gear and headed home.

FORTY-ONE

Among the worries keeping Cardinal Boyle awake at night was how he would come up with the money necessary to settle the latest wave of civil claims against the Archdiocese brought by victims sexually abused by several of its priests. He saw what was coming when he arrived in town five years ago. In fact, dealing with the crisis was a big reason for his papal appointment.

His first step was to shutter several churches and schools. He claimed it was necessary because of a drop in the number of parishioners and students. That was true, but not the whole truth. He also needed to build a war chest to settle these pedophile claims. There was no way that he could appeal directly for the funds. No one would buy that, although through some sleights of hand, he was able to redirect a limited amount from his annual "Open Hearts" charitable campaign and from his yearly dinner. But these steps were not nearly enough.

His general counsel, Bernard Fegley, had been busy selling off Archdiocesan real estate while fending off the dozens of plaintiffs awaiting justice. Fegley had been able to raise about thirty-seven million dollars from these fire sales while also negotiating down the demands of the aggrieved parties. However, he recently advised the Cardinal that they were still about five million short. He also recommended that the Archdiocese maintain a reserve of at least another ten million on the prospect that some additional victims might come forward.

The Cardinal had been stymied as to what to do until last week. The idea came during a private lunch with Ben Anderson. The Senator thought he might have a solution. His good friend, Max Grabel, was the biggest nursing home operator in the state. For years, the Archdiocese had operated Samaritan House, its own senior care facility. If the Cardinal needed a quick sale, Grabel might be interested in it.

Since his meeting with Anderson, Boyle had reviewed all the financials on Samaritan House. It was a two-hundred-unit facility which also included an assisted living component with a memory care center. It was fully occupied with a long list of prospective residents.

Most of the hundred or so employees were paid not much more than minimum wage. With steady revenues coming in from both private payers and public subsidies, the facility was the only Archdiocesan property that turned a profit. Beyond that, it sat on ten acres of highly valuable real estate.

The Cardinal's accountants told him that the facility had a market value between 25 and 30 million dollars. Of course, that depended upon a sale to a willing buyer in a competitive market, and only after the buyer had conducted a lengthy "due diligence" investigation.

Both the Cardinal and the man sitting outside his office knew that the Archdiocese needed money fast and that the transaction had to be as confidential as possible. That meant that Max Grabel was the only prospect in town.

The Cardinal and Grabel now sat opposite one another in the Cardinal's conference room. Just the two of them. Both had done their homework and were ready to deal. The Cardinal began by carefully skirting what was driving his decision to sell. He didn't have to explain. Grabel knew exactly why he was there.

"Max, I appreciate your coming today. I am also grateful for your support of my annual charity dinner. You have a proven track record as a nursing home operator, so when I decided it was best for the Archdiocese to divest itself of Samaritan House, I knew that you were the first person I should speak with."

Grabel smiled and nodded graciously.

"Cardinal Boyle, I have been an admirer of yours from the day you arrived here. You were dealt a tough hand, and you have played it as well as could be expected. Both of us are 'bottom line' types. I know more about Samaritan House than anyone else on the outside, so tell me what you want."

The Cardinal reflexively ran his fingers across the table for a moment, perhaps just a habit, or more likely a subtle acknowledgement of his weak bargaining position.

"My staff informs me that the facility, including land, has a current value of as much as 30 million dollars. However, I am concerned that a responsible operator like yourself take it over. I also would prefer that the sale be accomplished quickly and in a confidential manner. Therefore, subject to resolving certain details, including disposition of the current staff, I am prepared to sell it to you for 25 million."

Grabel stared across at the Cardinal for a moment, his face expressionless.

"Your Eminence. First, I would not be concerned about how your employees will be treated. We will keep everyone on for at least thirty days. They will be evaluated. Those found to be satisfactory will be retained. The others will be given an appropriate separation package. From what I know about your current pay scale, many of those retained will get an increase commensurate with what our existing employees receive. But, as to the purchase price, I am afraid that I cannot come close to your asking price. I was considering a price more like twelve million."

Cardinal Boyle was known to be a good poker player but this time he could not mask his feelings.

"Good God, man! You know it's worth much more than that. You must understand that I have a fiduciary duty to my flock."

"I understand that," Grabel responded, "but I also know that you need this sale to hold that flock together. As a businessman, you cannot blame me for negotiating the best deal available under the circumstances."

The Cardinal leaned back in his chair, defeated. "Well, can you do any better than that?"

Grabel summoned his most sympathetic smile. "I can go as high as 15 million, but no more. With closing in sixty days."

FORTY-TWO

OR THE FIRST FEW WEEKS, JAKE SPENT MOST OF HIS TIME shadowing Emil and his winter crew, Israel Jackson and Martin Ramser. Gradually, he became marginally useful, helping with the plowing operation by adjusting the snowplow blades and filling the hoppers of the spreaders with sand or salt. He also worked on the pre-season maintenance of the logging equipment which included a variety of chainsaws, handsaws, axes, picks, hooks, cables, and chains.

Jake had a chance to see how the latest, computer-driven logging machinery operated. One day, Emil took him on a trip north to watch the clear-cutting of a range. It was a massive operation. Sitting up inside enclosed cabins, operators worked keypads and joysticks to fell, strip, haul and load massive timber in machines called harvesters, feller bunchers and forwarders. Not only were these machines more efficient, Emil explained, but they also kept more workers off the ground where the overwhelming number of workplace accidents take place.

Although Emil and a few of his crew were trained in the use of such machines, and Emil sometimes leased such equipment, they would be using them only on a limited basis on the current assignment. Both the steep terrain and the required selective cutting meant that Emil's crew would rely on chain saws and other hand equipment to a great extent.

On the way back, Emil described to Jake how the work would flow.

"To oversimplify things a bit, this is how we will operate. Iz, Martin, and Nelson are my most experienced workers. Iz and Nelson will be the timber fallers, operating large chain saws. Felling timber is not as easy as it might look. First, the timber faller makes sure he has escape routes to avoid danger when the tree drops, and always aware of the location of everyone around him. Then, an angular notch is cut into the tree at the right height and location. The location dictates the direction the tree will fall, at least most of the time. Then a back cut is made on the opposite side. That cut should extend into the tree so that it meets up with a wedge of wood between both cuts. It creates a hinge allowing the tree to fall cleanly. If it isn't done right, then all hell can break loose. The tree can go any which way, sometimes getting hung up against another timber and causing what we call a 'widow-maker,' a timber that can fall unpredictably. We can also have a 'barber chair' fall when the trunk slides back, often splitting and potentially crashing down on the faller."

Jake's reporting skills kicked in as he took in Emil's every word. It was important for his story, but more than that, Jake realized the advice might one day save his life.

Emil continued. "When the tree is down, that's when the timber bucker takes over. That will be Mig and my son, Matt. They cut or 'buck' the tree, delimbing it and then cutting it into prescribed lengths.

"Finally, we have a system to remove the fallen timber. We will have tracked machinery at the top and bottom of the slope, each anchoring a forty-eight-foot tower. An overhead cable connects each tower with a remotely run, motorized drop cable dragging the felled timber down the slope. Martin operates it from the top, and I run it at the bottom. Only one can do it at a time so that we each can supervise the work of the choker setter and chaser and shut it down quickly in case of danger. The choker setter, Jimmy, attaches a heavy cable or 'choker' to the timber using a large hook at the top and then you, as the 'chaser,' remove it at the bottom. The whole thing sounds simple, but it's not. It requires you to fix the choker and remove it just at the right time. Then, get the hell out of the way. If you do it wrong, you might have several tons of timber coming down on you or be lashed by a swinging cable."

When Emil's tutorial was over, Jake just nodded and looked out the truck window.

He thought to himself, "So, this is why logging is the most dangerous occupation in America."

Until warmer weather permitted the start of logging operations, they were still called out for the occasional late season snowstorm. Jake would ride shotgun for hours as Emil, Iz, or Martin drove. Under their direction, he would jump out of the cab from time to time to adjust the height of the plow to account for changing road conditions.

Sometimes, they would need to swerve to avoid roadside hazards hidden by the storm but known to the driver through countless hours traveling familiar terrain. The drivers enjoyed having Jake on board to relieve the monotony. It also gave him an opportunity to learn more about them, and they about him.

One night, Jake was riding shotgun with Israel Jackson. They had been on the road for several hours, both fighting fatigue and the monotony of watching the narrow band of road as it wound through sheets of snow. Every few hours, they would stop for coffee and a bathroom break. In between, they shared their life stories.

Jake talked about his upbringing, his brief marriage, and his career in journalism. He stayed clear of the circumstances surrounding his departure from *The Times Union* and his breakup with Tess.

Iz couldn't help but ask him why he decided to take on his current assignment.

"Boy, do you realize what you've gotten yourself into? I have watched you over the past few weeks, and I can see that you are not allergic to hard work. Just look at the callouses on those hands. They don't look like they belong any longer to somebody punching a keyboard all day. But you are about to find out how hard this job can be. And there won't be any break-in time. From day one, you will have to listen hard, watch everything going on around you, move fast, muscle heavy cables or a downed timber, and then get out of danger's way. If you don't, you are going to be in some serious shit, and you might take somebody else along with you."

Iz continued the lesson.

"There are more ways a man can get killed or maimed on a logging site than you have fingers and toes. We wear hard hats, heavy chaps, gloves, ear and eye protection, and steel toe boots for a reason, but none of that will protect you from a falling tree, a bucking saw, a swinging cable or a hundred other hazards. So, ask questions if you're unsure about something and don't do stupid shit."

Jake listened and then nodded solemnly.

Now, it was Iz's turn to tell his story. He had met Emil Brunson in the Marines. Iz was one of his platoon sergeants in Iraq. Iz was married and had a child, but when he returned to the States, he found out that his wife had gone off with another guy from the base.

"When I got back, I was pretty screwed-up. PTSD, drugs, and some real shit-shows. After two years, I started to turn it around. I spent six months in rehab, and then looked around trying to figure out what I could do. Captain Brunson had kept in touch with me, and he asked me if I wanted to try logging. So, I came out here, and that was sixteen years ago. Turns out that logging for Emil Brunson is not that much different than humping around with him in Iraq. It's challenging and I guess I'm turned on by the danger. Besides, by now, I don't think I could work for anybody else."

Jake couldn't help himself. "Iz, I couldn't help noticing that you are the only Black man I've seen in Schuyler. In fact, you are the only one I've come across since I left Missoula. How do you deal with that?"

Iz couldn't disguise the smirk on his face.

"It's no different here than anywhere else. Whether in the military or civilian life. People's attitude about race is based on their upbringing and experiences. I can tell how a person feels about my color within the first five minutes. If they just don't like Black people, I let them be. Over time, some of those people come around. Most not. But there have been enough good people around here to make my life more than tolerable. I know that you have been to Cupid's Place a few times. Cupid Kincaid and I have been together now for about seven years. Most of the locals have come to accept a Black man and a White woman living together. We try to stay away from the others, but if you have learned anything about Cupid so far, the ones who don't like it better keep their distance."

FORTY-THREE

Ttorney General Mary Beth Karpinski sat at the head of the conference table as her staff reported on the status of their ongoing investigation of alleged abuse of minors by Catholic clergy in the state. Their conversation was interrupted by a call from her administrative assistant.

"I have a Reverend Austin Cabot on the line who identifies himself as the private secretary to Cardinal Boyle."

Karpinski's eyes widened.

"Tell him to hold. I'll be right out."

She quickly walked into her office and closed the door behind her. Picking up the phone, she began in her usual professional manner.

"Good morning, Father. This is Mary Beth Karpinski. How can I help you today?"

She was unprepared for the response.

"Attorney General Karpinski, I have some information which you may find useful. I would like to share it with you on a confidential basis."

Late that afternoon, they met in the rare book room of the city central library. It was discretely arranged through Karpinski's sister, the library's assistant director, who added the nice touch of placing a sign in front of the door "Temporarily Closed to the Public." Father Cabot came alone; Karpinski was accompanied only by her senior deputy.

Cabot got right to the point.

"For some time, I've known that the Cardinal has kept a separate set of files on priests accused of abusing minors. You will recall his recent release of the names of all priests credibly accused of misconduct over the last fifty years and his public statement that there are no longer any such individuals in church ministry. I now know that statement is not true."

Karpinski and her assistant were momentarily dumbstruck. She could only mutter "Please, go on."

"Two weeks ago, a woman called the Archdiocese hotline. She was apparently very distraught. She claimed that her twelve-year-old daughter was leaving the confessional when one of our priests asked her to touch his privates. The woman and her daughter were later interviewed by a counselor for the Archdiocese specially assigned to handle these matters. The counselor found the young girl and her mother to be highly credible. The Cardinal shared this news with me yesterday. Afterward, I did something highly irregular. While the Cardinal was at a medical appointment, I opened his confidential files and found a record of this priest. Over the last decade, he was accused on at least three occasions of fondling young girls."

"The stories were very similar. In each case, the parent or guardian was persuaded to let it go. Despite that history, this priest continued to be assigned to parish work. He is now associate pastor at Saint Timothy's Church. His name is Father Mike Randall."

Karpinski was about to respond when Cabot cut her off.

"And one more thing. The Cardinal and Randall go way back. They roomed together in Rome when the Cardinal worked in the Vatican. I can only judge that their long friendship prompted the Cardinal to exclude his name from the list of accused priests and why he was continued in active ministry."

Karpinski was a veteran prosecutor. Nevertheless, she could not conceal her shock.

"Why have you come forward with this information?"

"I have only been a priest for five years. To some of my brother priests, my assignment as the Cardinal's private secretary means that I am on a fast track toward becoming a prelate of the church. Really though, I am a glorified manservant. I drive his car. Carry his vestments. Mix his cocktails, and, on an occasional, unguarded moment, I hear things that I shouldn't hear. Having learned this awful truth, I can't stay silent even if it means the end of my priestly vocation."

It was now Karpinski's time to confess.

"Father, I too have a bit of history with the Cardinal. He may not remember me, but he taught me in high school. He was handsome back then, with a charismatic personality. Many of us had a semi-secret crush on him. I can appreciate how easy it might be to be drawn into his web. Thank you for meeting with us. We will be acting on your information. I can't tell you exactly what we will do with it, and when, or whether you will need to go public yourself. I will give you advance notice though if that's necessary. You have shown great courage today. Personally, I will keep you in my prayers, and I would ask that you do the same for me."

Smiling wistfully, Father Cabot nodded and stood to leave, when he suddenly stopped and turned back.

"I almost forgot. I have something else that may interest you. I took screenshots from my phone of the summary sections of each of the prior investigative reports on Father Randall. If you would like, I can send them to you by text."

The AG could hardly believe her good fortune.

"Yes. Please do."

FORTY-FOUR

BEN ANDERSON HAD LEARNED THE HARD WAY THAT TIME DOES NOT heal all wounds, but sometimes, it can at least stop the bleeding. It was now a month since his disastrous performance at the senate gun control hearing. His chief of staff, Meg Holland, had taken that long to stop browbeating him over his egregious act of political malpractice. She had suggested that he draw on his senatorial campaign funds to conduct a private opinion poll of suburban women voters to determine what impact the very public dressing down he received after the hearing might have on his chances for statewide office. It showed that he still retained a fifty-five percent approval rating within that critical demographic.

It was now nearly April, and the gubernatorial primary was less than three months away. Governor Hickey had been better than his word. He had obtained a commitment from his Lieutenant Governor, Nick Fazio, not to enter the race. He promised Fazio that he would appoint him to succeed the current United States Senator, Matthew Berry, if as rumored, Berry retired in mid-term for health reasons. The only other possible primary opponent was a second term state representative with little name recognition whose only initiative was a radical proposal to require all welfare recipients to reimburse the state from future earnings. It was important now for Anderson to get out of the gate first.

Moving into her new role as campaign manager, Meg Holland went about orchestrating Anderson's announcement of his candidacy. It was scheduled for April 10 and the venue would be the city convention center. Anderson's next step was to transfer to a new campaign fund the remaining $800,000 from his senate campaign account and to name Max Grabel as his finance chairman. Holland and Grabel arranged for a private fundraising dinner with an assortment of political high rollers, and Anderson walked away with another $500,000. With few exceptions, Anderson's senate campaign staff was still in place. They had been supplemented with veteran campaigners from other parts of the state to convert his little machine into a statewide juggernaut.

To fill the cavernous convention center ballroom, Holland enlisted the help of various county chairpersons to dragoon their workers into attending. She also contacted friendly labor leaders, especially the heads of the state-wide police and firefighter unions, who promised to enlist their rank and file. Grabel put the arm on several corporate executives, pressuring them to encourage their workers to attend, while drafting more than a hundred of his own employees for the event.

Finally, Anderson personally contacted the Cardinal. Although he understood that the Cardinal could not appear himself, he promised Anderson that he would get the word out, especially to key officials of the various pro-life organizations in the state. It was all beginning to come together, almost too easily.

April 10 was a big day for the Anderson campaign. Governor Jim Hickey lauded the candidate before a boisterous crowd of some three thousand, many holding signs reading "Anderson Gets It Done" and "Women United for Anderson." Hickey's praise was so effusive that it seemed he was speaking of his own son.

The Governor's other protégé was next to speak. Nick Fazio's tribute was so fulsome that a political naïf might judge these two pols to be loving brothers, rather than the second coming of Cain and Abel. Finally, in a particularly deft overture toward the women's vote, Brooke Anderson took the stage to introduce her husband. Never had the public seen a political spouse show such loving fealty to her husband, at least, since Nancy Reagan gazed adoringly up at her Ronnie at his inauguration.

Anderson's formal announcement was nearly anti-climactic. It contained no memorable phrases, but it did the job. After thanking a litany of people for helping him along the way, including a second-grade teacher, Anderson pledged to unite all the people of the state, to expand opportunity while keeping taxes low, end hatred and bigotry as it was so tragically displayed at Mount Zion AME Church, and follow Governor Hickey's example of fostering public integrity. At its conclusion, the crowd cheered wildly as if they had heard something new and exciting.

During Anderson's speech, all eyes had been rivetted on the candidate, except for Steve Chadwick. He may have been the only one who observed Max Grabel and Brooke Anderson standing in the shadows just off stage. Grabel had his arm placed not so discreetly around the waist of the candidate's wife.

FORTY-FIVE

An early April morning thaw brought a slowdown in operations at the nearby ski resort, and on that Monday, Miguel Ramos and Nelson Begay showed up at the Brunson Logging Company to start their summer jobs. After years spent in the mountains, both men were sunburned and windblown. Leathered frames of knotted muscle. Neither spoke except when they found it necessary, and they initially kept a distance from Jake, as if he were an exotic animal. As Jake had accomplished with the others, it would take a few weeks before a dependable work performance would overcome their initial misgivings.

Six weeks had passed since his arrival in Montana. Somehow, it felt longer to Jake. Tess remained in his thoughts constantly, and he wondered on occasion what Hunter Dane may have done with his investigation of Ben Anderson. Almost every day, he pulled up the digital edition of *The Times Union* to follow the reports on Anderson and his nascent bid for the governorship. Apart from his current focus on the lives of loggers, Jake had decided that he would not publish his exposé about Anderson's secret life. Maybe, he would never know why Dane seemed reluctant to run the story that day. Still, he just couldn't believe that the old man would let Anderson off scot-free.

With each day, the pace of work quickened. As long as the weather held and the ground continued to dry out, the Brunson crew would start felling timber in the next few weeks. Jake was excited and a little scared. He was not so much frightened of the physical risk he was taking on; he just didn't want to let Emil Brunson and the other men down.

The day arrived sooner than Jake had thought. Emil Brunson gathered the crew together on a sun-filled afternoon in the first week of May. Tomorrow, they would do a final equipment check, gas up the vehicles, and pack their gear to be ready to move out at daybreak the following day. All of them were excited, and as they did this time every year, the crew would gather at Cupid's that night for steaks and beers.

Iz had called ahead to alert Cupid, so they had the far corner of the bar set up for the five of them—Iz, Mig, Nelson, Martin, and Jake. Pints of cold brew arrived quickly, and the veterans took the opportunity to bust on Jake, referring to him by his new nickname "Rabbit," a term applied by Nelson one day as he watched Jake's fast pace moving from one job to another. Then, somebody decided he might be "Jake Rabbit," but most of the time it was simply "Rabbit."

As they talked about what Jake might expect on his first day, Iz commented, "I guess we'll see how quick Rabbit really is tomorrow when that choker cable comes swinging in his direction."

That brought a laugh from the others, except Jake, who struggled to force a smile.

Looking down the bar, Jake recognized a few faces. Laughing and pointing toward them was the skinny, greasy-haired guy with the high, nasal-sounding voice that Jake had encountered on his first night at Cupid's. He was back again with his two friends. Jake watched the man's prominent Adam's apple bob up and down as he guzzled his beer.

He asked the others if they knew this character. Martin nodded with a look of disgust.

"That's Abner Thornberry. The youngest of the notorious Thornberrys who staged a showdown with the National Park Service a few years ago. His old man has been at war with the federal government his whole life. Doesn't believe there should be a federal government, or really any government at all. This last time, he and his boys had gone on NPS land and poached several tons of prime timber. When the feds arrived on Thornberry land, they were met by forty self-proclaimed patriots, heavily armed. The stand-off lasted several days. Old Man Thornberry was arrested but he eventually got off with a heavy fine that, to my knowledge, was never paid."

Their steaks arrived along with another round of brews and the conversation shifted to the physical attributes of one of the waitresses. Jake looked back again down the bar and noticed that Abner's seat was empty. Suddenly, he heard that nasal voice coming from behind him. "Hey, Pilgrim, looks like you've fallen into some questionable company, hanging out with people like Mig, the Nig, and Tonto."

Martin Ramser wheeled around and in a single motion hit Thornberry with a right hook to his jaw. The man's head snapped back, striking the back wall as he slid to the floor. But he soon bounced up, and this time he had a six-inch blade in his hand. He moved menacingly toward Martin when suddenly the cavalry arrived in the person of Cupid Kincaid who pointed a sawed-off shotgun just below Thornberry's belt buckle.

"Abner, if you so much as twitch, I'll eliminate any chance of you ever fathering a child."

Thornberry froze, deathly still.

"Now, get the hell out of my place. Take your friends with you, and if you ever come in here again, there won't be another warning."

Thornberry slunk away, but then turned back and snarled, "Boys, this ain't over. Not by a long shot."

FORTY-SIX

HUNTER DANE HAD FOUND HIMSELF WRAPPED IN A COLD blanket of despair many times before. When he left the seminary after realizing that his desire to be a priest was just an illusion. When he discovered that his daughter, Fiona, was pregnant at the age of nineteen, without someone who would accept responsibility for fathering the child. When he held the papers as she signed away her rights and obligations as a mother. When he buried her two years later after the drugs had their way with her. When his wife walked away from their marriage after the seemingly interminable arguments over who was responsible for their daughter's death.

But this time seemed different. There didn't seem to be a single reason for his melancholy, but if he could point to a triggering event, it would be the day that Jake Morris walked out his office door. Hunter had high hopes for the young man. To Hunter, Jake's departure signaled the triumph of some spreading malignancy that couldn't be stopped. It seemed to him that every day at the paper he gave more ground to this growing despair. Sure, he still had his friends and Bern at home at night, but it felt like the rest of his world was imploding. He forced himself to push those thoughts away. Almost everyone had left the newsroom for the day and now Hunter followed behind them.

The night was unusually warm for early May. Hunter drove with the windows down and the sun visor shielding him from the glare of a golden sunset. He traveled across town to Finn's Seafood House, one of his favorite spots. As his eyes adjusted to the change in lighting, he made his way down the long aisle separating the bar from a string of booths, all of it encased in dark mahogany. In the back, a booth was occupied by his old friend and co-worker of many years, Peggy Opdyke. Hunter dropped into the seat across from her and flagged down a waiter. He was back in a few moments with a single malt scotch and a second glass of chardonnay for Peg.

"How is Tom responding to the proton therapy?"

Peggy shrugged.

"I suppose it's doing its job. He's suffering with terrible fatigue though. It's just his luck to embark upon retirement only to find out that he has prostate cancer."

"How's your assistant working out?"

"He's brilliant, but he's only twenty-eight, and as we both know, gray hair brings with it a more mature perspective on life. You read his editorials. What do you think?"

Hunter swirled his drink, taking a moment to respond.

"I like his work but he's no Margaret Opdyke, at least not yet. How much time does he have to get there?"

"Hunter, that's why I asked you to join me for dinner. I plan to step down at the end of the year. I think that Tom will beat his cancer, and I've got my Type 1 diabetes under control for now, but Tom just turned seventy and I'm sixty-eight. If we are ever going to travel to the places we've talked about, I think we better get started soon. But I could be available for occasional guest editorials if you think that would work."

Hunter was not surprised by the news. Peggy had been hinting at it for some time.

"I understand, Peg. You've got six months to whip that young man into shape. After that, I'd appreciate it if you could turn in one of your inciteful opinion pieces from time to time."

Peggy was watching Hunter closely, hesitating for a moment to bring it up, but she plunged ahead anyway.

"Speaking of young men in need of perspective, what do you hear about Jake Morris?"

Hunter winced at the mention of his name.

"He's left the area. Taken an assignment to embed with a logging crew in Montana and write about that life. He had been seeing a young woman here, but my sources tell me they've broken up."

"Hunter, you invested a lot of yourself mentoring that young man. I have watched you these last few months, and I can see how much his leaving has affected you. You need to let him go."

"You're right, Peg. It's just that he had so much potential. I would like to have done more."

"It's a big disappointment, I know. Funny. I saw a lot of you in that young man. You were just as hot-headed as Jake when I first met you. In fact, you haven't changed all that much."

"I can always count on Peggy Opdyke for an honest opinion, even if it's not welcome. Let's order."

FORTY-SEVEN

Steve Chadwick and Ellen Conway had become an item, professionally speaking. At Hunter Dane's behest, they had been meeting a few times each week at their favorite diner to share information and advice. Most of the time, they met for breakfast or lunch. Today, it was breakfast, and Ellen was already attacking her eggs and scrapple when Steve arrived.

Ellen hardly paused as she ingested her meal.

"So, what's the latest?"

Steve raised a hand to alert a nearby waitress. After he placed his order, he returned to business.

"Remember that old adage, hell hath no fury like a woman spurned?"

"I think the word is scorned," Ellen interrupted.

"Well, whatever. I found one in Grabel's office. A couple weeks ago, I covered Anderson's election announcement. While he was on stage, I spied Grabel and Anderson's wife cozying up offstage. Later, at the reception, I chatted up Grabel's administrative assistant, an attractive woman who appears to be in her late thirties. I started innocuously enough, commenting on how close her boss had gotten with the Andersons. I suppose she had a few drinks, but just that one remark lit the fuse. She said something about Grabel taking a very special interest in Brooke Anderson. She mentioned that they both would be attending a national conference on memory care in Las Vegas this week. Well, I called the conference a few days ago. Both are registered at the conference, but only Grabel has a room reserved in the headquarters hotel. So early yesterday, I called Grabel's room. A woman answered. I asked to speak with Brooke Anderson. The next thing I heard was the sound of a click as she disconnected me."

Ellen was so overcome that she dropped her fork.

"Outstanding! So Grabel is not satisfied owning just the Senator. He also has his wife on personal retainer. If you keep this up, Chadwick, you are going to wind up at *The National Enquirer*!"

"Great. What do you have to show for yourself, Conway?"

"Alright, I admit that it is not nearly as titillating, but I think I've pinned down that Grabel bought the Archdiocese's nursing home for a comparative song, and that Anderson put the deal together. Here's how. We know that the Archdiocese sold Samaritan House for 15 million. But on the suspicion that it's worth a lot more, I got Dane to authorize hiring a consulting firm to check the financials for the operation. They were able to pull from various public files things like building records, patient censuses, insurance reimbursement rates, staffing costs based on industry standards and other price indicators. Their assessment is that the place has a current value of 28 to 30 million."

Steve was equally impressed.

"So how did you find out that the Senator brokered the deal?"

"Just like you, I resorted to old-fashioned journalism. I asked someone. I know a woman who is a lawyer in the office of the general counsel for the Archdiocese. She worked on papering the transaction. She said that her boss was praising Senator Anderson for bringing Grabel to the table. I then asked the Cardinal about it. He squirmed a bit, but he must have figured out that I already had a source, so he acknowledged that the Senator was instrumental in putting the deal together."

Steve called for the check.

"I think it's time for us to meet again with the Great White."

FORTY-EIGHT

LARRY SHAPIRO HAD BEEN A UNITED STATES ATTORNEY THROUGH the administrations of two Presidents of opposing parties, a rare accomplishment in the hyper-partisan world of contemporary politics. After undergrad at Pitt, he earned his law degree from Michigan and then clerked for a federal judge. At the end of his clerkship, he began his career as an Assistant US Attorney prosecuting drug lords, armed robbers, and corrupt politicians. He had been the first head of the office's public integrity unit, earning a reputation for both tenacity and even-handedness. After twenty-three years in the office, the last six as US Attorney, Shapiro was known as "a prosecutor's prosecutor". He had also developed a refined sense for detecting a politician who had gone off the tracks, and Shapiro was now beginning to suspect that Senator Ben Anderson might fall into that category.

A few weeks after the opening of Anderson's primary campaign, Shapiro met with his chief of staff, Russ Harrington, and his first assistant, Anthony Capriotti. Each of them had reviewed the dossier built up over the last few years detailing the Senator's relationship with Max Grabel. A separate file on Grabel included an ongoing investigation of possible tax fraud. But, today, the trio focused upon the extent of Grabel's contributions to Anderson's political campaigns and their social interactions. They knew about their trips to Grabel's villa in the Turks and Caicos, the golfing and womanizing that went on there, and the ski vacations with their wives at the Grabel chalet in Wyoming, all paid for by Grabel. They had also reviewed the record of Anderson's intervention with state agencies on Grabel's behalf and his legislative efforts to shield Grabel's nursing homes.

Shapiro started things off.

"Alright, based upon what we have learned, what are your views about whether we can make a case under the Hobbs Act? Do we have enough to show that the benefits Anderson has received from Grabel constitute acts of bribery to perform 'official acts' under the statute? Also, do these benefits constitute undeclared political contributions in violation of the law?"

Capriotti responded first. "We are all aware of the recent Supreme Court holding interpreting 'official acts' narrowly. Nevertheless, free transportation, lodging, and entertainment, not to mention procuring prostitutes, are things of value. I think we can establish that there was a *quid quo pro* based upon Anderson squelching the nursing home investigation, even if his efforts to intervene on Gabel's behalf with state agencies might not meet the new restrictive standard for 'official acts.'"

Shapiro looked across at his chief of staff. "What do you think, Russ?"

"Well, you both are aware of the aphorism 'if you're going to shoot at the king, don't miss.' Based upon what we have now, given the high standard of proof, I think there's a good chance we would miss."

Shapiro thought for a moment.

"I agree. But stay on these two. We'll eventually have enough to move on them. Also, keep working with the IRS criminal investigation unit on Grabel's tax issues. If we can tag him with tax fraud, we'll have the leverage to flip him into incriminating Anderson on the other charges."

FORTY-NINE

O N THE SURFACE, TESS REILLY DIDN'T RECOGNIZE MUCH DIFFERENCE in her life in the three months since Jake Morris left. She wondered every day how he was making out on assignment in Montana, concerned about what might happen to him, but otherwise her routine was much the same. This morning though, as she sat at the kitchen table sipping her coffee, waiting for her mom to return from daily Mass, she was swamped by the worries she usually suppressed. At that moment, she was forced to acknowledge that her life was changing and, events might overtake her, and she would no longer be able to protect her little family. She mentally ticked off the many domestic threats.

Uppermost were her thoughts about Mikey's future. His cerebral palsy would require extensive care over his entire life. Despite a weekly regimen of physical, speech, and occupational therapy, his muscular atrophy seemed to be getting worse and his speech was significantly impaired. Mikey's tests showed no intellectual deficit, but Tess could see the frustration in his eyes as he attempted to make himself understood. He had just turned seven and he was growing fast. It was getting more difficult every day to maneuver him in and out of his wheelchair and, especially, to bathe him. It was tough enough for Tess, but nearly out of the question now for her mother.

Mary also worried her. She was seventy-two now and afflicted with osteoarthritis, especially in her hips and back. Nevertheless, she was doing the work of a young woman every day. Mary was tenacious, never complaining, but how long could she keep it up?

Thomas would be turning nine in September. He did well in school, enjoyed sports, and he especially loved his little brother. But Tess wondered as he got older if he would pay a price for all the attention directed toward Mikey and, perhaps even more important, the lack of a mature male influence in his life.

Finally, she wondered about herself. She was burning out as a bartender at Toppers. She had seen enough of how that business breaks down the bodies and the spirits of those who try to make a living at it. Although she hoped to continue with her college courses, leading to a career in teaching, that depended upon her holding together the rest of her life. If not, she would probably have to find some other line of work that would also give her time to be a mother. Likely one that paid less than tending bar. No wonder she was so short-tempered these days.

Fortunately, at that moment, Mary burst through the door.

"Would you believe it? Once again, Pat Flynn had to go over to the rectory to pull Father Skelly out of bed. You can't even count on the clergy today to set an alarm clock."

As they shared a laugh, Tess was reminded that it was time to get the boys up. So, she shook off the doldrums and went upstairs to roust them.

FIFTY

HUNTER DANE DID NOT ENJOY THE LIMELIGHT. HE DIDN'T CONSIDER himself an eloquent public speaker although that opinion was not generally shared by the audiences he was called upon to address from time to time. So, he approached the podium at the annual dinner of the local chapter of the League of American Journalists with his usual trepidation. He was there, though, for a cause close to his heart.

Each year, the chapter awarded a scholarship to a journalism major at a local university. In the aftermath of the Mount Zion Massacre, he had convinced the chapter officers to designate the award as the Liz Schiller Memorial Scholarship. Hunter was asked to introduce the first recipient. He was especially hesitant because he would also be speaking about Liz, and as he looked out across the crowd, he could see Barry and Rachel Schiller and Esther Washington seated together at one of the front tables. He began his presentation with some difficulty, picking up strength as he recognized its effect upon his listeners.

"The Liz Schiller Memorial Scholarship honors a student who has demonstrated in the study of journalism an ability to tell a story accurately and in a compelling manner while observing the highest ethical standards of the profession. During her tragically brief career as a journalist, Liz Schiller met and, in fact, exceeded those standards. Liz also brought to this pursuit an awareness that the subjects of her reporting were fellow human beings with strengths and frailties that we all share. She was not easily intimidated but she never lost her sense of compassion toward others. Liz may have only been with us at *The Times Union* a short time, but her memory will linger long after her passing. She helped make us better journalists, and more than that, better people. She is a worthy role model for the young woman we have selected tonight for this scholarship."

As Hunter returned to his seat on the dais, he scanned the audience. Among the attendees, seated at separate tables, were Senator Ben Anderson and Cardinal William Boyle. He wondered whether either man was aware of what was now barreling toward them.

FIFTY-ONE

THE RUN-IN WITH ABNER THORNBERRY AND HIS BOYS DID ONE GOOD thing. It got the Brunson crew members back to the bunk house early and relatively sober. They would all need as much rest as they could get. Jake had asked a lot of questions about what he might expect on the first day of logging operations so he knew enough to realize that the mobilization and set-up of the operation on site would move quickly. As a rookie, he would need to do what he was told or otherwise get out of the way. He lay on his bunk and felt the excitement building inside. He hoped he would do his part tomorrow. Finally, after a few restless hours, he was able to shut down.

Everyone was up and moving by 5:00 a.m. Mig made huevos rancheros with fried sourdough bread, and Jake brewed coffee so strong that a spoon could stand upright in it. They assembled in the garage yard by 6:00. There, Emil Brunson took a few moments to review with them the day's work program.

Brunson ran his logging operation with the precision of a military campaign. Over the last week, he had conducted training exercises using a map of the logging site. They would be working on a ridge accessed by a single lane dirt road about a half mile from the highway leading north from Schuyler. The southern edge of the road bordered a river now swollen from snow run-off. The ridge was steep and heavily wooded, extending about two miles east to west and ranging from 1,500 to 1,800 yards from the ridge top to the road below. The US Forest Service had established three fire breaks running roughly parallel to the road at 400-yard intervals up the mountain. Machinery and equipment could be moved up the ridge only one way. A narrow dirt road extended up the ridge providing access to each of the fire breaks, with switchbacks veering left and right to permit vehicles to manage the steep elevation and to reduce erosion. A flat area off the access road would be used for parking and as a laydown area for heavy equipment.

In addition to having marked those trees selected for logging, Brunson had broken the area down into a system of twenty grids. Each was roughly 400 yards square and bordered by one of the fire breaks. They would work one grid at a time with the active logging operations moving toward the top and the timber collection area below.

Brunson now focused on the first grid nearest to the access road. Although Brunson had described the operation to Jake on one of their earlier trips together, Jake's jaw dropped as he took it all in.

The operation required close communication among all the participants. Any missteps could put lives at risk, not to mention the prospect of heavy financial loss due to damaged machinery and operational downtime, so Brunson had run them through their assignments on several occasions. Today, he would find out if the lessons had stuck.

FIFTY-TWO

MAX GRABEL WAS IN THE BATHROOM SHAVING WHEN HE HEARD the hotel phone ring. He quickly finished up and walked toward the bed where Brooke Anderson sat, her face frozen in fear, still holding the handset.

"Who was that?" he asked, in a tone intending to convey a sense of calm, attempting to draw Brooke back into the moment.

"I don't know. He didn't say. He just asked for me."

Grabel's demeanor remained unchanged. "What did you tell him?"

"Nothing. I just hung up."

Throughout his life, Max Grabel had relied upon his unerring ability to size up situations quickly and to master the moment. That instinct kicked in immediately. He knew that he had to calm Brooke down and reassure her that he was in control. He lifted her up from the bed and held her in his arms in a manner both paternal and sensual.

"Listen. Let's not jump to conclusions. Remember. You originally reserved this room before you canceled, and I put it in my name. This guy could be somebody you met at the conference who just got bad information from the front desk. Now, let's get dressed and get some breakfast."

As they stood in the elevator, Grabel mentally ran through all other possible explanations for the call. Obviously, it could be a member of the media looking for a juicy political scandal. It could be an investigator working for either one of their spouses. Or it could be someone in law enforcement. He decided that the last two possibilities were unlikely. His wife had long since given up any concern over his indiscretions, and Ben Anderson was too occupied with his campaign and his own personal arrangement with his chief of staff to consider having the two of them tailed. Grabel was constantly under an IRS audit. In fact, one was underway now. But he was exceedingly careful in his business dealings, and he considered a criminal investigation unlikely. It could well be a press snoop, but tracking the two of them down in Las Vegas would have entailed more effort than he would have expected from the hometown corps. He decided that further speculation now was a waste of time. He would take this opportunity though to reset his relationship with Brooke Anderson.

Grabel was not a man who was content for very long with any sexual partner. He had enjoyed his romps with Brooke, especially since it was a by-product of his manipulation of her husband. But he could see that Brooke was beginning to think that there was something more to it. And there was another reason. Over the last few months, he had observed the barely contained fury of his administrative assistant, Marla Burton, as she watched Brooke walk breezily into his office for their thinly disguised business meetings. Over the last ten years, Burton had become a confidant, both professionally and personally. She knew the most intimate details of Grabel's business, and they both enjoyed pleasuring one another when Grabel was not otherwise distracted. Burton had not seemed to mind sharing him with others until now, but she clearly thought of Brooke as a rival. Grabel had learned the truth of the adage about a woman scorned from his first wife. It had cost him a boatload, including the boat.

He recognized now that he was in too deep with Brooke. At breakfast, he would gently suggest to her that they put the brakes on their private encounters until after the election. He hoped that change would be enough to bring Burton back into line. Unfortunately, as he would soon find out, he was too late. Burton had already played her hand.

FIFTY-THREE

BEN ANDERSON CONTINUED TO PLUNGE AHEAD IN PURSUIT OF what an unfriendly editorial in *The Times Union* described as his "Grand Obsession." The primary was a month away. From the look of Anderson's campaign schedule, you would think he was locked in a tight contest. In fact, internal polling showed that his opponent's name recognition was holding steady at a feeble fifteen percent. With no money and no message, his presence on the ballot only afforded Anderson the opportunity to build on his favorability among likely voters moving into the general election season.

His shuttling back and forth across the state left Anderson little time for concern about what his wife or kids might be doing. He would stop back to the house once or twice a week to pick up fresh laundry and maybe spend the night. The rest of the time, his evenings were spent in hotel rooms, holding staff meetings, and strategizing with his inner circle led by his ever-present chief of staff and campaign manager, Meg Holland.

One evening, after everyone had left, Anderson and Holland shared a bottle of wine, trying to relax after yet another long, adrenaline-fueled day. Holland had just changed into her standard night wear, a T-shirt and sweatpants. Anderson was down to his underwear. As they sat on the bed, Holland began to pinch a bit of stomach roll that Anderson was developing after several weeks of a steady diet of fast food. She was hoping that a friendly tussle would lead to a few moments of furious lovemaking before they collapsed in exhaustion. Anderson, though, was not ready to suspend operations for the evening.

"Did we get the opposition research on Faith Campbell?"

Campbell was now his odds-on opponent in the general. She was a West Point grad who had done two tours in Afghanistan before graduating from Harvard Law. After a few years as a federal prosecutor taking down a human trafficking network, she had entered the state legislature where she earned a reputation for sponsoring bills to combat spousal abuse and expand health care access for families. Suburban women and minorities loved her. Anderson knew that he was in for a tough fight in November.

Holland gave up.

"Nothing so far. We had some guy from her high school class who claimed that she was an easy lay and maybe smoked some grass. We are running down her college and law school friends now, as well as her army buddies. We'll find something. There's always some scandal out there, and if there's not, we'll make one up."

FIFTY-FOUR

JAKE SAT IN THE BACK SEAT OF EMIL BRUNSON'S EXTENDED CAB pickup, with Matt Brunson and Jimmy Maxwell on either side. Martin Ramser was up front, and he and Emil were discussing plans to deploy the equipment on their first day. The rest of the crew traveled behind in Israel Jackson's truck. It was a warm spring morning with the high expected to reach the mid-sixties. A few days more of this weather and most of the remaining snow at the ridge top would be gone.

Jake felt a bead of sweat run down the middle of his back. He knew it was not because of the weather. He hadn't felt jitters like this since he waited at the start of the eight hundred meters final at the Penn Relays his senior year at Dartmouth. Thankfully, the others on the crew did not pick up on it.

As they drove into the parking area off the access road, Jake saw that the leasing company had delivered the two tractor yarders. One was positioned in the timber collection area next to the first grid and the other above, on the first fire break. Emil and Martin would only need to make minor adjustments to set up the cable system. The rest of the operational vehicles were parked nearby. All the hand tools and remaining gear were stored in a van that would be kept in the parking area. Men and the equipment they needed each day for the active logging area would be transported up the ridge in a military surplus Humvee. Finally, there was a tracked loader parked near the collection area to collect timber for delivery to the sawmill.

During the operation, another truck would be located near the active logging area. It contained firefighting equipment. Jake had learned about the many ways that logging operations could set off a wildfire. Brunson, Ramser, and Jackson were all certified firefighters. They had given the rest of the crew elementary training in fire prevention, containment, and escape techniques. Jake had gone online to expand upon that training. He learned to appreciate how quickly fire could spread in a forest like the one where they would be working.

As he looked up the ridge that morning, Jake knew that the dense forest above would be a natural accelerant if anything set it off. Although the risk was low now, with the coming of summer, daily temperatures would rise and the humidity would drop. The forest would dry out. Fed by high winds, any spark generated by man or nature could produce a conflagration in a matter of minutes. The machinery and equipment they would be using might also precipitate such a firestorm, so they had to be ready.

As the rest of the crew positioned trucks and equipment near the initial work area, Emil and Ramser scoped out the location of the cable run. Iz and Nelson went about felling any trees which would be in the way. When the path was clear, Jake, Jimmy Maxwell, and Matt Brunson lugged the long section of cable up the ridge. Emil and Ramser then attached it to the yarder, and the boys fed it down to the collection area for attachment to the second yarder down there.

It took them about two hours before they were ready to begin felling trees and transporting them down to the collection area. With the initial set-up completed, Iz and Nelson stepped in with their heavy chain saws and began taking down trees. Miguel and Matt then stripped the trees of branches before they were sawed into uniform lengths. Jimmy attached the choker around three to five lengths at a time. The cable system picked the logs up and transported them as if they were oversized pick-up sticks. From there, Jake removed the choker, freeing the cable to return upslope to deliver another load. When the felled trees at the collection site had built up sufficiently, Emil operated the loader machine which stacked them in a trailer adjacent to the access road. At the end of each day, a truck arrived to transport the day's harvest to a nearby lumber mill. Such was the routine they had embarked upon.

The first day passed quickly. Emil had taught Jake the hand signals he would give to direct Jake when it was safe to step into the area where the load had been dropped and remove the choker. Once it was removed, Jake had to move quickly away and out of range of the choker as the secondary cable was raised upward. Most times, the choker cable was held down by the weight of the timber, and when pulled upward, was caught until it broke free from the timber pile. Then, for a moment, it whipped wildly and unpredictably.

Nervous in the beginning, Jake's movements soon became routine. As soon as he released the choker, he quickly stepped away to avoid the cable's whiplash. After a while, he had to remind himself not to lose his concentration for a moment. "Focus," Iz had told him, and Jake intended to.

Early in the day, Jake had his first close call. He removed the choker but then tripped over a log as he attempted to make his getaway. The heavy choker cable swung violently toward him, passing only a foot or so above his head. Any lower and his hard hat would not have prevented a concussion. Still lower than that and Jake would have become a part of the grim statistics proving that lumberjacks are the most endangered workers in America.

FIFTY-FIVE

MIKE RANDALL COOLED HIS HEELS OUTSIDE THE CARDINAL'S OFFICE for twenty minutes. He had been expecting this summons since he was informed of the recent accusation against him. That was two weeks ago. He knew that the young girl's mother had been interviewed by a representative of the Archdiocese, and he suspected she may have spoken with the Cardinal himself. In the past, official expressions of sympathy and reassurance were enough to satisfy some aggrieved parties who were told that steps would be taken to prevent further harm without the need to bring in the civil authorities. As much pain as they felt, they were convinced that it had to be borne to preserve Holy Mother Church. Sometimes, a confidential settlement was required to buy their silence. Randall assumed that, as in the past, he would be given a new posting sufficiently distant from Saint Timothy's so that there would be little chance the scandal might follow him.

When he was finally asked into the Cardinal's office, he found his old friend, Bill Boyle, sitting behind his desk. Randall's attempt at a friendly greeting was not reciprocated. Boyle simply looked up from some paperwork and silently directed Randall toward a chair. The Cardinal wasted no time on pleasantries.

"When I came to this Archdiocese, job one was dealing with our priests who were credibly accused of abusing minors. I've done my best to remove them from positions where they might do further harm while resolving claims against them in a way to avoid a public scandal that would undermine the Church's mission. However, you are my greatest failure. When you were last accused, perhaps because of our old friendship, I very reluctantly agreed to your entering a six-month program of intensive therapy. When you got out, your therapist certified that he considered you a very low risk of relapsing, and you promised me that it would never happen again. Sadly, I believed you, and now a young girl must pay a steep price for my mistake. Well, I will not allow it to be repeated. I have applied to Rome to begin proceedings leading to your laicization. You can oppose it, but that will just delay the process for your removal from the priesthood. Meanwhile, effective immediately, I am transferring you to Joseph's House where you will serve as chaplain for our retired priests. You are not authorized to say Mass publicly, and you will not leave without my express permission. If you do, I will do what I should have done five years ago. I will report this accusation to the civil authorities."

Randall had slumped down in his chair, stunned for a moment.

"I guess you've left me with no other option. Have you thought about what happens to you if this goes public?" said Randall.

The Cardinal was not surprised that Randall played that card.

"I know where I stand. If it comes to that, I am prepared to accept the consequences," the Cardinal answered.

Recognizing that their conversation was over, Randall stood and was about to leave when the Cardinal stopped him.

"I have just one more question, Mike. Why do you do this?"

Randall slumped back down in his chair.

"I have had years of therapy, and I still don't know why. You and I have known each other for over thirty-five years. We have seen the various ways that our brother priests attempt to deal with their sexual drive, given their vow of chastity. Some find relief in drink or drugs. The scholars hide among their books. Others gain gratification through occasional encounters with parishioners, other priests, prostitutes or just themselves. But some are obsessed with young children. Early in my priesthood, I was overcome by fantasies of young girls. There was something alluring about their innocence. They looked upon me as God's representative on earth. It was a power over them that I couldn't ignore. They were forbidden fruit, and try as I did, there were just times when I felt like I was caught in a vise and couldn't break free."

Cardinal Boyle had heard enough.

"At least now, you will no longer be viewed as God's representative on earth. Mike, I will pray for you as well as for all those you have harmed over the years."

FIFTY-SIX

B EN ANDERSON HAD JUST SKATED THROUGH THE PRIMARY. HE crushed his opponent, winning by twenty points. To his supporters, it seemed that Anderson needed only to pick out new drapes for the governor's office. But all that was about to change. The investigative reporters at *The Times Union* had missed their self-imposed deadline to release their findings before the primary but they pressed ahead now with increasing urgency.

Steve Chadwick had plied Grabel's assistant, Marla Burton, for evidence of any connection between Anderson's shutting down the recent nursing home investigation and the various perks Grabel had thrown his way. Eventually, she produced an email exchange between Grabel and Anderson. It was dated a week before the senate committee had scheduled a hearing about staffing shortages in state nursing homes. Its message was not subtle.

"Ben, what do I pay you and your wife for? If this investigation continues, I stand to lose millions. You better find a way to bury it."

Anderson responded tersely.

"Call me on my cell."

The hearing was postponed two days later because of supposed scheduling conflicts. The senate adjourned a month later, and the hearing was never rescheduled.

Chadwick had found another discovery based upon an off-the-record discussion with a mid-level administrator in the state's Department of Health and Institutions. When asked about any communications with Anderson and his staff on behalf of Grabel and his nursing homes, he revealed that there were a series of calls last spring from Anderson's office seeking to have the Department withdraw an investigative report on one of Grabel's homes. The inquiry had disclosed overcrowded conditions and poor sanitation. Despite persistent efforts to squelch it, the report resulted in a heavy fine and a compliance directive to the home's administrator.

When Chadwick shared this news with the Great White, Hunter knew that it was time to break the story. Although the decision was his alone as managing editor, he decided to convene a meeting with the paper's publisher and a small group of advisors beforehand. If he somehow got all this wrong, Hunter knew that it could destroy *The Times Union*. Over a long career, he had worked hard to establish the paper's record for accurate reporting. He intended to end his tenure with that reputation intact.

The next day, the small working group convened in the newspaper's boardroom. The publisher, Pamela Bessington, presided at the head of a long conference table. Its general counsel, George Orbach, sat on her right. Hunter brought Steve Chadwick and Ellen Conway. Ellen would share her work regarding the Cardinal's involvement with Anderson and Grabel. He had also asked his good friend and editorial page editor, Peggy Opdyke, to sit in.

Hunter meticulously laid out the results of the investigation begun by Jake Morris and now completed by Chadwick and Conway. He went through a detailed chronology, showing how Grabel had showered Anderson and his wife with numerous gratuities, including visits to the gentlemen's retreat in the Turks and Caicos, the vacations at the ski chalet in Wyoming, and finally the hundreds of thousands paid to the Andersons through the non-profit, Senior Moments. He also described Grabel's history of campaign donations to Anderson and his role of bundling contributions from others.

Next, Hunter asked Chadwick to describe Anderson's role in ending the Senate nursing home inquiry and his failed efforts to derail the investigation of one of Grabel's homes. Chadwick shared the critical email exchange between Grabel and Anderson where Grabel questioned why he was paying Anderson and his wife. For the sake of completeness, Chadwick also revealed evidence of a seamy affair between Brooke Anderson and Grabel.

Pamela Bessington had taken over the paper upon the death of her father three years ago. *The Times Union* had been controlled by the Bessington family for several generations. In her early forties, Bessington had overseen the family charitable foundations until her father's passing. She had no prior journalistic experience. After a few skirmishes with Hunter Dane, she backed off and pretty much relied upon his judgment. Bessington quickly recognized now how serious the matter was for Dane to have her share in what was his decision to publish the story.

Bessington turned to Orbach.

"What we may do will destroy the reputations of a candidate for governor and a very powerful businessman. What are our risks?"

After a slight pause, Orbach replied. "We could be sued for libel, but the law is in our favor. Both Anderson and Grabel are considered public figures and, even if our facts are ultimately found to be wrong, they would have to show that we had no reasonable basis to believe in their truth and had acted out of actual malice—a very high bar to cross. From a political perspective, Anderson and his supporters could still attempt to destroy the paper's reputation but, from what we have just heard, I believe they would lose the public relations battle also."

Bessington's focus shifted to Opdyke.

"Peggy, you've been around here just about as long as Hunter. What do you think?"

Peggy didn't hesitate. "I think if we don't run this story, then we might as well close up shop."

It was now time for Hunter to retake control of the helm.

"Ms. Bessington, I'm afraid we're not done yet. Ellen Conway has been assigned to report on the state grand jury investigating the Catholic hierarchy's role in the clergy sex abuse scandal. Although we have no hard news yet, it appears that Cardinal William Boyle may be at the heart of the inquiry. Ellen has uncovered, though, a close association between the Cardinal, Anderson and Grabel. She has confirmed that Anderson brokered the sale of the Archdiocese nursing facility to Grabel for cents on the dollar. That association will be laid out as sort of a subplot in our investigative report."

Pamela Bessington had heard enough.

"Looks like you and your associates, Hunter, have done some Pulitzer Prize-worthy work here."

"Thanks for the compliment, Ms. Bessington, but we have one more responsibility. We have two more days until Sunday's publication of the first part of a four-day series. Now that we are committed to moving forward, we will contact the Cardinal, the Andersons, and Grabel directly. We'll lay out what we have and then ask them to respond. My bet is that the Cardinal and the Andersons will refuse to comment and that Grabel will not even take our call. Unless they have anything material to offer, we'll proceed as planned."

Before adjourning the meeting, the publisher had one more question for her legal counsel.

"What are the legal implications for these three?"

George Orbach thought for a moment.

"Senator Anderson will confront demands for a senate ethics inquiry. After some effort to hold that off, he will have no choice but to suspend his campaign for governor. All of them will lawyer up, get ready to plead the fifth, and await whatever may come out of the US Attorney's office and, in the Cardinal's case, the state Attorney General. There are a host of possible criminal charges facing the Andersons and Grabel, including possible bribery, wire fraud, and campaign finance violations. Each of them has serious criminal exposure. As for the Cardinal, he has no immediate legal jeopardy; however, disclosure of his arrangements with Anderson and Grabel will certainly add to his troubles as he anticipates whatever Mary Beth Karpinski may have in store."

Pamela Bessington stood and thanked everyone. Hunter and his reporters hurried out. They had work to do.

FIFTY-SEVEN

AFTER HIS NEAR-MISS WITH THE CHOKER CABLE THAT FIRST DAY, Jake soon developed what Brunson described as "situational awareness," an acute perception of danger. Other than an occasional stumble scampering across a timber pile, Jake was able to avoid any more mishaps, keeping clear of swinging chokers, shifting timber, and any heavy machinery lumbering his way.

Apart from his duties as a choker chaser, Jake, along with Jimmy Maxwell and Matt Brunson, would lug the heavy cable when the transport system had to be relocated along the ridge. He would also load smaller branches and other debris, called slash, onto a large basket for transport down the ridge and later grinding into mulch. When collected timber was loaded onto the trailer for delivery to the mill, Jake stood near the huge claw, a long heavy pike in hand, to pull away logs interfering with the pick-up. It was exhausting work.

By the second week of the operation, the weather had turned warm, bringing a new distraction. Clouds of black flies swarmed around Jake and the rest of the crew. Jake quickly learned that bug spray was no deterrent. In fact, it seemed to attract them. They got under your clothes and into your mouth, eyes, and ears. Swatting at them did no good at all. Jake eventually gave up the fight and tried just to focus on the job at hand.

The other rookie on the crew, young Jimmy Maxwell, had his own challenges. Everyone knew that Jimmy had just been released from a half-way house, conditioned upon him passing random drug testing. He knew he was being watched so he tried harder to do his job, even to the point of getting in the way of others doing theirs.

On the second day, his need for acceptance nearly cost him his life. Not content to stay on the periphery until it was time for him to set the choker for delivery of a load down the ridge, Jimmy stepped into the felling zone to help clear away slash. With the task completed, he lingered nearby, mesmerized by the buzzing sound and spray of sawdust as Nelson Begay cut through a thick trunk. When the tree fell, it caught for a moment on a heavy branch of a nearby timber. The branch came crashing down, landing with a thud within a few feet of where Jimmy stood. Martin Ramser stopped the cable and rushed toward him, fearing that he had been struck. When he was sure that Jimmy had escaped injury, Ramser took him aside for a few moments.

Jimmy's hands were shaking. He was breathing hard, and Ramser could see fear in his eyes.

"Listen, Jimmy. Take a deep breath. This one didn't get you, but the next one might. Do your job, pay attention, and don't try to do the work for anyone else. I'll tell you when you need to step in. Now, get back up there and get ready with that choker."

The days assumed a certain routine. Up at 5:00. On the ridge by 6:30.

The crew would work its way up the ridge to the next fire break. Upon reaching the ridge top, they moved westward to the next grid and began again the inexorable climb to the top. At 4:00, tree cutting operations shut down, and the day's harvest was transported to the sawmill. Equipment was stored away in the tool truck, vehicles were refueled for the next day, and the Humvee transported the crew down the ridge. They were all back at the Brunson Logging Company by 6:00.

Each of them had assigned chores back at the bunk house. Miguel Ramos and Iz Jackson divided up the cooking, Jake and Jimmy Maxwell cleaned up afterward, and Martin Ramser, pulling rank, set up the card table for some low-stakes poker after dinner. Nelson Begay spent most of the time on his cell checking in with his wife and kids. Later, Jake would find a quiet corner to get on his laptop to connect with friends back home and record his observations from the day. The other guys were curious to find out what he might be writing about them, but they kept a respectful distance. Nevertheless, they took full advantage of him at the poker table. After a week, Jake was down $6.50.

When they got back to base at the end of the second week, Ingrid Brunson was there to greet them.

"I know this is short notice, but you all are invited for a little dinner tomorrow night. My records tell me that it is Jake Rabbit's birthday. So, bring your wives and girlfriends over, and we'll celebrate Jake's second week at a real job."

The crew cleaned up well, shaved and wearing their best shirts and jeans. With the sole exceptions of Jimmy Maxwell and Jake, they came to the party with the woman in their life. At work, Jake had been impressed with how well the crew veterans got along. It was not just that they were used to each other's habits. Despite their different backgrounds, it was apparent that they also respected one other. Beyond that, they enjoyed themselves, constantly needling one another, but knowing when to back off. Jake could now see that their women got along just as well. They operated as a family and the fact that they were all here to celebrate Jake Rabbit's birthday meant a lot to him.

As the sun dropped beneath a nearby mountain peak, the women put on sweaters or jackets, and the men gathered around a fire pit to talk about their week. Among Emil Brunson's many talents was his reputation as a braumeister. On tap was a keg of Emil's favorite pilsner, and it was apparent that the pale lager was a big success.

A long table had been set on the lawn, and as the guests took their seats, Ingrid Brunson, her daughter, Sarah, and Ingrid's younger sister, Lisbeth Mueller, proceeded from the kitchen, each carrying plates and serving dishes. The food was spread buffet-style on a nearby sideboard.

Ingrid had been taught to cook by her German mother. She had been at work all day preparing Jake's birthday dinner. The fare included all her Mutti's favorite recipes: spaetzle, sauerkraut, bratwurst, knockwurst, and hasenpfeffer. Ingrid was especially proud of the fresh farmer bread, called bauernbrot. It took hours to bake but it was a favorite at every family dinner.

Emil began with a blessing and then asked everyone to raise their glasses in celebration of Jake's birthday.

"Now that we have that out of the way, enjoy the best German cooking west of Bremerhaven, especially Ingrid's favorite, hasenpfeffer, made specially for Jake. For those of you who don't speak German, that's rabbit stew."

Cupid Kincaid then chimed in. "And save room for dessert. In Jake's honor, I made carrot cake."

That was only the beginning of what turned out to be a good-natured roast extending long into the evening. At one point, Nelson Begay stood, and with everyone's attention, he presented Jake with a small package. When he opened it, Jake was holding in his hand a small lump of white fur.

"What's this?"

Everyone else was laughing at him.

"Boy, are you clueless," Iz Jackson chimed in. "It's a rabbit's foot for good luck, Jake Rabbit. I think you ought to hold onto it."

Near the end of the meal, Jake struck up a conversation with Lisbeth

Mueller, Ingrid's sister. She sat across from him and had been watching Jake as he good-naturedly absorbed the barbs thrown his way. While the table was cleared and the rest of the men adjourned to watch baseball on TV, Ingrid directed them both to stay seated and continue their discussion as she and the other women cleared the table.

"So, Jake, how did you take on the moniker, Jake Rabbit?"

Chuckling softly, Jake replied, "I guess I acquired it the hard way. The guys started it even before we began work on the ridge, but I really earned it on my first day of logging. I was a half-step late getting out of range of a swinging cable. It just missed me, and since then I have learned to scamper out of harm's way. There was a time when I was considered pretty quick, and I guess I haven't lost more than a step or two. So now they call me Rabbit, or as Emil refers to me 'Jake Rabbit.' I guess I'll just have to live with it now."

Lisbeth smiled and pulled back a strand of long blonde hair that had fallen over her eye.

"Do you have any aliases you'd like to share?"

"None I would feel comfortable sharing with you at the moment, but my friends call me Beth."

Jake studied the young woman for a moment. "Well, can I call you that?"

"Sure. Why not?

Over the next hour, they spoke about how they each had made their way to Schuyler, Montana. Beth described how she and her sister were born and raised in Milwaukee. Ingrid had finished nursing training when Beth was still in grade school. Ingrid then went into the navy. Emil had been her patient when he was hospitalized in Germany with battle wounds from his time in Iraq. After his recovery, they became engaged, and Emil brought Ingrid out West to his home in Schuyler. They were married here by Emil's father, an ordained minister. After college, Beth taught school in Milwaukee until a year ago, when her husband walked out on her. Newly divorced, at her sister's urging, she moved to Montana to start a new life. She was renting a home near town and teaching at the local school.

It was now Jake's turn. He told her a bit about his upbringing and his brief marriage. He mentioned that he had left his job with the newspaper over an editorial disagreement and made no mention of his recent breakup with Tess. He said that he was excited about the opportunity to write about the logging industry and his new co-workers.

Beth had been listening intently, and he sensed that she was aware that he was holding back on the full story. She did not press him though.

"Jake, I have just one question. What is the most important thing you have learned so far through this experience?"

Jake paused for a moment.

"I realize now how much in life I've taken for granted. Life can change in an instant. I guess I'm just a bit less cocksure than I was before I arrived here. I think that's a good thing."

Beth reached across the table and gently tapped his hand.

"Well, we are all glad to have you with us, and we trust you to tell our story. Meanwhile, I have been shirking my domestic duties. I need to get back in the kitchen. I've enjoyed our conversation, Jake."

FIFTY-EIGHT

A s Hunter Dane predicted, none of the subjects of the newspaper's investigation responded to Steve Chadwick's requests for comment. The first part of the story hit the digital edition of *The Times Union* late on Saturday night. It summarized the results of the probe into the tangled connections between the Andersons and Grabel. A separate column described the Cardinal's involvement with them. Future segments would drill deeper into the mire in which the four principals had sunk.

Almost immediately, the story caught fire on the network news and social media. News reporters and camera crews staked out the residences and the offices of the four, each of whom were hidden away outside the public eye. The only official responses were from Anderson's chief of staff and from the Archdiocese legal counsel. Both offered bland statements seeking to normalize whatever was revealed in the press account.

Chadwick's call to Anderson was fielded by Meg Holland late Friday afternoon. He simply asked to speak with the Senator about his relationship with Max Grabel. Holland hung up after coolly responding that she would pass the request along to her boss. She then walked in on Anderson as he was about to leave the office.

"Ben, we've got a problem. *The Times Union* is about to print a story about you and Grabel, and they want to talk with you."

"Holy shit, Meg. What should we do?"

"Senator, I think what you should do is calm down for a moment. We know generally where this is going, but we don't know yet how much they have. If you call back now, you are likely to confirm or deny things that you will want to evade if you can. I recommend that you have me call the reporter back with a brief statement. Something like 'Senator Anderson has enjoyed a personal friendship with Max Grabel for several years. Mr. Grabel is a well-respected businessman who has also been a loyal supporter during the Senator's long career of public service. The Senator has no further comment at this time.'"

"That sounds good, Meg. Do it. Otherwise, what's our next step?"

"Senator, I recommend that you prepare your wife, as best you can, for what comes next. Then, I would reach out for an attorney, and if I were you, I'd pick one who is experienced in defending high-profile cases. One that has a reputation defending clients accused of white-collar crime. Meanwhile, after I release your statement, I will schedule a meeting of our campaign staff for early tomorrow morning. You should go home. Stay there and keep out of sight. Now, get the hell out of here."

Anderson pulled into his driveway, parking next to Brooke's SUV. He walked quickly inside, looking back, and half-expecting to see the media horde which he would soon confront. Fortunately, Blake and Brittany were spending the summer along the Jersey Shore with Brooke's parents. He would have a chance to speak with Brooke alone. Things had not been good between the two of them for a long time, but he knew this news would take their relationship to another place.

When Anderson walked through the kitchen door, he found Brooke sitting at the counter with a glass of wine in hand. From the look on her face, he could see that someone had already done his work for him.

"Do you know about the newspaper story?"

"Yes."

"How did you find out?"

"Max told me. He called a few minutes ago. He said that *The Times Union* is doing a piece about the three of us. He hasn't spoken with anyone, but he wanted us to know."

Anderson opened the refrigerator and grabbed a beer. Sitting down next to Brooke, he stared into her eyes, not really needing to ask why Grabel reached out to her and not to him. At least he would not have to face an angry blast of recrimination. They both knew there was enough guilt on both sides. Not yet knowing the specifics of what they would face, their conversation moved to the task of preparing the children as best they could. Neither of them chose to speculate about the future. Unspoken were questions of how this would impact his political career, their household, their marriage. And then there was the pervasive fear of legal jeopardy. All of that now hung in the air.

Meanwhile, at that moment, Max Grabel had just finished a round of golf and was now drinking a scotch and playing poker with his buddies in the men's locker room. He was confident that he would be able to navigate through this turbulence, even if the Andersons might not.

FIFTY-NINE

S SOON AS JAKE GOT BACK TO THE BUNKHOUSE FROM THE PARTY, he pulled up his emails. One immediately caught his attention. It was from one of his friends at the paper. The title read "Check This Out!" Jake clicked on the link to the latest digital edition of *The Times Union*. Its headline read "Senator Anderson's Questionable Connections." What Jake Morris thought would never come to light was now on full display. Jake raced through the story and then he went back again, reading more carefully now. Hunter Dane had not let Jake's story die. He had handed it to Jake's successors, and Jake could see that they had built upon what he had uncovered before he left the paper. The story they presented revealed the full scope of the corrupt relationship between the Andersons and Max Grabel, encompassing both their public and private lives. It was devastating. As a journalist, Jake was impressed not only by the depth of the research but also by the clear, succinct presentation. There was no reason to engage in sensationalist prose. Just a spare recitation of the facts was sufficient.

Jake sat back and tried to absorb what he had just read. He thought about what would likely happen next. What could Anderson possibly do by way of damage control? He would probably wait a few days to gauge public reaction. "Wishful thinking," Jake thought. The firestorm of criticism would build as more details came out in subsequent articles, adding fuel to the flames. The Senator's political enemies would pounce immediately. Friends like Governor Hickey would hang back, giving Anderson a chance to respond. He would offer a pallid justification for his actions. Anderson would claim that he and his wife simply exercised poor judgment, clouded by their longstanding friendship with Max Grabel. It wouldn't work, and the Hickeys and others would begin distancing themselves from Anderson and his candidacy.

Within a week or so, Jake judged that Anderson would be forced to suspend his campaign. Next would come demands for an ethics investigation. By then, the Andersons would have retained legal counsel and been directed to withhold further comment. US Attorney Lawrence Shapiro would likely step forward. Jake had no idea what more Shapiro might have, but he was certain that a grand jury would be convened. Subpoenas would be issued, and the press would begin its death watch, fully expecting that criminal indictments would be forthcoming.

Jake thought for a moment about the other principal players. He sensed that Hunter Dane had recognized the importance of the connection to the Cardinal. The Cardinal's involvement with the others had been limited, but the nursing home sale was further evidence of how beholden Anderson was to Grabel. It also shed light on the mutual backscratching going on among the three of them.

Jake could only imagine the story's other repercussions for the Cardinal.

Finally, there was Max Grabel. Jake judged that Grabel could survive a nuclear holocaust. From what he could see, Grabel did not give a fig about his reputation. Unless the feds had something more on him, he'd likely sail away leaving the Andersons in his wake.

Jake closed his laptop. It was nearly 2:00 a.m. The kitchen was dark except for the illumination offered by the outside security lighting. He could hear Jimmy Maxwell's light snoring coming from the bunk bay. Everyone else had gone back to their homes for the evening. Jake sat back and reflected upon the story that he had intended to write about Ben Anderson.

He thought little of the Senator when he was covering him for the newspaper. In fact, he had come to despise him for his raw ambition and ruthlessness. The man showed no sense of empathy for anyone, including his family. Jake was eager then to bring him down. But now, Jake felt a bit differently. He thought about what this story would do to Anderson and to his family. Surprisingly, he felt a twinge of sympathy, knowing that the man's life would likely crumble under the weight of these revelations. His family would suffer also, and they'd probably turn their backs on him. Maybe they all deserved whatever they would get, but Jake couldn't help feeling depressed. For some reason, he was relieved that Hunter had hesitated to have him write the story, whatever his reason had been.

SIXTY

IKE THE OTHERS, CARDINAL BOYLE HAD BEEN ON EDGE SINCE THE call on Friday afternoon. A *Times Union* reporter wanted his response to an upcoming story about Ben Anderson and Max Grabel and any connections he had with them. His private secretary relayed the message, and Boyle simply directed him to respond that the Cardinal would have no comment. That night, he checked online but so far there was no story. He spent a restless day in his residence and had just said goodnight to his usual Saturday dinner guests. He had been distracted all evening, so much so that one of his guests asked if he were well. Now, he retreated to his study, smoking a cigar, drinking a scotch, and wondering why the publication was delayed. Then it occurred to him. This story was big enough for *The Times Union* to stretch it out over several days. The first segment would come out tomorrow in the Sunday edition. It would be fresh on the minds of his flock as they gathered throughout the Archdiocese for Mass.

He drew on his cigar and pondered what the articles might say. He had no idea what specifics would be revealed about the others, but as for himself, he had a good idea. He would be portrayed as a power broker, wheeling and dealing with a politician and a cutthroat businessman.

"Well, they would be right about Grabel being cutthroat," he thought, as he reflected on their one-sided negotiation over the nursing home.

As for that deal, the story would likely lay out how one-sided it was. It would be portrayed as a desperate effort to get cash to settle the current lawsuits against the Archdiocese. Which he had to admit was the truth. Boyle knew that he was holding onto his job these days by the skin of his teeth. This investigation would make it even tougher for him.

The Cardinal poured himself another drink. He knew the digital edition of the paper would be out within the hour.

"Might as well stay up and await my fate," he thought.

SIXTY-ONE

J AKE AWOKE EARLY. DESPITE HAVING BEEN UP WELL INTO THE night thinking about the Anderson story, he found that he could no longer sleep past seven. Based upon his weekday schedule, seven felt like noon. Sundays were quiet at the Brunson place, especially with most of the crew away. They'd straggle in later in the day to get ready for the new week, but until then, Jake was pretty much on his own. He washed up, dressed, and then made some coffee. After working on his logging crew notes for a few hours, he filled a backpack with a few water bottles and some snacks. He hopped into his truck and headed out of town.

Before Jake left the party last night, Beth Mueller asked him if he would like to join her for a hike the next day. He welcomed the invitation. So now, as he drove through Schuyler, passing the town limits, he was looking for a yellow bungalow. He quickly found it. Beth was waiting for him on the front porch. She hopped into the truck cab, and they were on their way to Flathead Lake, about fifty miles south toward Missoula. The sky was cloudless and the temperature was in the mid-sixties, a near perfect day. Jake opened the windows and the roof hatch, and they settled back for a relaxing drive.

The ride gave Jake and Beth a chance to pick up where they left off the night before. Jake found it easy to talk with Beth, just as it had been with Tess. In fact, apart from their differences in appearance, Beth reminded Jake a lot of Tess. Both had a directness that appealed to him.

As he drove along, Jake looked down at the rabbit's foot he had left in the center well of the truck last night. "Everyone has been so kind to me," he thought, and now Beth. It left him a bit confused, but one thing was certain. He had not been this happy since he first met Tess.

They traveled through Whitefish and Kalispell, and within the hour, they had their first view of Flathead Lake. It is the largest, natural freshwater lake west of the Mississippi, 200 square miles with over 185 miles of shoreline. They parked the truck and walked a short distance to the water's edge. The blue-green lake was so clear they could see fish swimming several feet below the surface. Spread across its great expanse were a string of small islands.

After some time to take it all in, Jake and Beth set out for Bear Dance Trail. It afforded magnificent views of the Mission Mountains to the east and the Salish to the west. They seemed to be the only ones there. They took their time, stopping frequently to observe the wildlife. At one turn in the path, Jake and Beth looked up to find two longhorn sheep balefully staring down on them from a rock ledge. Later, a red fox darted across the trail, and a mule deer wallowed in a nearby mud pool.

It was now midday, and the sun's heat was bearing down on them. They were debating turning around when they saw ahead a large ugly lump of what was obviously bear scat. That was enough to make up their minds. It could have been from a black bear or a grizzly, but, either way, neither of them wanted to find out. So, they headed back.

After arriving at the car park, Beth retrieved an ice chest from the truck. They found a nearby picnic area and sat down to eat the sandwiches she had made. Afterward, they lingered to take in views of the lake for a few more minutes. Then, Beth broke their silence.

"Jake, I know what your assignment is, but why did you really come out here?"

Once, Jake might have been irritated by such a question. Not this time.

"I'm not sure how to answer you. I walked out on a dream job, and I was dumped by a woman I loved. All over the space of a few months. The first mistake was because I'm a hothead who doesn't stop to consider other viewpoints. The second was because I failed to appreciate the needs of the lady in question. I guess I tend to be a bit self-centered at times. I thought that going away, stepping into a totally new environment, and taking on the challenge of learning how to be a logger, might be good for me."

"Well, has it?"

"I'm not sure. At least not yet. But I do know that I feel like I've joined a family here rather than just being an observer reporting on the lives of people who mean nothing to me. I know that probably violates some rule of journalism, but I don't care. That's how I'm going to write this story."

"Jake, you're an interesting guy. I'm glad we've met. I must admit that it's been tough for me since I got here. There are very few guys that would interest me, even as friends. You're different. I can tell that you are still in love with the lady back East. If that changes, let me know. Otherwise, I'm just happy to be your friend."

The sun was sinking into the Salish range to the west as they drove back to Schuyler. Jake was blinded by the sun's glare, so he reached into the console for his sunglasses. That's when he saw the truck in his rearview mirror. It dropped back and then raced forward to within a few feet of them. Jake could see two figures in the front seat. He recognized one of them. Abner Thornberry. He and his passenger were laughing and pointing at them. Then the truck swerved into the left lane and sped up again until it was right alongside. Thornberry leaned toward them, shot Jake the bird, and then sped away. Jake looked across at Beth. She was visibly rattled.

"Who are those guys?"

"Abner Thornberry and one of his sidekicks. Remember I told you about the fight at Cupid's? Well, that's the guy."

"Stay clear of that one, Jake. I've got a bad feeling about him."

SIXTY-TWO

IN HIS THIRTY-SOME YEARS PRACTICING CRIMINAL DEFENSE LAW, Norris Black thought he'd seen it all. The long parade of clients included axe murderers, domestic terrorists, dirty politicians, and inside-trading hedge fund managers. But he never thought that he would have a cardinal of the Roman Catholic Church require his services.

Black now sat across from Cardinal William Boyle. He had suggested they meet in the Cardinal's office to minimize the chance of unwanted publicity. The Cardinal brought with him a subpoena *duces tecum* issued by a state grand jury summoning him to appear on a certain date. He would be questioned under oath as to any knowledge he might have regarding priests credibly accused of child abuse in his Archdiocese. It also demanded that he produce relevant documents in his possession. The Archdiocese had also been subpoenaed seeking such documents, but that was being handled by its general counsel, Edward Fegley. Fegley could not ethically represent the Cardinal and the Archdiocese, so he referred him to Black..

"Cardinal, if you will permit me, I will start by giving you my standard client introduction. As a criminal defense lawyer, I have a rather unique perspective on the truth. Theologically, I suspect you believe that there is such a thing as absolute truth. Not so, in my world. My job is to focus not on factual truth but what I call 'legal truth.' People can always disagree on the facts, but when a jury ponders the fate of my client, they must decide what is legal truth. Legal truth is a unanimous determination as to whether the state has proven facts beyond a reasonable doubt that satisfy each of the elements of a crime. Fortunately, for the folks I represent, that's not so easy a task. In fact, I make it as difficult as possible for the prosecutor."

"In this instance, I am here with you because the circumstances of your impending grand jury appearance raise the prospect of you being charged with one or more crimes. The first is, obviously, child endangerment. If it is determined that, in your supervisory capacity, through recklessness or indifference, you permitted or allowed someone to endanger the life or health of a minor, you face imprisonment of up to ten years for each such occurrence.

The second possibility is perjury, willfully telling an untruth under oath before a judicial body. If so found by a jury of your peers, you are subject to imprisonment for up to five years."

"Now, let me tell you about the truth as between you and me. I can only be of assistance to you to the extent that you allow me. I need to know everything you know or suspect regarding the subject of this investigation. Whatever you tell me will be kept strictly confidential. The attorney-client privilege is nearly absolute. Unless you tell me that you are about to commit a crime, I may not reveal to anyone anything else you say to me."

"If you believe that you are guilty, I don't need to know it. The matters you share with me could support that conclusion, but that doesn't mean that the prosecution will be able to elicit that information at trial, and with the other evidence presented, convince a jury that all the elements of a crime have been proved beyond a reasonable doubt."

"There are two absolute rules in this arrangement though. I will not represent anything to a judge or jury that I know not to be the truth. I would be suborning perjury. Second, hypothetically, if you would testify to a mistruth, thereby committing perjury, I would be obligated to withdraw as your attorney. Is all that understood, Cardinal Boyle?"

"Yes."

"Do you have any questions about what I have just said?"

"Yes. It's one I'm sure you've heard many times. How can you represent someone if you know they are guilty?"

"You're right. I get that all the time, and I have no difficulty answering it. In your line of work, I'm sure you are familiar with the expression 'judge not lest you be judged.' Well, that's how I operate as a defense attorney. In God's eyes, my client may be guilty, but I don't have divine knowledge. In our system of criminal justice, the only worldly judgment of guilt can be assessed by a jury after a fair trial."

"A fair trial entails a careful examination of the facts as presented from two conflicting points of view. A jury is required to sift through the evidence presented by both sides and determine what they believe to be what I call the legal truth. That's how our system of justice works. Not perfect, but better than any other invented by man. Even if my client admits to me that he is guilty, I will still do my utmost to compel the state to prove that to a jury, beyond a reasonable doubt, and there's almost always a doubt. "

"Why do I do it? Because if we acted otherwise, defense counsel like me are left to playing God, representing only those accused whom they believe are innocent. All the others are denied justice, many of whom may actually not be guilty under the law. Any other questions?"

"No."

"Fine. So, let's begin. Tell me everything you know about suspected child abuse by priests of your Archdiocese."

When they finished some four hours later, the Cardinal was thoroughly drained and cast into throes of depression. Norris Black leaned back in his chair, thought for a moment, and then looked intently at his client.

"Cardinal Boyle, it is my best professional advice that you exercise your Fifth Amendment right not to testify before this grand jury."

After Norris left, William Boyle looked about at the trappings of his office, his degrees on the walls, photos of him with the pope and other clerics, and various mementoes of his life as a priest. He was left with a decision which, however made, would utterly change his life, and with only a few days to make it. He would need to take it to prayer.

SIXTY-THREE

THERE WAS A SENSE OF ANTICIPATION AS FATHER NICK MARINO convened the monthly meeting of the Sole Survivors. All the usual attendees were there, along with a few who had not been seen in some time. They filled a long table in the back of the dining room, as they awaited the arrival of Hunter Dane. Hunter arrived about fifteen minutes late, having stopped at the bar for a scotch. He was greeted with a smattering of applause which he brusquely waved off. They all had read the four-part series in *The Times Union* concerning the Andersons, Max Grabel, and their old classmate, Cardinal Bill Boyle. Now, they wanted to hear the backstory from Hunter. But he made it clear from the outset that he was in no mood to discuss anything about it.

"Boys, give me a break tonight. You might think that I would be riding high at this moment. Well, I'm not. I am proud of the work done by my paper on this story, especially the talented young reporters who broke it. But whatever can be said about the four people who are the subjects of this investigation, I know that at least some of them are suffering right now. It can't be helped, but I guess I'm suffering a bit along with them. So, let's focus on the results of our latest prostate tests and tonight's specials on the menu."

SIXTY-FOUR

BY THE TIME *THE TIMES UNION* PUBLISHED THE RESULTS OF ITS investigation, the US Attorney's office had uncovered enough information on its own to open a criminal case against Ben and Brooke Anderson and Max Grabel. The troika of US Attorney Larry Shapiro, his chief of staff, Russ Harrington, and his first assistant, Anthony Capriotti, had traveled to Washington D.C. to meet with the Deputy Attorney General to review the evidence and to obtain authorization to proceed with a case which could incriminate a current candidate for governor.

They had spent weeks evaluating the evidence and devising a strategy most likely to produce convictions. As Shapiro anticipated, it all hinged on tagging Grabel with tax fraud. In prior cases asserting a conspiracy to commit bribery under the Hobbs Act, the prosecution failed because it could not drive a wedge between the corrupt politician and the person doing the bribing. At trial, juries tended to believe that the benefits offered were just gifts among friends. They had to put enough pressure on Grabel that he would give up the Andersons to avoid significant prison time. And they now believed they had sufficient evidence to do so.

Under the guise of what appeared to be a periodic civil tax audit, FBI agents, working with IRS auditors, were able to cajole and coerce Grabel's administrative assistant, Marla Burton, into sharing a separate set of financial records maintained by Grabel. They showed that Grabel had passed off as business expenses hundreds of thousands of dollars in renovations to his principal residence and vacation homes. Beyond that, they also uncovered thousands more in other personal expenses charged to Grabel's business. When Grabel was confronted with the proof, they hoped to put enough pressure on him that he would agree to testify against the Andersons. He would state that his payments on behalf of the Andersons were made so that Ben Anderson would use his office to protect and promote Grabel's business. For his testimony, Grabel would be given a favorable plea offer on the bribery-related charges and immunity from any possible prosecution for tax fraud.

Larry Shapiro's principal target was the Senator. Grabel was mainly a run-of-the-mill tax fraud. But a state senator who was also a candidate for governor, bought, and paid for by a corrupt businessman, had to be stopped. Put simply, Anderson's conduct undermined our faith in democracy. Shapiro viewed Brooke Anderson as collateral damage. Although she was implicated in the scheme, he had no appetite for pursuing a case against her unless she did something to obstruct his work. Besides, Shapiro did not like the optics of potentially putting away both parents of two children still in the household.

SIXTY-FIVE

Every morning at 7:00, Austin Cabot said Mass on the cathedral's side altar. Most days, he presided over an assembly of ten faithful worshipers. Seven were seniors, three of whom leaned heavily on canes for support. Two others were women in their thirties. One was dressed for business; the other had a toddler in tow. Finally, there was a young man who appeared every day in coat and tie. Austin knew nothing more about these people, except that they relied upon him to help sustain them in their daily lives.

As always, in concluding the rite this day, he raised his right hand and making the sign of the cross, intoned the words of benediction. In response, the congregation blessed themselves, murmuring "amen." As he left the altar, some knelt again in silent prayer while others made their way down the aisle and out the door to start their Friday.

Austin watched them walk out into the sunlight, thinking to himself, "I hope I've helped to bolster their faith, but it's mine that needs prayer." His was teetering on the brink. Austin was secure in his belief in God, but not so much these days in the Church founded in His name.

By mid-morning, Austin was driving north on the turnpike toward his hometown. The Cardinal had released him for the weekend so that he might officiate at the baptism of the first child of his closest high school friend. Austin also looked forward to seeing his family and old friends. Above all, he welcomed the chance to get away for a few days.

It was a clear morning. The air was cool and dry. Austin opened the windows and felt a rush of air on his face. He took a deep breath. It felt like his first in a long time. In the two weeks since his meeting with the Attorney General, the tension between the Cardinal and him seemed to build by the day. The Cardinal had accepted in silence the newspaper article about his relationship with Anderson and Grabel. But something else appeared to be working on him. Boyle was increasingly distant, almost becoming a recluse, spending hours alone either in his office or the chapel. It could be that he had become aware of Austin's disclosure of his secret, or perhaps something else was on his mind. Whatever it was, Austin felt that things would be coming to a head soon, perhaps as early as next week. He needed to prepare himself for whatever lay ahead.

Once again, Austin considered his decision to open up to the Attorney General. At first, he had harbored a vague feeling of guilt, as if he were a modern-day Judas Iscariot. He had what in the seminary was referred to as a "scrupulous conscience." But now, he no longer viewed it as an act of betrayal. Hadn't Jesus said that anyone who harmed a child would be better off if a large millstone were hung around his neck and then drowned in the sea? Pretty strong language from someone who spent his ministry forgiving sinners. Jesus had also counseled his disciples to suffer the little children to come to him. Austin was sure that he did not have in mind the suffering of a young girl because the Cardinal had placed her in the hands of a predator priest. No, what he did had to be done. No matter what will happen now to the Cardinal and to the Church. Austin also wondered what the consequences might be for him. Would he be permitted to continue in the priesthood? Would he even want to? He prayed now that the events of this weekend would help him to understand what God had in mind for him.

Austin did reach one decision on the drive back home. He owed it to the Cardinal to tell him what he had done.

SIXTY-SIX

THE SLEUTHS AT IRS HAD COMPLETED THEIR INVESTIGATION OF Max Grabel. They were ready now to pursue a criminal prosecution. In addition to a passel of phony business deductions for personal travel and entertainment, they had affidavits from Grabel's assistant, Marla Burton, and several contractors documenting over $800,000 in improvements to Grabel's residences that were charged to his business. They coordinated their work with the US Attorney's office investigating Grabel's connections with Senator Anderson. Both agencies agreed that if Grabel pled guilty to one count of bribery and testified against Anderson in a public corruption trial, he would be given a favorable deal. He'd have to pay back taxes and a heavy penalty, but the tax fraud charges would be dropped. Instead of facing decades in federal prison, Grabel would likely get thirty-six months in a minimum-security facility. He might even have an opportunity to sharpen his golf game while there.

After a final meeting with US Attorney Larry Shapiro and his staff, the IRS sent a letter to Grabel. It referenced certain unspecified discrepancies in Grabel's tax audit and requested a meeting to review these findings. Ominously, it urged Grabel to bring legal counsel with him.

At the appointed day and time, Max Grabel and his attorney, Marvin Rothko, appeared at the regional office of the IRS. They were ushered into a conference room where they were greeted by four agents led by Special Agent in Charge William Maxwell. After brief introductions, Maxwell methodically laid out the IRS's tax case against Grabel. The presentation lasted an hour, during which Grabel didn't as much as flinch, except at one point to ask for a glass of water.

When Maxwell was finished, he suggested that Rothko and his client might want to meet privately to discuss what they had just heard. Rothko agreed that might be a good idea, so the agents excused themselves. After another hour, Rothko stepped out of the room to invite the agents back in. This time, they returned with reinforcements. They were joined by First Assistant US Attorney Anthony Capriotti and two other staff attorneys.

Again, Maxwell led off. He introduced the representatives from the US Attorney's office and indicated they were there because they were pursuing a companion case against Grabel and Senator Ben Anderson. Grabel's attention shifted from Maxwell to Capriotti. Looking across the table, he swallowed hard and took a long sip of water. He was beginning to see where this was going.

Anthony Capriotti led Grabel and his attorney through the results of the Feds' probe into the activities of Grabel and Ben and Brooke Anderson. Although Capriotti was known as a tenacious litigator with a penchant for courtroom drama, his recitation of the facts now was more like what might be expected from a diligent law student presenting a comprehensive case study. He didn't need to resort to any histrionics to demonstrate the strength of his case. Finally, he advised Grabel and his lawyer that the government was prepared to charge Grabel with several offenses, including conspiracy to bribe a public official, plus wire and mail fraud.

Capriotti then threw out the bait.

"Mr. Grabel, as I'm sure your attorney will advise you, these are serious charges. If convicted, you face the prospect of a decade or more in federal prison. These charges are independent of the tax fraud liability that Special Agent Maxwell previously discussed with you. You would be tried separately for those offenses. If you are convicted in both cases, your incarceration will likely extend well beyond your life expectancy. To avoid prison altogether would be the equivalent of rolling the dice twice and coming up with seven both times. However, we do have an offer for you to consider. If you agree to plead guilty to a single count of bribery, and to cooperate fully in our prosecution of Senator Anderson, testifying truthfully to your dealings with him and his wife, we will recommend to the court a sentence of thirty-six months in a minimum-security facility. The tax fraud prosecution will then be dropped upon payment of outstanding taxes and a significant penalty. We know that you will want to discuss this matter with your attorney, so I suggest that we end this meeting now to afford you that opportunity. Please contact us within seven days if you intend to accept our offer. Otherwise, we will proceed with both prosecutions."

Marvin Rothko asked for a few moments to speak with his client. When the prosecutors returned, he indicated that his client would consider their offer, and he would advise them of his decision within the week.

SIXTY-SEVEN

MEG HOLLAND BET ON THE WRONG HORSE. SINCE *THE TIMES UNION* story three weeks ago, her boss had acted like a beaten man.

"Because he is," she reminded herself.

In the first few days after its publication, she encouraged Anderson to come up with a coherent response to the allegations. Tell people that Grabel was just sharing his wealth with an old friend. What assistance you gave him was nothing more than what you would do for any other constituent, even though Grabel may have bragged once or twice that it was more than that. And the money given to Brooke's non-profit was a legitimate grant used to advance a worthwhile cause. At Holland's urging, the Senator had put out a statement along those lines, but it was not enough to stem the torrent of calls, letters and editorials calling for him to withdraw from the race and resign as Senator.

After a week of relentless criticism, Holland and Anderson agreed that he had no choice but to suspend his campaign.

"… until the Senator has an opportunity to clear his name," his statement would read.

They both knew that would not happen anytime soon, if at all. The announcement was a tacit acceptance that his campaign for governor was over. Donors had run for the hills, and party leaders were pressuring Anderson to withdraw formally. Since his resignation would come after the primary, a new candidate would be chosen by the various county political committees.

Now, Meg Holland was at her computer putting the final touches on that announcement. She tried to make it sound noble, a step reluctantly taken so that the Senator's "personal circumstances would not serve as a distraction from the critical decisions the next governor must make on behalf of the citizens of this great state". The media was advised that the Senator would be making a statement at one o'clock. She only hoped that Anderson would be able to get the words out without losing it altogether. She would then wisk him away before reporters would have a chance for questions.

Although he stumbled a few times, Anderson got through it. He then turned from the bank of microphones set up outside his offices and fled inside. Meg was left to cover his retreat, offering a few non-responses to the shouted questions.

Anderson's senatorial staff feigned busyness as he swept past them. He would hide away until the coast was clear for him to duck out. Only one more appointment was scheduled that day. He and Brooke were meeting with a lawyer.

When Anderson left and the staff ended their day, Meg Holland sat back at her desk and contemplated her situation. Anderson faced an uncertain future. The Senate would launch an ethics investigation. There were even rumblings that the US Attorney was preparing a criminal case. She opened her bottom desk drawer and pulled out a half-empty bottle of bourbon. After a healthy pour, she leaned back and took a sip.

"This ship is going down, but it's not taking me with it," she thought.

She picked up her cell phone. As she dialed, she took another sip. She identified herself, and her call was quickly put through.

Meg got right to the point. "Lieutenant Governor Fazio, I'd like to help make you the next governor of this state."

SIXTY-EIGHT

ONE MORE SHOT WOULD WIN IT. AUSTIN CABOT WAS DOWN EIGHT to nine in a hotly contested backyard game of hoops against his two nephews. They sensed blood on the water. If they could only stop their uncle one more time, they would finally post a win against him. Austin could see that they had upped their game since his last visit home. He always played them two on one, since it required these two pre-teens to do something that they were otherwise not inclined to do—pass the ball. They had apparently learned that lesson since his last visit. They had him on the ropes now.

Their fathers hooted at Austin from the sidelines and chanted, "Defense!"

In this game, each basket counted one point, and a basket from outside a rough arc they established scored two. He knew he had to make one from downtown to win it.

Austin took the ball out from beyond the arc, and his nephews immediately swarmed around him. He faked a drive to his right, establishing some separation from the defenders, then raised up and let fly. Swoosh. Nothing but net. The boys and their fathers howled like a pack of wounded animals. Fortunately, a call to dinner brought an end to their protests.

Austin's dad had been busy barbequing ribs and chicken, and his mom and two older sisters prepared the rest: potato salad, cole slaw, and corn on the cob. This family loved their food, and more elbows were thrown grabbing dishes at the picnic table than on the basketball court. It was a classic Cabot family gathering. Bantering back and forth, while the adults were silently brimming with curiosity. All of them wanting to ask Austin what was really on their minds. "What was going on with the Cardinal and the Archdiocese"?

Austin knew he would have to fend off some hard questions later.

As the boys went inside the house to watch TV and the women cleared the table, Austin's dad broke out a bottle of Jameson and the interrogation began.

"Austin, as the Cardinal's private secretary, you know what is going on behind the scenes. It's obvious that the Archdiocese is near bankruptcy, what with the shuttering of the churches and schools and now the sale of the nursing home. A lot of people believe that this pedophile thing is not over. What do you see?"

Austin wiped his mouth with a napkin and placed it on the table.

"I can only tell you this. Pray for the Church, but most especially its people, who are hurting badly right now. As for me, I have never felt more pressure in my life. I'd ask that you keep me in your prayers, too."

He was exhausted, and he used that excuse to retreat to his old bedroom. It felt good to be back home.

Austin slept late on Saturday and then took his mom out to lunch. As they lingered over dessert, Austin could see the look of concern on her face.

"Austin, you've lost weight, and despite your efforts to disguise it, I know you're not happy. Your father and I were shocked when you entered the seminary after college, but we supported your decision then, and we're behind you now. If you're having second thoughts though, understand that we are with you whatever you decide."

Austin reached across the table and took his mom's hand.

"You are the best."

That Saturday night, Austin had plans for pizza and beers with three of his old high school friends, including Andre Thomas, whose daughter he would baptize the next morning. Andre and Austin had been inseparable in high school, both on and off the basketball court. Andre had lived in a neighborhood across the highway from Austin, separated by real estate and race. Still, they were able to bridge those different worlds. They practically grew up in each other's homes. Then, as now, there were people in town who didn't appreciate a Black boy and a White boy hanging out together. The only exception was on the basketball court. Austin and Andre were known as "Double A" or sometimes "Salt and Pepper." Austin played point guard, and Andre was the shooter in the backcourt. Andre was the scoring leader. Austin led in assists. They took their team to the state championship, and then they were off to college. Andre to Colgate and then to Fordham Law. Austin to Villanova and afterward the seminary.

Andre had returned home to practice law and to marry his high school sweetheart, an attractive Italian girl with high cheek bones and stunning brown eyes. Austin knew they were meant for one another, even back in high school, and even as they endured the ill will of many in both communities. Somehow, rejection drew them closer together.

Austin was sure their new baby would be a beautiful child, combining both Andre and Mia's striking features. If she also inherited their backbone, she would be well prepared to face an imperfect world.

Families are bound by love, reinforced through shared obligation. True friendships, however, come with no such constraints. Such was the relationship between Austin Cabot and Andre Thomas. That was made clear as Andre opened his front door and found Austin on his doorstep. They threw their arms around each other, rocking back and forth.

"Come on in, Austin, we can keep the rest of them waiting at the bar a few minutes longer. Mia wants to introduce you to our newest family member."

Austin sat down on the couch as Andre called out to his wife. Within a minute, Mia was there with little Mara. Austin stood and embraced them both, kissing Mia on the cheek. She carefully placed the baby in his arms. He looked down at her angelic face.

"She's even more beautiful than I thought she would be."

Mia asked them to stay a few minutes more. She went out to the kitchen and brought back three iced teas.

"I know that you are anxious to start your little reunion, but I have a question for you, Austin, about tomorrow's baptism. Would it be possible for you to both officiate and be Mara's godfather? Andre and I would be honored if you would. We can't think of a better choice to guide our daughter in the future."

Austin was shocked.

"But don't you already have Andre's brother lined up?"

"We do, but we told him that we would ask you first. If you can, he's fine with it."

"Well, first I am humbled by your offer. Since fatherhood is not in my future, this would be an opportunity at least to pinch-hit for my best friend. But frankly, I am not sure that this has ever been done before, or even if it's allowed. As I think about it, though, I am not aware of any canonical obstacle. It just may be, as with so much else in life, that it is better to ask forgiveness afterward than to seek permission beforehand. Sure, I'll do it. Only, to avoid any awkwardness during the ceremony, I will not join with the godmother in responding to the promises elicited by the officiant. It would look stupid for me to answer my own questions, even though I have a habit of doing that during my quiet nights alone in the rectory."

After a short drive, Austin and Andre were greeted at the door by the manager of Suds and Slices. Pete Marchione, whose family owned the place, happened to be yet another high school classmate of theirs. For years, it had been the best spot in town for pizza and cold drafts. There was a time when Pete would sneak Austin, Andre, and their buddies in without them being carded. No need for that now, but Pete couldn't resist having some fun at Austin's expense.

"Padre, are you here tonight undercover to see firsthand what life is like in the real world?"

"No, Pete. I'm here to find out how much weight you've put on since my last visit."

The place was usually packed on a Saturday night. A band was scheduled to play in an hour, and the tables were filling up quickly. Their two other classmates were waiting for them at the bar, and Pete escorted the group to a table near the dance floor. Dan Mullins was another ball player in school who now was a successful real estate agent. Angel Vasquez had been a math whiz who now worked as a software engineer. Both were married with kids. The group quickly fell into conversation as a round of drafts arrived at the table followed by two large, thin-crust pizzas.

Austin had not seen any of them in six months, so there was a lot of catching up to do. Andre spoke of the frustrations of being a junior associate in a stodgy law firm. Dan complained about how cutthroat the competition was among real estate agents, and Angel lost all of them as he attempted to describe what he was working on, something called a block chain. Dan thought that was something you kept in your car trunk in case of a heavy snowfall.

Another round of beers arrived, and the band started up before the conversation could shift to Austin and his current circumstances. The dance floor was now full, and the group's attention was drawn to a comical group of young women dancing with one another. There were four of them, each wearing a bright orange, pageboy style wig. One of them also had a cheap plastic tiara on her head and was waving a silver wand. A sign on the table they occupied read, "Theresa's Last Night of Freedom. Apply here." They all were having a little more fun than they could handle.

Austin's group had finished their pizzas, and they were unable now to hear themselves over the noise. Andre flagged a waiter down and asked for the check. But before it could arrive, something happened that they would all talk about for years. The tiara-crowned, bride-to-be got up from her table, took each of her attendants by hand and led them to another table where she tapped a gentleman's shoulder, inviting him to dance with the young woman. As it happened, one of those gentlemen was Austin.

The young women stood before Austin, as his friends erupted in laughter. The women expected a surprised reaction. Maybe, an awkward moment with some silly jokes. But neither of them had any idea why they had prompted such a thunderous response from the three guys surrounding the selected partner. Austin rose quickly, took the young woman's hand, and escorted her to the dance floor.

Suddenly, Austin was transported back to his senior prom. It felt so strange. He placed his right hand on the young woman's back and cupped her offered hand lightly in his other palm. He was back doing the old box step. Across, back, across, forward, but trying not to think about it. He felt her warmth and detected the scent of a vaguely familiar perfume.

"This is the longest song ever," he thought.

When it ended, he apologized for his friends' behavior. Fortunately, the band chose to take a break. Austin escorted his partner back to her table, thanked her, and returned to his old friends.

"Alright. You've had your fun. Now let's get out of here before the band comes back. You've embarrassed me enough tonight."

On the ride back to the city the next afternoon, Austin had some time for reflection. The weekend brought no epiphanies, but it did offer him plenty of opportunity to reconsider his current direction. His role as a clerical bureaucrat had squeezed all the joy from his life. He knew he had to get away from that. But to what? Would a new assignment restore his conviction to be a priest? Or were the experiences over the weekend a sign that his future happiness lay in being a husband and a father? He felt that longing when he held little Mara at her baptism, and a different longing, briefly, on Saturday night. But he also felt a power working within him as he poured the holy water on his little godchild. To Andre and Mia, he was a priest bestowing a spiritual blessing, but he was also one of them. Maybe, that was his special gift as a priest. His ordinariness. His human connection.

As he arrived back at the rectory, Austin decided that he would talk to the Cardinal the next day. But before going inside, he sat for a moment behind the wheel. He offered a quick prayer for tomorrow. He wanted to be truthful, but non-judgmental. After all, Cardinal Boyle was just another stumbling sinner, like himself.

SIXTY-NINE

IT WAS 10:00 A.M., AND BROOKE ANDERSON HAD GONE OUT FOR A run. Then she had breakfast and answered some emails. Her husband though was still in bed. Each day, he seemed to get to the office later and return home sooner. He told her that everyone he encountered either looked on him with sympathy or contempt. When he mentioned that to her one night, she wondered to herself which category she fell into. Sometimes, she despised him for what he had done to her and the family. But other times, she could not help but feel sorry as she watched him slowly retreat within himself.

Where would this end? They had spoken about the possibilities. Ben might be fined by the senate Ethics Committee. He might be driven out of office, or just hang on there for three years, treated as a pariah until the voters threw him out.

The most terrifying prospect was a criminal case that might be brought against them both over the payments from Grabel. It could mean financial ruin or worse. That was brought home when they sought legal counsel. After the facts were laid out, the attorney tactfully attempted to advise them that they would need to consult separate counsel. It would be a conflict to represent them both since they could wind up on opposing sides.

They drove home from the lawyer's office in silence, both privately considering the prospect that they might become adversaries in a criminal case. As they pulled into their driveway, Brooke suddenly turned toward Ben.

"I won't do it."

"Won't do what?"

"I won't get a lawyer, and nobody will get me to turn on you. We both have made a hash of this marriage. I'm not sure it's retrievable, but regardless, I'm going to stick it out if you're willing."

Ben reached out for his wife's hand.

"Let's go inside and figure out what we need to tell the kids."

There was no sudden rapprochement in their relationship. But slowly things changed. They stopped bickering, becoming more considerate toward one other. Nevertheless, the household was draped in sadness. As they sat together having dinner, conversation would sometimes trail off and they would brood silently. Both wondering what would happen next.

Ben started drinking more. In the morning, Brooke would often find a bottle of scotch and an empty glass next to the couch in the den. Sometimes, she would also find Ben there asleep. She did not come down hard on him, but when she told him she was worried about it, he told her it helped him to sleep, especially since his chronic back pain was flaring up.

SEVENTY

SHE LOOKED UP FROM HER WORK AND SAW HIM COMING. AS HE passed, she looked into his eyes, and she knew that he knew. A few minutes later, Marla Burton was called into Max Grabel's office. Without a word, she sat down, and he looked up from something he was reading. He could see that she did not regret what she had done. In fact, she had an air of defiance.

"I am giving you a promotion."

Defiance turned to shock.

"What?"

"I will be going away soon for as much as three years. As you so ably demonstrated recently to the IRS, you know how this business operates as well as I do. So, I am going to need you to run it while I'm away. I'm promoting you to Vice President of Operations. In the time I have left, I will fill you in on what I see as problems and opportunities facing us now and in the future. While I'm away, you will brief me regularly, and you can also rely upon our legal counsel, Marvin Rothko, for advice. That's all for the moment."

As she got up to leave, he stopped her.

"One more thing. I know why you did it, and I'm sorry. I took you for granted. I won't do that again."

That afternoon, Rothko called the US Attorney. He asked to be put through to Larry Shapiro.

"Larry, my client will take the deal."

When Shapiro hung up, he sat back in his chair, savoring the moment. He could now move against Senator Anderson. He got his deputy, Anthony Capriotti, on the line.

"As soon as we have Grabel's guilty plea, send out our standard target letter to Anderson."

SEVENTY-ONE

Emil Brunson was pleased with his crew and their progress selectively clearing timber from the ridge. He had no doubts that his regulars would perform, and he knew he could count on his son, Matt. But both Jake and Jimmy Maxwell had come along quickly. Except that Jimmy could get a bit jumpy at times.

They had worked their way through several grids and were now in an area high up on the ridge and farthest away from the access road.

It was mid-summer, and it hadn't rained in weeks. The woods were dried out, and Brunson was increasingly concerned about the risk of wildfires. He was an experienced firefighter, having worked for a few seasons when he was younger as a Hotshot, part of an elite firefighting unit sponsored locally by the US Forest Service. He still kept up with those guys, and he was now chief of the Schuyler Volunteer Fire Department.

Brunson always kept track of regional fire reports. There had been a fire a few weeks back about forty miles south. Lightning was the apparent cause. It burned out five thousand acres. Twenty homes were lost; however, no one was killed or seriously injured. It could happen anywhere now, so he continually reminded the men to keep alert, and he drilled them weekly on what they would need to do in a fire emergency.

Meanwhile, Jake was becoming something of an older brother to Jimmy Maxwell. Both on the job and back at the bunkhouse, he had looked after the younger guy. Jimmy had opened up to him, sharing his background, his difficulties in school, the conflicts with his father it brought on, and the drugs that had gotten him into trouble. Jimmy was subject to random drug testing, and when he got the call, Jake volunteered to drive him to the rehab center in Missoula. That night as he drove back to Schuyler with Jimmy, he looked down at his phone and saw that he had a voicemail from a number with a familiar area code. He listened to the message. It was from Peggy Opdyke at *The Times Union*.

"Jake, when you get this message, please call me."

SEVENTY-TWO

AS SHE EXITED THE PARKING GARAGE, SHE NOTICED ON HER PHONE that the heat index was still above ninety degrees even though it was almost 8:00 p.m. She turned the air conditioning on to maximum and headed for home, looking forward to a cold white wine with her husband.

It was not to be. Her phone rang. As she looked down on her console, she could see from the number that it was the paper.

"Hello, Peggy Opdyke."

"Peggy, it's Steve Chadwick. Pull over as soon as you can. I have something important to tell you."

"OK. I'm safely on the shoulder. What is it?"

"Hunter's dead."

"Oh my God! What happened?"

"Shortly after you left, I went in to see him. He was slumped over his desk. Unconscious and unresponsive. I immediately called 911, and the EMTs were here within ten minutes. They tried to bring him back, but he was gone. They are waiting now for the pronouncement of death. They're pretty sure it was a stroke. They tell me that what they call post-mortem imaging should confirm it."

"I'm turning around now. I'll be back in a few minutes."

While driving back, Peggy dialed up Father Nick Marino, one of Hunter's oldest friends. After the initial shock, he agreed to meet Peggy at the paper.

Father Nick was waiting for her in the lobby. They went up together and found Hunter's body lying on the carpeted floor. The EMTs had collected all the materials they had used to attempt to revive him. Everyone was waiting now for the doctor's pronouncement of death.

Peggy and Father Nick knelt by the body. Hunter looked as if he were asleep. Father Nick opened a black bag and removed a small vial. He proceeded to anoint Hunter's forehead, quietly reciting the Church's prayers for the dying. He then stood, and he and Peggy stepped out of the room.

"Peggy, I will drive to Hunter's home and break the news to Bern. I'll then call our little circle of friends. I'm sure you have a number of things you'll have to do. Let's talk tomorrow."

Peggy called Pamela Bessington, the paper's publisher. She then asked Steve Chadwick to assemble a few others to work on the report of Hunter's death which would run first in the digital edition. After that, she returned to Hunter's office. Everyone was standing outside, so she had a few minutes alone. She knelt again and looked down at her old friend. She wondered what may have gone through his mind in the last moments, knowing it was the end. She hoped that death came quickly.

Tom had humorously called him her second husband. He was certainly not that, but next to her husband, Peggy respected no one more than Hunter Dane. Looking down now, her eyes filled as she said goodbye. She leaned down and kissed him lightly on the cheek. Then she got up, walked out, and brought together her reporters.

SEVENTY-THREE

WHEN JAKE GOT BACK, HE DROPPED JIMMY MAXWELL OFF AT THE bunkhouse and remained in his truck. Somehow, he suspected why Peggy Opdyke called him. Jake had been thinking about Hunter Dane often as he read follow-up stories about the political scandal back home. He wasn't bothered any more about missing out on that scoop, but he had come to regret how he left the paper. How he had turned his back on his mentor. Jake wondered now if something had happened. Maybe he wouldn't have a chance to make amends.

His suspicion was soon confirmed. The door had closed. No more chance for reconciliation. Peggy told him of Hunter's death earlier that evening.

"Jake, I know how things fell apart between you two, but I had to let you know myself. More than anything Hunter may have said to me, I could feel something between the two of you. He really cared for you."

"Thanks, Peggy. Will there be a funeral service?"

"There'll be a private service in a few days and then a more public celebration of Hunter's life sometime in the future. I'll keep you posted."

Jake thanked her, hung up and then sat for several moments in the cab. He had no coherent thoughts, just a jumble of emotions. Random recollections of their time together.

He had to talk to someone. Jake thought first about calling Tess. He began to punch the number, then pulled back. They hadn't spoken since the breakup. He wasn't sure if she would even take his call, and if she did, it seemed selfish to pull her into his grief now. His next call was to Beth Mueller, and it went through.

"Beth, do you have time for me to stop by tonight? I need to talk about something."

"Sure. I'll open a bottle of wine."

Beth was sitting cross-legged on the floor, playing with her cat, when he came through the screen door.

"Jake, you look awful. Go into the kitchen and pour us both a glass."

When he returned, he sat down beside her.

"Beth, I've not told you much about the circumstances that brought me here, but I need to now".

For the next hour, Jake talked without interruption, describing how he had come to work at *The Times Union* and the reason why he left. He spoke about his times with Hunter Dane, what he had learned from him about journalism, and about the man himself.

"And now I learned tonight that he's dead."

Beth Mueller was a good listener. That's all the good she could do for Jake that night.

SEVENTY-FOUR

When Austin Cabot awoke on Monday morning, he was surprised to learn that the Cardinal had already left for Washington to meet with the Papal Nuncio. Theresa shared the news as she served Austin breakfast. The Cardinal planned to return on Wednesday after stopping on his way back for a short visit with his sister in Maryland. Austin thought it strange that, as the Cardinal's secretary, he would not have known about the trip beforehand. Meetings with the Holy Father's representative to the American bishops were normally scheduled well in advance.

The next day, *The Times Union* reported the sudden passing of its managing editor, Hunter Dane. As he read the obituary, Austin noted that Dane had once been a local seminarian. It seemed strange now that the Cardinal had never mentioned that to him, especially with all the attention the paper paid to the Cardinal recently.

After Mass, Austin left for his weekly shift as a chaplain at the city's public hospital. Typically, he would walk the halls for several hours, looking in on patients, briefly introducing himself and asking if they had a moment to talk. Most of them were elderly. Some had been there for weeks, and he was their only regular visitor. Austin gave communion to those Catholics who requested it, but he was happy to spend time with anyone who was open to him.

He experienced moments of joy. His visit to a man who had been estranged from the Church for decades but now wanted to reconcile. A woman on life support who wished to receive the Last Rites. But then, sometimes things didn't go so well. He was surprised at first at the number of people with a longstanding grudge against the Church. If those folks didn't show him the door immediately, he was resigned to sit patiently as they told their bitter stories. Often, their words came slowly, haltingly. The details confused, but the message generally the same. They had needed comfort and understanding at a time of crisis in their lives, but they were left to feel condemned and rejected. Many times, Austin could offer only a sympathetic nod and a prayer for them. He was not able to tell them what he really felt.

They were often right. The Church, in the person of a stiff-necked cleric, had abandoned them.

When Austin got back to the residence that afternoon, he changed his clothes and took Seamus, the Cardinal's black Lab, for a long walk. He might be the Cardinal's dog, but Seamus knew who fed him and walked him. Some nights, he would wander away from his owner and make his way to Austin's room, lying next to the bed. The Cardinal grudgingly came to accept this shared custody arrangement. Tonight, with the Cardinal away, there would be no need for Seamus to engage in any subterfuge.

SEVENTY-FIVE

BEN AND BROOKE ANDERSON HAD TAKEN TO JOGGING TOGETHER early in the morning. Although Brooke was in better condition, she adjusted her pace and distance to accommodate her husband. When they got back from their run that Tuesday morning, Brooke went upstairs to shower while Ben made coffee. He poured a cup and sat down at the counter, opening the morning paper. The headline read, "Veteran Journalist, Hunter Dane, Found Dead at His Desk."

Ben put down his cup, his focus now on the accompanying story. When he was finished, he looked out the window for a moment at a pair of blue jays in a nearby tree. He thought back to his encounters with Hunter over the years. It had begun when Ben was a young man. Hunter helped him get out of a real jam. Then, when Ben entered politics and would run into Hunter on occasion, neither of them ever brought up that earlier experience. Hunter had obviously marshalled the investigation which imperiled him now, but Ben did not hold that against him. Hunter Dane was a professional and a gentleman.

Much had changed in the Anderson household. Over several nights, they tried to game out their future. Their past infidelities were never mentioned. Meg Holland had now left for a more promising future as Nick Fazio's campaign manager. Privately, Ben was relieved. Mutual ambition had been the aphrodisiac drawing them together, but Ben could no longer offer her a path to power. For her part, Brooke realized that she had been played by Max Grabel. Her excuse, at the time, was that she was lonely. The truth, though, was that she had prostituted herself while helping Grabel sink his hooks further into her husband. Both Ben and Brooke were unsure of a future together, although they both wanted a try at it. But first, they would have to confront the consequences of their actions.

The publicity subsided after a few weeks, but the ripples of notoriety spread widely. They tried to prepare the kids who were summering on the Jersey Shore, but Blake and Britney were quickly barraged with comments from their friends on social media. Both were understandably furious, wondering how the scandal might impact their plans for school in the fall.

In the last few months, Brooke had become a passionate advocate for her dementia clients; however, she now faced the loss of funding for her non-profit. In response, she worked even harder on behalf of families seeking help for a loved one, and she scoured the community of charitable donors to find a replacement for Grabel's foundation. But those efforts were made more difficult now. Some folks were no longer very trusting of Senator Anderson's wife.

Ben faced similar challenges. He assigned Stan Mosca as his new chief of staff. In some respects, that job was a lot easier now. The legislature was not in session for much of the summer, and Ben was no longer able to advance policy initiatives anyway. He decided one thing he would do is provide even better constituent services. So, he doubled the number of hours for visits from the public. Both he and Stan ran down even the most insignificant requests. Ben figured it was the only practical step he could take to attempt to repair his reputation. Besides, it kept his mind off other things.

Ben also had to deal with his law partners. Obviously, they were not pleased with the negative publicity brought on by their high profile, low billing partner. He met with the firm's Executive Committee, and in carefully couched terms, they advised that since his time was now freed up from running for governor, they wanted him to spend more time in the office performing real legal work. Although Ben had worked for years as a commercial lawyer, he had not drafted a contract in a long time. Well, he was told, he would now. And they also strongly recommended that he maintain a low profile while doing so.

Looming over all for Ben and Brooke was the thought of what the US Attorney might do. But it seemed now that question may have been answered.

One afternoon, Ben arrived home from his law office with a stunned look on his face. Brooke recognized it as he walked through the kitchen door.

"Ben, what's happened?"

Ben headed for the fridge, grabbed a beer, and slumped onto a counter stool.

"One of my partners told me today what he just heard about Max. They both belong to the same golf club. They have a mutual friend who has been part of Max's regular foursome for years. He said that Max abruptly dropped out of the group and that he's suspended his membership at the club."

"Well?"

"Well, Max would never have done that unless something had changed dramatically in his life. Like cutting a deal with the feds that will send him away for a while."

"But Ben, there could be other things."

"Sure, but it's another example of Occam's Razor."

"Occam's what?"

"It's a principle in philosophy. Basically, it holds that the simplest explanation is usually the correct one. We both know the feds need to get through Max to get to us. I think they found a way to do it."

SEVENTY-SIX

WHEN AUSTIN CABOT RETURNED FROM MORNING MASS ON Wednesday, he saw that the Cardinal had returned. The time had come to tell him what he had done. As he nervously pushed around the bacon and eggs on his plate, Theresa came into the kitchen.

"The Cardinal would like to see you in his office when you're finished breakfast."

Austin found the Cardinal seated at his desk, looking out at his garden. He turned as he heard Austin come in.

"Austin, please sit down. I have some things I need to share with you."

The Cardinal paused for a moment, seeming to collect his thoughts.

"Last Sunday, I said Mass at Saint Barnabas. When I was walking out of the church afterward, a woman approached me. I judge she may have been in her early sixties. She asked if we could speak for a few minutes. We sat together in the back pew as she told me her story. Her son had been abused by a priest when he was a young altar boy. For years, he received counseling, but ultimately, it did no good. Six years ago, he took his own life. Fighting back tears, the woman said that she wanted to thank me for all that I had done to protect other children from predator priests. She asked me to pray for her and then hugged me as she said goodbye. That's when I knew what I had to do."

"Do what, Eminence?"

"When I came to the Archdiocese five years ago, I announced that all priests credibly accused of sex abuse were removed from the ministry. That was a lie. As you know, Father Randall has recently been accused by a woman of molesting her daughter. Father Randall had prior complaints lodged against him. I knew that when I came here, but I allowed him to remain in his parish after getting therapy. Because we had known each other for many years, I trusted him and his therapist when I was told he was cured. Austin, there is no cure for what he has. I should have known that. That woman finally caused me to face up to what I've done. I allowed a young girl to fall into the hands of a predator. I pray that she does not suffer the same fate as that woman's son. And I pray there aren't others out there who have been victimized by Randall because of me."

"What can you do?"

"Randall has been transferred from his parish to a place where he will be confined until he is formally removed from the priesthood. But that's not enough. I have been called by Attorney General Mary Beth Karpinski to testify next Thursday before a state grand jury. One of the small ironies in life is that I taught Mary Beth many years ago. I plan now to tell my former student the truth about Randall and my role as his enabler."

"What happens then?"

"I don't know, exactly. My meeting with the Papal Nuncio was to advise him of this beforehand so that he can alert the Holy Father. When I have unburdened myself to the AG, I will submit to the Holy Father my resignation as Archbishop and as a member of the College of Cardinals. I will be a simple priest then, Austin, like yourself."

"How do you think the AG will treat you?"

"Like anyone else in similar circumstances who pleads guilty to child endangerment. I do not intend to bargain with her. My lawyer tells me that I will likely face some period of incarceration. I am prepared to accept that."

"Austin, I haven't told anyone yet but the Papal Nuncio, and now you. I wanted you to know because you have been good to me, even at times when I didn't deserve it. You may not know it, but you've played a part in bringing me to this point. You are a good priest. Whatever may be the Church's future, it will need priests like you."

"I do have a few requests though. I suspect that soon I will no longer be able to care for Seamus. He's an old dog, and I don't want him to fall into the hands of strangers or worse. I'd ask you to take over as his master, formally now, since he spends more time with you these days anyway. And, finally, I would like you to hear my confession. I have sinned grievously against God and His people."

SEVENTY-SEVEN

*T*HE *TIMES UNION* STAFF WERE STILL IN SHOCK TWO DAYS AFTER Hunter's death. But none of the paper's readers would have known that anything was different except for the report of his passing. The staff's ability to deal with the shock was itself a testimonial to him. On Wednesday morning though, Steve Chadwick and Ellen Conway came up with an idea to allow their co-workers to share their grief. They circulated an email among the editorial staff, inviting them to an informal gathering that night at Bennie's Bar.

Bennie's was a beer and whiskey joint down the street from the paper. For decades, it had been a safe harbor for reporters celebrating a good story or nursing life's inevitable bumps and bruises. Soon the invitation spread to all the paper's employees and even some of its retirees.

By 5:30 that night, they were three deep at the bar and filling up most of the tables. Bennie Jr., who had taken over for his father some years ago, could not believe his good fortune. Behind the bar in his trademark black pants and open white dress shirt, he was busy serving drinks while his wait staff handled sandwich orders.

Soon, without any prompting, the stories began. Tales of memorable encounters with the Great White. Each one culminated in a toast to his memory. After several had taken their turn, the crowd called on Harry Schneider to address them. Harry was the paper's long-time copy editor and a particular target of Hunter's ire over the years. He was also the funniest man who ever passed through the paper's doors.

"Alright, settle down now for a little history lesson. Let me give you the benefit of my many years surviving under the Boss's scrutiny. But first let me remind all of you of what I do on behalf of this publication. My job is to act as the final gatekeeper to eliminate any typos, misspellings, or worse things that could get the paper sued or otherwise make us a laughingstock in this city. I'd like to think I've done that well, but sometimes I must admit that I was not up to Hunter's high standards. On those occasions, many of you in the newsroom had an opportunity to overhear the Boss's reprimands, even with his office door closed. So let me share with you now some of the more memorable snafus in my time with Hunter."

"There was the Halloween edition of the paper when we ran a photo of the police chief handing out candy to young trick-or-treaters. A nice human-interest feature which, unfortunately, was placed on the front page immediately below a headline reading, 'Sex Offender Apprehended.' The police chief and the mayor were engaged in a running battle at the time. The mayor loved it; the chief not so much. After that, you can bet that Hunter and I made sure not to speed on city streets."

"Then there was the innocent typo that caused a volcanic eruption. We ran a story in the Community section about some high school boys who had started a band. We listed all the band members and their musical instruments but, unfortunately, we concluded by identifying the group's drummer, let's call him Timmy Morrison, as 'backing the group on drugs.' When Timmy's mother was through with Hunter, he started in on me. He used words I had never heard before. When he was done with me, we had to figure out a way to issue a correction. Which was a challenge in and of itself. What could we say? 'We regret that we said Timmy was on drugs?' And how did we even know that he wasn't? Finally, we agreed upon a tactful solution. 'We regret that the paper misidentified the musical instrument played by Timmy Morrison in the new youth band Purple Crush. Mr. Morrison is an accomplished percussionist.'"

"Hunter Dane fancied himself a literary lion. He loved the occasional pun or play on words. One day, our sports editor found his sweet spot. Some years ago, we had in town a talented young right fielder by the name of Johnny Balz. Hold on now, I can tell that some of you are getting ahead of the story. Well, one night, Balz made a dramatic catch on the warning track to prevent a three-run homer. Amazingly, our photographer caught the moment as Balz jumped, catching the ball just above the top of the outfield wall. The next day our readers saw that moment recreated in our morning edition with the headline, 'Balz to the Wall.'"

"I will leave you with this. I would not trade my time with Hunter Dane for anything in this world other than my family. He was a lovely man."

With that, everyone raised their glasses.

The evening concluded with a benediction of sorts from the newly appointed successor to Hunter, the acting managing editor, Peggy Opdyke. She approached the bar, set down her gin and tonic, and turned to the crowd.

"Many of you know how far back I go with Hunter. We've been through a lot together. With it all, Hunter held a steadfast belief in the power of journalism to improve people's lives. Sure, he was hard on us at times, but he reserved the lash only for when he believed that a talent was being wasted. And he was there when we needed him, never drawing attention to himself. Like the time that he stayed with a young reporter all night at the hospital while his wife went through a difficult delivery. Or the check that turned up to help one of our circulation people whose house had burned down. That man never knew where the money came from, and I only learned of it later by accident. There were many other instances of Hunter's compassion which we will never know about. But there is one area where Hunter clearly fell short. Despite all his efforts, whether he knew it or not, he was never able to convince us that he didn't love us. Every one of us."

SEVENTY-EIGHT

THEY HAD NOW BAGGED MAX GRABEL, OBTAINING A SIGNED PLEA agreement and a detailed affidavit listing all the gifts he provided to the Andersons, his motivation for doing so, and the various actions Ben Anderson had taken on his behalf. US Attorney Larry Shapiro and his staff now shifted their attention to the Senator.

As Shapiro sat with his chief of staff, Russ Harrington, and his first assistant, Anthony Capriotti, they reviewed one more time the potential charges against Anderson and, for each charge, the facts demonstrating probable cause that a crime had been committed. From the beginning of this investigation, they were aware of the recent Supreme Court decision limiting the ability of law enforcement to proceed against a public official for what an ordinary person might judge to be official corruption. Even if a prosecutor could show that benefits were provided to that official for the purpose of obtaining special treatment and not based simply upon friendship, more had to be shown. There needed to be an "official act" undertaken by the pol on his benefactor's behalf. The Court had narrowed that definition. Anderson's many interventions on Grabel's behalf with various state agencies did not qualify as "official acts." However, Shapiro and his people were confident that Anderson's decision, as chair of the senate Health and Institutions Committee, to drop an investigation into nursing home safety met that standard.

They recognized that this case would not be a slam dunk. Grabel would testify that his arrangements with the Andersons were not driven by friendship, but by a desire for special treatment for his businesses. They hoped that any half-awake juror watching Grabel testify would conclude that he did nothing in his life out of the kindness of his heart. But Anderson and his wife would likely testify that they believed otherwise. Both could make compelling witnesses.

Shapiro had investigators monitoring the Andersons' movements since *The Times Union* story came out. They still lived together in the same household, and there was no indication of a continuing breach in their marriage.

He surmised they may have reconciled. Together, they could evoke sympathy from a certain sort of juror. The defense needed only to persuade one juror to vote against conviction on all charges in order for the judge to declare a mistrial. In that event, the government could retry Anderson, but Shapiro knew that was unlikely, both because of the cost and because of the likelihood it would appear to the public that the prosecution had turned into a persecution.

Shapiro recently received a call from Cynthia Everett. He worked with Everett when they both served in the office as assistant US Attorneys. After a decade there, she left for private practice. Everett was now a high-profile, white collar defense attorney. She had called as a courtesy to advise Shapiro that she now represented Senator Anderson so that if there were any need to contact him it should come through her. Decoded, she was saying that any target letter to Anderson should go directly to her.

With that additional intelligence, Shapiro and his staff plotted their next step. The target letter would go out that day. Inevitably, arrangements would be made for a meeting to discuss the possibility of a plea. Larry Shapiro always took the same approach to plea negotiations. Unlike some prosecutors, Shapiro did not believe in over-charging defendants. "Running up the bill" he called it, by coming up with an array of claimed offenses that had little merit and even less chance of producing a conviction. Shapiro found it unethical. Besides, it rarely stampeded a defendant into accepting a plea on the core charges, especially when that person was represented by someone like Cynthia Everett.

After much back and forth, Shapiro and his assistants agreed upon their negotiating strategy. Although a conviction under the Hobbs Act could result in imprisonment for up to twenty years as well as a hefty fine, Shapiro would offer the prospect of a recommendation to the court of forty-eight months. That decision was driven not only by the factual and legal challenges of the case, but also by the deal given to Grabel. He got three years. Anderson could be offered no less than four.

There was one other factor which the prosecutors discussed. Brooke Anderson. Conceivably, she could be prosecuted as an accessory. While Shapiro had decided not to take that step, he would not commit openly to that, nor even bring it up in the negotiations. Some other prosecutors might, but he would not employ brass knuckles with Anderson. He knew, however, that the possibility would weigh on Anderson as he considered whether to accept a deal, even if Everett tried to convince him otherwise.

Larry Shapiro sat back in his chair after the others left the office. He swiveled around and looked out at the river in the distance and the boaters cruising by.

"What would I do if I were the Senator?" he thought.

SEVENTY-NINE

CALEB THORNBERRY WAS CALLED AWAY TO ATTEND A MEETING OF the Pioneer Patriots, a loosely organized group that opposed federal ownership of land in the American West. For the next week, his ranch would be in the unsteady hands of his youngest son, Abner. Abner had one assignment: to repair a stretch of fence on the south side of the property. He had enlisted the help of his usual drinking buddies, J.D. Calloway and Toby Grimes. Neither had much use for a hammer, but they knew there would be beers awaiting them when the work was done.

On Monday morning, they got an early start and were able to repair about a hundred feet of fence by mid-day. It was a hot one. Temperature in the mid-nineties. Thankfully, a dry heat. Nevertheless, it had sucked out of Abner whatever enthusiasm he had for the project.

"Boys, I've got a better idea than spending the rest of the day out here sweating our balls off. We have more than enough time this week to complete the job before my Pa gets back. I say we hop in my truck, buy some beer, and go for a ride."

Ten minutes later, they were pulling into the Gas n' Go and buying a cold case of beer. Toby sat in the back with the beer and passed two cans forward to the others. Abner headed north out of town, knowing where he wanted to go.

"Let's go check out our friends on the Brunson crew."

Abner had been out to the work site several times, careful not to be seen, so he knew that the crew was now working high up near the ridge. They could drive onto the access road without being observed and park near the crew's staging area.

Abner pulled over to the side of the road and stopped about forty yards behind two trucks which he recognized as Emil's and Jake's. He shut off the engine, and they each popped another cold one. The windows were open, but they were still baking in the cab. They got out with the case of beer and found a shady spot to squat. Even with the rushing sound of the river behind them, they could hear in the distance the whirring sound of saws and the thud of falling timber. Abner judged that the Brunson bunch were near the northwest corner of the mountain, close to the ridge top, about a mile away as the crow flies, but three miles or more on the switchback road leading back to the staging area. They would be undetected, relaxing with their beers.

Abner Thornberry was not much for relaxation though. After twenty minutes and two more beers, he suddenly got up and turned to his friends with a mischievous smile.

"I gotta pee, but when I get back, I've got an idea how we can have some fun. I've been trying to figure out what I can do to pay that bunch back for that night at Cupid's. I think I got it."

When Abner returned, he grabbed another beer and then sauntered down to the two trucks with J.D. and Toby trailing behind. When he got there, he pulled his knife out of his boot and scratched "Asshole" on the driver's door of the first truck.

"OK, boys. Let's see what you can do."

Both of them pulled out a set of keys and got to work. Soon, they had crudely fashioned on the sides of both trucks images of penises, female breasts, and KKK and Nazi insignia. They stepped back, took a sip of their beers, and admired their work.

"You know, boys. This is the sort of thing we would have done back in school. But I think we can do better."

With that, Abner walked back to his truck, returning a few minutes later with a five gallon can of gasoline and two dirty rags.

"Here's my thought. Toby, see that pile of hay bales in the back of Brunson's truck? Well, pull one out. Break it up into two sections."

When Toby did what he was told, Abner soaked both clumps of hay with gas and placed one under each truck. He then soaked the rags to use as wicks.

"OK, now. Toby, you go back and start my truck. Turn it around so we are set for a quick getaway. J.D., you take Brunson's truck. I'll take the other. When I say so, both of us will light these rags, throw 'em under the trucks, and then we'll haul ass."

Minutes later, they were back in Abner's truck looking behind at the conflagration, giggling, and sharing high fives. Soon, the trucks' gas tanks exploded with a deafening boom, and plumes of thick black smoke drifted upward.

"Oowee! Sweet! Now, that got their attention. Let's get the hell out of here."

As they pulled onto the main highway, Toby stopped on the side of the road.

"What the hell! We left some good beer back there."

Abner blew up.

"Damn you! Step on it! I've got plenty more beer back at the ranch."

Abner and his boys enjoyed a fine show, but they missed the finale. When the hay bales in Brunson's truck caught fire, burning shafts of hay drifted upward into the air. Caught in a strong wind from the southeast, they floated across the road and landed among some low brush at the bottom of the mountain slope. Soon, fire spread among the brush, moving up the slope and stretching wide as it climbed, searching for rich fuel among the tall timber.

EIGHTY

IT WASN'T THE FIRST TIME IN HIS CAREER THAT ONE OF NORRIS Black's clients declined to take his advice. Black had just finished a long, draining session with Cardinal Boyle who informed him that he would not plead the Fifth before the state grand jury. In their last meeting, Black had explained that at this juncture there was no way of knowing what, if anything, the Attorney General knew about the Cardinal's dealings with Father Randall. It might just be a fishing expedition. The only way to know what cards the AG was holding would be through discovery of the state's files, and that would only happen if she decided to prosecute. Black suggested that they call her bluff.

Today, however, the Cardinal explained what Black already understood. If he refused to cooperate and pled the Fifth, it would be universally seen as a tacit admission of guilt. He would no longer have the moral authority to serve the people of the Archdiocese. Besides, he no longer wanted to live his lie.

Grudgingly, Black came to understand.

"Well, then, let me start a conversation with the AG about a possible plea bargain. I might even be able to get a recommendation of probation in return for your testimony against Randall."

Black was shocked at the Cardinal's response.

"No. I don't want you to bargain on my behalf. If you can, please set up a meeting with Ms. Karpinski. I would rather do that than appear before a grand jury. I will tell her everything, and, if necessary, I will testify truthfully in any proceedings against Father Randall. As for my disposition, I will leave it to the Attorney General and to a judge. I trust that they will treat me fairly, but whatever happens, it's in God's hands."

When Norris Black and his client entered the conference room, Attorney General Karpinski stood and reached across the table to shake their hands. Black could see that she was visibly shaken, as if she were the person about to plead guilty to a crime.

"Cardinal Boyle, perhaps, you remember me from another time."

"I certainly do. I remember you as one of my best students when I was teaching at Saint Peter's High School. It's good to see you again, although I would prefer it were under different circumstances."

"I couldn't agree more, but we find ourselves here, so let's begin."

When it was over, William Boyle felt an overwhelming sense of relief despite all that lay ahead of him. He would now submit to the Holy Father his resignation as Archbishop and as a Cardinal, hoping that he would be allowed to continue in the priesthood in some capacity.

He left the Cardinal's residence that day with only a single suitcase. Arrangements were made to stay temporarily in the home of a former priest. He would offer a written statement of his guilt and remorse to the people and the clergy of the Archdiocese, and then he'd attempt to fade into obscurity.

In the coming months, William Boyle would be sentenced to one year in state prison at a facility mainly occupied by non-violent offenders. Father Randall would plead guilty to one count of child molestation in the most recent case, and he would be removed from the priesthood. The statute of limitations prevented prosecution for his earlier offenses. Randall would be sentenced to seven years' imprisonment at a facility housing serious sex offenders.

EIGHTY-ONE

T HE PROTECTIVE EARMUFFS ATTACHED TO THEIR HELMETS prevented the Brunson crew from hearing the exploding gas tanks as they were busy felling and hauling timber. With Brunson and Jake facing upslope as they received timber coming down, it was a few minutes before Martin Ramser, perched on the upslope yarder, looked up to see two plumes of black smoke below. He called Brunson on his headset.

"Emil! Quick! Turn around."

Emil soon figured out what had happened.

"Our vehicles have been torched. The wind is picking up and headed in our direction. If it hasn't happened already, the fire will leap across the road and into the trees. We've got to get out of here. Fast. Have the men collect up the tools and be ready to go. Jake and I will get up there as quick as we can!"

They moved up the ridge as fast as they could, picking their way through stumps and standing timber over the four hundred yards to the work site.

When they got there, Emil quickly brought the crew together.

"We've got a wildfire on our hands. It will be moving quickly in our direction. Our best chance is to try an end around. If we can out-race it before it spreads across the eastern side of the slope, we might be able to escape by going back down the switchback. But we have to move fast. Everybody in the Humvee, except Jake. You go with me in the fire safety truck. Everything else stays behind. Now, go!"

The first leg was east along the fire break until they reached the switchback. Then they had a crisscrossing route of some two miles down until they reached the access road about fifty yards east of the fire's origin. Emil did the calculations in his head. Maximum safe speed on the rough roads was about twenty miles per hour. They would have about fifteen minutes to get there. It would be close.

As he led the crew down, Emil got the district interagency dispatcher on his speaker phone. He gave the location coordinates and described what he had seen.

"A vehicle fire has triggered a wildfire traveling north to northwest up the range. Winds appear to be gusting up to twenty miles per hour. I've got an eight-man crew traveling down to the access road, and we'll try to get there before we're cut off. If we can't, we'll retreat to the ridge top and try to find an escape route up there. Deploy all available personnel, including the Hotshots. Also, we need aircraft to dump water and chemical retardants as soon as possible."

In the Humvee behind Emil, the men silently looked out over the treetops below at the thick wall of smoke, seeded with flaming embers, headed their way. The wood line was broken at certain points by gullies, dry now, but carrying natural run-off down the mountain in the wet season. There they could see the full fury of the inferno. Boiling flames, thirty feet high, rolling toward them. They were deathly quiet, except for Jimmy Maxwell.

"How are we going to get out? I don't want to die like this."

Iz Jackson did his best to calm down Jimmy and the others.

"I was with Emil Brunson in Iraq. He got us out of tougher spots than this. He'll find a way."

Five minutes later, Emil stopped the truck and got out. Ahead of them about two hundred yards, he could see that the fire had crossed the road and was headed eastward. It must have been a momentary wind shift. Although the flames were not as intense on the roadway, a large flaming timber had fallen, blocking their path out by that route.

Maybe, they could have outraced the fire in their vehicles if the road were not blocked. But they had no chance on foot. After spreading eastward, the wind had shifted back to the northwest. The fire had collapsed in on itself, looping around and creating a noose for them to step into.

It was almost as though Emil had been drawn into a game of chess with a demonic creature.

"Checkmate," he thought.

Emil walked quickly back to the Humvee to tell the crew. Then, as he stepped into the fire safety truck, he gave Jake the news.

"We can't get around that timber, and trying to hike out to the main highway would be suicide. We can't out-run this thing. Our best chance now is to turn around, head back up, and look for a back door out at the top."

Both vehicles slowly turned around, carefully avoiding the steep drop-off on either side of the dirt road. The Humvee led now, with Emil close behind. Emil got back on the speaker phone to advise interagency dispatch of the change of plan. This time he was patched through to the fire management officer, an old friend.

"Sam, we're not having a good day here. The fire has blocked our way to the access road, and we can't chance trying to hike around it to get out to the main highway. It's moving too fast. We're headed now back to our work site high on the northwest side of the range, farthest from the fire's path. We'll hike from there up to the ridge top. Our hope is to find a route to the other side. It's rocky near the top and all rock on the opposite face. So, if we can pick our way down the back slope, we'll be safe. If not, we're left to hunker down and do what we can to survive a burn-over."

"I think that's all you can do, Emil. You know that we don't have enough time to chopper your crew out of there, and the Hotshots and their back-up won't be able to bring this thing under control for some time. It's a raw deal, but if anybody can find a way to pull through this, it's you. We'll get to you as fast as we can. Meanwhile, let's stay in touch. God bless, you all."

Emil thought through his plan on the way back. He had learned that fighting wildfires was a lot like his combat experience in Iraq. You had to assess the enemy's strength and intent. Then figure out whether your resources gave you an advantage in a firefight. If they didn't, then you considered a plan for tactical retreat. If that wasn't feasible, you had to make a stand, knowing the terrain, and taking advantage of it to improve your odds of surviving the battle. That's what Emil and his boys faced now.

Emil certainly knew the terrain. The highest and steepest part of the range was mostly boulders and loose rocks with scattered pygmy pines and dry brush. On the other side, it was all boulders, but it was so steep that at most points the drop-off was a hundred feet or more.

When he scouted the area in planning the logging operation, he saw a few locations where the grade was not so steep. If they were able to find one of them, the crew could scramble to safety. But they wouldn't have much time. The wind was picking up in the late afternoon. It would accelerate even more as it moved upslope.

Emil judged they would have no more than a half hour to hike to the top and search for an escape route. He decided that he would scout for the opening. The rest of the crew would be busy preparing for their final option. Hunkering down, shielded by emergency shelters, and hoping that they'd survive the burn-over.

He had never been trapped in a wildfire, but Emil knew the stories of others who survived a burn-over and of those who had not. He understood that the conditions at the top would increase their chances of survival since there would be less fuel there to feed the beast. He would have the men do whatever they could to reduce the available fuel even more. They would pile up rocks to surround themselves in case they had to deploy the emergency shelters he had trained the crew to use. Sometimes those shelters worked, and sometimes they didn't.

Emil glanced at Jake. His eyes were fixed on the road ahead. Emil had long since learned to read men under stress.

"I won't have to worry about him," he thought.

When they reached the worksite, Emil gathered the men around him. He looked into their faces and was reminded of the young Marines he had led into combat. The same look of fear; each man struggling to control it in his own way.

He briefly explained the escape plan to them and the last-ditch alternative.

"Go to the back of the truck and pull out the emergency shelter packs. Grab two hoes, two shovels, and two Pulaski fire axes. Each of you carry one tool. Martin and I will bring along drip torches. Now, move. The fire's on its way."

It took them about ten minutes to get to the top. Immediately, Emil put them to work under Martin's supervision. They established an area where they would deploy their shelters, if necessary. Three of them used shovels and hoes to hollow out the space, building up a low wall of rocks around the perimeter. The others fanned out, chopping down any nearby small trees and dragging them down slope.

Martin used a drip torch to burn out as much nearby brush as possible.

Meanwhile, Emil quickly walked along the ridge top, looking for a safe passage. He first traveled west, farthest away from the fire's approach. After five minutes without success, he turned back and moved east. He hadn't gotten far when he realized that his time had run out. He looked down the slope and saw that the fire was approaching the fire break where their vehicles were parked. The break would only slow it down for a few moments and then it would be within four hundred yards of them. Emil turned back and brought the crew around him.

"I couldn't find a way out. We don't have much time now. Drop your tools and deploy the shelters."

Each of them pulled out a thin blanket faced with aluminum foil and backed by a silica weave.

"OK, just as we trained, unfold it completely. We are all going to lie prone together on our stomachs in the hollow facing away from the fire. Make sure the shelter covers you entirely and pin it down with your head, hands, elbows, and feet. Try to get your face as close to the earth as possible. The air will be coolest there. And whatever happens, don't move. Stay there until you hear me tell you to get up. Remember, without these shelters we have no chance."

By then, they could see the creature bounding toward them. The boiling black cloud with flames rising thirty feet; the roaring sound it gave off increasing by the moment. Emil waited to deploy until the last moment to be sure that everyone else was covered. Then he dropped down under his shelter next to his boy and prayed.

Jake lay in his shelter and waited. The roar grew louder, and he felt embers dropping on him, spewed into the air by cyclone wind pushing the inferno toward them. The sensation of warmth on his legs and back grew in intensity until it became nearly unbearable. Jake began to fear that the shelter had failed him and that he was now ablaze. He fought off the urge to break and run, knowing that if he did, he would soon be overcome by toxic fumes or superheated air would scald his lungs. Pressing his face further down into the earth, Jake tried to find distraction from the searing pain. He thought of Tess. Of what could be or might have been. At that moment, Jake's mind drifted back in time, reaching out to a prayer from his youth.

It might have been ten minutes or a half hour. Suddenly, the wind dropped, and the demon roar began to fade away. Emil stood above them, calling for them to leave their shelters. The crew stood unsteadily and looked out across a spectral landscape. Smoke rose from the blackened earth, barren except for a charred stump here and there. The blaze had shifted its path and was now moving farther west along the range.

Emil took stock of his men. Their faces were covered in dirt and caked with sweat. They were unnaturally calm, with no life in their eyes. Emil had seen this in men before. They were all in shock, probably a good thing for the moment. Most of them were burned and the shock would mask the pain for a while.

Suddenly, Emil recognized that one of them was missing. Jimmy Maxwell. Emil looked about and could find no evidence of him except for his shelter on the ground some distance away. He must have panicked and tried to run. Emil turned and walked up to the ridge top. He looked down, and there was Jimmy some eighty feet below. His limbs were splayed. One leg was twisted so badly that it appeared as if he were attempting to walk in opposite directions at once. Emil could see that Jimmy's head had been crushed against the rocks.

Emil forced himself to turn away.

"My God. What am I going to say to his parents? He was doing so well, and now for nothing."

It wasn't long before they saw the two medivac choppers in the sky, the whump-whump of their rotor blades growing louder until they hovered overhead. The steep terrain prevented them from landing, but one dropped a cable, and a rescue worker was lowered down. He moved quickly among the crew members, assessing their conditions and identifying those to be evacuated first.

Of the seven remaining crew members, only two escaped injury. The others suffered burns of varying intensity. Three of them had what appeared to be more serious burns. One of them was Jake.

Transport baskets were lowered, and the rescuers began the laborious task of carefully lifting the injured crew members. The choppers then flew them to a staging area set up a few miles away where a medical team provided emergency treatment. The injured were then shuttled by ambulance to a hospital in Missoula.

One chopper circled back to the site to remove Jimmy Maxwell's remains.

The Hotshots and their support teams were now coming on the scene. Firefighters were being dropped by helicopter into areas ahead of the blaze to set up fire breaks. Two planes flew passes over those areas, dumping tons of water and retardants to slow down the fire's progress.

Meanwhile, since the area was within the jurisdiction of the National Park Service, based upon preliminary reports, federal arson investigators were called to the scene. They were there by early evening. First, they cordoned off the location of the truck fires to preserve all possible evidence there. They would meticulously pick through the charred shells of the vehicles the next day. Then, because the surrounding area had largely been spared the effects of the wildfire, they conducted a cursory examination of the ground. They soon discovered several beer cans in a grassy area by the river. Nearby, they found a five-gallon gas can lying in the river shallows. With that evidence and interviews of the survivors the next day, they were on the way to solving the case.

EIGHTY-TWO

PEGGY OPDYKE INVITED STEVE CHADWICK AND ELLEN CONWAY into her conference room for a working lunch. She called out for sandwiches which the three nibbled on as Steve and Ellen reported on the status of their investigations. A few days ago, the paper had run Steve's story recapping the entanglement between Grabel and the Andersons. Legal experts were quoted as to the prospect of a federal prosecution. According to one former prosecutor, the US Attorney would attempt to flip Grabel to get to the Senator.

Chadwick took a sip of water.

"As usual, my sources in Shapiro's office are dead to me. One thing you can say about Larry Shapiro is that he does not tolerate leakers. We've seen recently that public corruption cases have become harder to prove, so my bet is that Shapiro is going to offer Grabel a light sentence for his agreement to testify against Anderson. If he brings Grabel into line, he'll offer Anderson a plea with real jail time, but much less than he might get if he went to trial. Shapiro will give him a little time to chew on it. If he doesn't take the offer, then he'll be indicted, and maybe Brooke Anderson too. I think all this will play out within the next few weeks."

Opdyke looked across at Ellen.

"What have you got on the Cardinal?"

"I've had a little better luck working my insiders in the AG's office. I found out that the office has issued a subpoena to the Cardinal to appear before a state grand jury. If the Cardinal's clean, then it's just a bad day for him and more negative publicity. As if he could handle any more embarrassing headlines. But if Karpinski has anything on him, then we just may have one of the highest-ranking clergy in the American Catholic Church charged with a crime. In that event, like with the Anderson investigation, it will hit the fan soon."

Peggy Opdyke was proud of their work.

"People, it seems we have an embarrassment of journalistic riches. Two consequential stories with significant national interest, possibly breaking at the same time. We need to prepare now. I am reassigning every available staff member to work under your direction. Each of you has to game out possible outcomes, whether it be a plea or an indictment.

"For instance, in the Cardinal's case, what will be the reaction locally and what about the impact on the Church in America? How will the Vatican respond? In the case of the Senator, a companion story should explore his background and his swift fall from grace. Future governor to accused felon in a matter of weeks. We need to work on each of these possible sidebars and others that may come to mind. We won't have time when the storm hits. I know that we operate within a tight editorial budget, but we are on the brink of the two biggest stories this newspaper has ever covered. I sure wish that Hunter were here now to experience it with us."

EIGHTY-THREE

IT WAS OVER A TWO HOUR RIDE TO THE HOSPITAL IN MISSOULA. However, for Jake, there was no awareness of time. As with the others, the EMTs had stripped away his clothes, carefully cutting around those areas of his legs, buttocks, and back where the cloth had adhered to his wounds. Exposed areas were covered with light gauze and an IV was set up to prevent dehydration and possible shock leading to cardiac arrest. Jake lay on his stomach during the trip, lapsing in and out of consciousness. Despite the meds, in his waking moments, the searing pain was nearly overwhelming.

He awoke the next morning in a hospital bed with various tubes connected to him. Someone was standing nearby, checking read-outs on a monitor above him.

"Jake, I'm Doctor Ross. Can you tell me how you feel?"

Jake responded dreamily.

"The pain is real bad."

"I'm sure. If it's any comfort, it would be a lot worse if we didn't have you on a morphine drip. You have suffered second degree burns of most of your back side, with some blistering. But there are a few areas of third degree burns on your legs and buttocks where the heat has burned through both layers of skin. Our biggest concern is infection, so we are applying an antibiotic cream called Silvadene.

"The less serious burns will heal on their own in time, but the deeper ones will require intervention. After a few days, we will consider debriding the areas of dead skin and applying synthetic grafts to promote healing. Meanwhile, we need to keep you as comfortable and still as we can. Hold onto this button. If the pain becomes too much, press it and one of us will be in to adjust your medication."

Of the other crew members injured, after examination, three were treated and discharged. Two others, Nelson Begay and Matt Brunson, were admitted with second degree burns, their conditions less serious than Jake.

Near the end of the day, Emil Brunson stopped in to visit. Jake was a bit more alert and beginning to cope with the constant pain. He asked Emil about the rest of the crew.

"You appear to have gotten the worst of it, Jake."

Emil paused for a moment wondering whether to go on.

"Except for Jimmy."

"What happened to Jimmy?"

"He must have lost it as the fire came on us. When it had passed, I looked for him. His body was on a ledge below the other side of the ridge. Once he got out of his shelter as the fire approached, he didn't have a chance."

Jake struggled to find the words. "So sad. I really liked that boy."

EIGHTY-FOUR

ITHIN A WEEK, THE ARSON INVESTIGATION WAS WRAPPED UP. THE guy behind the counter at the Gas n Go identified J.D. Calloway as purchasing a case of beer around noon the day of the fire. J.D. was well-known as one of Abner's sidekicks, and several crew members recounted the incident with Abner Thornberry at Cupid's some weeks back. An investigator spoke with Jake briefly, and he volunteered that Thornberry had menaced him recently on the drive back from Flathead Lake. Calloway was brought in for questioning. He cracked fifteen minutes into the interview. He laid it all out, hoping somehow to maintain his innocence because he was in Thornberry's truck when Abner and Toby started the fire.

Abner was a little bit tougher nut to crack. His story broke down when investigators showed him the records of his father's purchase of the gas can from a local farm supply dealer and the forensic report matching his truck's tire treads to prints on the access road.

Two weeks later, the US Attorney for the District of Montana indicted Abner Thornberry, Tobias Grimes, and Jefferson Davis Calloway for arson, felony murder, and related lesser offenses.

Meanwhile, the story of the Brunson crew made the national news. It was especially featured in *The Times Union* because of Jake Morris's local connection.

Tess Reilly heard about the fire from one of the paper's reporters who was kind enough to call her before the news got out. When she ended the call, Tess retreated to her bedroom. A half hour later, she went downstairs to find her mother.

She broke the news and then said, "Mom, I've made a decision. I'm going to Montana. I need to see Jake."

EIGHTY-FIVE

ELLEN CONWAY'S SOURCE IN THE AG'S OFFICE GAVE HER A HEADS up. The AG would hold a press conference the next day to announce that Cardinal William Boyle pled guilty to child endangerment. Also, she would reveal that another priest of the Archdiocese had been indicted for alleged child molestation.

Ellen contacted Peggy Opdyke, and a meeting of the team of reporters working on the story was quickly convened. Although they did not yet know the identity of the indicted priest, they were prepared to swing into action regarding the Cardinal. One reporter had already written a bio of him with a special focus upon his tenure in the Archdiocese. Two others identified who they would contact for comment to gauge the public's reaction to the news. Another reporter wrote a piece providing an overview of the priest pedophile crisis in America and around the world. Ellen would attend the press conference and attempt to quiz the Attorney General, with particular attention paid to any sentencing recommendation for the Cardinal.

Ellen arrived at the offices of the Attorney General the next morning two hours before the appointed time. It was a good thing that she did because news of the announcement had spread among the media, and soon there was an overflow crowd spilling out of the briefing room. Ellen had staked out a seat in the front row, the only local reporter to secure premium seating. Looking around, she found herself among reporters she customarily saw on the national news.

There was a heavy tension in the air as Attorney General Mary Beth Karpinski made her way to the podium, flanked on both sides by three of her senior attorneys and the chief of the state police. She paused for a moment before beginning.

Karpinski had been in office for four years now, and she had presided over many such occasions. She had learned to avoid using these press conferences as an opportunity to take a victory lap. The circumstances might vary from case to case, but she was always presiding over a human tragedy, and there was never a reason to gloat.

That was especially true here. Karpinski was sympathetic to the victim, an innocent young girl, as well as her mother and the rest of her family. She felt nothing but disgust toward Father Randall, but the Cardinal was a different story. The AG recognized what it had taken for the Cardinal to come forward and accept responsibility without any preconditions. Although what Boyle had done was wrong, he was also a victim, brought down by his own hubris, and he would now pay a heavy price.

When it was Ellen's chance, she asked the Attorney General if her office had decided on a sentencing recommendation for the Cardinal.

"Our recommendation will await the completion of the Cardinal's pre-sentence report; however, I can tell you now that it will include a request for some period of incarceration."

A hush came over the room as the assembled reporters absorbed the news that, for the first time, an American bishop, a cardinal in fact, a Prince of the Roman Catholic Church, would likely be going to prison.

While she still had the floor, Ellen followed up with another question.

"Madam Attorney General, how does it feel to be in the position of prosecuting someone who many years ago was your high school teacher?"

Mary Beth Karpinski did her best to hide her shock that Ellen Conway had uncovered that part of her past.

"I have good memories of the days when I was taught by then Father Boyle. Nevertheless, I have a job to do on behalf of the people of this state, and I will not let my past association with the Cardinal get in my way."

Shortly after the press conference concluded, Austin Cabot performed his last service as the Cardinal's private secretary. At the Cardinal's request, he called Ellen Conway and told her he would be emailing her a statement from the Cardinal, including his apology to the child and her mother and to the people of the Archdiocese. When pressed by Ellen, Austin informed her that the Cardinal would not be available for an interview, nor would he have any further public statement. Ellen asked about the Cardinal's whereabouts, but Austin simply replied that he was in seclusion.

Before his resignation took effect, as his last official act, Cardinal Boyle arranged for his assistant to be re-assigned as pastor of a poor, inner-city parish. Austin could not have been more grateful.

EIGHTY-SIX

Before heading to work that night, Tess called her manager and asked if she could have the next four nights off. With his approval, she arranged for other bartenders to cover her shift. Next, she contacted her two sisters-in-law to help Mary with the boys while she was away. Then she booked a flight to Missoula for the next day, leaving at 9:40am ET with a stopover in Denver. With luck, she would arrive in Missoula around 4:30pm MT. Finally, after a few misfires, she was able to contact Emil Brunson. He told her about Jake's current condition. He had just undergone a procedure to remove dead skin at two burn sites and have synthetic grafts placed in those areas.

"We'll make this a surprise. Jake's gonna be out of it pretty much for the next day or so anyway. I'll arrange for someone to pick you up at the airport."

The next morning, Tess got the boys up and made them breakfast. While they were eating, she casually explained to them that she would be away for a few days to visit a sick friend and that Aunt Carol and Aunt Dottie would be helping Gram out. Neither one of them seemed concerned enough to stop working on their cereal.

Mary drove her to the airport. On the way, she asked Tess what she thought might come of her visit.

"I don't know, Mom. I just know I have to do this. I've had almost six months to think about my breakup with Jake. I've also thought a lot about Paul and how he left the boys and me. It's five years since I threw him out and three since his death. The boys were young enough that only Thomas has any memory of his father. Seems like Thomas has recovered well, but I don't think I have. You saw it all. Paul nearly destroyed me. In fact, for a while, I thought he had. I vowed that I would never let anyone else do what Paul did to me. I'd never be hurt like that again. But since Jake left, I've come to understand that the pain I feel after sending him away is worse than the worry that he might let me down again. Does that make any sense?"

"It makes a lot of sense. Your father let me down many times during our marriage, and I suppose I did that to him on occasion. But I wouldn't trade our life together for anything in this world."

"Mom, I don't know how Jake feels now. I don't know if he's moved on, or whether he's found someone. What I do know is that by going out there, I will finally get over the fear that Paul left me with. He will no longer control my life. Whatever happens."

Tess arrived in Missoula on time. She was halfway down the escalator to the baggage claim area when she saw an attractive woman about her age looking up toward her. She held a cardboard sign reading, "Tess Reilly."

Tess walked up to her. "I'm Tess Reilly."

The woman stuck out her hand.

"It's so good to meet you. I'm Lisbeth Mueller, Emil Brunson's sister-in-law. But just call me Beth. I'm here to take you to Jake."

As they drove out of the airport, Beth glanced across at Tess. She felt her unease, knowing Tess might be wondering what this stranger is doing here and her possible connection to Jake. It would be too awkward to broach the subject now, so Beth resorted to casual conversation.

"How was your flight?"

"Wearisome, but it could have been worse. We were delayed leaving, so I had to race for my connecting flight in Denver. As a kid, I remember being excited the few times I flew with my family. But today it's an ordeal."

Tess told Beth she had gotten a report on Jake yesterday. She asked if there was any change.

"Not much. The operation yesterday to debride the two worst burns seems to have gone well. The grafts will accelerate the healing process. Meanwhile, they are concerned about the possibility of infection, so, in addition to the other tubes they've set up, Jake is receiving antibiotics intravenously. Anybody visiting him must wear a mask and other protective gear."

"How are the others doing?"

"Nelson Begay and Matt Brunson were the only other crew members hospitalized, but they were released yesterday. The others are recovering quickly. You probably know of the death of Jimmy Maxwell though."

"I did read about him. It must be awful."

"Emil and his dad are close friends. Emil and Ingrid have been over at the Maxwells much of the past few days. Jimmy was their only son. He had some problems recently, but Emil had brought him on the crew, hoping the experience would help him. Emil's taking his death especially hard.

Meanwhile, we've all been looking in on Jake every day. You know Jake, so you can appreciate that he has found a place for himself here. He came as an outsider some months ago, and we were a little wary because he would be reporting on his time with us. But we're all past that now."

Tess looked across at Beth, continuing privately to assess her motives. "Seems like Jake has made some good friends out here."

Later, Tess and Beth walked into Jake's hospital room, clothed in protective gear. He had been placed on his side facing the window.

Beth called to him. "Jake, I've brought you a special guest today."

Beth gestured for Tess to move to the bedside. Jake looked up and seemed to be confused for a moment. Then it registered with him.

A smile formed and he murmured groggily, "Tess."

Beth stepped back and quietly left the room.

"Jake, I'm so sorry for what has happened."

"I am too."

"I mean about your injury. Well, really that and more."

"I know."

"Let's not talk now. You need to rest. We'll have time."

Jake nodded and closed his eyes. The smile remained until he drifted off. Tess sat with him for another hour until medical staff arrived to rebandage Jake's burn sites. Tess blew Jake a kiss.

"I'll be back to see you tomorrow. Meanwhile, try to rest."

Tess found Beth in the waiting area.

"Beth, I forgot to ask you. Do you have any recommendation for a motel near the hospital?"

"You won't need a motel room. You're going to stay with me while you're here. I won't take no for an answer."

The drive north to Schuyler gave them an opportunity to talk. Gradually, Tess became more relaxed with Beth. She was beginning to like her.

When they arrived home, Beth showed Tess her bedroom, and while Tess unpacked and freshened up, Beth opened a bottle of wine. Tess then rejoined her in the kitchen. Beth offered her a glass and said, "I hope you like white?"

"I like every color of wine."

"I also hope you like pot roast. I've had it in the slow cooker all day."

"It sounds delicious. Can I help?"

"You could set the table. The flatware is in that first cabinet drawer."

After dinner, the two settled in the living room, Tess on the couch and Beth nearby on a lounge chair.

"Tess, I want to tell you something, and I am not sure how to say it. I guess I should just come out with it. I had a crush on Jake, but before anything might get started, he made it clear that there was only one woman he was interested in. You. He didn't share much with me, but it is clear he's hoping that there is still a future for him with you. Jake and I have become good friends. Obviously, I hardly know you, and I don't want to interfere. But I also hope that there is a chance for you two."

"Beth, thank you. You've been so kind. Let me just say that I wouldn't be here if I didn't hope for the same thing."

The next morning, Beth told Tess that she would be occupied all day preparing for Jimmy Maxwell's funeral. After the service, the Brunsons were having the mourners back to their house for lunch, and Beth had to get over there to help Ingrid with the preparations.

Beth and Tess drove together to the Brunsons, and Beth introduced Tess to Emil and Ingrid. Then, Beth handed Tess the keys to her car.

"As you saw yesterday, it's a straight shot to Missoula and the hospital. Give Jake our love. See you back at the house tonight."

Tess was exhausted when she got back from the hospital, and she drifted off to sleep before Beth returned. When Tess awoke the next morning, Beth was already gone. She had left a note in the kitchen next to a very tempting blueberry muffin.

"K-cups are in the cabinet above the coffee machine. There's fruit and yogurt in the refrigerator. The car's yours again today. Hope Jake and you have a good day. See you back here tonight."

Tess resisted the urge to gawk at the sights on her trip south to Missoula. From her experience so far, she had come to appreciate the attraction of living in western Montana, except for those sub-zero winter mornings she had heard about. Off to the right, she could see what looked like a mother elk with her calf, both wallowing in the shallows of a river. To the left were successive waves of mountain ridges. In between, sloping pastures contained herds of cattle and fields under cultivation. In the distance rose jagged snow-covered peaks. Her attention was drawn to the wide expanse of Flathead Lake up ahead when, suddenly, the woosh of a northbound eighteen-wheeler caused her to re-direct her attention to the road ahead.

As Tess walked into Jake's room, she could see that he was more alert than the day before. The attendants had moved him onto his side, and he greeted her as she came through the door.

"So that's not an apparition I saw here yesterday."

"No, it's not. It's your friendly bartender from Toppers. From the look on your face and the absence of several tubes I saw yesterday, it looks like you've made some progress, my boy." Jake shrugged his shoulders.

"With another few weeks of healing and rehab, I might be eligible for an honorable discharge. After that, there will be some weeks of outpatient physical therapy. The general idea is to maintain joint and muscle flexibility and minimize contraction of scar tissue. I've already started the therapy. I suggest you don't stick around during one of those sessions or when they change my dressings. They say I'm not too pleasant then."

Over the course of the morning, Jake asked about the boys and Mary. He wondered how Tess was handling the demands of her job, juggling it with school and the boys at home.

Tess wanted to know about his experience on the crew, what the work's been like, and how he had been treated by the locals. She avoided any discussion of the day of the fire.

A few times, Jake started to talk about their breakup, but Tess put a stop to it.

"Jake, as far as I'm concerned, there's nothing to say except that I was wrong. If it wasn't the girl at the strip club, it would have been something else. I was afraid that things wouldn't work out between us, so I had to find some excuse to bring it to an end. I just couldn't accept the risk of being unhappy, so I did something to guarantee it. Does that make any sense?"

Jake nodded. "Well, it worked. Now we're both miserable."

Tess smiled, not knowing what else to say. Her awkwardness was interrupted by the arrival of two nurses, there to change Jake's dressings.

"Just once, I would appreciate you ladies being behind schedule. Tess, this hit team will be a while with me. Why not get some lunch and check on me in an hour or so?"

Tess returned about 2:00. Jake was out cold, obviously worn out. He awoke about an hour later. Tess was absorbed in something she was reading so Jake took the opportunity to observe her for a few moments before interrupting the moment.

"Hi. I guess they had their will with me again. What's that you're reading?"

"Oh, it's a book of Irish blessings that speak to various moments in life. I've found it helpful these last months."

"Sounds interesting. I'll take an Irish blessing over a curse any day. Try one on me."

"This one's called 'For Healing.'"

When Tess finished reading, Jake lay there, silently looking out the window toward the distant mountain range.

"That's wonderful, Tess. I'd like to read more."

"How about if I leave it here with you. I can get it tomorrow. Meanwhile, I'd better get back. The Brunsons invited Beth and me to dinner. I tried to beg off because of all they've been dealing with, but they wouldn't listen. I would think they'd need some time alone after what's happened, but they insisted on having me over."

Jake reached out his hand for Tess.

"Look forward to tomorrow."

It was late afternoon when Tess got back to the Brunson house. The luncheon guests had left, and Emil and a few of the other crew members were loading up tables and chairs for return to the rental company. Ingrid was cleaning up the mess in the kitchen with help from Sarah and Beth. Tess pitched in.

When the work was done, the adults gathered on the front porch. Ingrid handed Tess a plateful of leftovers.

"I thought you'd be hungry."

Emil grabbed a cold beer and served wine to the ladies. As they sat on the front porch, Tess reported on Jake's progress and asked about Jimmy Maxwell's funeral.

Emil sighed and took a sip of beer.

"Well, it went about as well as could be expected. Reverend Thompson selected a few uplifting Scripture readings and did as much as he could to offer comfort to the family. About a hundred family and friends were there to lend their support."

"And Emil offered a eulogy for Jimmy," Ingrid added.

"I have certainly not been a stranger to death in my life but speaking about Jimmy today was as tough a thing as I ever had to do. Pete and Sally were grateful to hear about how well their son performed on the crew and how we had come to rely upon him after his earlier setbacks, but I still can't help feeling that Jimmy would be alive today if I hadn't offered him a job.

But then my faith tells me that God has a plan for each of us. Although we will never know why in this world, this was God's plan for Jimmy."

Ingrid turned to Tess. "Tell us what you will be going back to."

"Chaos."

Tess talked about Thomas and Mikey, her mom, her job, and her ambition to be a teacher. She left out her relationship with Jake, but she got the sense that she didn't need to go into that. Whatever Beth may have shared with the others, they had apparently figured that part out already.

"I want to thank all of you for making me feel at home, especially at this time."

Emil responded with a gentle smile. "The Gospel of Matthew encourages us to welcome the stranger. That's how we live. It was easy in Jake's case, and you fit in pretty well yourself."

Beth asked Emil about his plans for the business.

"Well, I think we're going to pull out of this, but it's going to take time. I'm glad I paid all those insurance premiums over the years though. We'll be able to replace just about all the lost vehicles and equipment, and I'll be able to draw on business interruption insurance. In addition, the folks at the Forest Service have been good to us. They are paying me for all the completed work on the ridge, and they've been able to amend our contract to have us clear away all the debris from the fire. Fortunately, except for Jake, the other survivors have recovered, so none of my boys will miss a paycheck. But, I will be glad when I don't have to spend much of my day talking to lawyers, accountants, and insurance people."

Tess could see the exhaustion in their eyes.

"Beth, tomorrow is my last day with Jake before I leave. Would you mind if we head back to your place early?"

Beth seemed relieved. "Sure. I also have a busy day getting my school room ready for the beginning of class next week. Let's head out."

As they stood up, Emil got in the last word. "Tess, despite the circumstances, it's been good to meet you. We won't have a chance to see you again before you leave, but we want you to know that we hope you visit with us again, whether you bring Jake along or not."

The next morning, Beth drove Tess down to the hospital, stopped in to visit Jake for a few minutes, and then excused herself.

"I'll be back to pick you up at five."

Hospital visits can take on a tedium of their own, but Jake and Tess filled their time together that day with conversation that covered parts of their lives not shared in their previous times together. Tess could see that Jake had more energy than when she first visited him. He reported that they planned to discharge him the following week and he would be able to stay with the Brunsons for the weeks of scheduled outpatient therapy ahead. After that, he expected he would be ready to travel back East. He was anxious to finish his story for the magazine.

Around five, there was a knock at the door. Somehow, four of his crew-mates had gotten past security for a visit. Each of them took the opportunity to poke fun at Jake Rabbit. When it was Nelson Begay's turn, he opened his hand to reveal a familiar object, the rabbit's foot he had given Jake.

"Jake, I found this near your bunk. Now, remember to carry this with you next time."

Jake smiled and reclaimed his good luck charm.

Soon Beth returned and it was time for Tess to leave. The boys said goodbye, and Beth stepped out to leave the two of them alone for a few moments.

"Tess, there is no way for me to say how much your visit has meant to me. Please tell your mom and the boys I asked for them. When I get back home, I hope we can see one another."

Tess leaned over and kissed Jake's forehead.

"I hope so too."

After Tess left, Jake soon fell off to sleep, but when he awoke, he saw that Tess had left her book. When he opened it, a note fell out. "Jake, get well and come home as soon as you can. Meanwhile, enjoy reading these blessings and sharing them. Return it when you get back. If it's not in my hands in two months, I will charge a late fee."

EIGHTY-SEVEN

EN ANDERSON'S FRIDAY MORNING BEGAN WITH A VISIT TO HIS attorney's office. Cynthia Everett agreed to meet with him at 7:00 a.m. Ben requested that time because of an exaggerated concern that his visit might attract media attention. Everett represented many high-profile clients so she was used to accommodating requests which others might dismiss as baseless paranoia.

After offering Ben a coffee, Everett escorted him into her office and quickly got to the point of their meeting.

"Senator, I have received an offer from the US Attorney which I need to discuss with you. The government is prepared to recommend to the court a sentence of forty-eight months' incarceration in return for your resignation from office and a plea of guilty to one count each of conspiracy to commit bribery under the Hobbs Act and wire fraud. Before you react, let me lay out your options."

"If we reject the offer, the case will not go to trial for several months. During that time, we will file discovery requests to attempt to learn every-thing that Larry Shapiro has uncovered. We will likely engage an investiga-tor of our own to probe any weaknesses in the prosecution's case. There also may be the need to file certain pre-trial motions. I know that you and your family have already had to deal with the pressures of public scrutiny, but you can expect it to intensify leading up to the date of trial and continuing for several months afterward, whatever the outcome."

"Now, let me talk a bit about the merits of the government's case, as we know it so far. To prove a violation of the Hobbs Act, the US Attorney must show beyond a reasonable doubt that you performed an official act on behalf of Max Grabel in return for financial and other benefits that he otherwise would not have supplied you and your wife."

"As we've discussed before, some of the efforts you undertook on Grabel's behalf can be explained away as things that you would have done on behalf of any other constituent. But at least one is more problematic, your action as chair of the Health and Institutions Committee to stop the nursing home investigation."

"Although our pre-trial work may uncover additional defenses, we don't have the benefit of that now. At this point, it seems that our best hope is to attempt to show that your close friendship with Grabel was the motivation for his largesse. I am sure that Grabel has cut a deal with the feds and will testify to the contrary. The jury will learn about that arrangement, but they will be left to choose between believing you and your wife or Max Grabel. Facts such as your shared vacations could support the conclusion that you were close friends. Or it could be viewed as part of a deliberate effort to influence the exercise of your official duties."

"It is hard to assess how Grabel's involvement with your wife will be judged; however, you and your family will need to prepare yourselves for testimony of an extra-marital encounter. There is no way to predict how all of this might shake out, except that, as you know well as a practicing attorney, the burden of proof is on your side."

"If the jury finds in your favor, it's over. I can't begin to predict the impact of a finding of not guilty on your political career, or even the effect upon your standing as a member of the bar, but you will be a free man otherwise."

"Another possible outcome is a mistrial because the jury has failed to reach a unanimous verdict. In that case, the bar against double jeopardy doesn't apply, so the feds could choose to retry the case. However, because of the inordinate expense and the appearance that the government's case had become a persecution, that's doubtful. I've known Larry Shapiro a long time, and I don't think he would go down that road."

"If the jury finds against you though, subject to any limited prospect of a post-judgment appeal on legal grounds, you face a sentence of up to twenty years in prison. That is the limit, but realistically, you would likely face a sentence in the range of ten years."

"At this point, I need to interpose a practical consideration. When you initially retained me, you agreed to an initial payment of fifty thousand dollars. You supplied that, and obviously a part of that is already expended. If you decide to go to trial, I will require an additional retainer of three hundred thousand dollars which will be non-refundable, regardless of the outcome of the case."

"Now, let's talk for a moment about what will happen if you decide to take the government's offer. First, as a condition, we will extract a commitment that the US Attorney will decline to prosecute your wife. I don't think that is a practical possibility, whatever happens to you, but we will want to pin it down. Next, we will negotiate the minimum fine that can be imposed under the circumstances. Then, we will try to arrange for your assignment to a federal facility which is the least restrictive and most convenient for family visitation. And, of course, you will be required to resign your office and will most certainly be disqualified from any right to a public pension. Do you have any questions at this point?"

Ben just shook his head. He hadn't heard anything unexpected, but just having all of it explained by Cynthia Everett had him reeling at the enormity of the decision before him and the consequences for him and his family. Ben's face was flushed, his palms were wet, and he was glad that he had skipped breakfast.

"Well, I know that you will want to discuss this with your wife, and perhaps others, but you should know that we are now on the clock. I have committed to provide the US Attorney with our response by the close of business next Friday. Call me at any time if you have further questions. Otherwise, I will expect to hear from you by Friday morning."

Ben somehow made it to work, operating on autopilot. Thankfully, none of the staff had arrived yet. He immediately walked into his office and shut the door. Each day had gotten harder to get through since the first disclosure in *The Times Union*. Some days he came close to drafting his resignation letter, but he knew that he would have to stay in office if he were to decide to fight. Right now, he didn't know what he would do, except that he had to talk it over tonight with Brooke.

Meanwhile, he would do his best to get through the day. The worst would be the need to attend a farewell lunch for a summer intern, a young woman who had become close with his former chief of staff, Meg Holland. Meg was long gone and now managed Nick Fazio's campaign for governor. But Ben was pretty sure she was keeping tabs on him through the intern. Maybe Meg even told her about their personal involvement. Ben stopped himself. He had to put it out of his mind. It didn't matter now.

As Ben pulled into his garage to begin the weekend, he looked through the rearview mirror, watched the electric door come down, and half-expected to see a news reporter follow him inside. He sat behind the wheel and welcomed the silence, only interrupted by the muffled thump of the washing machine in rinse cycle upstairs. As he had all day, his mind played the continuous loop of advice offered by his defense counsel that morning. Once again, he asked himself the same questions.

What will happen to Brooke and the kids if I go to prison? Where will they get the money to survive? Maybe, his marriage could survive a four-year stretch with him away, but what if it's a decade? Would Brooke want a divorce?

If so, he wouldn't blame her. As for the kids, he didn't have much of a relationship with them, especially these days. Would there be any chance for one if I went away? Would the feds decide to go after Brooke also? How do I come up with the money if I decide to fight?

Ben forced himself to shut it down, if only for a few moments. He felt the stabbing pain in his lower back, a condition that had worsened recently. He reached into his jacket pocket and removed a pill from a small vial. Oxycodone prescribed by his orthopedist. The thought of turning the engine back on and bringing it all to a close flashed through his mind, but he couldn't do that to Brooke and the kids. He slowly exited the car and opened the door to the kitchen where Brooke was waiting for him.

"Ben, you look exhausted. Why don't you go upstairs and take a shower. Then, come down and join me for a glass of wine."

EIGHTY-EIGHT

WHILE BEN'S ATTORNEY HAD BEEN DISCUSSING HIS LEGAL OPTIONS that morning, Brooke awoke remembering a long discussion with Ben the night before. As she stood at the kitchen counter waiting for her coffee to brew, she was surprised by the lightness of her mood. She felt exhilarated, and she couldn't quite figure out why. Both she and Ben had been publicly humiliated. Her husband faced the prospect of a long prison term. She and the kids might be left to struggle financially, possibly being thrown out of their home and the kids' college plans placed in doubt.

So why did she feel so good? Suddenly, it came to her. Sometime during their encounter last night, Brooke discovered that she was still in love with her husband.

It could have turned out otherwise, but neither of them chose to blame the other. There were no recriminations. They were reunited by grief. For the first time in a long while, perhaps ever, Ben was not in control. He was struggling to accept that he was no longer a powerful man. And he seemed to be relieved. For her part, Brooke was coming to terms with her reduced social status. They both confessed their unfaithfulness, offering no justification for it. Although Ben was likely the only one facing legal judgment, they were both equally culpable. Finally exhausted, they lay together, and Ben had reached out to touch Brooke's hand. For now, that moment would suffice.

EIGHTY-NINE

RESH FROM HIS SHOWER, BEN CAME INTO THE KITCHEN AND Brooke greeted him with a light kiss and a glass of merlot. They knew that they had some hard choices to make, but they agreed to postpone that discussion until after dinner.

Brooke prepared one of Ben's favorite dishes, meatloaf and mac and cheese. During the meal, they did their best to divert one another with small talk, but not very successfully. After the table was cleared and the dishes stacked in the dishwasher, Brooke poured them both a refill, and they sat down together at the kitchen table.

Ben methodically laid out Cynthia Everett's advice. Although not a lawyer, none of it was a surprise to Brooke. When he finished, Brooke was quick to offer her opinion.

"I think we should fight."

Ben was shocked by the conviction in her voice.

"What's your theory?"

"From what I understand, the prosecution rests on the conclusion that what you did for Grabel was a *quid pro quo* for the benefits both of us received from him. But it's not that simple. We both know how persuasive Grabel can be. Although there were moments when the relationships were purely transactional, there were other times when each of us genuinely believed that Max was doing these things because he was our friend."

"And we both know how huge his ego is. I can't imagine he could resist the desire to testify about his success in gulling both of us. I admit that the truth cuts both ways, but as you well know, the government's burden is to show evidence beyond a reasonable doubt that each of us offered Grabel our services, if you will, for a price. I am not sure myself of the answer to that question, but I bet there are prospective jurors out there who might be equally in doubt."

Ben was impressed but not totally convinced.

"What if they are not on our jury panel? What happens if we lose, and I go away for ten years or more?"

Brooke was quick to reply.

"I don't think that it will happen, but if it does, we'll get through it somehow."

"Will we?"

"Nothing is certain in life, but sometime last night, I remembered why I married you. My recent behavior would not inspire confidence, but if you're found guilty, I will stay with you."

"What about the kids?"

"It's already been hard on them. They are tough though, and they have the benefit of youth. We need to make this decision for ourselves."

"Where can we get the money to pay the legal fees?"

Brooke had that figured out as well. "I've already talked to my parents. I don't need to tell you that they have not been your biggest fans over the years, but they know how important this is to me. They would offer us a loan to cover all of it, and, at worst, it just comes out of my inheritance."

"Just one more question. Can you handle sitting in a witness chair and having our lives portrayed in the tawdriest way possible? What has come out so far is nothing like what you should expect on cross-examination."

"Our lives really have been tawdry recently. It will be excruciating for all that to play out. I will feel terrible, especially because of what it will do to the kids and my parents. But I have already accepted my own guilt, morally and ethically. I believe I can face up to admitting it publicly."

They had moved from the kitchen to the TV room and settled together on the couch. Ben had moved on to scotch, while Brooke continued to sip her wine. They were both exhausted. Brooke dropped her head on Ben's shoulder, and he cradled her in his arms. They sat in silence for perhaps ten minutes, but it could have been longer.

Finally, Brooke announced she was heading up to bed. She turned toward Ben, and he leaned down to kiss her on the forehead. Brooke looked up, and they shared a lingering kiss, sealing their truce.

As she stood and turned toward the stairs, she reminded Ben not to make it an all-nighter on the couch.

"I promise. I'll just tune in the ball game for a few innings."

When Brooke awoke the next morning, she was not surprised to find the other side of the bed empty. Ben had taken to sleeping on the couch lately, especially because of the recurrence of his chronic back pain.

As she walked down the stairs, she first noticed the sound of the TV.

Ben was lying on the couch, facing away from her. On the coffee table was a half-empty bottle of scotch and an open vial of pills.

Brooke shook Ben softly but got no response. Her shaking became more insistent. Finally, she pulled Ben over. His eyes were closed, and he was unresponsive, his skin pale and cool to the touch.

She quickly called 911 and then placed her palms down and began to press hard on Ben's chest. After a few moments, seeing no response, Brooke arched Ben's head back, opened his mouth, and attempted to breathe life into his lungs.

Brooke continued her efforts while she waited for the emergency response. The EMTs were there in fifteen minutes. They quickly placed defibrillator paddles on Ben's chest, hoping to shock him back to life. After several attempts, it was apparent that their efforts were futile. Ben Anderson was gone.

NINETY

Beth Mueller sat in her car, her eyes fixed on the hospital portico. After two weeks of treatment and physical therapy, Jake was being discharged. But he would need a few more weeks of healing before he would be ready for travel back East. The Brunsons and Beth had talked about Jake's living arrangements in the interim. Ingrid and Beth together could look to Jake's daily needs, including wound cleansing and travel for therapy and doctor visits.

The delicate question was where Jake should stay during that time. Emil and Ingrid were aware of the earlier dynamic between Beth and Jake. They didn't want to do anything that might undermine the tentative reconciliation they had witnessed between Jake and Tess. Yet, there wasn't any good arrangement for Jake in the Brunson household. Jake would have to stay for a short time at Beth's place. There was no other option.

During the day, Ingrid would spell Beth as Jake's caregiver when Beth was teaching school. Then Beth would take it from there. She worried about that as she waited for Jake to be brought down. Would being together in the same house trigger something between them? Even if it didn't, would Tess assume that it had?

Beth had prudently called Tess the night before to advise her of the need for the arrangement. Tess seemed to understand. But everything could change in a moment, and Beth was torn. She knew what she ought to do, but part of her wanted something else.

Beth pulled up to the entrance as a hospital attendant wheeled Jake out the door. The attendant opened the passenger door and eased Jake into the seat. He was pale and a bit thinner. He leaned over and gave Beth a kiss on the cheek.

"It is so good to be out of there. Thanks so much for helping me break loose."

"How are you feeling, Jake?"

"A bit weak and a little unsure on my feet. I have a cane, but I try not to use it. The burns are mostly healed but I need to exercise the muscles in the back of my thighs. If I stick with my exercises, I should be back to normal soon. Except the docs have also scheduled some counselling sessions to deal with the psychological effects."

Beth pulled into traffic and then broke the news.

"Between Ingrid and myself, we'll get you to your appointments. Meanwhile, for the next few weeks, I'm afraid you're going to have to put up with my cooking most of the time. Because of the cramped quarters at the Brunsons, you'll be bunking at my place until you're ready to travel."

"I am grateful for all you've done for me, Beth. You and the Brunsons."

"It's been our pleasure. In fact, you've become almost like Emil's younger brother over these last months. Consider us family."

It was a warm afternoon, and Beth had the car windows open as they traveled north to Schuyler. She was in mid-sentence when she looked across and found that Jake had nodded off. Sometime later, the rushing sound of a southbound truck awakened him.

As they passed Flathead Lake to the east, the setting sun cast a golden shimmer across its surface. Beth saw something in Jake's eyes, and she suspected he was thinking of the idyllic Sunday they had shared there just a few months ago.

Their silence was unbroken until they reached the outskirts of Schuyler.

"Jake, we need to stop at the Brunsons so that you can pick up the things you'll need during your stay at my place. Ingrid has prepared a light supper for us."

Jake reluctantly accepted Beth's help getting out of the car, but he was able to make his own way across the grass and up the stairs of the Brunson home, his steps tentative while using the cane for support.

Ingrid greeted him at the door with a hug.

"Jake, it's so good to have you back with us again. Emil is finishing up in the office and should join us in a few minutes. He'll be happy to see you."

The three of them were seated at the kitchen table when Emil came in a few minutes later. He placed his hand on Jake's shoulder, giving it a gentle squeeze.

"Maybe I can get a little more work out of you before you head out."

Jake and Beth had little to say on the way home. It was as if there were a third person with them. Whatever prospects they might have had as a couple, Tess's visit had changed all that. When they got inside, Beth helped Jake carry his things into the spare bedroom.

"If you need anything during the night, Jake, just yell out and I'll be there. Otherwise, sleep well." Jake thanked her and turned hesitantly to give her a hug, but she was gone.

When Jake awoke, he discovered that Beth had already left for school. She left a note on the kitchen table, telling him where he could find food for breakfast and advising that Ingrid would be by to pick him up at noon.

When Jake finished breakfast, he shuffled back into his bedroom and set up his laptop. As he did each day, he checked *The Times Union* website. Its headline read, "State Senator Ben Anderson Dead at Fifty-Two."

Jake stared at the screen in disbelief for a few moments before reading the accompanying story. No cause of death was given although an autopsy had been ordered. The story recounted Anderson's political career with a particular focus upon his pending criminal investigation.

Jake shut down the computer. He looked out his window at a bright September morning and reflected on the path his life had taken. It was about a year ago that he chose to delve into Ben Anderson's involvement with Max Grabel. Subsequent events showed that he was onto something, but his abrupt decision to quit the paper had brought an end to his investigation. Although Jake had suspected the worst about Hunter when Jake stalked out of *The Times Union*, Hunter had restarted the investigation and shepherded it to its conclusion. Hunter must have known something then that caused him to hesitate about publishing the story. But now both Hunter and Anderson were dead, and he supposed that he would never know the truth behind it.

Ingrid arrived on schedule.

"I thought you might be willing to help me in the office this afternoon, Jake, but before we go, let me draw on my skills as a former nurse and dress your bandages."

Jake changed into a pair of gym shorts and lay across his bed as Ingrid removed the wraps on his back thighs, cleaned the areas and applied new dressings.

As she worked, Jake asked about her nursing experience.

"I was a navy nurse for six years. That's how I met Emil. I was stationed at the Landstuhl Medical Center in Germany. Emil had been shot up pretty bad in Iraq, and he was sent to Landstuhl for treatment. He was there for six weeks. After he was shipped back home, we kept in touch. One thing led to another, and this Wisconsin girl wound up in Big Sky Country."

Ingrid finished her work.

"How's it feel now?"

"Feels fine."

"Good. While you're here, I'll take over this job. It's outside Beth's area of expertise anyway."

Jake spent the afternoon helping Ingrid wade through the mountain of correspondence in the aftermath of the wildfire, including such things as workers compensation forms and insurance reports..

He quickly came to understand the Brunsons' additional burden as they tried to keep the business alive. Emil was out on the range with the crew clearing dead trees and other timber slash to promote regrowth. That emergency contract with the Forest Service and a few smaller jobs were keeping the company afloat for the moment as they waited for the insurance claims to be processed.

Beth arrived about five after completing her teaching day, and Emil followed a bit later. As Ingrid and Beth retreated to the kitchen to prepare dinner, Jake and Emil shared a beer on the porch.

"How's the crew, Emil?"

"Well, we're down to five now that Matt has gone off to college. It's enough for what we're doing now."

"I mean how are they dealing with…things."

"As best we all can. They're pretty well healed physically. But I've seen the effects of PTSD before, and they're all suffering now."

Emil got up to get another round, obviously wanting to change the subject. When he returned, he inquired about Jake's day.

"Well, it started off with a shock. Remember, I told you about the story I was working on before I came out here?"

"You mean the political investigation that got you fired?"

"No. The investigation that prompted me to quit. Well, I learned that the state senator at the heart of that story died suddenly, just as he was apparently about to be indicted."

"Any connection?"

"Don't know. But it's a tragedy either way."

"If I recall, you told me that your former boss also passed away recently."

"Yes. Under totally different circumstances. But the upshot is that I'll never know why my boss hesitated to run my story."

"Jake, maybe it's better that you don't know. Some things in life should be left alone."

"Maybe that's what Hunter Dane thought."

Jake took a sip, reflecting on the wisdom of that for a moment.

His hand swept the vista before them. "I'm going to miss all this. I know that I have a good story to tell about this experience when I get back East, and you can be sure I'll do right by all of you."

"I have no doubt about that. Jake, you've made your mark out here. If you ever get tired of civilization, you'll always be welcome among us."

"Thanks, Emil. I came out here to learn about men in the timber business. Men with the most dangerous occupation in America today. Boy, did that prove to be true. But I wound up learning a helluva lot more."

In the week remaining, Jake's days took on a certain urgency. In addition to his final therapy sessions and helping in the office with Ingrid, Jake had more work to do on his story. With the national press coverage of the wildfire, his editor encouraged him to extend the scope of his article to cover that incident. Jake scheduled sessions with Emil and the crew members to record their accounts of that fateful day, and he expanded his story to encompass the tragedy. For now, Jake just wanted to get it all down. He would do the final editing when he got back East.

Meanwhile, Jake and Beth maintained a friendly distance although it was difficult in her small cottage. Beth was away at school most days, but the evenings brought them together. After sharing dinner, Jake would retreat to his room under the guise that he needed to work on his article. All true, but not his real reason. He was afraid to share with Beth his true feelings toward her. Jake was still attracted to Beth, but he knew now that Tess was the one for him. Beth deserved to hear it from him, but Jake was afraid that it might come out the wrong way, especially if he opened up to her while they were alone together at her place. He promised himself that he would find an opportunity before he flew out.

The Brunson's held a farewell party for Jake on his last night. All his fellow crew members were there along with their partners. As usual, Beth assisted Ingrid with the preparations. After the meal, each of the men took the opportunity to offer a few words about him. Iz Jackson said it best.

"Jake, when you came out here, we didn't know what to expect. You were a stranger. We all thought we had nothing in common with you. But all that's changed now. You are one of us."

As always, Emil had the last word. "Let's all raise a glass to Jake. Jake, remember that you will always have a home with us. Whatever lies ahead, we hope that you'll find your way back here someday."

Beth took the next day off so that she could drive Jake to the airport. They both were unusually quiet on the way into Missoula.

When they got there, Jake asked Beth if she could pull over into a waiting area for a few minutes. He had something to tell her.

"Beth, I don't quite know how to say this, but I hope it comes out right. When I arrived here, I was pretty much a broken man. I had failed in my responsibilities as a journalist, and I had let a person whom I loved slip away. You and the others patched me back together. I learned about making commitments and then keeping them. I saw in Emil and Ingrid a marriage that can stand up against life's toughest challenges. I saw the same spirit in you. But then a tragedy brought with it the opportunity for me to have a second chance with Tess. And I knew I had to take it. Who knows how things might have turned out otherwise? I will always remember you, Beth, and I wish you all the happiness that you deserve."

Beth was fighting back tears, and she knew she would have to be brief.

"You will always have a place in my heart, Jake. I wish you and Tess a wonderful life together, and I hope that you both will come back to visit someday."

She helped Jake with his baggage and then they stood together in the terminal for a moment. They embraced, and then Beth turned and walked back to her car. Jake lingered for a moment to watch her drive away.

NINETY-ONE

TESS WAITED IN THE QUEUE AT THE BAGGAGE CAROUSEL AND watched the few remaining passengers come down the escalator. Jake was next to last. He was moving a bit slowly but was obviously much stronger than when she last saw him. She ran to him and held him close.

They kissed, and he whispered, "I'm so happy to be back home…with you."

On the drive to Jake's apartment, they tripped over their words, seeking to overcome their anxiety for what lay ahead. It was like two people whose dance has been interrupted. When the music starts again, where does the guy place his hands? Do they start off again cheek to cheek or do they work up to it? Whatever this dance was going to be, Jake was pretty sure it was going to be a ladies' choice.

Inquiries about Mary and the boys and questions about Montana were interspersed with trivia intended to fill a void until they had a chance to talk about the future. It seemed like love, a love tested by time, distance and near disaster. But now the hard work lay ahead, the living of everyday life together. Both had to decide what they were willing to give up for it to work. Those questions would not be answered quickly or easily. But they were ready to try.

Tess had not seen Jake's place before. She was not impressed. The disorder that Jake had left was now caked with several months of dust.

"Jake, how could you live like this? I'll leave you to wallow in this mess for now. You need your rest, and I've got to get to work. But I'll be back tomorrow morning, and when I'm done, you won't recognize the place."

Jake slowly regained consciousness the next morning, responding tentatively to the unaccustomed sound of his apartment's security system. He shuffled toward the annunciator on the wall, pressed the button and muttered, "Can I help you?"

"It's not about you helping me, buddy. I'm here to help you."

Jake buzzed Tess into the building lobby, and he barely had time to pull on a top and jeans before she swept into the apartment, brimming with energy and offering coffee and bagels.

"I am here on behalf of the county health department, but before I begin my reclamation project, I thought we could chat for a few minutes and share our expectations going forward."

Jake blinked and gulped. "I'm not sure I want to hear what's coming."

"Don't worry. This conversation isn't going to end with my invitation that we just be friends. I'm already your friend, Jake. Much more than that, in fact. It's just that I think we need to agree on our expectations going forward."

"I'm good with that."

"So, what I was thinking is that we take some time together before going public. I'd especially like some time before the boys see us back together. Just a few days at least, so that we are comfortable with this new start. It was hard on them both when we broke up. I don't want to go through that again, and I don't want it for them either. My hope is that you have come back into our lives to stay."

Jake gulped.

"Well, that's what I want also."

"OK, so that's out of the way. Now, step aside so I can do my work. I'll be back up in a few minutes with all my cleaning stuff."

Jake was sequestered in his bedroom, exchanging emails with his editor and reviewing comments on the latest draft of his story. He could hear the faint hum of a vacuum and then the slosh of a mop dropped into a bucket.

Suddenly, there was a loud thud coming from the kitchen and then a low moan.

Jake got there as quickly as he could to find Tess sprawled on the floor. She had apparently stood on a chair to reach a high place, then slipped and fell, turning her right ankle as she landed. Jake knelt and asked if he could help her up.

"I'm not sure I can stand, but let's give it a try."

Tess screamed in pain when she tried to place weight on her foot. She slumped back again on the floor.

"Jake, I think it may be broken."

After two hours waiting together in a hospital emergency room, X-rays confirmed Tess's original diagnosis. It could have been worse though. She was told it was a nondisplaced fracture of the lateral malleolus. There appeared to be no tear of the associated ligaments. Just a simple break, according to the young doctor on duty.

Over the next two hours, Tess was fitted with a walking boot, prescribed a mild pain reliever, and discharged. Jake assumed responsibility for the drive back to Tess's home. Tess called ahead to Mary to break the news and let her know to expect Jake with her. On the way, they discussed how Tess would handle her employer. She was expected behind the bar at Toppers in a few hours, but she would obviously be a "no show" that night. In fact, she would be out of commission for several weeks.

"Jake, my boss has been great, giving me time off to visit you in Montana and an occasional night off when one of the boys was sick and Mary couldn't handle things herself. But I don't know how he will deal with this. He just might have to let me go. And I need that job."

Jake thought for a moment and then responded. "I've got the solution. It's been a while, but I tended bar in college. It was an upscale place, the Hanover Inn. I may be a little bit rusty, but I'm sure I can handle your shift for you until you are back on your feet again—literally. If they can do without you tonight, ask your boss if he'll consider giving me a try-out."

"Jake, that's a kind offer but you are already fully committed to your writing project."

"I have enough flexibility to do both. Besides, with you unable to drive for now, Mary will need help ferrying the boys and doing other chores. I want to do this, Tess."

Tess smiled and patted Jake's hand. "Thanks. What a strange twist. I guess we can forget about a staged re-entry."

Tess picked up her cell to call her boss, but then put it down.

"I've got to say something before I call in to work. We haven't talked directly about it before, but before you left for Montana, I had become concerned about your drinking. I don't know how you are now, but I'm worried about you taking over for me at Toppers temporarily. Can you handle being in that environment?"

Jake thought for a moment.

"I think so. As I look back, even before we met, I was sliding into addiction. But after my epic performance that night at the strip club, I found myself in a place that allowed me to taper off. Out West, I had time for a few beers with the guys. Maybe, a glass of wine or two with the Brunsons. That was it. I was happy with my days. Physically active by day, and busy at night with my writing. I also had plenty of time to think of the role alcohol played in my downfall. I think I can control my drinking now. But I won't know until I try. I've learned a few things about drinking. You should never drink alone. And you never drink at any place where you work. I do know if I wind up behind a bar for the next few weeks, that will be the test. I'll soon know if I can handle it. If I can't, I promise you I'll get help, and I'll do whatever's necessary to stop altogether. I'm not going to screw this up."

When the door opened, Thomas and Mikey turned from the TV screen and stared blankly at Jake for a moment. Thomas was the first to recognize him. He ran to the door and wrapped his arms around Jake. Mikey smiled and began to chant "J-J-Jake."

Mary had been in the kitchen, but she quickly came out, wiping her hands with a towel and reaching out for a hug. Jake could feel each of the bones in her back. Her face seemed pinched; the eyes not so bright as he remembered. He took it all in, glad to be back.

NINETY-TWO

Business was slow at Toppers as the remnants of the lunch trade lingered at the bar and the staff prepared for happy hour. Tess and Jake found Marty Popovitch in his squalid little office off the back kitchen. There, they made their pitch.

When they were finished, Marty took over. "Alright. This can play out in one of two ways. I don't have anybody on staff to fill in for you over the next four weeks, so I would have to hire somebody, temporary anyway, to cover your spot. If they're good, then I'm under pressure to keep them on. If you come back then and your position has been taken, then maybe some slimy, hack lawyer sues me for God knows what. I won't have to worry about that with Jake here, as long as he can pour a draft, mix a Moscow Mule and make change. And as long as you both keep this arrangement among us. I don't want anybody else here thinking they can have family and friends fill in for them just because they want to spend a week at South Beach. Do we understand one another?"

Both nodded on cue.

"Good. So, Jake. Get your ass back here by five. I want you to learn the ropes before the night crowd arrives. And I want to see if you know as much about tending bar as you say. You're filling in for one of the best."

When Toppers shut down at 2 a.m., Jake settled with Marty on his receipts and staggered out the door. He had forgotten how exhausting tending bar at a busy spot can be. He hadn't screwed up too badly. Otherwise, Marty would have sent him down the road.

Of course, Marty didn't know about Jake's minor miscue with a bunch of young ladies out celebrating a promotion. One of them ordered a glass of red wine and a Coke on the side. In the blur of the moment, Jake wound up mixing the two. Fortunately, from the other end of the bar, Jake could see the twisted expression on the girl's face. He was there before she had time to make a fuss, and he quickly replaced both drinks, with the next round on the house. Otherwise, he picked up a steady pace and was able to keep the customers at bay.

Jake was still operating on Montana lumberjack time, so he was wide awake at eight the next morning. Maybe, it was the experience of sharing housekeeping with his bunkmates, but the first thing he did was finish the chores that Tess had begun. Then he sat down with a cup of coffee and looked toward the river. College crews were out on the water, and he renewed his ritual of watching their rhythmic movement. He thought about what lay ahead. Unlike the last time, Jake now had a rough outline of a plan. But, as Tess's mishap revealed, all plans are fluid.

Later, Jake checked his phone. He had received a voicemail and multiple text messages from Henry Battalini, his trust attorney. With the excitement of his return and the shock of Tess's accident, Jake had ignored them earlier. But now he scrolled through. The last text read, "Jake, please contact me at your first opportunity. I have some papers that you need to sign. Henry B."

"Damn, he's persistent. I'll get back to him when I can."

Battalini had certainly kept his word. While Jake was away, he had faithfully paid the rent and utilities on Jake's apartment from trust proceeds. Jake now found himself in much better financial condition than when he left for Montana. *Stalwart* magazine had paid a $20,000 advance on Jake's story. Since Jake's housing was covered by the Brunsons, most of that advance remained in the bank. Jake was obligated now to produce a final draft of the expanded article over the next six weeks, but the media attention garnered by the wildfire had produced its own firestorm of public interest. The magazine increased its final payment to $60,000, and Jake was recently contacted by a film producer wanting to negotiate the screen rights.

So, Jake had to produce. He planned to spend each morning writing before heading over to Tess's house in the early afternoon to help with the boys. And now that he had agreed to spell Tess at Toppers until her ankle healed, Jake just had no spare time. He emailed Battalini, explaining his circumstances, and promising to call for an appointment as soon as he could.

NINETY-THREE

IT WAS ONLY A WEEK SINCE THE ACCIDENT, AND TESS WAS NOT tolerating well her enforced confinement. She had to rely on crutches, and her armpits ached from trying to keep up with the boys. But in spending more time around the house, she saw something else of concern.

Yesterday, she was sitting in the kitchen when she heard a muffled buzz. She got up and hobbled about until she located the source. Opening the refrigerator, she saw Mary's cell phone next to the milk.

Mary was upstairs helping the boys get ready for school. At first, Tess thought she would take advantage of the situation to tease her mom about her ditsy lapse. But then, Tess thought otherwise. There was the car door left open overnight a few weeks ago. Before that, it was the mail stuck in a pile of dirty laundry. Tess thought she knew what she needed to do but she wanted to talk to Jake first. Maybe, he had experienced something like this with his parents.

Tess got her chance after they delivered the boys home from school. Mary was upstairs napping, and Thomas was doing his homework while Mikey watched a nature film in the living room. Jake sat at the kitchen table as Tess joined him to share a coffee before he left for the night shift at Toppers.

"Jake, I need your advice. I think my mom is starting to slip."

She recounted what she saw yesterday and on those other occasions over the last few weeks. Jake sipped his coffee, remaining silent for a few moments.

"I had similar experiences with my dad in his last years. You need to get her evaluated professionally."

Tess grimaced. "You have learned enough about my mom to know that she'll chain herself to this table before she'll agree to that."

"I've seen where you get your stubbornness if that's what you mean. The same look when those Irish eyes turn emerald hard. But you've got to get her there. Maybe there's medication that can slow things down. Besides, you can't just sit back and wait for something more serious to happen. After all, Mary serves as the boys' caregiver a good part of the time."

"I understand, but I don't know how I'm going to pull it off."

Jake looked across the room and saw Mary's cell phone resting in its charger.

"I've got an idea. You need to take that phone and put it where you found it yesterday. When Mary comes down later, ask her to get something out of the refrigerator. You be right behind her when she opens the door. You'll both discover the phone there together. That will give you the chance to convince Mary that she needs help."

Tess stared at Jake. He saw her eyes turn cold and then narrow.

"That is a horrible idea. How can you be so cruel?"

Now, it was Jake's turn.

"Cruel? How do you think you are going to get help for Mary if you don't force her to confront her problem?"

"Not by setting her up like that. Jake, I guess I don't really know you."

Jake put down his cup, stood, and walked toward the door.

"The person you just called a stranger has got to get ready to cover for you tonight. Think about what I said and why I said it."

He was out the door without another word.

Jake's mind raced as he drove back to his apartment to change. He was furious with Tess. She asked for his advice, and he gave it. As harsh as it was, it was not meant to hurt Mary or her. He knew enough to be sure that it was the only way Mary would acknowledge she needed help, short of getting caught blowing a red light with the kids in the car.

How would things play out between the two of them now?

He thought back to how he dealt with conflict in the past. His first wife. The headmaster at Christian Brothers Prep. Hunter. Given a choice between fight or flight, Jake chose flight every time. He wouldn't do it again.

Looking back, he mishandled every one of those situations. As upset as he was, he silently pledged to himself that this time would be different. He would take a deep breath. Maybe several. He'd give Tess space and hope they'd find a way to work through it.

It was a big crowd for a Tuesday at Toppers, and Jake was glad to keep moving. It didn't keep him from thinking about Tess, but the work helped to distract him. Late in the shift, Jake got a text from Matt Simonetti, the groom who infamously arranged Jake's one and only lap dance.

"When you finish, join us at Liam's to celebrate my upcoming fatherhood."

Jake thought, "Why not?"

"I'll be there by 1:30 for a drink."

At this late hour, Liam's Hideaway was a refuge mainly for the rejected, neglected, and disaffected. Matt and the boys occupied a booth in the back, and as Jake joined them, he could see that sobriety had called it a night hours ago. Apparently, their waitperson had fallen behind since there were several spent glasses in the center of the table, islands in a sea of spilled Guinness.

Matt leaned over to give Jake a hug, breathing gusts of stale stout, and welcoming back home the local hero. There was a time when that would have been enough for Jake to sign on to this ship of fools. But not tonight. Jake caught the eye of one of the veteran waitresses he knew. He raised his right index finger and within a few minutes she was back with a pint. He placed a ten in her palm, wiggling the same finger as if to say, "That will do it for me."

Jake was at the keyboard working on story edits the next day when he heard the buzz. He walked to the door and pressed the button.

"Can I help you?"

"Jake, please let me in. We need to talk."

When Jake opened the door, Tess hobbled past him toward the kitchen where she drew a glass of water and sat down at the table, motioning for Jake to do the same.

"I'm sorry. What you said yesterday was not cruel. How I reacted, now that was cruel. I know I've got a problem with Mom. No, we've got a problem. Because I hope we can face it together. But I know I've got a bigger problem. I thought about it all night. I still have trouble trusting. Anybody. Even you. And when I feel threatened, my Irish temper flairs up, as you correctly pointed out. So, again. I'm sorry. I need your help."

Jake reached across the table and covered Tess's hand with his.

"I think we can work on both problems together."

Their conversation over the next two hours was painful but necessary. Both revealing their wounds. Those that had scarred over and those that were still raw.

At one point, Tess broke down and threw her arms around Jake as he softly stroked her hair. Tess asked if she could excuse herself.

"I must look like a mess."

When she did not return after ten minutes, Jake followed after her. He found her lying in his bed, her clothes cast on a chair nearby, the sheet pulled up to her chin. When Jake walked in, Tess smiled gently and pulled the sheet away.

"I've been waiting for you."

Jake could find no words to respond. He removed his clothes and slid beside her. They began to move together slowly. For a moment, they were distracted by the humorous impediment of Tess's ankle boot. But they soon were fully engaged. When it was over, they lay together in silence as Tess turned and nestled into the curve of Jake's body.

NINETY-FOUR

WHILE MOST PEOPLE WERE BEGINNING THEIR WORKDAY, BROOKE Anderson had already spent an hour on a video call with a prospective grant provider. She then worked on her cash flow projections for the upcoming quarter. Next, she reviewed her notes for scheduled interviews that afternoon with three families seeking help in handling family members recently diagnosed with dementia.

It was four months now since Ben's death. The US Attorney had dropped his investigation, and Brooke was working hard to overcome the fall-out for Senior Moments. With funding from Max Grabel dried up, Brooke scoured the non-profit world for another source. Most people were understandably skeptical, but Brooke was able to continue operating for a while by using personal funds.

When it appeared as though Ben would be prosecuted, their financial prospects were bleak. Ben's death, however, unexpectedly turned that around. Brooke was shocked to discover that Ben had maintained a five-million-dollar life insurance policy through his law firm. Initially, the insurance company had balked at paying since the circumstances of Ben's death appeared suspicious. Suicide is a standard exclusion to coverage. But the autopsy performed after Ben's death confirmed that cardiac arrest due to a congenital defect was the cause of his demise. So, Brooke and the kids would not have to deal with any financial pressures.

However, Ben's notoriety remained. Brooke and the kids faced the occasional odd look or off-putting remark but that would fade over time. What they were left with was an unexpected sense of loss. A family that had been bound together by a complicated set of transactional expectations had now imploded. But both Brooke and the kids were finding a new reason for staying together. It was not the money. In their own way, they had each discovered that they missed Ben, not for what he was, but for what he might have been. That shared loss brought them back together as a family. It was Ben's last and greatest gift.

Before Brooke left the office for a meeting, she checked her voicemails. One was from a very sincere-sounding woman. She needed help dealing with her mother, who was showing signs of early dementia. Brooke wrote down the number for Tess Reilly. She would get back to her later that day.

NINETY-FIVE

"WHAT IN THE NAME OF GOD WAS I THINKING?"

Peggy Opdyke was reaching her limit. It was five months since she agreed to step temporarily into the managing editor role at *The Times Union* after Hunter Dane's passing. Her assistant on the editorial page assumed her former role, but he wasn't ready yet. So, Peggy was constantly talking him out of quitting, answering his frantic calls and emails, editing his pieces and, generally, still doing her old job while assuming a new one.

Even worse, the paper was belatedly catching up with the world of digital journalism. Instead of meeting just one daily deadline for the print edition, stories online were constantly being updated, so her work literally never ended. She was stretched thinner than ever, and she could see that it was beginning to show in the product.

Peggy kept an old pair of bedroom slippers under her desk, and as the day wore on and with all the staff meetings concluded, she flipped off the heels that had hobbled her all day and surreptitiously slid into the slippers. She rested her half-glasses on her forehead, pulled her silvery hair back into a knot and spun her chair around toward the window. The setting sun created shafts of light cast through the looming darkness of nearby buildings.

"I wonder how Tom made out at the doctor's today?" she thought. Peggy had texted her husband earlier and he'd responded, "OK."

Typical for Tom. His cancer had been in remission now for three years. They both avoided discussions about it, just as they avoided discussions about Peg's shifting retirement schedule. Most recently, it had been pushed back because of Hunter's death. Hunter had always been the other man in their marriage. Peg knew that Tom never suspected any infidelity, and had no reason to, but Hunter had been his rival just the same. And he continued to be so in death.

NINETY-SIX

JAKE TOOK NOTE THAT NOTHING HAD CHANGED IN HENRY BATTALINI'S office since he was last there. At least the aesthetics hadn't changed. Same carefully maintained plants on the side tables next to the client couch in the waiting room. Same magazines on the coffee table. Though, maybe later editions. The same pleasant and efficient assistant ushered him into Battalini's office.

The trustee looked very much as Jake remembered him. Banker's gray suit with a conservative club tie. Receding gray hair, meticulously combed. The same inscrutable demeanor. With a slight smile, Battalini offered Jake a chair in front of his desk.

"Jake, I am certainly glad that you survived that episode out West. It must have been quite a scare, and I'm sure that the healing process has been painful."

Before waiting for a response, the trustee launched into an explanation for their meeting.

"As you know, I used certain trust funds to maintain your apartment during your absence. I expect that you have been able to draw upon personal income for your other living expenses. But I have asked you in today to inform you that the trust has recently been terminated, and I will no longer be serving as trustee."

"Why? What happened? Have the funds been exhausted?"

"No. The creator of the trust has died, and under its provisions, the trust has been closed out. Although you will be given a full accounting, the trust proceeds, totaling some seven million dollars, will shortly be transferred to you outright."

Jake struggled to process the news. After getting himself together, he asked Battalini the question he had struggled with since their first meeting.

"Can you tell me who created the trust?"

"I can now. The trust was created by Hunter Dane."

Jake stared at the attorney for a moment, expressionless, as if he had not understood. Then, he stammered, "Why did he do it?"

"Because Hunter Dane was your grandfather. Don't ask me for any details because I don't know."

NINETY-SEVEN

BILL BOYLE DID HIS BEST TO PREPARE FOR HIS TERM OF incarceration, three hundred and sixty-four days in Oakwood, the state's minimum security work camp for low-risk, non-violent offenders. He read online advice from various former inmates. He reviewed a flyer from the state Department of Corrections describing the intake process, the camp's facilities, and its operating rules. He knew that he would be addressed simply as Boyle, William, Inmate Number O-22-217. The initial letter connoted the name of the facility, the next two numbers the year of admission, and the last three his place in the line of convicts sentenced to Oakwood that year.

As his reporting day approached, Boyle, now Father Boyle to the outside world, felt both a growing apprehension but also a sense of relief. Since his guilty plea and his resignation as both an archbishop and a cardinal of the Church, after a short stay with a friend, he had been living with his brother Pete and his wife in a community about fifty miles from the city. His self-imposed isolation seemed almost a part of his sentence. He wanted to start his prison time, and yet, despite everything he had read and heard, he was still anxious about what it would be like.

But now, the wait was over. He sat in the passenger seat of his brother's SUV on a bright September morning, a small canvas bag on the floor between his legs, as they pulled off the main highway and onto the "campus" as described in the DOC flyer.

As they drove slowly down the main drive, he could see men in tan work clothes on tractors mowing acres of lawn. Others were part of a crew patching potholes in the roadway surface. There were no walls or fences. Only a cluster of squat, tan brick buildings up ahead. It looked to Boyle almost like a seminary where he taught early in his priesthood. He was sure he wouldn't find anybody here like the self-consciously pious seminarians back then.

Bill's brother turned right at the first intersection, following a sign directing them to the administration office. They stopped in front. Bill reached across to shake his brother's hand. Pete pointed to the bag at his brother's feet.

"Have you got all your meds, Bill?"

"Yup. I'll call you as soon as I'm permitted. Please pray for me, and I'll do the same for you and Betty."

He walked up the steps, opened the door, and was greeted by a man who, since he was wearing the same tan uniform as the other workers, was obviously another inmate.

He gazed at Boyle for a moment and then simply said, "Sit down over there. Someone will be with you shortly."

He picked up the phone, and within five minutes, Boyle was directed into a conference room for his first meeting with the intake unit. His fellow inmate continued to watch Boyle's back. With a low whistle, he softly said to no one, "So the 'Prince of the Church' has arrived."

Over the next three hours, Inmate Boyle underwent the same intake process that every new resident of Oakwood Correctional Camp experiences. He was briefly introduced to several administrators whose roles seemed obscure in the tension of the moment. Boyle was then sent to a nearby room with no windows where an officer directed him to remove all his clothes while another officer carefully went through the contents of his carry bag. He stood before them nude, so nervous that small puddles were forming on the floor as perspiration dripped from his forehead and armpits.

"Run your fingers through your hair five times."

Boyle complied.

"Lift your penis."

He did as he was ordered as one of the officers scrutinized that part of his body.

"Bend over and spread your cheeks."

He stretched his legs wide and immediately felt from behind the pressure of a probing gloved hand. When they were finished, Boyle was led to a small, open cubicle where he was directed to put on his prison uniform—the same tan short sleeve shirt, khaki pants and canvas low-top sneakers all inmates wore. He was then ushered back into the conference room for further processing, including swabbing for DNA, fingerprinting, and a brief medical and psychological assessment.

Finally, he was interviewed by a counselor tasked to determine his occupational assignment as an inmate. The counselor quickly came to the obvious conclusion that Inmate Boyle should serve as a chaplain's assistant, as well as a member of the staff at the facility's library. For the first moment since he arrived, Bill Boyle felt a momentary flush of reassurance. Finally, he was dismissed and directed to report to the cafeteria for lunch.

He walked into a room filled with some two hundred men in the same tan uniforms, some filing through the chow line, others seated at long tables eating their meal. First, only a few heads turned toward him, but soon the others followed. Conversations stopped and, for a moment, no one moved. They all stared at the newest inmate and then, one by one, they resumed their activities. Inmate Boyle walked to the back of the chow line and picked up a tray. But he knew one thing. They had been expecting him.

NINETY-EIGHT

JAKE MORRIS TOOK THE ELEVATOR TO THE FOURTH FLOOR OF THE parking garage, found his car, and slid behind the wheel. He sat there, engine off, just staring at the blank wall in front of him for several minutes.

"Hunter Dane…my grandfather?"

It seemed incomprehensible but he had no reason to question Henry Battalini. Jake replayed in his mind his many encounters with Hunter. Looking back, was there a sign of anything more than a professional relationship? Had Hunter treated him any differently than others at the paper? Jake often felt Hunter had been tougher on him than his peers. He thought it was because Hunter recognized his potential. Maybe, that was just Jake's ego, but maybe it was something else. He now had another reason to consider.

Jake had never shown much interest before in tracing his heritage, but now he was asking himself questions that he had ignored all these years. He always knew he was adopted, but why didn't his parents tell him about how he came into their lives? Who are his biological parents? Are they even alive? If so, can he find them? What role, if any, did Hunter play in his adoption? Why did Hunter keep silent all these years? And what was behind his behavior that last day at the paper? Suddenly, he had an overwhelming need for answers. He'd have to launch another kind of investigation, and he knew he had the tools for it.

Jake then considered his other dilemma. What would he do with all this money? How will Tess deal with it? Jake knew that money could create as many problems as it solved.

In the weeks since his return from Montana, Jake had spent the bulk of his days editing his story about Emil's logging crew. Much of his spare time was spent with Tess, helping her out with the boys and supporting her as she came to grips with her mom's advancing dementia.

As Mikey got older and bigger, he was more of a challenge, and Tess was becoming more reluctant each day to leave Mary alone in the house. Tess needed Jake, and she often expressed her appreciation for his help, but Jake also picked up some reluctance on her part. Tess had been pretty much on her own for a long while, and she valued her independence. She had been able to get by until now, with some help from her mom and her sisters, but that was no longer enough. Jake had to help Tess come to grips with that and allow him further into her life. But Tess still found it hard to trust a man, even Jake. This financial windfall could go a long way toward easing her burden, but Jake wondered how Tess would react upon hearing the news. Would it bring them closer or drive them apart? Jake had wanted to ask Tess to marry him since the afternoon she visited him in the hospital. Since returning home, he had been looking for the chance, but now the money could complicate things.

NINETY-NINE

Tess could no longer put it off. She and Mary were alone in the kitchen fixing dinner. As she prepared the salad at the counter with her back turned toward her mother, she tried to make it sound like a casual request.

"Mom, can you pour the milk for the boys?"

Mary shuffled to the fridge, opened the door, and saw her cell phone on the shelf next to the milk. "Why, that's crazy. Who would have put my phone in here?"

Tess had rehearsed her response, but it was all she could do to stick to the script. She hated herself for setting her mom up, but she knew that it had to be done. "Mom, who would have done that except you? We need to talk about this after dinner."

Despite her feeble effort to point the finger elsewhere, the shocked look in Mary's eyes was unmistakable. It wasn't an "I've got cancer" look but it clearly showed that Mary understood the implications of what had happened. Tess was relieved.

Dinner was a somber affair. Mary was always a picky eater, but tonight she just took a few bites and then moved the rest of her food around her plate. As soon as the boys finished, Tess shipped them off; Thomas to his bedroom to finish his homework and Mikey to the family room to work on a numbers game.

After the dishes were cleared, Tess made them both a cup of tea, and they sat back down at the table. Mary stared for several moments into the bottom of her cup. Then she looked up at her daughter.

"Don't think I don't know what's going on. I've seen the same thing happen to a few of my friends, and it scares me."

"Mom, I've been reading about this illness and talking to some people who know a lot about it. It takes many different paths and moves at its own pace. There are also therapies available. They can't stop it, but they can slow it down."

"Tess, you know I'm a fighter. I will do everything I can to stay here and help you and the boys. But when the time comes, I want you to promise me that you'll find a place that will take me in so that I don't pull you down with me."

Tess bit her lip hard to hold back tears.

"I have spoken with someone who runs an agency that helps families like us. She has put me in touch with a doctor who specializes in dementia treatment. If you're willing, I'll set up an appointment for the two of us."

Mary nodded, then stood and took the cups over to the sink. She didn't seem fazed by Tess naming her condition.

ONE HUNDRED

Bill Boyle spent his first afternoon in prison alone in the chapel office. The chaplain was a retired minister from the area who came in every Sunday for an interdenominational Christian service. Boyle was told that he usually drew a crowd of twenty or so. Also, there were about five inmates who gathered in the cafeteria on Fridays to read the Koran. The rest of the population kept any religious observation to themselves.

Anticipating his arrival, Reverend Stanton left a list of tasks for his new assistant. First, Boyle went through the pages of several well-thumbed Bibles to make sure they were in good order. Although it hadn't happened yet, the chaplain wanted to be sure that no one had either defaced them or left any objectionable message inside. The texts were then stacked in a box at the chapel entry. Then, with the chaplain's express permission, he opened several pieces of mail from either inmates or their families, most of them seeking support for a prisoner's early release. Those requests ranged from the pathetic to the comical. Stories of dying parents, failing businesses, and children requiring discipline from their incarcerated parent. One inmate, though, pleaded for the chaplain's help so that he could be released before the start of the football season. He wanted to take advantage of his season tickets.

Boyle attempted to prioritize the requests so that the chaplain could quickly deal with them after the Sunday service. The Reverend would soon learn to delegate to his new assistant the task of responding to these letters. Finally, Boyle set up the letters and numbers on the wall board identifying the Scripture readings for next Sunday.

His work completed, Boyle realized that he still had about ninety minutes until supper. He could go back to his suite, but he wasn't quite ready for what he expected to be awkward introductions there. He had brought his breviary along, so he sat down to read the divine office, the prayers and readings that had been a part of his daily experience as a priest for over forty years.

When he finished, he headed to the dorm to take care of some chores. Frank Majewski was folding his clothes in the laundry when Bill Boyle walked by. Everyone else was either still at their job or in the cafeteria. He looked up and then quickly turned and put his folded laundry in a basket. He wanted to get away from the priest as quickly as he could, but Boyle walked into the room and stuck out his hand.

"Hi, I'm Bill Boyle and, as I'm sure you figured out, this is my first day here."

Majewski hesitated for a moment and then, tentatively, accepted the handshake.

Boyle saw it in his eyes. The man didn't want to have anything to do with him. For a moment, Boyle thought he might even throw a punch.

"We've all been expecting you. Some of us more than others. Me among them. I used to be one of your parishioners, and my older brother was once a seminarian."

Boyle was as uncomfortable as his new acquaintance.

"I know that this situation is difficult for everybody. I'll do my best not to make it any worse."

Majewski shrugged and then turned away.

It was not until the next morning that Boyle was able to get onto the prison library computer and look up Francis Majewski. He was a disbarred lawyer who had stolen hundreds of thousands from his clients. Majewski was serving a three-year term for wire fraud.

But then Boyle came upon another Majewski. Stanley Majewski was one of the plaintiffs in a settlement reached by the Archdiocese five years ago, before Boyle arrived as Archbishop. Majewski alleged that a priest in the seminary raped him, resulting in years of psychiatric treatment and alcoholism.

No wonder his brother was not so friendly. "I wouldn't be either," Boyle thought to himself.

ONE HUNDRED AND ONE

JAKE HAD BEEN FAMOUS DURING HIS DAYS AT DARTMOUTH FOR pulling all-nighters—heroic efforts to cram for final exams after weeks of academic neglect. Although he'd thought those days were over, he came back to his apartment after his shift at Toppers and remembered that the final edit of his Montana story was due at the publisher by the end of the day. He'd done some of his best work under pressure, and it worked again this time. By mid-afternoon, Jake had finished a last read and then hit "send"on his computer. He had a few hours before returning to his tour of duty at Toppers, and he lay back in his bed hoping to take a brief nap.

It was not to be. His mind was racing as he sorted things out, trying to envision what lay ahead. What future did he have with Tess? What direction would his career take? What would he do with this sudden financial windfall? And, finally, what about this sudden revelation?

Jake was beginning to understand that Hunter Dane had been the invisible hand guiding his life's path. He wished he could draw upon his grandfather's wisdom now.

Jake finally stopped staring at the ceiling. He got up, showered, put on a fresh shirt and pants, and headed out to attempt, once again, to slake the unquenchable thirst of his customers.

He thought about the money on the drive to work. Rather than manna from heaven, Jake began to think of his new fortune as forbidden fruit. It had been three weeks since his meeting with Henry Battalini, and he knew he could not postpone a discussion with Tess much longer.

Battalini directed him to a tax lawyer, and the two attorneys structured the transfer of funds to minimize tax consequences. But Jake asked Battalini to take another step on his behalf.

"I don't know whether I'll have a future with Tess and her sons, but, either way, I want to make sure those boys are financially secure. I'd like to use some of this windfall I've received to do that. So, Mr. Battalini, perform your legal magic."

A trust was created on behalf of both Thomas and Michael Reilly. Again, it would be a sprinkling trust, with Battalini serving as trustee. There would be a fund of two million dollars available to both boys. Recognizing that Mikey's needs would likely be greater than Thomas's, Battalini alone would determine when and how much would be applied for each of their interests.

Jake struggled over how to tell Tess about the money and the trust he had created. She already thought of the boys and herself as a charity case. He had not yet been able to dispel that belief despite doing everything possible to let her know how reliant upon her he had become. He wanted her to know that both boys would be taken care of, even if she decided not to marry him. Because that's what he intended to ask her whenever they could find time to be alone together.

ONE HUNDRED AND TWO

TESS HAD INITIALLY GONE TO BROOKE ANDERSON FOR PROFESSIONAL advice. Brooke was instrumental in arranging for Mary's dementia screening and then enrolling her in a course of cognitive reinforcement sessions. But at their first meeting, Tess and Brooke each saw something in the other that soon led to a casual lunch.

It took a second meeting for each of them to tell their story, or at least pieces of it. Brooke was shocked to discover that Tess knew nothing about her late husband's scandalous fall from power and sudden death. Tess shared some of her struggle to raise her boys after a disastrous marriage. Both had faced tragedy, and that shared experience brought them closer together.

Today, Tess walked into Cachet, a small café popular with ladies dining out. She headed for a small table by a window where Brooke was occupied responding to emails. Brooke looked up, smiled, and gestured for Tess to join her. Soon, they were sipping Pellegrinos as they scanned the menu.

"How's your ankle healing?"

"Almost back to normal. I expect to ditch the boot next week. I'll soon be back behind the bar taking abuse from lecherous drunks."

The waiter arrived, took their luncheon orders, and the chatter picked up again.

"Tess, how are things developing with the man in your life?"

"I don't really know. I don't get to see him much these days."

"Well, that's because the poor guy is dead on his feet after covering for you at the bar. It seems to me that you struck gold there."

"You may be right, but how do you really know before it's too late to turn back?

"Girl, it's never too late to turn back, but you need to trust your instincts at some point. God knows, I screwed up my marriage to Ben. The shame is that we were finally ready to make it work, despite the obstacles, when the curtain fell. Don't look for guarantees. There are none. From the little you've told me about this guy, he seems like the one."

"Thanks, Brooke. I'm starving. I hope the quiche is as good as promised."

They had finished lunch and ordered coffee when Tess's phone rang. It was Jake.

"Hi. I know you're at lunch with your friend, but I need to get you some disability forms so I can take them with me to work tonight. Can I drop by and have you sign them?

"Sure. We're finishing lunch at Cachet but you're only about 15 minutes away. I'll wait for you."

Tess and Brooke were into their second cup when Jake arrived. As he approached the table, in the moment before the ladies looked up, Jake recognized that Tess's new friend was Brooke Anderson. He had only a moment to collect himself.

Brooke did not have the luxury of time. She looked up with a slight smile, as Jake approached the table. She remembered him. Suddenly, she was looking into the face of someone she associated with the pack of jackals at *The Times Union* who had helped bring her late husband down. She forced herself to attempt a pleasant expression that looked more like a grimace.

"Brooke, this is my friend, Jake Morris. And Jake, Brooke is my new friend who has been so helpful with Mom."

Both Jake and Brooke looked at one another and, instinctively, entered into a silent pact. They would leave for another day any explanation of how they knew one another. Maybe it wouldn't be necessary at all. For now, they said what they needed to say under the circumstances, acting as if they had only just met. But anyone closely observing the two would recognize it was a staged performance. Fortunately, it escaped Tess for the moment. She signed the forms and Jake was on his way.

ONE HUNDRED AND THREE

Despite the tedium of daily life at Oakwood Correctional Camp, Bill Boyle could hardly believe that he had completed the third month of his sentence. The monotony of each day reminded Boyle of the seminary in some ways. Only he couldn't remember his fellow seminarians getting into fights, as happened here from time to time, or surreptitiously passing a joint after the lights were doused at ten each night. That was pretty much the worst of it, at least so far.

Prisoners were permitted to receive visitors on Saturday mornings. Boyle's brother had come already, sharing news of the family and bringing along his wife's cookies. The cookies were confiscated immediately.

However, this Saturday, Boyle had an unexpected visitor. He arrived at the reception center to find Father Austin Cabot waiting for him. Austin wore khakis and a sport shirt under a windbreaker to protect against a late autumn chill.

Boyle thought how odd it was that priests often felt that they could go under cover by wearing civilian clothes. Most people could spot them right away. Maybe, it was their expression, that look that betrayed their separation from the rest of the world. Even Austin Cabot, whom Boyle knew was more in touch with reality than most every other priest he had known. Austin looked a bit older, a bit drawn. Boyle could see that his hair color was beginning to turn to salt and pepper.

"Austin. So good of you to come. How's the life of a parish priest?"

"Eminence, you should know."

"I don't know. I spent too much time playing clerical power games. When I was a young seminarian, I became friends with a wise old nun. We would walk behind the bishops in their regal purple garb. Some priests were more ambitious than others. My friend said that they were 'diving for purple.' Well, as it turned out, I became one of them. I've dived pretty deep, but I think I've hit bottom, and now I'm struggling to reach the surface. And stop calling me 'Eminence'. I'm just a foot soldier now like you. From now on, it's Bill. OK?"

"OK, Bill."

They sat in a corner of the reception area for an hour. Austin described his challenges as pastor of an inner-city parish.

"It's mostly poor Black and Hispanic families. They have no money, bad schools, poor health care, and little chance that anything will change. How do you give these people any hope when everything is stacked against them? I do my best to live their experience and to remind them that Jesus lived a life much like theirs. But how can the prospect of salvation in the next life sustain them in the world they face every day?"

Bill placed his hand on his young friend's shoulder.

"You are doing the work that many others in the Church should be doing. Whatever chance your people have, they will have none unless you hold on. There will be some small victories. You'll see."

On his way back to his dorm, Boyle passed several families visiting inmates. Across the room, he saw Frank Majewski sitting with a man and woman. Majewski looked up at him and stopped talking. He then said something, and the other man turned and stared at Boyle. They both had the same blank expression.

As Boyle passed, he thought to himself, "That's got to be his brother, Stanley."

ONE HUNDRED AND FOUR

PEGGY OPDYKE WAS DESPERATE. SHE HAD SPENT SEVERAL WEEKS looking for her replacement, and, as far as she could tell, no one in the world of journalism was interested in becoming the managing editor of *The Times Union*. Would they haul her out like they did Hunter? Then, suddenly, the thought occurred to her. She had one last chance. It was so obvious that she didn't think of it until now. She grabbed her phone and left a message.

"Jake. It's Peggy Opdyke. I wonder if you would like to get together to catch up on things. Give me a call when you can."

Fittingly, they met at Benny's Bar, the refuge for journalists seeking an escape and the site of Hunter's testimonial. Jake had the night off from Toppers, so he was not in any hurry. Peggy ordered a martini and Jake a draft. She did her best to appear casual as she eased into her real purpose for their meeting.

"Jake, you look well. It's been over a year since you left the paper, but it seems like a decade. How are you?"

"I'm ok. A lot has changed in my life and much of it for the better. I've had sort of an epiphany through my magazine experience in Montana. My article is finished and scheduled for publication next month. It seems to have attracted a bit of a buzz, and I'm fielding calls from a producer who wants to turn it into a screenplay. More important, I've met a woman whom I hope to marry. I'm about to find out if she wants to marry me."

"I am so happy for you, Jake. I remember the day you walked out. You were a mess then, and I wasn't sure you would right the ship. I regret though that you didn't stick around. You are a damned good journalist."

"Well, I'm not sure Hunter thought so."

"Jake, you will never know how much Hunter respected you."

"I hope he did, Peggy. I sure respected him. But something has happened, and I hope you can help me figure it out. After my mom's death, I met a lawyer who told me that many years ago someone had set up a trust to provide me with financial support. Under the terms of the trust, he couldn't tell me then who my benefactor was. When I came back from Montana, I found out it was Hunter. When I asked why, I learned that it was because Hunter was my grandfather."

Jake looked across at Peggy, searching for her reaction. She was gob-smacked. It took her a moment to find the words.

"You know that Hunter and I were very close. Throughout my career, he was always there to support me. He saved my job more than once, and he also saved my son when he was caught up in drugs for a while. We spoke a lot about you, but all that time, he never let on that you were his grandson. Thinking back though, something came over Hunter whenever your name was mentioned. Barely detectable, but I could pick it up. Hard to describe now. But let me tell you why I wanted to meet. Ironically, I'd like you to con-sider taking your late grandfather's job. You'd be great at it. The paper needs you. This city needs you. And I need you to allow me a few quiet years of retirement with my husband."

By now, they both had finished a second round. The conversation fell away, and Peggy looked across expectantly at Jake, hoping for some encouragement.

"Peggy, all I can say is I'll think about it. I do miss the newspaper busi-ness, assuming it will survive for a few more years. I hope to have a family soon, and I certainly can't have that and travel around as an investigative journalist. Besides, my prospective wife has two young sons. They are rooted in this area. So, give me some time. I'll let you know."

"I will hold out until then, but I hope you do this. You have an ineffa-ble quality that reminds me of Hunter."

Jake found that amusing.

"I don't know about that. I think I'm pretty effable. What I do know is that Hunter would never use that word to describe anybody."

Jake insisted on picking up the tab, and then they walked out together. When they stepped outside, Jake had one more question for her.

"In your many conversations with Hunter, did he ever say why he may have been reluctant to run my initial story about Ben Anderson?"

"Jake, I'm sorry. It never came up. But I know that Hunter left a wife. You might find out that way."

ONE HUNDRED AND FIVE

Bill Boyle's life at Oakwood might not be comfortable, but it had become tolerable. He kept busy performing his duties as chaplain's assistant and helping at the library. The administration permitted him to say Mass on Sunday at 9 a.m., just prior to the interdenominational service conducted by Reverend Stanton. Although the Reverend was initially cold toward him, they gradually formed a partnership. Boyle was allowed to preach on occasion, and one weekend when Stanton was away at a conference, Boyle was left to conduct the entire service himself.

Boyle had also adjusted to his living arrangements. He occupied a suite with three other inmates. Their quarters were twenty feet wide and twenty-five feet long. Each prisoner had a chair and low dresser next to his bed. At the end of the room was a common area with two built-in desks and a small sitting area in the center. Natural light was admitted through three windows above eye level.

He now lay on his bed as the winter sun dipped below the dorm windows. He had a half-hour before supper, and he was finishing his daily prayers. His suite mates were busy elsewhere. It took a while, but he had achieved a certain accommodation with each of them.

Albert Pincus was halfway through a three-year term for defrauding his financial clients to the tune of $1.3 million. Most of his personal assets were gone, either to his lawyers, his wife's alimony settlement, or for restitution to his former clients. A man in late middle age, slim with thinning gray hair, Pincus spent his free time at the library's computers, still playing the market. Only now, it was for the sole purpose of keeping up his skills as an investor. He held onto the illusion that he would regain his license as a financial advisor after he'd served his sentence.

Martin O'Malley was a former cop who shielded a high-end prostitution ring in return for some $75,000 in bribes and personal services. He was big and beefy and was struggling to get back in shape. He often dropped for push-ups and crunches next to his bunk, in addition to time each day in the prison gym. He had another year to figure out what he could do when he returned to civilian life.

Finally, there was the most colorful character of all, Nicodemus Winston... "the Reverend Nicodemus or Nic the Rev." He'd been the charismatic pastor of a large African American church whose sermons were broadcast on a local radio station, until his congregants found out about his condo in the Bahamas. Eventually, it was discovered that, over the years, Nic the Rev skimmed some $400,000 from the collection plate. He had nine months left on a two-year sentence. Nic made much of the fact that their suite was home to two men of the cloth, and Boyle and he had struck up an improbable friendship.

As for the general prison population, outside the chapel and library, Boyle pretty much kept to himself.

Boyle's reflections were interrupted now by Nic the Rev who tapped on his bunk. He handed over a chocolate chip cookie he had pilfered from the kitchen.

"Thanks, Nic. You know that I'm trying to lose weight while I'm here."

He took the cookie anyway.

"Bill, what's it like to live amongst us mere mortals?"

"I'm adjusting, Nic. At times, I do miss the gourmet meals cooked by my personal chef. But no, really, I don't miss any of the Church trappings. I actually feel like I've been freed from bondage."

"Free at last. Free at last. Well, brother, I'm happy for you. Maybe you can arrange for me to preachify at next Sunday's service. I'll show you how to get those dead asses up off their seats and speakin' in tongues."

ONE HUNDRED AND SIX

TESS SCHEDULED HER FINAL VISIT WITH HER ORTHOPEDIST FOR A Monday afternoon, a day when neither she nor Jake was needed to keep the booze flowing at Toppers. After her boot was removed and she was cleared to return to work, Jake picked her up and quickly announced that he had made reservations at Emilio's for dinner, the site of their first date, a time that seemed like a lifetime ago.

"Don't give me any grief, Ms. Reilly. Mary's given her blessing. She's got the boys in tow, and we are free to celebrate both your recovery and my liberation from the job you will return to tomorrow."

As Jake made his way through commuter traffic, he organized his thoughts. He hoped they would have a lot more to celebrate by the end of the evening.

After a delicious meal, a bottle of wine and some light conversation, Jake suggested that they adjourn to a corner table in the bar for a nightcap. As they placed their order, Tess could see that Jake had taken on a more serious demeanor. He tried unsuccessfully to hide his nerves. Tess began to suspect why.

"Tess, I have some news to share with you."

Despite his efforts to rehearse his presentation, everything tumbled out at once. Their drinks arrived but neither of them looked up. Their eyes locked upon each other.

Jake told her about his trust, his dealings with Henry Battalini, and his last encounter with him. He shared with her the revelation that Hunter Dane had set up the trust for his benefit.

"Tess, he did that because I am his grandson."

Tess did not react immediately. She lifted her glass while silently holding her gaze upon him.

His thoughts jumbled now, Jake described his encounter with Peggy Opdyke and her request that Jake come back to the paper and take on Hunter's role as managing editor.

Finally, Jake reached the most critical bit of news.

"Tess, I don't know how all of this might change my life, but I am sure of one thing. I want to marry you."

With that, Jake placed a small ring on the table.

"Tess, this was my mother's. I would like it to be yours now."

He looked at Tess, seeking something that might predict her response. She took on a somber expression, her eyes filling up. Tess sat motionless and silent. It seemed that his hopes were dashed. She looked at the ring and then again at Jake.

"I don't quite know what to say."

"Please say what's on your mind."

"I've thought about this for a long time. But now that the moment has arrived, I'm struggling for words. My first thought is that I love you, but I wonder if that's enough. I loved Paul, but love wasn't enough then. Too many things got between us. Will that happen again? As you know, I come with baggage. Two boys, one of them seriously disabled. A mom with early dementia. You have done so much to turn your life around, but will you fall back into your old habits? You are now a successful journalist, and with the funds from the trust, a very wealthy one. Do you really need to take all of this on?"

"The short answer is yes. Tess, my Montana experience showed me that almost nothing is certain in this life. But what is certain for me is that I love you. Sure, we'll have challenges. But we need to trust one another. I pledge to you that this time your trust will not be betrayed. As for the money, it gives us the chance to do a lot for the boys and Mary. It also would give you the chance to finish school or do whatever you'd like to do outside our home. I didn't plan on it, but I'm prepared to get down on one knee and embarrass you if I must."

That brought a smile.

"Spare me. You have made your case, and I accept. You know what you're in for living with a hardheaded Irishwoman."

Jake had some more news. He told Tess of his creation of a trust for the boys.

"You did that before hearing my answer?"

"Yes."

"You're a good man, Jake Morris."

ONE HUNDRED AND SEVEN

Bill Boyle was feeling especially drained lately. He had just finished writing next Sunday's sermon, and he looked forward to a hot shower before turning in. He padded down the hallway in his robe and slippers, towel in hand. It was late, almost curfew time, so he had the shower room to himself.

In the months since his arrival at Oakwood, he had become oblivious to the constant presence of overhead cameras watching the population's every move, so he didn't notice the towel which had been placed over the camera covering the shower area.

As the steam rose and Boyle lathered up, he reached out to adjust the heat, when he suddenly was thrust forward. His head struck the faucet, and he crumbled to the floor. Looking up, his eyes veiled in blood, he could just make out the dim figure of a man looming over him. Suddenly, the man turned, used a mop pole to remove the towel from the camera, and then was gone. After a few moments, Boyle was able to crawl over to a bench. He took his towel and applied it to the area where blood was streaming from his forehead. He then staggered into the hallway and collapsed.

The next morning, Boyle awoke in the infirmary with a blinding headache. He felt the large gauze bandage on his head covering what he would later learn were six stitches needed to close the gash. Despite his fogginess, he prepared his story for the interrogation he expected would come.

After a brief afternoon nap, Boyle found Deputy Warden Howard Rosen and an assistant standing at the foot of the bed. "Father Boyle, how are you feeling?"

"About as well as could be expected under the circumstances. I guess I'm just a little bit embarrassed.

"Why is that?"

"Well, I had a senior moment last night. I just remember that I dropped the soap, and when I leaned down to pick it up, I must have lost my balance."

Rosen didn't buy it for a moment.

"Was anybody in the shower with you at the time?"

"Not that I can recall."

"We have a camera monitoring activity in that area but, mysteriously, it wasn't operational for about fifteen minutes last night. Just about the time you would have been there. Are you sure you were alone?"

"As best I can remember."

"Well, Father, you contact me if your memory improves."

As Rosen walked back to his office, he commented to his assistant, "I've been lied to by hundreds of inmates over the years, but this is the first time by a priest. And he was pretty good at it. Guess they don't like snitches in the Catholic Church either."

ONE HUNDRED AND EIGHT

THERE WERE TIMES IN LIFE WHEN JAKE MORRIS FELT THAT HE was stuck in neutral, waiting for some event that would allow him to shift gears. Like after he left the newspaper and met Tess. For months, he had weighed his options as a writer, hesitant to make a move. And for an even longer time, he had wondered whether he would have a future with Tess. But now, suddenly, things were falling into place.

After their memorable dinner, Jake and Tess settled on a small wedding over the upcoming Thanksgiving weekend, only six weeks away. It was a bitter pill for Tess, and even more so for Mary, but a Catholic wedding was ruled out because of Jake's divorce. They found an Episcopal priest who agreed to preside over their exchange of vows.

Jake sought Tess's counsel regarding his opportunity to return to the paper. He shared with Tess his concerns about taking on the job. A lot of people would consider it a bad move. Print media was dying. He knew that. But that didn't mean the end of journalism. Like other papers, *The Times Union* was transforming itself into a digital outlet. The trick was to do it without sacrificing the quality of its reporting. They decided together he should give it a try.

In his new role, Jake might not have to rule out other writing assignments. His piece about the Montana logging crew was about to come out, and he expected that it would attract an audience. At least, he'd finish that project.

He had the luxury of making this career decision without wondering how he would provide for a new family. With the money from the trust and income from his Montana piece, he and Tess would have more than enough to live on. In fact, they planned to move into a bigger home to accommodate an expanded family. After their discussion, Tess gave her notice to Toppers.

Peggy Opdyke was overjoyed to hear that Jake would be coming back to the paper. Her publisher was delighted also. Jake would soon be sitting behind the Great White's desk. How would that feel? He didn't know yet, but he had come to realize that Hunter's shadow would follow him whatever path his life might take. He would learn to live with it, and, in fact, take comfort in it.

He had discovered a lot about himself over the last year, but he had one more mission. He needed to visit Hunter's widow.

ONE HUNDRED AND NINE

WHEN BILL BOYLE ENTERED THE CAFETERIA, CONVERSATIONS stopped, and heads turned. He had just been discharged from the infirmary, and his forehead was still swathed in gauze. Rumors had spread about his injury, and there were several theories about who did the job. He set his tray down at his usual table among his suite mates.

Martin O'Malley decided to break the ice. "Bill, did you get the license number of that truck?"

"I didn't, Marty. Must have been blinded by the headlights."

Albert Pincus chimed in.

"Come on, Bill. Who did the number on you?"

"Fellas, I'll tell you what I told the warden. I leaned over to pick up the soap and went ass over teacup."

The jury didn't buy it, but they realized that there was no sense in pursuing it further. Bill Boyle had taken a vow of silence.

After a few weeks, the sutures were removed. The wound healed, only to leave a slight scar. Boyle still had to deal with the occasional interrogation from other inmates, but one who asked no questions was Frank Majewski.

Boyle did, however, observe a subtle change in Majewski's demeanor. When they passed, Majewski no longer scowled at him. Once, Boyle looked up from his work in the library and saw Majewski staring intently at him. Something had changed.

Another change at Oakwood Correctional Camp involved its chaplain. Reverend Stanton announced that he was retiring from the ministry. The administration asked Boyle if he would step in as chaplain. Stanton had been easing back lately, allowing his assistant to do more, so the promotion would not cause much of a change in Boyle's work schedule.

Also, as he began to contemplate his return to the free world, the Archdiocese had taken a greater interest in him. The new Archbishop was sensitive to the publicity that his scheduled release would generate. What could he possibly do with this notorious priest? The answer came as a surprise to both the Archbishop and his predecessor. Father Austin Cabot approached the Archbishop with a request. He needed help serving the people of his inner-city parish. Could Father Boyle be assigned as his assistant? Boyle could also continue to serve as chaplain at Oakwood.

Both Austin and Bill were overjoyed with this arrangement, but no more so than the Archbishop. He could spin this assignment very nicely. Father Boyle would be portrayed as the rehabilitated cleric, continuing to serve his fellow inmates. Father Cabot's parishioners would likely not raise a ruckus having Boyle in their community, like many other uptown parishes might. The scandal Father Boyle had visited upon the Church would simply fade away.

Bill Boyle now looked forward to the Christmas season. As a priest, he had quickly learned to accept the increased demands of the holiday. Folks he had not seen in several months would suddenly show up at church, not to return until Easter, if then. It was much the same at Oakwood.

In the weeks before Christmas, more inmates sought his counsel and the numbers on Sunday spiked. So, it was no surprise when he showed up at his office one morning to find an inmate waiting for him. He was shocked though to discover that it was Frank Majewski.

Majewski stood as Boyle approached him.

He smiled slightly and said, "Father, could you please hear my confession?"

ONE HUNDRED AND TEN

IT WAS AN ESTABLISHED NEIGHBORHOOD OF WELL-MAINTAINED, older homes, each one on an expansive lot with mature trees affording a measure of privacy. Jake parked his car at the curb and walked down a long flagstone path to the front door. He rang the bell, and after a few moments, a man opened it. He was of slight build, with the look of a retired academic.

He smiled and asked, "Can I help you?

"Yes, I am looking for Hunter Dane's widow."

The man could see that his visitor was already looking past him, expecting someone else to appear at any moment. He recognized a bit of confusion, something he had dealt with often over the years.

"I'm Bernie McAvaddy, Hunter's widow."

Jake tried but failed to disguise his shock.

"Don't be uncomfortable. Come on in. But could you please introduce yourself?"

"I'm sorry. I'm Jake Morris."

"Of course. I have been expecting you. Please come in."

Jake was ushered into a room off the main hall. It had a desk at one end with bookshelves behind it. He could see several photographs on the shelves, some of Hunter and some of Bernie at various ages. There were a few photos of what appeared to be a family with children. At the other end of the room was a sitting area, with a small couch and two easy chairs surrounding a coffee table.

"Please sit down and be comfortable. I've just brewed a pot of tea. Can I interest you in a cup?"

"Yes. Thank you."

Bernie excused himself but returned a few moments later with a tray.

As he poured the tea, he asked, "Jake, tell me what you have been up to. Hunter spoke about you often, but I've heard nothing since his death."

Jake was still recovering from his shock, but he managed to say, "A lot has happened. I hardly know where to begin."

By the time they had both finished a second cup, Jake had covered much of what he'd experienced since leaving the paper. Bernie was aware of most of it, and Jake realized that Hunter had followed his exploits closely, most likely through Henry Battalini.

Jake told Bernie of his upcoming marriage and of his decision to return to the paper as managing editor.

"Jake, I must tell you that your grandfather would be overjoyed to know that you are stepping into his shoes at *The Times Union*. Even though you were unaware of it, Hunter watched you from a distance your entire life. He was so proud of you. If you'll excuse me for a moment, there are some things I need to show you."

Bernie returned a few moments later. He carried a box containing several files, each neatly labeled by hand. He placed it on the floor next to Jake.

"I think you'll find this interesting. I've got some cleaning up to do in the kitchen. I'll be back in a while."

Jake picked out a file labeled, "Jake's Early Years." It contained a variety of items, including baby photos, First Communion and Confirmation announcements, school assembly programs, little league team pictures and other memorabilia. Other files documented Jake's high school and collegiate record. It included candid photos from Jake's graduations that obviously were taken by Hunter. There were newspaper articles reporting on Jake's accomplishments on Dartmouth's track team and copies of articles he had written for the college newspaper. Yet another file documented his work as a reporter for *The Times Union*, including his recognition as a Stapleton Award winner.

Finally, Jake opened a file marked "Jake's Adoption." It contained several legal documents including a lengthy petition in the name of Brian and Rosemary Morris, as adoptive parents. Jake skimmed over several legal recitals until he reached the part of the petition which contained the biological parents' written consent to the adoption . It was executed by Fiona Dane as the mother. It also contained the signature of the father. Jake let out an audible gasp when he read the typed name under the signature, "Benjamin Anderson."

He dropped the papers and sat back in his chair, unable to focus upon anything except the enormity of this disclosure.

When Bernie returned, he could see that the experience had left Jake shaken.

"Jake, I know that this is a lot for you to absorb. Please take these files. They belong to you. Let me know if there is anything more I can do to help."

Jake got into his car and sat transfixed behind the wheel for several minutes, struggling to replay each of his encounters with Hunter. He fixed on their last meeting in Hunter's office. He now knew that Hunter was searching for a way to keep his grandson from writing a story that would bring down his birth father. Unwittingly, Jake provided the solution when he blew up and quit on the spot. Hunter hadn't pulled the plug on the story. Jake had. Hunter, wisely, waited to assign the story to someone else, and Jake was grateful for that now.

What was it like for Hunter to watch him over the years, having set up a financial safety net for his grandson, but then stepping away and never revealing his secret role in Jake's life? The full truth would never come from the mouth of Hunter Dane. But Jake had now discovered that truth. The question now was what he would do with it.

He started the engine and soon was on his way. He had received a text. The managing editor of *The Times Union* was needed back in the newsroom.

When he arrived, Jake was greeted by the paper's newest reporter, an eager young woman freshly minted from UNC's journalism school. In addition to being eminently qualified, Paige Andrews was scary smart and devastatingly attractive. She only lacked experience.

Jake thought of what she would face in her new job. She had so much to learn, and he couldn't teach her everything. She would have to pick up a lot of it on her own. There were those who would attempt to take advantage of her inexperience, and she would need to deal with them.

Jake put those thoughts aside as he escorted the young woman into his office. Making sure that his door remained open, he settled into his chair and looked across the desk at his new pupil.

He reached reflexively for the baseball kept in the unused ashtray on his desk. He looked down at the faded inscription on its cover. "To my good friend, Hunter. Lefty No. 32."

Turning the ball over in his hand, he reflexively practiced his curveball grip for a moment, as he weighed his words.

"Ms. Andrews, you have an impressive resume, and I believe you will make a great addition to our reporting staff. However, I think you'll find that your academic experience has not prepared you fully for what you will face at *The Times Union*. You will be starting here covering community events.

You may consider that inconsequential, but I assure you it is not. Our readers depend upon this paper to chronicle local events which are more important, for many of them, than what happens in Washington or Moscow. If you do the job right, you will learn what makes this city such a special place. If you don't, you can be assured that you will hear about it from me. Any questions?"

"No, sir."

"Then, I'll leave you to settle in. Remember though, I'm here to support you. So, don't hesitate to call on me if you need help. I want you to succeed."

As Paige Andrews stood and turned toward the door, Jake had one more bit of advice to offer.

"I know all about the grammatical tools we have on our computers, but that will get you only so far. I read everything we print in this paper, and you should know one more thing about me. I am a stickler for punctuation."

ACKNOWLEDGMENTS

Here we go again. Another "lose, lose" situation. This novel had an unusually long gestation period. Along the way, it had several midwives and "midhusbands." Several friends offered advice, and I'm happy to say I'm still on their Christmas card list. Among them are Joyce and Howard Loughlin (Joyce is responsible for greatly improving the story's ending, I think.). Dottie Fiedler, Ellen Pospeich, Bill DeConcini, Jamie Mulholland, Ken Calemmo, Jerry Gross, and Padgett Gerler. Thanks to all of you for your encouragement and, even more, your friendship.

My editors, Alice Osborn and Bob Lijana, deserve special recognition. Both are talented and understanding folks, and I have benefited from their collaboration. Alice, by the way, is also an accomplished singer-songwriter, and Bob is a gifted musician in his own right. I am also grateful for the technical assistance my daughter-in-law, Andrea Armstrong, provided during the last stages of publication. Andrea, you are a wonder!

And so, I end as I began. With thanks to my wife, Val. Stephen King speaks of his wife, Tabby, as his "ideal reader." Val is mine. Innumerable times, she's pulled me out of the valley of despair, only the next day to topple me from the summit of my fragile ego. It's the story of our marriage, and it's worked so far. So, thanks again, Val. But don't wander too far. Hopefully, there's more to come.